The Cliff

Christie A.C. Gucker

Pagan Writers Press

Houston, Texas

Library of Congress Catalog Number: 2012949579

ISBN: 978-1-938397-31-8

Published by Pagan Writers Press, Houston

Edited by Toni Rakestraw
Cover by Christie A.C. Gucker
Typeset by Angelique Mroczka

Printed in the United States of America

To my inspirations:
my daughters, Samantha and Sydney, and my husband Chris.

Thank you for being there through this whole wonderful ride with your love and support. I could not have done this without you, my biggest fans. And you know I'm always your biggest fan and supporter.

With much love, I give this book to you.

Contents

Acknowledgements

I wanted to take a moment to thank a few people for being a huge part of my journey up *The Cliff.*

Thank you, God, for everything.

Thanks Mom and Dad, for always standing by me and accepting me for everything I am, have been, do and have done. I'm glad we all survived my youth. Thank you for letting me be me, no matter how insane I drove you, because it is this very reason I am who I am. Dad, you might not be here with me physically, but I feel you every day and I know your arm is around my shoulder to let me know I did a good job. I want to thank ALL my family for being there and not laughing at me for trying my hand at yet 'another new thing'. Kat (love ya, sis), Darren, Chelsie, Callie, Dot, Don, Judi, Erica, and Shannon. And of course I have already dedicated this book to my husband Chris, and my two daughters, Samantha and Sydney for putting up with my sitting at my computer writing (I KNOW AND TWEETING). LOL Without you, I am nothing.

To my best friend, Jennifer Ambrose Schimmel, I love you so much and you are my "other sister". Thanks to all my friends and family who have supported me throughout my life and continue to today.

To Angie Mroczka, my publisher, who not only had faith in my talent and this story once, but twice, thank you, thank you! I feel lucky to now call you my friend.

Thanks Toni Rakestraw, my amazing editor, for making my book the best it could be. I so enjoyed working with you and our banter! Thanks for being gentle with me, since you were my first! HAHA

Special thanks to my proofreader Lacey Wolfe for helping put the finishing touches on this baby!

To my personality Doppelganger Sarah Carr. Ummm...WOW! LOL We scare me!

Thank you Stephen King who showed me what a storyteller is.

Special thanks to a few friends, who I've never met in person. Without you this book would not be here. You pushed me, cried with me, and gave me the strength to give it a try: Gina Bennett, Cheryl Chere, Nicole Harlow and Katie Melton. What an amazing ride – I hope it never ends!

Thank you to my readers for thinking this book was worth reading!

—Christie A.C. Gucker

Prologue

The Past

It was a warm morning, and the breeze off the ocean was enough to give you just the slightest chill. I lay there on my back, wiggling my toes and feeling the warmth of the two boys with me, one on either side. I was comfortable. I was happy. I loved them. They were my boys and I was their girl. We did everything together and had since our births. On my left was Dane Voight and on my right was Grant Bennett.

Our parents were all best friends when they were growing up and had started a business together. They had each built a house on the cliff when their business took off, making them all very wealthy. Three beautiful houses, each with its own distinct personality, just like Grant, Dane, and me.

Our mothers thought it would be fun to have children at the same time so we could grow up as one big extended family together on our isolated cliff. We all ranged within a year of age between us. Grant was the oldest, then Dane and then me, Lanie Rhodes.

My house sat in the middle. It was a beautiful stone beach cottage, with a slate roof and peaks everywhere, including a widow's walk, which was my favorite place to be. My father, Jack, had given me the room to do what I wanted with—he just couldn't go there after my mother, Nicole, passed away from breast cancer when I was twelve. None of us were ever quite the same after that, but that room made me feel like she was there with me.

I spent my alone time there, sketching, daydreaming, or having conversations with my deceased mom. I painted the room her favorite shade of blue, somewhere between the sky and the ocean, and plopped a big old papasan chair right in the middle. My dad bought me a mini fridge so I wouldn't have to run up and down the stairs, a small table and an old radio for music.

The inside of our home was very airy, with high ceilings and lots of windows. We had a gorgeous kitchen, which I often commandeered, that opened up to a sunken living room facing the ocean. The outer wall of the living room was completely glass, and you could see all the way to heaven from there. It had French doors opening to a very large terrace on the edge of the cliff, looking straight out over the ocean and the never-ending horizon. The bedrooms were all on the second floor. Mine was on the end to the right, closest to Grant's house. Almost every night, Grant and I would go to our windows, which were directly across from each other, to wave or hold up messages to read with our telescopes.

When I was a teenager, however, I did other things in front of the window, hoping Grant would be looking, somehow showing he felt the same. I would undress and linger in the dim light of my room, walk past the window with the translucent drapes exposing my body to him. I would run my hands over my small perky breasts and tight ass. I had a great body as a teenager, the kind of body other girls would call killer. I'm not sure if he was ever there to notice my window trysts, but in my head he was, and it would make my teenage blood rush to all the parts I was flaunting for him. I learned to take things into my own hands to satisfy my frustration. I would lie in bed and dream of Grant crawling through my window to kiss me, touch me and eventually to make love to me. I knew this would never happen, but it was my room and my fantasy. He never said anything about it and I never caught him looking. We did have a few innocent moments that I can recall, but something always happened to stop any progression.

Grant's house was much more modern. Wood that looked like teak, and glass everywhere. Clean and sharp and beautiful, just like Grant. Even with all the glass, it was always warm and comforting inside, as almost every room had its own fireplace. It was actually quite amazing! As were Grant's parents, Jennifer and Joe.

They were both stunningly handsome, and you could see where Grant got his good looks and grace. Grant was tall and muscular with a lean frame.

His eyes were a piercing blue, which were accentuated by his dark golden hair. He was normally a casual dresser, wearing mostly jeans and button down shirts, but enjoyed donning a high-end suit when necessary. His smile could knock any woman off her feet.

The Bennett house was always alive with family and friends; it was a great place to be. Joe's brother, sister-in-law, and their children were regulars on the cliff. I grew up with all of them. Grant's female fraternal twin cousins, Samantha and Chelsie, were two of my best friends. They came to the cliff often and remained in my life always. All the Bennetts were strong people who would do anything for those they loved, which seemed to be everyone on earth.

Dane's house stood on the other side of mine—with quite a presence. His house was more like a mansion, with huge steps leading up to giant wooden doors that belonged on a fortress instead of a house, with very large metal knockers so big I couldn't lift them when I was little. We loved to bust on Dane about his mom's huge knockers.

Everything about Dane's house was grand, from the front entrance hall to a mini ballroom for entertaining business guests. Dane was a perfect match to his abode. His short black hair, dark eyes and quiet demeanor made him seem unapproachable at first, but he was actually quite easy-going and very funny. He was meticulous with his appearance, preferring to dress in suits or khakis and polo shirts.

We usually had our holidays at the Voight house, since the dining room was huge and housed a very long table seating at least twenty. Despite the foreboding feeling you got when you first entered the house, its inhabitants didn't seem to match the décor. Dane's parents were sweet and warm people, and the house was always filled with laughter and the wonderful smell of something baking. It was Dane's mother who taught me to cook.

My connection with Grant had always been different from the one I had with Dane. Grant and I were tender and sweet with each other. He and I shared all our secrets and could never run out of things to talk about. With Dane, everything had always been about having adventures and finding reasons to laugh at just about anything. He also had a way of making anything bad go away. I crushed on both of them at one point or another, maybe one a bit more than the other, because it never went away.

My feeble attempts at flirting with either of them were pathetic in my eyes, so I never pursued my feelings for either in any way for fear of ruining our happy threesome. Worse yet, I didn't want to find out neither looked at me that way. So they remained just for me.

That morning, while we lay together on the edge of the cliff with our feet dangling close to the edge watching the clouds lazily pass over us, we made a lifelong pact. We would never leave each other, never leave our homes, and always be a family, no matter what. We promised nothing would ever come between us, the three musketeers forever. No secrets, no lies. Except for one. Ours wasn't the only pact made that day.

My boys made one too, earlier: Grant and Dane had promised each other that neither of them would vie for more of my attention than the other, neither would ever be my boyfriend or lover because they never wanted the other to feel left out and didn't ever want to know who I loved more. With both pacts made, we lived our lives together, inseparable forever.

The Present

I was jarred from my childhood memories as the plane began its descent and my ears plugged up. God I hated that, and I hated flying even more. I felt like my brain was going to start leaking out of my ears. I had spent the past six months flying around the world, visiting our satellite offices. But now, I was going home to my two guys. At least I hoped so. After being gone for so long, even with all the emailing, texting, and phone calls, I knew some things had changed. And some of those changes I was not ready to face. There were people I did not want to see.

I departed the plane, and as I entered the baggage claim area, I saw our limo driver, Pierre, who had somehow already managed to grab my bags. Pierre had been driving for our family since I was ten. He was like an uncle to me. He smiled his huge New Orleans Mardi Gras grin at me and then grabbed me in his arms and said in his Creole accent, "Lovely Lanie, running' round gettin' business straight, only to come home 'n have to do it dere, too, eh? You have been missed. Things just not been 'de same since you left! Glad you're home, my baby. Now she goin' to make things right again."

And there it was. I could feel all the blood draining from my face just hearing him say it out loud. I knew it already, but he just had to say it. *Great, this is just great.* I followed Pierre to the car, climbed in and prepared for the hour-long drive home from the airport and for what or who waited for me when I got there.

Chapter 1

I'm Home, Anyone There?

The closer we got to the cliff, the more my stomach tightened. I couldn't tell if it was excitement or paranoia giving me some six-pack abs. *I wonder if I could market that?* I felt the car shift from a smooth ride to a rough one as Pierre made the turn onto the gravel road that led up to the cliff top. My heart rate accelerated. I began to gather my things and check my hair and makeup in the window. *Like I could see how tired I probably looked.* I know I felt it.

I looked pale in the dim light, but I was light-skinned to begin with. I grabbed my blush and eyeliner out of my purse for a quick touch up. My light green eyes actually did look tired, so I gave them a quick outline in black. I pulled my long, caramel-colored hair out of the bun it was presently in, and let it fall in loose waves over my shoulders. I finished off with some lip gloss and a quick check on my clothes. I stared at my reflection in the window of the car. I was a pretty girl whether I was dressed to kill or in my most comfortable sweats with no makeup at all. I had no shame in saying this, because I looked like my mother and she had been beautiful.

As the car ambled up the drive, even in the twilight, I could see it. The widow's walk, it beckoned me. I realized how badly I had missed being home. As we came around the final bend, I said aloud, "I'm home, anyone there?" and then my heart sank. No one was there.

When one of us was away, the homecoming was quite a production. Everyone would be waiting with hugs and kisses. Since our parents had all moved to warm sunny places and each of us had taken over ownership of our respective childhood homes, it was a smaller reunion. Of course, I can't forget to add in any "peripherals" that may have attached themselves to my guys … *whatever*. No one had lasted very long—so far. But my boys weren't here to greet me, neither of them.

What the hell? I had texted them both when we pulled away from the airport. I had received a reply from Grant. But he was a no show. *Damn. They blew me off.* I could feel my eyes welling up with tears and I bit my lower lip to help hold them back. I was an emotional lip nibbler. I couldn't tell if I was pissed at them or sad. I had been really looking forward to seeing them.

The car rolled to a stop in front of my cottage. I opened my door too quickly and literally fell out, trying to rush inside. They didn't come see me, so my intention was not to let them see me. *So there!* I think I actually stuck my tongue out. Pierre just smiled, helped me up and went to get my luggage.

I headed to the door and tried to open it, but something on the other side was blocking it. I gave a little push and it gave way. The house was pitch black. I reached for the hall light and felt something that should not have been there.

The air rushed out of my lungs until there was nothing left to scream with. I heard myself gasping for breath and then something else. *Was that a snicker or a growl?* I turned to run out the door, but the door closed in front of me. And then I felt it. A hand. I began to flail my arms wildly at nothing, hoping to fight off my invisible assailant, but then I felt a very familiar tingling.

"Grant? Is that you?" I pleaded the question to the ghost. He began to chuckle.

"Yes, Lanie, it's me. You look hysterical boxing nothing. I've been waiting here in the dark for half an hour for you, eyes all adjusted," and he proceeded to flip the light switch.

There he was, Grant, and he had seemingly spent the past six months getting hotter. I threw myself into his arms and inhaled the sweet scent of him. His arms returned the wrapping and he nestled his head into my hair, then planted a kiss atop of my head.

"We really have missed you, Lanie, you have no idea. It's not the same without you," he said in a soft, smooth voice, right against my ear.

"We, huh?" I said sarcastically as I reluctantly released him. "And who is we? Because I only see you here." *Did I just make a hmph sound?*

"Well, that is a very interesting story I plan to share with you after you get yourself showered and I make you dinner. How does Bennett's famous baked mac and cheese with warm garlic twists sound?" He literally drooled out the words, but I could tell he was craving it, and I was more than happy to let him pamper me with comfort food.

"Sounds perfect. Can you give me about an hour to get myself together?"

"You look pretty together to me, but of course," he said. "And I have a special welcome home present for you, too, something to keep you here."

My head began to feel a little light, and things started running through it. I felt like a little girl again, all giddy about what it could be. But it was something from Grant, something he wanted to give to me, so the anticipation got the better of me and I pushed him out the door.

"Hey, where are we eating?" I shouted as he skipped down the stairs.

"You've done enough traveling; dinner will be served for you here, madam," he said with a slight bow and a rolling salute. *Wow, that was charming.* I couldn't help but blush slightly. I turned and ran up the stairs.

I took a long, hot, soapy shower and threw on my favorite gray sweats and a tank top à la commando. The house was warm and cozy and so was I. Running a brush through my towel-dried hair, I let it air dry into soft waves.

I would have loved to curl up in my bed. *God, I had missed my bed.* But I had missed Grant more, and I was famished. I rubbed some vanilla lotion I had picked up in Paris on all my exposed skin. The sweet fragrance made my stomach growl. I went downstairs and decided that eating at the table was completely out of the question. So I grabbed plates, forks, and glasses, then took them into the living room. We were going to eat on my big squishy couches with a nice roaring fire. I grabbed the fireplace remote and pressed the switch. *Voilà.* Instant ambiance.

I heard the front door open. Perfect timing. I scooted to help him with everything he was balancing. I started to empty the containers from the bags and he smacked my hands and gently pushed me onto the couch. Again there was that tingle. *Stop that*, I thought to myself. *What is wrong with me? I must be on a second wind or something.* He proceeded to divvy up the food into heaping portions on each plate and then pour some black Shiraz he knew I loved.

We just kind of stared at each other while we shoveled food into our mouths, barely speaking. Occasionally one of us would grunt. When I could not eat another bite, I grabbed my wineglass and stretched out. I patted my belly and thanked him for the extra ten pounds he just packed on me. *Grant packing me. Oh, damn it! I did it again. Sleep deprivation must make Lanie a horny girl.*

I cleared my throat and tried to sound as calm and disinterested as I could. "So, you said something about an interesting story to tell me? And something else about—what?"

"Nope, that doesn't sound familiar to me at all." He smiled and then looked like he was going to pounce. But then he eyed the wineglass in my hand and shifted back. *Damn, I knew I should quit drinking.* I loved a good Grant wrestle. I had loved wrestling with Dane and Grant since we were little kids, playful, rough and tumble, and then more flirty when we were teenagers. This would have been much more fun.

"Fine, mister liar, no dessert for you!" I teased.

"What? But I ate all my dinner," he mocked back.

"Surely you can't expect any sweets until you add the sugar," I purred.

"Fine! I'll tell you, and stop calling me Shirley," he bantered back. "What do you want first?"

Hmm, what do I want? I want a man to touch me in the most intimate of ways. Any man at this point, or this man … but I digress.

"Well, I'm sure you're wondering why it's just you and me, kid," he said, his tone just edging towards serious.

"That would be something I'm wondering, all right." And that was it, our first in-person secret after six months. "Spill it, dagnabbit!" I demanded with a smirk.

"Seriously, did you just say dagnabbit?"

"Focus, Grant."

"Fine, but you can't get mad at me. Promise."

I raised my right hand and stated, "I promise not to get mad at the messenger." This had been our standard secret-telling rule since we were seven.

"Well, Dane has been keeping some 'particular' company with—"

"No. No. Don't you even say her name!" I interrupted him.

"I won't say it, but you wanted to hear, so I'll just say Sally instead, okay?"

I glared at him.

"Umm, Dane ran into *Sally* at a recent work function and they went for drinks after."

"And?" I was really not in the mood for this to be the news I came home to. And I was dreading to hear it confirmed by Grant. Now the paranoia was not paranoia any more, it was the real deal.

"And well, they came back here after drinks." I pursed my lips so tight, Coach would have been proud.

"Here? At my house?"

"No, of course not. I meant here on the cliff. His house."

"Okay, there has to be more to it. What's more to it?"

"Well, um, Sally has been here ever since."

"Dane is shacking up with her? Are you kidding me?"

"No, I would never do that. Especially where Sally is concerned. And of course, Dane as well."

I just stared at him and shook my head. *No, please, not here. Not her on my cliff with one of my guys.* And what was worse was Dane knew how I felt about her and he had the nerve not to show up tonight. He chose her over me. That was always the way it was when stupid-Sally-selling-herself-by-the-seawhore was around. *Ha, ha.* I made myself laugh.

"Lanie."

"No, I don't want to talk about this anymore. We're done." He could tell I was fuming inside.

"How about that surprise I have, to make everything better?" he teased.

"No, I don't want anything right now."

I could tell I hurt his feelings by the way he just kind of dropped his eyes from mine and cleared his throat. I felt bad. It wasn't his fault. And I really, really wanted to see what he got me that would, and I quote, 'keep me here.'

"I'm sorry, I feel bad now." I pouted. I even did my best boo-boo lip and then bit it and then kicked him. "Give it to me." *Wow, I wish I could say that in other ways!*

His eyes lit up, and he jumped up and ran out of the room. I heard a door open, and then close and footsteps back.

"Close your eyes, no peeking. Promise."

I raised my right hand like the good girl I was and stated flatly, "I promise not to peek."

He told me to put out my hands. I complied. And then I felt something so warm and completely not what I was expecting …

Chapter 2

Knock, Knock, Who's There?

. . . because it was soft and warm and moving? Yes. It was definitely moving.

"May I please open my eyes now?" I said excitedly.

"Yes, Lanie. Please do." He snickered. And there in my hands was the tiniest, cutest, sweetest little black kitten I had ever seen.

"Oh my God! A kitten? You got me a kitten? You got me a kitten."

"You're great at this game," he chortled, "and now you can't leave or he'll be all alone. And he doesn't like to be left alone. So can you not leave for that long again?"

"Grant. I love him. He's adorable. I've always wanted a kitten."

"Yes, you need some protection with that wolf in sheep's clothing hanging around here."

"Did you say woof? I'm pretty sure you just said woof in sheep's clothing,"

"I said w-o-l-f. Wolf," he said, even though I swear I couldn't hear that *L*.

"Nope, you just said it again. Woof."

"Shut up," he whispered under his breath with a smile.

"I think that'll be his name. Woof."

"You're going to name your kitten Woof? That's absurd."

"Absurd and a done deal."

I put Woof on my lap and leaned over and gave Grant a soft kiss. And then it happened. He lingered. *Yes, I'm sure of it.* My sweet peck became a "linger." I couldn't bring myself to pull away. But after a few seconds longer, I felt his lips turn into a smile and he sat back, breaking our "linger" with what sounded like a sigh.

"I missed you. I have everything ready for him. Litter boxes, both upstairs and down, as well as bowls, food, and toys. I also took the liberty of stocking your fridge."

Did he just say he missed me? Oh and he took care of taking care of things here? This was a man any woman would fall head over heels over. *Pact. But not me, right? I was not falling head over heels. Was I? No. This was Grant. Pact. Pact. And more pact.*

"It's getting late, and you probably could use some sleep in your freshly sheeted bed," he stated. He really had all the bases covered.

"Please don't go. I haven't seen you for six months other than online video chat, and honestly, I really don't want to be alone. Please stay."

"Lanie, I have to get up pretty early to take care of the horses before my nine o'clock in the morning conference call." He sounded disappointed.

"Woof says pretty please. How can you resist him?" I said as I shoved Woof into his face.

"I wouldn't want to disappoint Woof. Let's watch some TV and hang for a bit. That work for you?"

"Yes!" I handed him the remote, grabbed my throw and snuggled into the side of him with Woof carefully cradled in my arms. I'm not sure how many seconds it took for me to start snoring, but I remember feeling Grant pick me up and carry me upstairs, lay me in my bed and tuck me in too. Somewhere I think I felt him stroke my hair and bless my forehead with a kiss. Or was I dreaming?

I woke up to Woof playing with a tendril of my hair that was across my face. He would swat at it and hit me in the nose. That was the cutest way I had ever been awakened. I looked at the clock and it read 6:45 A.M. I hit the bathroom and then jumped back in bed and shut my eyes, hoping to fall back to sleep for a few more hours. I had earned a late sleep. I deserved it.

After about half an hour, I heard a quiet knock on my front door. Then I heard it open. 7:13 A.M. I groaned. I heard a bunch of fumbling around in the kitchen. Woof and I looked at each other. I grabbed my robe and Woof and headed down the stairs. "Knock, knock. Who's there?" I called out.

There at my kitchen table were two cups of coffee, and I could smell bagels toasting. I turned towards the delicious smell and there was Dane. He looked like a little boy who had just been caught stealing cookies.

"Ah, the prodigal sister joins us again." He joked.

"Really, Dane? After you never came to see me last night? Or returned my text telling you I was on my way?" I said, slightly annoyed.

"I never got your text. I swear. I had no idea you were actually going to be home until late last night when I saw your lights were on. I figured I'd let you get unpacked and get some sleep and surprise you with breakfast."

"Grant got my text and you were on the same message. I'm sure it was the company you've been keeping who wouldn't let you come over. Hmmm? Come on, 'fess up," I said, poking him in the chest.

"Not at all, Lanie, I swear. She's not the same person from high school. She's matured. She's so sweet and open and really, I promise, you'll love hanging out with her."

"That is highly unlikely, Dane, but I would never stand in the way of something you seem so determined about. I'll give her a chance, of course." *I'm a sucker for my guys.* I hated this woman with all my being and he knew it, but if he was standing there asking me to give it a go, I just couldn't say no. He was so damn cute with his big puppy dog eyes.

He actually clapped. "Thank you. You're the best." And he proceeded to pull me into his arms. Those arms were twice the size they were when I left.

"Working out much?" I stammered. Any woman, even his mother, would feel flushed having those guns wrapped around her. He made me feel so tiny. He held me close, and was he pushing his hips towards me? *Nah.*

Then he finally released me. "Time to eat. I got bagels, cream cheese, whipped butter, and your favorite, fresh lox. Oh, and fruit and a box of coffee." Actually, if he wasn't going to make me breakfast, this was my favorite breakfast to nosh on.

"How could I possibly stay mad at you for you blowing me off, then waking me up early, and sleeping with my enemy for the past few months, when you bring me a breakfast like this?" I said in my most placating voice and then proceeded to grab a sesame bagel off the tray.

"Real nice, Lanie." He snickered and then winked.

"I'm kidding," I said, peering over my coffee cup at him while I took a nice long gulp. "Kind of."

"So. I was wondering if you and Grant want to have dinner over at my place tonight."

"Okay, but you'll have to ask Grant yourself. Not a double date, you know?"

"Oh, of course not. I just figured you'd want someone, you know, there on your side."

"On my side?" I cocked one eyebrow at him.

"You know what I mean. She's cooking. I'll even give her requests."

"No, that's all right. I'll come. I have to stop over at Grant's this morning to give him six months' worth of work crap, so I'll tell him about tonight." He leaned over the table and gave me a quick kiss and ran a finger down my cheek. *That was sweet.*

Dane was just too hard to say no to, ever. Made perfect sense for him to handle all the sales work for the company. He just had a pull about him. He always got what he wanted. And if he didn't, he'd just take it.

As soon as breakfast was done, I gave Dane a quick hug and scooted him out the door so I could get ready for the day. I ran upstairs and saw the phone sitting there, telling me to call Samantha and Chelsie. I had to get their feedback on tonight and also see if they wanted to help me look absolutely amazing. If I was going to face my enemy, I was sure as hell going to look hot. *It's a girl thing.*

Around one o'clock, Samantha and Chelsie were pulling in front of the house with bags of stuff. Grant had been standing outside and headed over to greet his cousins. After some quick hellos, they made him leave and busted right in.

"Lanie! I am so happy you're home. I missed you so much," Samantha chimed. She sounded like perfectly tuned wind chimes, whimsical and melodic. And for someone so tiny, she nearly knocked me down when she threw herself into a great big bear hug. I wondered how Dylan, her fiancé, dealt with that. Even though she was such a petite little thing, I was sure she dominated their bedroom.

"Hey sweetie, so glad you're home," Chelsie said. Now Chelsie was just a perfect specimen and so was her husband, Steve. They were Mr. and Mrs. Perfect, and I wanted to be them when I grew up!

"So, you want to look hot for your date tonight, huh?" Chelsie said, matter-of-factly.

"Date? You know it's nothing like that. I just have to look hotter than *her*." They knew the whole story.

"Are you sure? Because it sounds like a double date, and you know we would love nothing more than having you as actual *real* family," Samantha chirped while flitting through everything they'd brought.

"Samantha. Don't go there."

"But, Lanie, it's perfect. The pact is broken once one of them is taken." Of course my girls knew about the pact.

"Don't push her. She'll come to her senses and realize Grant is the perfect man for her." Well there was Chelsie's two cents.

"You guys know Grant doesn't think about me like that." I raised the two-cent ante.

"I don't know, Lanie … he seemed awful lost without you while you were gone," Chelsie said.

"Oh stop it already. He sounded fine whenever I talked to him."

"Right, because you were talking to him. Whenever I talked to him he sounded all sad and gloomy." Samantha threw her two cents in, too. At this rate we would be millionaires. "And he made that comment," Samantha babbled some more.

"What comment?" I said as I pulled my knees up to my chest, feeling slightly uneasy.

"Nothing. No comment." Chelsie punched Samantha in the arm.

"Ow!" Samantha cried, "Fine. No comment."

"You are so telling me about said comment," I demanded.

"Dane was all sad, too. It was like 'who could be sadder that Lanie was gone.'" Chelsie ignored me completely. I had to get Chelsie out of the room so I could get loose-lips to spill it.

"Chelsie, did you see the kitten Grant got me?"

"Kitten? He got you a kitten? Where? I have to see him. I love little animals."

"Downstairs. You'll have to search him out." And with that she was gone. I turned to Samantha, who had the same sly look on her face I probably did. "About that comment you mentioned?"

"I have to do it fast. You can email me any questions. So the other day, Chelsie and I came to see Grant. We asked him when you'd be getting home and he actually said …

Chapter 3

I'm Sorry, What Did You Say?

… and I quote, 'I don't ever want to be without Lanie for any extended period of time ever again. Never without her.' Yep, that's what he said." I could hear her shit-eating grin.

My heart fluttered. *Or was that my stomach?* She had to be misreading what he meant.

"I'm sure he was talking generally. You know, about the business and things around here. I'm sure it wasn't meant that way."

"Well, you think what you want, but I was there and I know what our conversation was, and …" She stopped abruptly at hearing Chelsie cooing while climbing the stairs, "And do with it what you will."

"I see you found my little Woof."

"I'm sorry, what did you say? Did you just call this cat a wolf? You do know it's a cat, right?" I exaggerated rolling my eyes. Apparently, that's just how their family said Wolf. Woof. Whatever.

After about an hour of looking through everything in my closet and all the garment bags the girls had brought, we all agreed on a slinky sapphire blue mini dress with black knee-high boots. Oh yeah, I was going to look hot. Samantha promised to stay to do my hair and Chelsie was all over my makeup. *Why did I feel like there was more to this dress-up game we were playing than outdoing Sally?*

After a lunch of laughter, girl gabbing and a hot shower, they began transforming me into a formidable force of hotness. I had to give myself this one. I really did look good. I was stoked.

Grant said he would swing past and get me. Of course he would, since he had to pass my front door to get to Dane's. So at about 5:30, the girls headed out right as Grant arrived.

"Ladies."

"Cousin."

"Have a really good time tonight," Chelsie sang.

"Don't do anything I wouldn't do," Samantha chimed in.

Grant laughed and shook his head. "What's up with those two?" He hadn't even looked at me yet, and when he turned, his mouth dropped open. "Wow. Who cares? You look amazing."

I smirked to myself, satisfied that we had accomplished our mission. If someone who saw me as a sister was mouth agape, then I knew I looked hot. He offered me his elbow and I slid my hand around. I wished I had someone to do this with all the time. *Hell, I wished I had Grant to do this with all the time, because he also looked quite fine on my arm.*

Did things seem different between us? No, I was sure it was just Samantha putting ideas in my head. Stupid Samantha! Why would she do that to me?

We walked to Dane's house, giggling all the way about what awful thing Sally would be serving for dinner.

"Can she even cook?"

"She probably ordered from a restaurant and is putting dirty pots around the kitchen."

"Can you get eye of newt and bat wings at the local market?"

"Those aren't hot dogs, they're the fingers of all the men she's dated."

"Dane Piccata on the menu tomorrow."

"Dinner is served! Bathroom to the right, coffins to the left."

By the time we got there we were in tears. We used Dane's mom's knockers, trying to be formal. Dane answered.

"Why did you use the knockers?"

"Who doesn't want to touch your mom's knockers before dinner?" Grant joked.

"I can play with knockers anytime I want." I smiled and walked in past them both.

I saw Grant and Dane share a smile at that one and then they followed me into the grand hall.

Dane's house was just over the top. He had marble floors and a huge crystal chandelier that gave a clear starry night a run for its money.

Although Dane was himself with us, he was all about image with other people. He had to have the expensive suits and the hottest sports cars (of which he had many), and he was ruthless when it came to making deals or taking down the competition. I was glad we were on his good side. And then I heard it. *Oh crap.*

"Lanie! Oh my God, Lanie. Look at you. You actually look so good, no more awkward tomboy." Lori threw her words at me.

There she was in her too-short skirt with her too-low top. Her hair was perfect and so was her makeup. I had to give it to her. She was a very pretty girl—on the outside.

"Yes, some of us just have good genes like that." I shrugged it off. This was about Dane's happiness and for Lori, that was as close to a compliment as it got.

Yes, Lori was Sally Seawhore. My enemy. I hated her. I hadn't always. We were good friends our freshman year of high school. We were always together and people referred to us as the twins. Not that we looked anything alike; we were just inseparable. We were so tight that even after spending the entire day together in or out of school, we would call each other the second we each got home. But then things changed.

Lori spent the summer between freshman and sophomore year away, and when she came back, she was a different person, cruel and mean-spirited. Then the shenanigans began. She stole any guy I was interested in. First there was George Long. She nabbed him by my locker for the girls' choice dance. I was shocked but chalked it up to "it happens." Then there was Mike Pucci. We were in a study group and she apparently needed some tutor time in her pants. This I just thought was humorous. Then there was Tom Loft, my prom date. That one infuriated me. I remember them going outside for a smoke and then they were gone. I waited by the dance floor for the big last dance and he just never came back. Dane had left early with his date, so I called Grant in tears to come pick me up. I stood alone outside waiting for him, my chest heaving from muffled cries. Everyone was coupled and leaving for after parties or hotel rendezvous. They looked and whispered or completely ignored me.

The car rolled up and Grant had to get out to help me in. I cried so hard when I saw him, I couldn't even see the door handle. We left and drove straight to the beach. He put his arm around me as we stared at the ocean while I cried out every last bit of liquid in my body.

He reminded me of how I had attended his senior prom with him and said I should hold onto that memory as my prom. And I do still, to this day. I also hold close what he told me that night.

"When we're married," he cleared his throat quickly and added some comment about how if we each never met the right person we would marry each other, "and have kids," again the throat cleared and he said something about our parents killing us if we never produced grandchildren, "I want them to see pictures of their parents together at the prom." Sweet. Grant was just so compassionate.

* * *

Grant walked up behind me and gave his polite greeting. Lori took one look at Grant and squealed as she flung herself into his arms for a huge hug. Lori had two very nice assets that I was not blessed with. And now she was rubbing them all over Grant's chest. I felt a serious pang of jealousy. *You can't have them both*, I thought.

There are only two ways to get boobs like that. You either have them put in or you're a little on the heavier side. Or sometimes God just graced certain people with cleavage. Lori was an hourglass and carried it well.

Although speaking of assets, my *ass*et blew hers away! I had been graced with awesome buttocks. I had legs that went all the way up! *Thank you, God.*

Grant was red in the face, so I jumped in to rescue him. "Lori, let's go get some girl talk on while we finish any last minute stuff for dinner." And I grabbed her arm and yanked her off Grant and toward the kitchen.

When dinnertime rolled around, we all took our seats so Lori could serve us. She gave Dane a healthy platter without asking him a thing. Were they that close now that she knew what he liked? Maybe she just felt he needed some of everything she had to offer. That's usually what she gave most guys. When it came to Grant, who she sat next to herself, she literally leaned down so he could see her heaving cleavage at eye level. "Can I offer you some sweet breast meat?"

"Hmm," escaped my lips curtly.

"Oh no, thanks, I'm more of a thigh guy myself," Grant said with a smile as he shot me a wink from across the table. *What did that mean? Why was I questioning everything suddenly?*

As the night progressed, I watched Lori fawn all over Grant instead of Dane. Dane seemed not to notice or mind. That was out of character for him. He did have a jealous streak. Maybe Lori really did make him happy. He planted himself next to me on the couch and Lori did the same with Grant. It seemed the "couples" were all sorts of mixed up. We talked about old times and heard a lot about everything Lori. She loved to talk about herself.

I was growing increasingly tired of her pawing Grant, and after coffee, I had had enough. "Grant, we need to head back. Remember, we have to get up really early."

"What? Oh, yes. Early. We should really head out. Dinner was really nice."

"Oh, we must do this all the time," Lori said, while she tried to touch him yet again. We gave Dane the double raised eyebrow look as we hugged him goodbye and headed out the door.

"Well, that was interesting," I said flatly.

"She was all over me, right? I mean, flirting and touching? And Dane thought it was cute or something, right?" He sounded completely confused.

"Yes. She was, he did, and I didn't like it." The words escaped my mouth before I even had a chance to think of what I had done. Grant stopped in his tracks and grabbed my arm and pulled me back to face him.

"Lanie? Which part didn't you like?" I put my eyes to the ground and watched as my boot made little circles in the dirt. He tilted my face so our eyes met. His fingertip was tingling where it touched me. Suddenly, I could feel my eyelids getting heavy and my breathing change. I was feeling something different. I mean, since I had been back, things with Grant seemed different. *Where was this going?*

"I didn't like her touching you like right in front of Dane like that." *Damn. I was a chicken.*

"I see. And that's all?" His eyes bore into mine searching for more. I could feel myself about to start babbling anything he wanted to hear. He was like walking truth serum.

"How about we go one-for-one. Shall we?" One-for-one was a game we had always played together. When something was hard to say, we would go one-for-one. You tell me something, and then I tell you. You show me yours and I'll show you mine. *Well, that would have been a lot more fun.*

"You go first," I said.

"All right. I missed you so much these past six months," he offered.

"I already know that; that doesn't count."

"But I don't think you know the extent or how."

"Okay … how then?"

"I don't ever want you to be away again."

"Grant, work will always cause one of us to travel for extended—" and he put a finger over my lips. I suddenly felt the urge to wrap my tongue around it.

"No, Lanie. I don't ever want you to be away from me; never again. I missed you terribly."

"Um, terribly*?" God I was so lame.* I stared into his eyes. The heat between us became intense, as if electricity was cracking there.

"Lanie, do I have to spell this out for you?"

"Yes, please. Spelling, definition, and then use it in a sentence."

And then he …

Chapter 4

Could You Spell That Again?

. . . just kissed me. It was a soft, gentle kiss that sent a shock wave from my lips right to my girliest of girl parts. When he pulled away, not very far away, he just stared into my eyes with something that was *not* looking at me like a sister. *What was he searching for?*

"Could you please spell that again?" I murmured. He relaxed and laughed softly and kissed me again, this time allowing his tongue to brush across my bottom lip. I was melting.

It took everything not to pounce on him and do all the naughty things that were suddenly running through my head right there on my porch.

"Use it in a sentence, please." I whispered with my eyes still closed, my head still tilted.

"Of course." And he crushed his lips to mine, pulling my body against his. I was lost in him. His tongue began swirling with mine and my head began swirling, too. We remained in this sentence, which was slowly approaching a paragraph. I didn't care, I would have been happy kissing a novella with him.

When our lips finally parted, I wasn't sure what to do next. "Would you like to come in?" I sounded like a complete idiot.

"Lanie, I'm not sure this is right or wrong. I just know it's what I want. *But* I want to go very slowly. I don't ever want to hurt you or ruin things between us. Maybe not tonight. Promise you understand."

I raised my right hand and stated, "I promise I understand."

And then his lips were on mine again. Reaching up, I curled my fingers into his hair and drank him in. I wanted to pull him inside to see where this would go, but I had promised. So I released him.

"I'll meet you at eight at the stables?"

"Yes, and don't be late. There's a huge nor'easter heading in, looks to hit the island head on. Might be a really nasty one and we have a lot to do to batten down the hatches."

"Sounds good."

"Great. Good night, Lanie."

"Good night, Grant." We watched each other as he headed home until he almost tripped looking back at me. I could see him shaking his head. I giggled. I got inside and ran for the phone to call Samantha. Voicemail. *Damn it.* So I found Woof and told him everything. He purred and rubbed against me and listened. He curled up in my lap and fell asleep while I tried to reach Samantha two more times and left a slew of excited messages.

I carried Woof up to my room and put him on the bed and dimmed the lights so I didn't wake him. He was just so damn cute. I began to undress and my thoughts shot back to when I used to window tryst for Grant, well at least in my head. *Maybe for old times' sake.*

I walked over to see if his light was on. It was but something was blocking it. *Was he looking at my window, too?* I started to undress and felt a little silly at first. But taking the chance he might be watching made my confidence boost. In a matter of moments, the boots and dress were on the floor and I put on the sheerest nightie I had. I went to the window and pushed open the French panes. Immediately the breeze blew the curtains back. I rested my hands on the sill and tried to appear like I was looking at something. Got to love that wind. It was kicking up from the oncoming storm and blowing my hair back like I was a model on a photo shoot.

I felt sexy knowing he was interested and the exhibitionism of the moment only added to it. I pulled myself up onto the sill to sit and listen to the ocean and give Grant a better view. I glanced over and I could see him.

He was watching! I saw him run his fingers through his hair, then down his face, and pace a bit. It almost looked like he was heading toward his door, but then he was back at the window again.

Now all sorts of things ran through my mind. *Did he know about when we were younger? Did he know I knew he was there? Was he on his way over?* I hoped he would get up the courage. And then the phone rang. *Oh my God, it must be him.* I could feel myself turn a bright red. I jumped down from the sill and grabbed the phone. It was Samantha. I proceeded to fill Samantha in on the entire night. And she actually made this squeal noise when I told her about the kiss. Then I fessed up the window thing.

"Lanie, I am so impressed! I didn't think you had it in you," she teased.

"Yes, Samantha. I am a slutty whore at heart. Are you proud?"

"Oh very. I can't wait to tell Chelsie."

"No! No. You can't tell Chelsie."

"Lanie, don't be silly. We need her help. We have to make sure you and Grant don't both chicken out. We need someone to whisper in his ear to egg him on." I pondered this for a moment. *Yes, that would be helpful. Have an insider's track on what Grant actually thought.*

"You can tell her."

"We'll be over for breakfast and you can tell her yourself."

"I can't, I'm meeting Grant at the stables. Plus we have that storm coming in and I don't want you to get trapped here."

"Lanie, you just gave me the best idea ever."

"What? What did I say?"

"You're going to get you and Grant trapped at one of your houses for the storm. It's perfect." I could hear her clapping over the phone.

"Samantha. We live right next to each other. How am I going to pull that off? That's silly."

"No, it's perfect. You'll have to tell him you don't want to be alone. Tell him the storm scares you."

"Samantha. I love storms. Grant knows that."

"It'll work. You'll think of something. You need to wear something really hot tomorrow." That was Samantha, always thinking about what outfit to wear for any occasion.

"I'm sure I'll have it covered. Look, let me get some sleep. I'll call you after the stables. You can call Chelsie now." I think I heard her say goodbye, but the phone went dead.

I snuck to the window to see if he was still there but his bedroom lights were out. Feeling a bit disappointed, I got into bed and spent the next hour lying there thinking about nothing but our kiss. I was so worked up and confused but happy and hadn't felt this happy in a long time.

My alarm cat went off at five in the morning. *Gee, thanks so much, Woof.* I couldn't go back to sleep and had a few hours to kill before I had to be at the stables.

I went down the kitchen and fed Woof, who was now affectionately rubbing all over my legs. I could feel him sticking to them and realized I needed to better prepare my body for anything that might happen today. I flipped the weather report on while sipping my coffee, I listened to them discuss the potentially damaging winds and storm duration.

So the storm would be here this afternoon. This storm was huge. They even predicted it could stall over us, which would mean possibly more than a few hours of hunkering down with Grant. *More like hunking down.* He was so hot. And presently, I sounded like a boy-crazed teenage girl. My hormones sure seemed to be in sync.

As the sun began to lighten up the sky, I could see the bands of clouds over the dark gray sky. They were moving pretty quickly. Stepping out onto the terrace to feel the warm breeze gently caress me, I was immediately brought back to Grant's hands on me last night. How reverently he had touched me while we kissed. As soft as this breeze. Like I was a china doll he was afraid to break. Did he really think I was so fragile? I would show him I wasn't today. I was going to give him everything I had pent up inside.

And then I thought about Dane. We had made a pact and Grant and I were going to break it. Maybe Dane wouldn't care. He had been with Lori for four months now, and apparently right before I returned home she had basically moved in. I had enough on my mind dealing with my feelings for Grant, and what was happening between us, to worry about Dane right now. I felt guilty, but I needed to focus on the things at hand.

It was still very early, so I grabbed Woof and my coffee and headed up to the one place, the one person, I had yet to visit since I'd been home, the widow's walk, and Nicole. Maybe my mom could give me some sort of sign. When I got to the walk, I realized it was the one place Grant hadn't prepared for my return. It was my private place and apparently everyone respected that. I sat in my big comfy chair and sipped my coffee while watching the night sky turn to day, while remaining just as dark. This was going to be one hell of a storm.

"Hi, Mom. I've missed you. I know you saw what happened between Grant and I last night. Am I doing the right thing?" She never replied. Well, that wasn't completely true. Thoughts that seemed not mine would always pop in when I spoke to her. Maybe it was just me working things out. It was comforting for me to think it was her, just the same.

I picked up my sketchpad and began to draw the angry ocean and sky. Whenever I drew something, I would go into some kind of trance. My mind would completely open and communicate directly with my hands; I was just a bystander watching. Very soon, my image turned into something other than the storm. There in the clouds were both Grant and Dane's eyes. *Huh.* Was this the sign my mom was subconsciously giving me? Showing me the storm on the horizon that would brew between my guys when Dane found out the direction Grant and I were headed? And where exactly were we headed? I stayed and sketched for a while longer and then headed down to get ready.

I showered and shaved everything all nice and smooth and applied some light make-up to look pretty but not overdone. I debated what to wear. *Right.* Guess I really didn't have it covered. I considered calling Samantha, but it was only seven o'clock, and she would be sleeping.

I opted for a tight pair of jeans that made my ass look even better than it normally did. And then I added a cute tight white V-neck tee shirt with a great push-up bra, jeans jacket and boots.

With almost an hour left to kill, I headed out to the stables early. They were situated behind Grant's house. We each had a horse and there were two spares for Chelsie and Samantha.

My horse, Magic, was a beautiful Palomino. His coloring was typical of the breed, but his legs were dappled and he had a gorgeous light cream mane and tail. I decided it had been too long since I rode and saddled him up.

I took the trail down the cliff and through the dunes until it opened up to a narrow stretch of beach. Magic moved with me like we were one. I loved riding him and imagined it would be the same when I finally rode Grant. *Wait. What was wrong with me? Why was I thinking like we're going to go all the way today?* It was Samantha's fault. In my head, I kept running over scenarios as to why we needed to ride out the storm together. *Riding. Riding Grant.* There I went again.

I ran Magic back and forth the length of the beach, which was walled in on either side by our cliff. I looked up and I could see Dane's house on one side, Grant's on the other and mine sitting cozily in the middle.

I had spent many days with Grant and Dane on this beach. This was our private beach. There was no way to get here except through our land, by boat or swimming. Perhaps one in the wrong frame of mind might consider cliff diving to get here.

I thought Magic had a good enough workout and being mindful of the time, headed back towards the trail and the stables. I felt like a little girl. The closer we got the more butterflies I felt.

When I reached the stables I was still about fifteen minutes ahead of Grant's arrival. I had time to remove the saddle and get Magic hosed off and back in his stall and then proceeded to feed and water all the horses. While pulling some of the equipment into the empty stalls, I could hear the wind kicking up even more. I loved the wind before a thunderstorm and was eager to stand in it until Grant arrived. Just as I walked out, Grant was walking down the path with two cups of coffee in his hands. He beamed at me when he saw me. Beamed.

"Hey," he said, handing me a cup. It smelled so good I immediately knew it was Kona coffee, my favorite. I just had a feeling this was going to be an epic day.

"Kona?"

"You're good."

"I know my coffee."

"And I know my stables. I see you've been busy. What time did you get here?"

"Well, the alarm cat you bought me works great. Woke me up at five o'clock, so I feel like I've had a full day already." I ran my hand through my hair and leaned against the side of the stable. "So, how was the rest of your night?" I looked at him through my eyelashes and hoped I wasn't blushing.

"It was quite an interesting night. I spent some time at my window." He put his forearm against the wall above my head and leaned into me. I froze. It was my own fault for leading the conversation. I looked down, sure I was blushing now, not sure what to say next.

"I was really enjoying the view. Stunning." He lifted my chin with his other hand and smiled this quirky grin at me. I could feel the flush all over now.

"Of course, it's not the first time the view out from my window has been so beautiful. I've been enjoying it for many, many years." He winked at me.

“I—Grant, I, Look, I—” I was at a loss. All I could do was stutter. This was me not being confident at all.

“Lanie. That is a view I hope to get a much closer look at. I’ve wasted too many years being a watcher and never taking advantage of the scenery.” I smiled and then his was gone. “I didn’t mean *take advantage of.* I meant …” he stumbled over his words.

“I know what you meant. And I like what you said. I’ll see if that can be arranged.”

He moved closer to me and pushed a stray piece of hair behind my ear before running his fingers across my cheek. I felt the warmth rising between us and then something interrupted the moment. Out of the corner of my eye I could see …

Chapter 5

You Smell Good Enough to Eat

… movement. Something was running towards us. I turned my head to see. So did Grant. Before we knew it, Dane was sprinting into the stable. Grant quickly stepped away from me as Dane slowed, sounding like he had just run a marathon.

"Hey. What're you guys doing here so early?" he puffed at us.

"Good morning to you too," I said.

"We're getting the stables ready for the storm."

"I see I'm just in time to help." He wiped the sweat from him brow with his sleeve. He certainly didn't seem dressed for a morning run or helping with dirty work.

"The more the merrier," I said and shot Grant a sideways glance. He smiled at me and handed me a pitchfork. I guess I was on mucking detail. *Oh joy.* I turned and headed to the stalls and glanced back to see both of them staring at my butt. I accentuated my sway for the fun of it. I released the horses into the paddock and began mucking. Grant and Dane moved anything that could be blown away inside and closed and secured any windows or doors. Around noon, we were about finished and I decided I was in need of another shower. I told them I was leaving and would be back in about an hour to bring the horses back in.

"Timing will be good. The storm looks like it's going to hit by then," Grant said and he gave me a little wave and a look. Dane had a look on his face, too. He looked … smug?

I headed home, discarded my boots at the door and went to the kitchen to grab something cold to drink and a quick bite to eat before my second shower of the day. I sat at my computer and quickly looked through a graphic presentation for our company, which had to be approved and sent by Monday. I was ahead of the game. It was only Friday. *Great.* Work done. Now I could relax.

I went through my routine again, this time opting for a white sheath sundress and brown cowboy boots. It was unseasonably warm, probably the storm. I sprayed myself with vanilla perfume. I loved smelling sweet.

The dress didn't allow for a bra. It was pretty thin material and the fabric rubbed against my nipples, making them hard. *Oh great.* I guess it added to the allure I was trying to accomplish.

I made sure to pair the dress with a cute white lace thong. I wanted to be prepared. I had every intention of making Samantha's plan come true. I looked like a virgin all in white. Heck, I practically was. It had been so long. I had only been with one man, anyway. He had definitely been a mistake.

I headed back toward the stables to gather the horses and saw they were no longer in the paddock. I entered the stable and there was Grant. He was also freshly showered and looked amazing. He was wearing a pair of black jeans and a button-up shirt. He looked up at me and smiled. I smiled back and walked over to him.

"Hey, where's Dane?"

"Funny thing about Dane. As soon as you left, he suddenly remembered something important he had to take care of and took off. He said something about having to go to see Lori's parents' house tonight and he would be back tomorrow."

Yes. The coast was clear. I didn't have to worry about Dane interrupting and catching Grant and I again before anything even got started. It had begun raining when I entered the stables and Grant walked over to the door to take a look.

"That puppy is going to come down in buckets any minute now." The doorway was pretty big. Big enough for horses to move through with plenty of room, yet Grant moved so he was pressing lightly against my back. I sighed when I felt him wrap his arms around me.

"Are you cold?"

"At the moment my temperature seems to be on the rise." I leaned into him and he tightened his grip.

"I smell cake."

"That would be me."

"Mmm. You smell good enough to eat." He said it in a low growl that made my heart stammer in my chest. *I love my vanilla perfume.*

The wind suddenly began blowing ferociously and the rain tried to rival it. I heard a rumble of thunder and then little clicks on the roof.

"Hail!" Grant said.

"It's getting mighty stormy out there, maybe we should make a run for it."

"Let's wait a bit, until the hail stops. I don't want it to knock any sense into you." He laughed and then gave me a gentle nuggie. I play-struggled enough to turn myself around and now we were pressed against each other face to face.

"Lanie," Grant was suddenly serious. He stared into my eyes and I could feel his hands moving down my back and pulling all of me closer to him. I could hear the rain become a downpour. My panties felt doused as well.

"Grant, it's really raining out there. We need to decide whose house we're going to spend the storm at. I need to run or you'll be able to see everything if this dress gets soaked."

"That's something I think I'd like to see."

"Oh really? You don't say." I poked lightly on the tip of his nose and he stuck his tongue out and licked it.

"You just licked my finger."

"You just poked my nose."

"You're changing the subject."

"No."

"Yes. You were supposed to tell me whose house we're running to before ... well you know."

"Yes. Interesting. You want to get stuck together during this entire storm?"

"Oh, um, I thought it would be fun to have company." My face flushed. I was pretty sure I wasn't misunderstanding his intentions, but I might be moving too quickly. He said he wanted to take this slowly. I think he could sense my sudden apprehension.

"Lanie, I would love to spend the storm with you. There is nothing I want more, except maybe watching that dress become transparent." His voice was velvety smooth and dripping with suggestion.

I had to tease him just a bit. "Is that a dare?"

"That is a triple dog dare." He cocked an eyebrow at me.

"Well, I for one, have never turned down a triple dog dare." I kissed his lips and pulled away. He seemed to not want to let go until the very tips of his fingers could no longer touch me. I stared into his eyes, and with a sly smile on my face, backed right out the door and into the rain. I was immediately pelted with huge drops. It felt more like stepping into a waterfall. I could feel everything getting soaked, and I mean everything. The expression on his face went from one of bewilderment to one of amazement. His eyes darted from my face to my breasts, which I knew were quite visible now. I could feel the fabric rub against them as his gaze burned into me. My dress was basically transparent now.

"Lanie, fuck." His lips parted, and before I knew what happened, he was standing against me in the rain, his hands grasping my face and our lips only millimeters apart.

He began to wipe my hair from my face. It was plastered there now. I wondered if my mascara was running, funny the things that women worry about. His hand trailed down my cheek and neck and rested right above my heart.

"You're so beautiful. Lanie, please, I don't know what to do here."

I pushed up on my tippy toes and pressed my lips to his, sliding my tongue between them, silencing him. I could feel his whole body shake as he returned the gesture. We stood in the middle of a storm, making out with his hand over my heart and I was sure he could feel how strongly it was beating. Water began to drip off our noses and it made me giggle.

"You're finding something funny?" His breath was warm and sweet and I felt myself longing for more of his kisses.

"We should go. I'm sure we would be more comfortable someplace other than out in a nor'easter."

"I don't want to leave this spot. Ever."

"Location has nothing to do with it. I promise to pick this moment right back up where we left off." I raised my right hand as I said it.

"Okay." He looked up at the two houses, his being much closer.

"Shall we head over to your house?"

"What about Woof?" He sounded worried. It was cute.

"He is fed, warm, and safe; we can always get back there if we need to. We can call if it makes you feel better."

"Yes, I'm sure he'll answer and tell us everything is fine, so we don't know he's throwing a party with all his feline friends."

"Maybe he's only invited one special kitty over. "

"I know my eyes would like to see a special pu—" Grant cleared his throat and seemed to think better of finishing that statement. "My place it is. On the count of three; one, two, three." He grabbed my hand and we made a dash for his house. By the time we reached the door, it looked like we had jumped into the ocean. We were both dripping wet, some of us, more than others. The thunder and lightning had picked up, and as we entered his dark house, it crashed, ushering us in faster. Divine intervention? *Oh, I hoped so.*

"We're soaked. How about we take a hot shower and put something dry on?"

I must have had a shocked expression on my face because he quickly followed with, "You can use the guest bath and I'll use the master bath." And then he gave me the most adorable sheepish grin I had ever seen. I wanted to kiss him. So I did. We kissed in his hallway until a small swimming pool had formed under our feet from our dripping clothes.

"Maybe we should discard some of this clothing here so we don't track it through the house."

"Grant, I'd pretty much be in nothing but panties if I did that." He groaned. Yes, he had just groaned. I smiled and started for the stairs. He stayed there for a moment, like he couldn't move. "Um, are you coming?" He groaned again.

"Geez, subtle innuendo much? Come on." But I had thought the same thing as soon as the words left my mouth. I smiled, secretly thinking if I had my way, he would be. He ran his hand over his face and then followed me up the stairs. He gave me a huge towel and told me he'd leave some appropriate clothes on the bed for me. That should be interesting. I tried to debate whether I wanted a hot shower or a cold one. I decided that no cold showers would be needed tonight.

The hot water felt good, but I didn't want to waste one second of the night ahead of us. I showered quickly. Maybe too quickly, because when I came back into the guest room, Grant was placing a few small piles of clothes on the bed. He was only wearing a bathrobe. Grant wasn't the bathrobe type, but Dane had given us all Turkish robes for Christmas the year before; nothing but the best for his pals. I entered the room in only my towel. We both stopped. I grasped the front of my towel and he wrestled the front of his robe to make sure it was closed appropriately.

This might be slightly awkward. We were both entering a territory neither of us had considered before. And of course we were thinking about how Dane would react and if we were doing the right thing. *But it felt so right.*

"I was just bringing you some things to choose from." He was blushing.

"Let me see what you have there." My mind was more focused on what was beneath his robe than any closet shopping he had done for me. I stepped closer and could feel the heat down below start to stoke. By the time I was beside him, it took all my strength not to throw him on the bed. His mind must have been in sync with mine because he reached out and grabbed the knot of my towel and pulled me close. My body was on fire. There was nothing but fluffy cotton between us. I wanted to feel his skin against mine. The ache was so real. I reached up and grabbed the edges of his robe and began to pull it open. He took my hands and stopped them.

"Lanie." His voice was gentle and soothing. He was trying to slow things down.

"Grant, I'm sorry."

"No, please don't be sorry. I didn't stop you because I don't want to or because I don't feel the same way."

I sighed with relief.

"Okay. Back to clothes then?" On the bed was a pair of pajama pants, cozy soft socks, a Ginny-tee, a button down shirt and a tee shirt. Oh and one more thing, a pair of biker-briefs. I immediately picked those and decided to pair it with the button down shirt and socks. I could make this sexy. I would feel sexy wearing his briefs. He watched me pick out my outfit and smiled when I grabbed his underwear.

"Those are very comfy."

"Yes, just like slipping into your skin," I purred.

He smiled at me. "I'll give you some privacy." He gave me a wink and brushed the back of his hand across my collarbone from one side to the other. I took a deep breath as his fingertips hesitated right above the knot in my towel … then he dropped his hand, turned and left. I dressed quickly and then stopped by a large mirror to see if I had indeed achieved sexy. *Yep, cute and sexy!* I did a little excited dance.

I headed down the hallway past Grant's room. His door was open, so I snuck a peek. I could see him. He was just pulling his sweats over his amazing behind! I should have blown off the mirror check. Two seconds earlier and I would have seen a new moon. He had no shirt on. I had seen him this way a hundred times, but tonight it made my head swoon. He started to move towards my direction and, not wanting to get caught, I turned quickly and ended up smacking my head on the door jam. It made a loud thump. He must have heard it, but I was already halfway down the stairs. Shortly after my escape, I heard Grant coming down the stairs.

"That storm must be knocking things into the house. Did you hear that huge thump?" He was laughing. *Damn. I was caught.*

"Funny, I didn't hear a thing."

"Really? You weren't storm watching?" he smiled. I wanted to play, but not like this. I had other things in mind. I backed Grant up against the wall and pressed my body against his. "I can't wait to see the storm in all its glory." Then I reached back and grabbed his beautiful moon and pulled it tight against me. "If you know what I mean." I reluctantly released it and headed towards his kitchen. I heard some air escape him and then he was right behind me.

"So how about some dinner?

"How about we just raid whatever munchies you have or heat up some leftovers, quick and easy? Maybe grab some liquor, or as I like to call it, Inhibition Remover." I shot him a glance but he was no longer where he had been standing. He was now rummaging through his liquor cabinet. With our arms full, we descended into his living room. It was a great place to watch a storm. Where my living room had a glass wall, his was completely glass except for the ceiling. He began working on a fire while I laid out our feast. We talked and laughed while we picked at our food. Grant had chosen sparkling champagne to have with our buffet, and we sipped from our glasses until we had finished off the bottle and started on the next.

The storm was raging outside and lightning lit up the room. Along with candles and the fireplace, it was romantic. As moments passed, we moved closer together on the couch. Soon our legs were entwined. At this point my inhibitions were almost out the door. I pulled away, leaned over to put my glass on the table, and made sure he could get a glimpse of my girls under my shirt. His eyes were in the right spot, but then he averted them.

I turned and began a very sexy cat-like prowl toward him on my hands and knees until I was basically in his lap. "So, I was thinking …" I ran my nose along his neck until my lips were right against his ear, "… about kissing you." I sucked his earlobe into my mouth.

I felt his whole body lean into me, and seconds later, I was flat on my back and he was on top of me. I was impressed with his moves. He pulled my hands above my head and held them there. He covered my neck with small kisses while he spoke, each breath driving me further to the edge.

"Lanie, I can barely stand it. I want to feel you. I need to." He pushed his hips against me. I moaned and softly pushed my hips back. Our kisses became more frantic. "God, Lanie, you're driving me crazy." He slid a hand up my shirt and stopped short of my breasts. He looked at me, I guessed for some type of permission.

"Touch me, Grant, any way you want. I want this."

"Lanie," he whispered, before crushing his lips to mine. Our tongues mingled while he matched the movements with his hands under my shirt and I arched my back, pushing my breasts further into them. He pulled himself up until he was straddling me. He slowly started to unbutton my shirt, caressing my skin as he uncovered it, savoring each inch with his hands and lips. It was amazing, bordering on agonizing, as I tried to maintain control.

I couldn't take it anymore and pushed him back, tearing his shirt over his head. I needed to feel his skin against mine immediately. He looked as though I took him off guard. We were playing a push and touch game and it was exhilarating. I shoved my breasts against him. We both groaned together as our skin touched and our hands began moving everywhere. We were frantic, neither of us able to get enough of the other.

My blood was boiling with passion and couldn't take it anymore. I wanted to taste him, feel him in every way. My next push put him on his back and I was again the aggressor. I had to slow myself so I could tease him. All we could hear was the storm and our heavy breathing.

I ran my hands down him until I reached the string of his sweats. Neither of us took our eyes off each other. Pulling the string slowly, I backed myself down his legs until my lips had access to his torso. I licked and teased him, kissing and nibbling anywhere and everywhere, all the while still holding the string.

He ran his fingers through his hair and then pulled me up to him, grasping my face and kissing me deeply. When I say deeply, I mean emotionally deep. I could feel everything he felt for me in that kiss. I felt safe and wanted. I felt loved. My eyes welled up with tears as he pulled me close to kiss me again, gently this time.

I had never felt this way before and it was utterly overwhelming. Soon I was sobbing and I realized, or rather, admitted to myself, that I had always loved Grant differently, and here he was with me; he wanted me, wanted to treat me in a way no other man ever had.

"Don't cry. I find it completely heartbreaking to see you hurt or sad in any way," he told me.

We were facing each other, inches apart, both on our knees. My arms hung limp at my sides as I became lost in feeling only him. His hands moved to my shoulders and he gently pulled my shirt down over them, removing it and tossing it to the side. He continued to kiss me, despite my tears, until my cries were nothing but little gasps of breath.

He slowly and reverently ran his hands over my back and neck, never breaking our kiss. He laid me back and slid next to me. I hitched my leg around him and he grasped it with his strong arm, holding it there while he slowly began to grind against me. Small moans escaped us both as we mimicked making love. I could have done this all night, but soon felt his hands move downward and touch the waistband of the briefs.

"Lanie?" It was more of a rhetorical question. I couldn't fathom this beautiful man, who could have any woman he wanted, whom I had known my whole life, needing to ask me for permission in any way, shape or form.

"Yes."

I heard a whispered sound come from him, but couldn't make out what he said, nor did I care at the moment. I just wanted to feel him.

He slid my bottoms off delicately; so sensual. And then I was bare underneath him. There was no awkwardness anymore, only he and I, as if it had always been like this between us. He slid his hand down my stomach slowly, right down to my folds. Once he touched me there, a wave of intense pleasure shot through my entire body. I held still, which at the moment was very hard to do.

He slid his fingertips up and down my lips. "Lanie, I can feel how much you want me." He slid a finger inside me and I groaned and writhed under his touch. He watched his hand intently and licked his lips. I could feel him getting harder against my side, and reached to touch him as he pushed against my hand. I began to stroke him through his pants and he made another quiet sound.

Reaching again I grabbed the string once more, looked at *him* for sort of permission and he nodded with a soft smile. I pulled at them and he lifted his body so they could slide off easily.

Once we were both completely undressed, we stopped to just feel each other like this for a moment. The connection of our skin felt so good, the heat intense, and I could feel him against me, hard and hot.

We continued to touch and kiss and writhe until neither of us could take it any longer. Like our minds were connected, we rolled so I was on my back and I wrapped my legs around him. He was right at my opening but waited. I wanted to push him inside of me; the anticipation excruciating and totally hot. I hadn't wanted anyone so badly in my entire life

He leaned up on his elbows and stroked my hair, nuzzling into my neck and whispered into my ear, "Lanie, I love you. I'm in love with you. It has always been this way for me." And with that, he pushed inside me. I felt like my entire body was alight with lust and desire as he entered me, moving slowly in and out. I could feel every inch of him. He seemed to strain to keep his pace as I lifted my hips to move with his and we rocked together. We were one, completely one.

I didn't even hear the storm anymore. My world at the moment was nothing but this, nothing but Grant making love to me. My heart strummed in my chest. There was no greater ecstasy, and if I died today, my life would feel complete.

He began more deliberate drives into me, faster and harder now. Muffled sounds of pleasure were coming from both of us. I felt myself edging closer to the brink of my climax. My stomach tightened and my body began to tense.

"Lanie, I want to hear you. I need to feel you come for me." That was all it took. I felt my orgasm immediately respond to his command and wash over me, ripping through my entire being until I could feel it in my fingertips and toes. I felt myself tighten all around his increasingly hardening member and I screamed out his name as I grabbed his glorious ass and pulled him as deep inside me as was humanly possible. I wanted every single cell of him to be part of me.

I held him there as my body convulsed with the pure pleasure of him and then he was shuddering with me. "Oh, Lanie ..." He pushed further inside me and with each surge, sending smaller waves of pleasure through me. Mini O's. We grasped each other in bliss until our bodies had ceased their pulsing. He held me for a very long time after, stroking my hair and showering me with kisses. I returned every single one of his gestures.

"I don't know about you, but I'm famished and I plan on a repeat performance, so we'll need some sustenance."

"Oh, Baby, I am so with you." He threw on his sweatpants and I threw on his t-shirt because it smelled like him, and his briefs again. He growled and pulled me close.

"Grant, I am more then happy to forgo food if you're ready to start all over again." His stomach answered for him. We giggled and headed for the kitchen.

"Lanie, I have no words for what I'm feeling right now," he said, but I understood, because I felt the same way.

"You know we need to talk about this. How to tell certain people?" He nodded. We needed to formulate a plan for telling Dane and what this all meant for us. I was not going to hide what I felt for Grant and there was no way I was ever letting him go.

"Yes. That is going to be quite a conundrum." I shook my head at his formality.

"He's going to freak out."

"Maybe not; he does have Lori now."

"So, do you think he just happened upon us at the stable today?

"I was wondering about that myself. No, it was unlike him. I'm not sure what prompted that." The conversation about Dane ended and we continued our evening, never discussing these matters again. We laughed, chatted, ate, touched and stared into each other's eyes.

Around 10pm, the phone rang. Grant pulled me into his arms. "Just let it ring."

"That was my intention." It stopped. Then it began to ring again. Stopped, and then rang again.

"Wow, someone sure does want to get in touch with you."

"I couldn't care less who it is. The only person I want to hear from is right here."

"What if it's Woof?" I giggled. He made an exaggerated sigh, pulled away from me and grabbed the phone. "Caller ID says it's Dane. I thought he was at Lori's for the night?"

"Maybe something's wrong. You'd better answer."

"Hello? Dane, everything is fine. She's right here with me. What do you mean why is she here? Please calm down; I don't understand why you're so upset. Of course you can speak with her." Grant shot me a perplexed look and handed the phone to me. "It's for you."

"Dane, is everything all right?" I questioned

"Lanie! What …

Chapter 6

Well That Was Bizarre

… the hell is going on? I've been trying to reach you all day!" Dane's furious voice boomed over the phone. I was sure Grant, and possibly Woof, could hear him. A knot formed in my stomach and I immediately thought he must know what was happening. I gave Grant a worried look and he quickly came over to me. That was a bit of a mistake, because as soon as he slid beside me, he began biting my neck and nibbling my ears, trying to make this conversation even harder. I giggled.

"Are you laughing at me?"

"Dane, no. What's wrong with you? What's the matter?"

"I'd like to know why you think it's okay not to answer your house or cell phone," he demanded. I realized I'd left my cell at home. It didn't matter, anyway. "Well? Are you going to answer me?"

Now I was getting angry. *Who did he think he was? What right did he have to be questioning me like I was a child?*

"Dane, I left my cell at my house. I've been at Grant's since the storm hit. We figured we'd watch movies to kill the time. Now what exactly is the issue?" Dead air. Nothing. "Dane?"

"I have that presentation on Monday, and you need to complete the graphics. I need to land this and you're not helping." *Okay, that's not where I thought this was headed.*

"I finished the presentation. I emailed it to you and about ten other people."

"I didn't get it. You need to meet me at your house right now so we can finish it."

"Are you kidding me? Have you looked outside? I'll do no such thing. It's done. And what's wrong with all your technology that you aren't getting texts or emails lately?"

"Nothing is wrong with my technology. It doesn't matter. I need to be prepared. This proposal is huge for us. Now get your stuff together and meet me here or at your house."

By now Grant was getting visibly angry. Maybe he was feeling protective. He walked over to his computer, switched it from sleep mode and opened his email. I saw him open my email with the presentation, hit forward and then write:

D

Here is the presentation. Please respond when you receive it to confirm. I have reviewed it and it is perfect as always. Now relax and enjoy the rest of your night. You and I are going to talk tomorrow.

G

He hit send. I actually heard Dane's email go off in the background. He must have been sitting at his computer.

"So, you have it now?"

"Yes. I got it."

"Now open it and look though it. I'll wait."

"It's impeccable, as always. Are you staying over at Grant's tonight?"

"Yes. Grant would never tell me to walk home in the middle of a huge storm. Not sure if it's really your business, anyway. So are we done here?"

"Yes. Done."

"Bye then." I waved to the phone and hung up, turned it back on, and placed it on the table until it went dead.

"Well, that was bizarre." Grant crawled next to me on the couch and began kissing my neck again.

"Yes. Bizarre. Who cares? I think we were in the middle of something?"

"Grant, you didn't find that phone call a complete moment killer?"

"Nothing could kill this moment." I smiled. There he was, being a complete sweetheart again.

"Come on. Let's go upstairs in case any storm-chasing peeping Danes show up." He grabbed my hand and pulled me upstairs.

"Grant, really, does that whole phone call not bother you?"

"What do I need to do to get that call off your mind? Wait, I have the perfect eraser: my tongue." He pushed me down onto the stairs and lifted my shirt above my breasts and began to bite and lick, making little circles with his tongue.

"Oh," I squeaked.

"Have you forgotten yet?"

"Nope, not yet. I think I need a lot more erasing," I snarked. He was kneeling on the stairs between my legs and looked up to cock an eyebrow at me.

"Really now. I'll have to try harder." He popped down a stair, smirked at me and then dove between my thighs, making O shapes with his tongue. My legs immediately began to shake. *Oh please take those stupid briefs off me.*

"How's that for brain bleach?"

"More," my voice croaked. It was the only word my mouth could form. I was jelly. As all great minds think alike, he ripped the briefs off me and buried his mouth on my sex. My buttocks came off the ground as his sweet mouth began tugging at my lips. I was afraid I was going to drown him I was so turned on.

This man knew how to pleasure a woman and I was so happy to be that woman. I could feel my toes curl as he slid two fingers inside me so I shoved my hands into his hair, pushed his head down and raised my hips off the steps to be even closer.

"Oh Grant, just like that." And then he would switch it up. I would be upset but then his new erasing would feel even better. "Oh Grant!" I screamed and his tongue picked up its pace. I could feel myself approaching orgasm, but I wanted to make love to him.

"Grant, I want you inside me. Please. Now." He obeyed my command, quickly crawled on top of me and thrust deep inside. I was immediately butter.

His eyes grew dark and his lids heavy with lust and he held me still by my shoulders so he could have full access to every bit I could offer his length.

"It's like you were made for me, Lanie," he whispered, and that made me orgasm again. Who knew Grant had the power to make women orgasm just by saying their name? I was going to make him say my name constantly. When we recovered enough to move, he pulled me to my feet.

"This has to be very uncomfortable for you. We should move things upstairs." His eyebrows shot up twice and I couldn't help but mimic back at him. My legs were weak from the amazing passion we had just shared in the middle of his stairwell and I had to steady myself against him. He smiled a genuine smile and I was giddy with the thought of making love to him all night.

"How about a nice, relaxing bath?"

Third cleaning of the day for me, which was fine, because I was feeling extra dirty. The bath in Grant's room was an oversized jet bath with a horizon pool on the sides. I watched as he ran around his room gathering candles, quickly placing them on the floor all around the tub and lighting them. In a matter of moments he had transformed his bathroom into a steamy, romantic cove.

We shed what remained of our clothes and I tossed a sock at his head. He grabbed me and kissed me urgently. When he released me, I tossed the other at him. He kissed me again.

He took my hand and helped me as I stepped up and into the tub. My muscles instantly relaxed as I hit the water. Apparently, lovemaking on the stairs had taken a bit of a toll on my body. I sighed in complete contentment as Grant poured in the bath salts.

"That's an interesting find in a bachelor's place," I teased.

"Chelsie dropped them off early this afternoon. She said I might need them. My cousins must have been planning for this to happen."

"For years." I grinned.

He climbed in with me and our bodies intertwined. I had never been this happy in my entire life as I was in this moment, this night with Grant. I was in a complete state of bliss and he seemed to be, too. We didn't speak much, but instead, whispered sweet nothings into each other's ears. I found it hard not to kiss him often. I felt his hands move to my breasts, where they remained, massaging and caressing until the water began to cool.

"To my bed?"

"Yes, sir, that would be wonderful." I think I was beaming.

His bed was a huge king-sized super cushy one and we sank into it together. He turned me on my side and spooned me. It was like our bodies were made for each other. A perfect fit. He stroked my hair and kissed my neck and soon sleep fell upon us. The storm still raged outside, but here with Grant, I was warm, safe and happy.

I awoke by being jolted out of sleep by a large crash of thunder. I felt Grant's arms tighten around me. This is where I belonged, in this man's arms. I sighed blissfully and turned over to press closer against him and quickly returned to a deep slumber.

When I awoke in the morning, I was alone. Sitting up quickly, I began to panic that the night before had all been a dream.

"Grant?" Then I heard his steps on the stairs and relief filled me. When he entered the room, he had a tray with a smattering of delicious breakfast treats, freshly brewed Kona coffee and a huge grin. He wore only the briefs

I had been wearing last night and it made me smile to think I was the last one wearing them. His body was perfect; lean and cut. He looked like some kind of mythical creature too beautiful for this world.

"Wow, breakfast in bed?"

"If I have my way, I'll be serving the next few meals to you right here." I smiled, ran a hand across his cheek and headed to the bathroom for a quick moment.

I used my finger to brush my teeth, splashed water on my face, put my hair in a loose knot and pulled on his Turkish bathrobe and then headed back to bed as fast as I could. We sipped on coffee and nibbled on fruit and chocolate croissants.

"So, chocolate croissants?"

"Chelsie again. She gave me quite a care package yesterday."

"I have to remember to call and thank her."

"And fill her in on all the delicious details?"

"Of course. Hopefully I can get her and Samantha at the same time so I can tell them how satisfying breakfast was."

When we had finished, we refreshed our coffee, placed the tray on the ground and cuddled back into bed together. It wasn't long before our coffee was abandoned and we were making love again.

"Grant, you said something to me last night. I just want to understand."

"I meant every word I said to you."

"But you said that you loved me. That you always have."

"And again, I meant every word I said to you." His gaze was intent, honest. I believed him.

I couldn't say it back even though I felt it. I loved him, but I wasn't ready to tell him yet. I wanted to be. This was all happening so fast and I wanted to make sure things would be okay with Dane. I didn't want to lose our little family or hurt either of them.

"Grant, you know I feel deeply for you, but …

Chapter 7

I Don't Understand

… I think we have to talk about all this. And then there's Dane …" Grant smiled at me but his eyes showed hurt. I wished I could tell him the words he wanted to hear and throw caution to the wind, but I couldn't do that, it wasn't who I was. I had to make sure nothing could go wrong. This was something I really wanted.

"I have every intention of speaking with him today," he said, his tone serious.

"Shouldn't we talk to him together?"

"We need to handle this very delicately. I need to be the one. It's a guy thing."

"You know I trust you. But I'm sure he's going to approach me at some point today. Shall I just play coy or clueless?"

"Neither. You won't have to play at all. Unless you'd like to play some more now?" He grabbed me and pulled me on top of him.

"I hate to say this, but we really should get out of bed. Although I wouldn't mind spending the entire day here with you."

"Yes. I know. Duty calls." I kissed him deeply.

"How about you come to my place tonight so Woof has some company?"

"I'm sure we'll be no company for Woof once we get going again." He ran his fingers through the ends of my hair, twirling them around his finger.

"We're still here, in bed." I was starting to feel anxious about seeing Dane. But Grant said he would handle it, so I tried to calm myself as well as yank myself away from him to find my clothes. When I was dressed, Grant walked me to the door and kissed me goodbye. I gave him a soft wave and headed home, carrying my boots in my hand. It was still stormy, but I walked slowly. Woof was waiting for me by the door when I got there. He didn't look worse for wear, so the storm must have not bothered him much. I headed upstairs to call my girls.

I reached for the phone and realized I had about twenty messages waiting. The first three were from a very panicked Dane. The next few were from Samantha, two from Chelsie with a squealing Samantha in the background, and then two more from a now angry Dane. Oh, and one more from Grant. He must have called while I was walking home.

"Lanie, I just wanted you to know I am thinking of you. Constantly. That I meant everything I said. And how beautiful I think you are. *Oh*, and last night was amazing. Let's have a repeat performance tonight. Okay? Good. I love you."

I played his message over and over again and then saved it. I was about to call the girls when the phone rang in my hand.

"What are you two, psychic? Or do you have cameras hidden around here?"

"I wish we had cameras. I would love to have watched you two last night instead of the very boring movie Dylan and Steve made us watch."

"Have a storm party, did we?"

"Oh, who cares about what we did? We're old news. We want to hear all about last night." I filled the girls in with a play by play of what happened without divulging the graphic details. There were whoots and clapping from the other end and then finally Samantha could contain herself no longer.

"He told you he loved you?" she said in a high-pitched loud voice.

"He what?" I heard Chelsie say from somewhere. She must have removed herself from the call at one point. "And?"

"And I couldn't say it back yet. I love him. I'm definitely in love with him, I think I always have been."

"Then why not?" Samantha sounded upset.

"We just started heading in this direction. I kind of want the whole wooing thing. Make him work for it a bit." I smiled. I wanted the whole real deal with Grant. I then told them about Dane's call and Grant's email and his intention to go talk with him today. I heard them cover the phone and a muffled conversation began.

"Umm, Ladies, I'm still here, you know. What are you discussing?"

"It's nothing, Lanie … we just agree with the whole make-him-work-for-it thing."

"Good! Well, I have to give Dane a call. I'll call you back. I need some ideas for tonight."

Samantha couldn't wait and started rambling. I heard Chelsie wrestle the phone from her.

"Okay, babe, we'll wait for your call back."

I stared at the phone. I wanted to call Dane, but I was still mad at him. And had we betrayed him? I kind of felt like we did. I went over multiple conversations in my head and finally decided now was not the time. I'd wait until Grant called to tell me what had happened. I took dinner makings out of the fridge and prepared a few things ahead of time. I went upstairs, picked out an outfit for dinner and then something sexier for dessert. I called the girls back and took complicated mental notes. *Wow, lucky Dylan.* Samantha was giving me *Kama Sutra* instructions over the phone. At one point, she had to email me some pictures, because I couldn't figure out what she was talking about.

"You can actually bend like that?" My head was tilted so far over I was almost viewing the image upside down.

"You get pretty limber after a few months of *Kama Sutra*," Samantha said nonchalantly.

"I bet you do. I think I have everything I need. I'll give you a call later to let you know how the body origami goes."

I hung up and started to mill around the house again, getting ready for the evening. I even tried to get myself into one of Samantha's positions. Yeah. That particular one was not happening any time soon. I needed to practice. There was a knock at my door. Thinking it was Grant, I ran to answer. It was Dane.

"Hey, come on in." *Oh man, how was this going to go?* I had no idea if Grant had spoken to him yet. He came in and plunked himself down on the couch.

"Lanie, I just had an interesting conversation with Grant."

"Oh, you did? And you're here because you'd like to talk to me about it?"

"Yes. I think it's only fair I hear this from you, too. I don't understand why you didn't come speak to me yourself."

"Dane, Grant said he needed to talk guy-to-guy with you first." I didn't mean to throw Grant under the bus, but he would understand.

"Lanie, why didn't you guys just tell me? I mean, I'm with Lori and it's pretty serious. And, well, if you aren't with me, then I couldn't think of two people I'd like together more. It's no biggie."

"Really? I mean seriously?"

"Of course."

"But we broke the pact."

"Grant and I made that pact so long ago, I'm not going to hold him to it."

"You mean we all made the pact."

"Oh wait. Grant never told you about our pact?"

"I don't understand. There's a different one?" My mind was racing. What was he talking about? Grant never said anything to me about a pact between just them. Neither of them had.

"Well, I'm going to defer that one to your boyfriend. So would you and Grant like to come over for coffee and cards tonight? As a double date now, of course."

"Oh, Dane, Grant and I were planning on being alone, you know, tonight."

"In other words, he plans on getting you into bed tonight."

"Why would you jump to that conclusion?"

"I just assumed, you know, based on Grant's past with other women, that he was planning on getting lucky tonight with you." Dane was referring to the time when Grant was, how shall I put this, kind of a male slut. He brought home a different girl every weekend and they would hole up at his place for the night. They never lasted past the weekend.

"Look, that was a long time ago. I would hope he doesn't look at me like that."

"Of course he doesn't." His tone was a little funky and I really didn't like it.

"So what was with your phone call last night?" I wanted to change the subject. I didn't want to think about Grant with other women. It bothered me more now than it did then.

"Did he tell you he loved you?" Why was he doing this if it was no biggie?

"Dane, I don't really want to discuss this with you right now. I want to talk about why you were so mad yesterday."

"I'm sorry, Lanie, I didn't mean to upset you. I was panicking about the presentation is all." I guess that was it, nothing to do with Grant or me, just nerves about the proposal, which was out of character for Dane. Nothing threw him.

"Listen, I have to start getting ready for tonight. I don't mean to push you out the door or anything." I felt bad, but I wanted to call Grant and find out what time he was coming and get ready without having to rush.

Dane laughed. "But it's just Grant. He's seen you covered in mud." I was a wee bit stunned. Yes, it was just Grant, and he had seen me lots of ways, even more so after last night, but it was different now; I wanted to look nice.

"Well, it's just Lori, but you probably try to look nice for her, right?"

"Are you jealous of Lori, Lanie?" Seriously, was that supposed to be some kind of dig?

"That's ridiculous. I'm happy for you."

"If you say so."

"I do say so."

"You go ahead and get ready for your date with Grant." He laughed. "Oh, and don't become another weekend romp." *Did he just suggest that Grant might only look at me like another weekend romp?* I could feel my blood pressure starting to rise a bit and needed to put this conversation to an end. It was only getting worse.

"Sure. See you later." He gave me a kiss goodbye on the cheek and headed out the door. I watched him walk home and he seemed really tense. His fists were clenched and he was walking quickly, with determination. I tried to block what he said out of my mind. I sure could use one of Grant's mind erasers right now. Bet I would get one later tonight. Just thinking about tonight seemed to do the trick.

Around four o'clock, the phone rang. I checked the caller ID and it was Grant. "Hey." I said it as sexy as one can say a one-syllable word.

"Hey to you, too." I could hear the smile in his voice.

"So what's our plan? Timing-wise. I thought we'd play the rest by ear, or whatever body part you were thinking."

"Lanie, you're being naughty and I like it. I just have to take care of something, shower, and I'll be over say around six or half past. Sound good?"

"Sounds fantastic. I'll have dinner ready to go by then."

"I can't wait to see you tonight."

"If you want to see me so badly, come over now."

"I'd like that; I'd like nothing more. However, good things come to those who wait. I'll be there by six-thirty."

"Okay, see you then."

Around six-fifteen, I had everything ready. Grant would be here soon and I was excited, so excited that I couldn't stop looking out the window for him. I saw Lori walk by and head towards Grant's. Wonder what she was doing? She must be going over to the stables; but she wasn't exactly dressed for the stables. I careened my neck and pressed my face up against the window, trying to watch her, but lost my view. *Must be nothing.* I decided to spend the rest of the time in the kitchen finishing up dinner.

> *6:30 - He should be here any second.*
> *6:40 - He must be running behind.*
> *6:50 - Picked up the phone and called him. No answer.*
> *6:51 - Decided to go over and see what was up.*
> *6:52 - I was out the door.*
> *6:53 - I was at his door knocking. No answer. And then Dane was there with me.*

"Hey. What're you doing here?" I was really curious because he knew Grant and I had plans tonight.

"Grant called Lori and told her he needed her to come over. She left half an hour ago, but never came back. I was coming to get her."

"Really? I'll check for them here. Can you go check the stables? Maybe they're there. Grant mentioned something about a saddle for Lori."

Dane headed off, so I let myself in. I heard the shower running. So Lori wasn't here. They must have run overtime and Grant was running behind. I thought it would be fun to be waiting there when he got out of the shower. I could be an appetizer. I started to head up the stairs and the shower stopped. I quickened my pace so I could catch him with only his towel on. But when I reached the room …

Chapter 8

This Can't Be Happening

… it was Lori who I caught in just her towel.

Lori and Grant were facing each other. She was holding her towel open and giggling. Grant wore nothing but his towel, standing there with his mouth gaping open like he just received the best surprise ever.

"This can't be happening." I rubbed my eyes and looked again, but it was. My stomach dropped and I got a serious wave of nausea. My body felt hot all over, yet cold at the same time. My breath was lost and my heartbeat was out of control. My chest was burning. My heart was breaking.

"What the hell's going on here?" It was Dane. *Where did he come from?* I had no idea what was happening. The time frame of events suddenly became disjointed.

I could hear them all. But everything sounded muted and distant.

The gasp from Lori at seeing Dane and I.

Her smug expression.

Dane's accusations.

Yelling.

Crying.

I think I was the one crying, but I couldn't tell.

The whole time I stood there, minutes or seconds—I couldn't tell—all I could see was Grant's face, a look of horror pasted on it. His mouth was moving, but nothing was coming out; at least I didn't hear anything. Dane was pushing at him, pulling at Lori. But Grant's gaze was focused on mine.

It was like a tunnel. Dane barreled over and grabbed my wrist, and yanked me toward him.

"Come on, we're going. We can leave them to whatever it was they were doing. We don't need them," he hissed.

I saw Grant grab his hair and he was hyperventilating. As Dane started to pull me away, I could hear Grant screaming while holding onto his towel for dear life. "Lanie, no! It's not what you think. I swear to you! Lanie, please. Oh God. Dane, please don't take her. She needs to listen to me! Please, Lanie!"

I heard him all the way down the stairs and out the front door, even as Dane pulled me down the walk and away from Grant. Dane dragged me past my house, and I struggled to release my wrist from his grasp, but he wouldn't let go.

"Lanie, come on."

"Dane, I need to talk to Grant. I have to talk with him."

"Lanie, nothing has changed with him. Same old Grant. Last night you, a little Lori in between, and then back to you. What is there to say?"

"No, I don't believe it. I have to go back."

"You saw it with your own eyes. What's not to believe?"

"But he said he loved me."

"Oh, classic Grant."

"No, he never told anyone that. I know it."

"Lanie, you're so naïve. When are you going to stop living in this little fantasy world of yours?"

His words lashed out and stung. It was all too much. I could feel the tears streaming down my face. He finally stopped to look at me.

"Lanie, I'm sorry. I'm taking my anger at the two of them out on you. It's not your fault. You're the victim here, just like me." His tone was softer.

"I get it. I just want to go home."

"I don't think you should be alone right now. I'm sure Grant will try and come over or call you. You don't need that."

"Dane, please, I need to go home. I want to be alone."

"Fine then," he said abruptly and released me. I walked slowly to my door, looking back between Dane and Grant's houses.

When I got inside, the candles were still burning, and so was dinner. I had left it on warm. I turned it off and threw all the food in the garbage and the dishes in the sink.

Woof sat nearby, watching me dismantle my romantic evening. I finally couldn't do anymore; my emotions were a mess and I was crying so hard I couldn't see. I slumped down on the floor against the cabinets. I felt sick to my stomach.

Woof padded over and rubbed up against me. I pushed him away. "No, go away. You're from him and I don't want you anymore." He just looked at me and gave me a small mew. He settled down against my thigh and began to purr. I knew it wasn't his fault, and he was mine now. I scooped him up and cried into his fur.

After a long while, the candles had almost reached their quick. I was still sitting on the floor and had no idea how long I had been there just staring. I pulled myself up and called Dane.

"I changed my mind. Don't want to be here. I don't want to be alone."

"Come over."

I made some sort of noise of agreement and hung up. Dane would make it better. Dane always seemed to make the bad things go away. I locked the door and I headed over.

When I got there, Dane was waiting for me. He moved aside to let me in. He looked around before closing the door like someone was watching.

"Hey, thanks. My head is all over the place right now."

"I know, mine, too. Maybe we should just sit and talk about how we're going to handle this whole thing."

"What's to handle? Grant and I were barely together. I mean, things just happened. What about you and Lori?" I lied. Of course there was plenty to handle with Grant.

"Lanie, he used you. He lied to you. He slept with you and it meant nothing at all to him." The weight of his words hit me like a ton of bricks.

"It's not true." I shook my head.

"Stop it, Lanie—stop sticking up for him. Things just happened and it didn't take him but hours to cheat on you. Or maybe his entire intention was only to get you into bed until someone better came along."

"Are you saying Lori is better than me?"

"That's not what I meant." Then he whispered under his breath, "Not to me."

"I just have to figure this all out in my head. There are pieces missing and I need to talk to Grant. Don't you want to talk to Lori?"

"Not really, no. I don't want to talk to either of them."

Dane's phone rang. "Hello? What do you want? She's here, but she doesn't want to talk to you." I started to protest but he put his hand up to stop me. "I don't want to hear your lies, Grant. Not from you or Lori. You made your bed, and now you can sleep in it with her." And he hung up. The phone rang again and Dane switched off the ringer.

I wondered if Lori was still there with him. I looked out the window and her car was gone. *Coward. Bitch.* She hurt Dane and was too self-absorbed to even try and talk to him. At least Grant tried to find me.

"Looks like Lori left."

"I'm sure she knows there's nothing more to do here."

"What do you mean, nothing more to do here?"

His answer was quick, "Meaning she did enough damage. Anything else would just make it worse."

Dane went over to the bar and reached for a glass. "You want a drink? Because I can't think of anything else I want to do more right now than drown my sorrows with you."

I considered this. A few drinks would make me numb, and if I drank enough, I possibly might pass out instead of thinking too much. "Yes."

He grabbed two glasses. "What's your poison?"

"Something strong. And bring the whole bottle."

"Slow down over there. I don't need a throwing up Lanie, just a calm one. Pace yourself."

He poured some pretty colored liquor over ice and handed it to me. He sat down close to me on the couch and put an arm around my shoulder. I leaned into him and took a sip. It didn't taste pretty, but I could tell it was strong. I downed it.

"That's how you pace yourself?"

"I needed a quick fix," I choked out.

He poured me another, and then it was gone. My glass had become endless as he poured drink after drink. Soon we were chatting about anything but what had happened. Deep down, the hurt was so raw I couldn't even think about it.

"Finished that one off," he said as he held the bottle upside down and grabbed our glasses. He went to find us a new poison. When he returned, he handed me the glass. This one tasted different, tasted funny. I didn't care. I just wanted to be numb. Soon my vision started to blur and I felt so tired. I couldn't focus on Danc anymore, and all I wanted to do was shut my eyes and sleep. I felt him stroking my hair and cheek as I drifted off.

I thought I heard voices. A man? A woman? I wasn't sure. My head was so fuzzy and I couldn't focus my eyes, so I just lay there drifting in and out of sleep. I must have been dreaming about Grant, because he was there with me then. I felt him touch my cheek and say my name. I reached for his hand and pulled him down to me.

"I missed you, Baby, kiss me," I mumbled to him.

"Yes, Baby, I want you, too." I felt a soft kiss on my lips.

"I want to feel you. Show me you want me." I felt my clothes being removed, soft kisses on my neck and brushing my lips. I opened my eyes, at least I think I did, and Grant was there. My shirt was being unbuttoned.

He was telling me everything was going to be okay. My bra was taken off.

He was telling me we were meant to be together. My pants were being pulled off.

He said he wanted to show me how much he loved me. My panties slid down my legs. His tongue was moving up my thigh.

My body was cold. I tried to reach out for something to keep me warm and then I felt Grant's body cover mine. I moaned slightly and moved my legs apart so he could slide himself between them. I felt his hot breath on my neck. I tried to kiss him, but ended up running my tongue down his neck.

"That's right, Baby. You know we're supposed to be together. Show me you want me. Let me make love to you." His voice didn't sound right to me, but my Grant was here, with me, not Lori. He wanted me and I felt warm and tingly. I tried as hard as I could to open my eyes, but the room was swaying. My head felt fuzzy. I tried to say something, but the slurred words I heard come out didn't have any meaning. Through my mostly-shut eyes, I thought I could see Grant's face, his sweet, beautiful face. But then I felt him twist my nipples, and nip at them. He was grabbing me all over and then settled between my legs. His hands were rough, moving too fast. It was not the same as last night. I tried to tell him to be gentler.

"Rough."

"Oh you want it rougher? Any way you like it, Baby."

“What?” I mumbled in confusion. Suddenly he was grabbing my hair and slamming his lips to mine. He was hurting me.

“Hurting me,” I slurred incoherently.

“Shhh, I’m just doing what we both want. Showing you how much I love you.”

I felt him spread my legs further apart and he shoved himself inside me, hard. I thought he would split me open. He was being rough and it hurt. He was just pummeling me. Grinding into me hard and fast. It felt like he was ripping me apart. Then I heard something else. Was that a whimper? I tried to turn my head, but his hands were holding my hair so I couldn’t move.

“No,” I heard Grant’s voice say. I peered to my side through my semi-closed lids and Grant was …

Chapter 9

Have You Gone Absolutely Mad?

… standing in the doorway. How could he be there and on top of me? He was making love to me, but he was standing across the room. I looked above me and a blurry Grant zoomed in and out of focus. He was Grant, but then he was Dane, and then Grant again; but Grant was at the door.

"Lanie, I'm so glad you finally told me this was what you wanted. I never would have done anything like this without knowing you wanted it, too."

No, that wasn't right. What was he saying? I was so confused and my head was thrumming. Something was seriously wrong.

"This is how it should have always been." But it was Dane's voice. I was still being rammed. The pain between my legs was becoming increasingly worse.

I had to get my bearings. I tried as hard as I could to pull myself out of my stupor. I tried to kick him off me using everything I had to fight. I scratched his face and his fist came down hard into my jaw. I heard fast footsteps. I started to scream, and then I felt him being ripped from me. I could taste blood in my mouth and intense pain. Then there was fighting. I tried to sit up and force my eyes to open. Dane and Grant were fighting. Punching each other, breaking things and knocking over furniture. I didn't understand where I was or what was going on. I was in a complete state of utter confusion. Suddenly feeling very exposed. I tried to find anything to cover myself with. I felt hands on me and cried out slapping at whoever it was.

"Shhh, Lanie. Stop. I'm getting you out of here." This voice sounded right to me.

"She doesn't want to be with you. You hurt her, you lied to her," Dane spat.

"No, Dane. Not me. You." Grant's words were filled with venom. He wrapped his jacket around me and picked me up. I threw my arms around his neck and breathed him in. This was the real Grant. He held me close.

"Lanie, what are you doing? Why are you going with him? What about us?" Dane sounded sickeningly sweet.

"Are you sick, Dane? This whole thing tonight, it's just so sick," Grant sounded disgusted.

"No, what you did to Lanie was sick." He blocked the doorway.

"Dane, I'm taking Lanie home. Get out of my way. Now."

"She doesn't want to go with you. She wants to be with me. You saw us. We were together. We were making love."

"Have you gone absolutely mad? Move. Move now or something we'll both regret is going to happen. Something far worse then everything that's happened so far tonight."

"Please, take me home," I barely managed. With my plea hanging in the air, Dane moved to the side. As Grant and I passed, Dane reached out to touch me.

"Don't! Don't you ever dare touch her again." His voice was gruff and low. I heard the door slam behind us. The night air was extremely cold, or maybe I was just chilled from lack of clothing. My head was still spinning. My eyes still couldn't focus.

"Oh God, Lanie. How can this all be happening? What the hell?" He pulled me even closer. He pressed his lips to the top of my head and didn't move them. *Was he crying?* My mind couldn't process it all. I thought I heard him sob.

I had locked the door to my house when I left earlier. Grant had to get the key. "Can you stand?"

"I don't know."

"We're going to give it a try, okay?"

"Okay."

"Keep your arm around me." He ever so gently lowered me to place my feet on the ground only long enough to grab the key and unlock the door. He swiftly picked me back up into the safety of his embrace. He held me there for a moment before opening the door, then entered my kitchen. I guess my dinner cleanup looked more like a temper tantrum. Food was on the counters and floors; dishes were in the sink, some of them broken.

"Lanie," he whispered in shock, "what the hell happened?"

I was in no mood to, nor did I think I could recant the evening's events. I didn't reply. He turned and headed for the stairs. This was what I wanted tonight to be like. Grant and I, home together, but that was all gone now. There wouldn't be anything for us tonight, possibly ever again. Pieces of my heart were now strewn all the way up my stairs. When we got to my room, he brought me right into the master bath and sat me on the edge of the tub.

"You're jaw is bruised. I need to get you some ice. Do you think you can stay right here without falling off the tub?"

"Yes. Don't leave me."

"I have to get some ice for your face."

"Fine," I said reluctantly. And he was gone. I tried to stand and the room swam. I took a deep breath in and grabbed the towel bar to steady myself. I made it to the door and grabbed my robe and put it on. I went to the mirror to see the damage. *Yep, I looked like I had been in a bar fight.* I made it back to the tub and sat down. Grant was back with a bag of frozen peas. I was hurt, not hungry.

"Lanie, this will mold to your face, so it shouldn't hurt too bad." He pressed the peas to my face. It did hurt and I jerked back.

"I'm sorry, Sweetheart. Here, you hold it on so you can press as much as you need to so it doesn't hurt."

He proceeded to wet the corner of a small hand towel and started cleaning the mascara that was probably halfway down my face. He was so gentle showing how much he cared for me in his touch. *Is that even possible? Why was he being so nice to me right now?* I could feel my eyes start to sting and the tears started to well in my eyes.

"Does it hurt?"

"No. It's not that." My words were lost. I didn't know how to tell him what I felt. I'm sure he sensed it. He stopped dead; his face went pale and he looked pained. Then his eyes got moist, too.

"What the hell happened tonight? Everything was perfect, then everything was wrong."

He grasped my shoulders, dropped his head and leaned it against my chest. I wanted to reach out and hold him. I didn't know what to do. My head finally felt like it was starting to clear.

"We have a lot to talk about," he said.

"I know. But I don't want to talk now. I can't. I just want to go to sleep. I want to go to sleep and wake up tomorrow morning from this nightmare." His sad eyes searched my face, but I'm not sure what for. I got up and my knees gave out. He grabbed my arm and helped me to the bedroom. I grabbed leggings and a big soft sweatshirt and pulled them on. Grant turned his back and looked out my window to his window across the way. One hand covered his face and the other hung at his side. He looked lost. I climbed into bed, pulled the covers up to my neck and curled myself into fetal position.

"I'm not leaving you alone. I'll stay downstairs."

"No. Stay here with me. Please." I closed my eyes. I felt him lay down on the bed at my feet and he curled himself around them.

Nightmares. Vivid visions splashed across my mind.

Grant with Lori.

His face when he saw me.

Dane above me.

Tom using me.

Lori giggling in front of Grant.

Lori walking out the door with Tom.

Grant seeing me with Dane.

My nightmare must have become a night terror, because I heard myself screaming and then Grant was beside me. Soothing me, waking me, telling me everything was going to be all right.

"I'm so sorry, Lanie. This wasn't the night I had planned for us," he whispered quietly into my ear.

"Grant, hold me. I need you right now. I'm sorry."

"Don't say you're sorry. I want to be here with you. I'll stay as long as you'll have me. "

Grant lay beside me and spooned me. We stayed like that all night. He never left my side and the nightmares stayed at bay. When light entered the room, I started to stir. The pain seeped into my consciousness. My jaw was killing me. My head hurt just as much. Grant was leaning up on one arm, watching me. I looked up at him for a moment, but the pain I saw in his eyes was too much for me. I looked away.

"I need to shower." I said.

"Maybe a hot bath would do you better. Soak for a while. Clear your head. How is your head?"

"I'm not sure. I'm still feeling fuzzy. Not like a hangover; I don't know."

Grant's hand clenched into a fist and then he quickly released it. I had to think he was trying keep calm for me.

"I'll start the water and then I'm going to attack your kitchen. Well, un-attack it. Looks like it was in a bar brawl last night. Can I get you some coffee?"

A million emotions ran through my veins and I just didn't know how to react. Part of me wanted to reach and out kiss him. Another wanted to yell at him for being with Lori. Another was ashamed of what happened last night with Dane.

"I can clean the kitchen. My mess."

"Lanie, please let me help you."

"I don't want your pity. I want everything to be like it was yesterday morning. I don't know what I want." And with that the waterworks started. I didn't want him to see me like this.

"Please don't cry. It's heartbreaking to me."

"I think I want you to go."

He looked hurt. More than he already did. I didn't want to hurt him anymore. I'm sure last night had devastated him as much as it had me.

"I think I need female company right now. Could you call Samantha and Chels for me? I need them here." I was suddenly desperate for them to be here. Before I could say anything else, he shot up and grabbed the phone.

"Chels, something happened last night. I don't want to talk about it right now. Lanie needs you and Samantha. Now, please." He hung up and looked at me. I couldn't look him in the eyes. The more last night's events came back to my memory, the more I wanted to crawl deep inside myself.

"Lanie, I'm going to go downstairs. I'm not leaving until they get here. Do you want me to come back later?" I didn't want him to leave. I didn't want him to stay. I didn't want to face any of this.

"Grant, I need some time. I need to straighten out everything that's going on in my head."

"Please, Lanie, give me a chance to tell you my side of this, when you're ready. This whole thing, I just don't know what to say to you right now."

"I'm not sure I could listen right now."

"Please promise me you'll give me a chance. That's all I'm asking."

I raised my hand. "I promise to hear you out. But you have to do the same for me. That's all I can give you right now. When I'm ready. Not now. I'm not even sure today."

He lowered his head and pulled himself up. He looked like he was carrying a great weight. He moved slowly and with much effort, like a magnet trying to pull away from its attractant.

"Grant, I'm not abandoning you. I'm not going anywhere. I just don't know where here is right now." I gestured to the space between us.

"I understand." He turned and left the room. My breath hitched in my throat and it took me a bit to recover from watching him walk away. I felt empty.

I started my bath and stopped to look in the mirror. I was mortified to see that my jaw had a black and blue bruise on it. I felt a pang of something, not sure what, that Grant had seen me looking like this. I needed to keep myself moving, so I got into the bath. I heard voices downstairs and figured Grant was filling Chelsie and Samantha in on everything. Suddenly I felt the need to scrub myself clean. I started to rub my skin furiously. I wanted to clean off the entire night's events. Dane touching me; Grant and Lori being together. I thought if I could scrub it all off, it would go away. My skin was starting to get raw and I was starting to get hysterical. Suddenly there was Samantha, her arms were around me and stopping me.

"Lanie, stop. You'll hurt yourself. That's definitely not the proper way to exfoliate, and it won't make anything go away."

"Samantha, I just want to wash it away," I cried. I broke down and grasped onto her. She just held me. I could hear Chelsie and Grant now outside the bathroom door.

"Grant, she doesn't need you to see her like this."

"I can't stand to see her like this. I just want to make it all go away."

"This is not the time. There isn't anything you can do for her right now, and you're a big part of this, too. We'll take care of her. You should go."

"Chels, please."

"Grant, we'll take it from here. You need to go home. And stay away from Dane's. Do you hear me? You just stay home until one of us comes to you or calls. Go." Chelsie's voice was strong and full of command.

"Chelsie, I can't …"

Chapter 10

It's Never Going to be the Same

"... ever be without her again. Not now. Not after things finally started."

"Grant. I promise. I'll call you." Her voice was calm and reassuring.

The door opened and Chelsie came into the bathroom to join us. She wound her arms around me, too, and they both held me as I cried. We stayed like that for quite a while. Eventually, Chelsie got up to leave.

"No, please don't go."

"Honey, I'm just going to get something for you to wear. You need to get out of that tub. You're pruning. Let's not add insult to injury. Then we'll talk. I'm also making a pot of tea." Chelsie was always the voice of reason. Blunt was more like it. She was a no-bullshit kind of gal, and I loved her for that.

I got dressed with a watchful Samantha, who just looked at me with sad eyes. I could tell her heart was reaching out to mine, but my heart was temporarily closed for business. I finished and sat on the edge of the bed.

"Sam, it's never going to be the same, not ever." I was feeling pretty weepy, but who could blame me?

Samantha pulled up behind me and put her arms around me, her chin on my shoulder. "No, Honey, not the same. It will be different. But that doesn't mean it can't be better different."

"How can it ever be better? It's probably over before it even got started."

"It's not over. Only if you both decide that's what you want. Things happen and we grow from it." I was totally not in the mood for a pep talk.

"Oh screw that, Sam. How are Grant and I ever going to get past this?"

"Enough, Lanie. It's time to talk." It was Chelsie with her matter-of-fact attitude, "Downstairs. Let's go sort this all out."

We sat at my now clean kitchen table. Chelsie or Grant had returned my kitchen to its sparkly clean state. I was grateful, but said nothing. I didn't want to think about my burned dinner and ruined night. But that was not going to happen, because the girls wanted a play by play. It was hard to go through it all, really hard. I started from the beginning. I told them about Grant telling me he had to take care of something and seeing Lori and being late for dinner.

"So I went over to see where he was."

"Deep breath, Baby," Chelsie said when I faltered in my thoughts and words.

"I caught him with Lori."

"What?" Samantha was horrified, "No, Grant wouldn't do that." I described the scene. I told them how Dane said Grant had called for Lori to come over.

"No, that can't be. Grant and I were on the phone, and then the computer for at least an hour or so." Chelsie was pretty sure of the time frame.

"You were? Are you sure it was the same time?"

"Lanie, we got on the phone at 5:30 or so—I know because the game was on and it had just started. At 6:15, he started freaking about how he had to get in the shower. But we weren't finished. I made him run late."

"So how did he end up in the shower with her then?" I winced.

"Honey, I have no idea. It was about 6:45 when we got off the phone. He said he was going to power shower."

"Then what happened?" Samantha wanted to know.

I told them about Dane showing up there at the same time I did. I told them how I found them, how Dane was suddenly pulling me out, and me wanting to be alone.

"Something is just wrong with this whole thing. Grant hates Lori. He always has, ever since your prom."

"Grant hates Lori? Because of what she did to me prom night?"

"Lanie, Grant has always had strong feelings for you. Not that it's my place to tell you, but I think it's about time you hear it. He's been too damn chicken to tell you all these years. Those stupid pacts."

"Pact. Everyone keeps saying pacts. Plural. There's only one."

"Nope. There's more than one, but that's for another time. Let's finish this first. What happened next?"

"Then I proceeded to destroy my kitchen and cry. Then I called Dane, told him I didn't want to be alone and he told me to come over."

"Hmm. Convenient. More." The wheels in Chelsie's mind were turning. Samantha had a strange look on her face, too. The whole thing wasn't adding up to them, or me, for that matter.

"And when I got there, he told me we should drown our sorrows together and I thought that would be a good idea."

"How much did you actually drink?" Chelsie had heard a brief run down of the night already from Grant. She had an idea of what happened next.

"I don't know. We finished one bottle that was already open. And then I had one from a new bottle. I don't know what it was. It tasted terrible. I remember that. Everything else afterward is really fuzzy."

"Let's walk it through. You were drinking. You both drank a lot. Then what?"

"We were on his couch in the den. We were just joking about old times, trying not to talk about what had happened and then suddenly I got really tired."

"Just like that? You just suddenly got tired." Chelsie seemed angry.

"Yeah. And the next thing I knew Dane and I were …" I couldn't say it. "I don't even remember how it happened. I thought he was Grant and then suddenly I was …" I couldn't finish.

"Lanie, did you sleep with Dane?" Samantha's voice was like a weak whisper.

"No. Yes. But at first it was Grant. I was sure it was him. But it was wrong. He was rough, nothing like the night before. And then I heard Grant, and he was across the room. And it was Dane I was having sex with."

"Oh my God." Samantha was beside herself.

"Lanie, maybe Dane slipped something into your drink."

The thought had crossed my mind last night when I couldn't function. I had been drunk many times in my life, but it was never like that before. I hadn't had enough to drink to make me pass out.

"No. Dane would never do that."

"Lanie, try to remember how things got to that point."

"I just don't know. I think I let Dane have sex with me and Grant saw us. How is Grant ever going to forgive me?"

"Lanie, are you insane? You were out of it and thought he was Grant. Why would Grant ever hold that against you?"

"Sometimes the heart and the brain don't see eye to eye, Chels. Might be too much for the brain to handle right now."

"When did Dane hit you?" Samantha said under her breath.

"I realized it was him and he was being rough, and I got angry and tried to hit him. I think I scratched his face. He must have just reacted. It's all so surreal."

"That was a pretty crappy reaction, so don't you dare stick up for him. I have a mind to call him up and give him a piece of it."

"Chelsie, please don't."

"Only because you don't want me to, for now. But as soon as you say, I am so calling him out on this. I want to send Steve over to have a little talk with him."

"Yeah, Dylan isn't going to be too happy, either."

"No, please don't tell them. I'm ashamed."

"Lanie, stop it. You have every right to be upset, but not with yourself!" Samantha was pissed now.

"I'm going over to Grant's. I think he needs a shoulder, too. Sam, Lanie is all yours; work your magic".

A part of me longed for Grant to be here with me, to make this all some awful nightmare. But that wasn't possible. We could only heal, either together or apart. I just wasn't sure which.

"Lanie, you need to eat something. When was the last time you ate?"

"I don't remember. Yesterday morning?" Honestly the thought of food made my stomach lurch. It wasn't going to happen. Samantha started making me some toast to go with my tea. "Buttered toast always helps."

"Really? Singed bread with globs of fat makes everything better?"

"Yep. Sure does. In the same family as ice cream, chocolate in any form whatsoever, French fries and alcohol. But we're not going there with you today on that last one."

"Let's see how I feel. Maybe later. So, can you put melted chocolate on the toast?"

"Don't laugh. It's been done," she mused. She plopped my feel better meal on the table.

I sat and picked at the toast. It really did taste great where the butter had soaked through. Samantha knew everything. I was hoping she could help me with my make-up to hide the bruising. I think I wanted to see Grant later, but not looking like a truck ran over my face.

"Lanie, is this whole thing bringing up bad memories? Tom memories?"

"Uh, yeah. Lots. All last night I had nightmares. Everything was jumbled between the past and the present. It was terrible."

"Well, at least you were able to sleep. Gotta find that bright side."

"Bright side? You think there can be a bright side to any of this?" I snapped at her.

"I guess not. But I'm going to do my best to help you, whatever it takes. I'll get you whatever you need; chocolate covered anything, new shoes, a gun, even a chocolate covered gun. You name it and it's yours!"

Samantha really was trying. A chocolate gun. I'd have to think about that one. I wasn't sure what to do. *Should I go see Grant? Should I go see Dane?* I had a zillion questions and I wasn't sure I was prepared for the answers. Actually, I wasn't really prepared to see either of them. *Maybe I should just stay away from them both for a while.*

"Sam, I think I want to go up to the walk for a bit. Would you stay here? I might change my mind about being alone."

"Can I have access to your internet for some shopping? This whole thing has me utterly depressed. I need to buy you something to make you feel better!"

"Sure, shop away. Buy me something completely silly."

"I'm more about sexy, but given the circumstances, I'll see what I can do. Call me if you need me." With that, I proceeded to climb the stairs to the walk. I needed to think, or not think. I needed to draw. I think I needed Nicole.

The day was as gloomy outside as it was inside. There was a steady patter of rain on the roof and the ocean was too lazy to do much. Maybe Nicole was sharing her feelings, too. *No.* She'd be pissed, more like another nor'easter. I grabbed my sketchpad and graphite and started to sketch. But nothing came to me. There was no inspiration in this mess, so I decided to just think.

Grant said he loved me. It seemed like he did. But then he was with Lori—or maybe not. Dane apparently wanted me, too. But I'm pretty sure his chances were non-existent at this point. I just didn't feel that way about him. I was in love with Grant. I wanted to see where things were headed. However, everything on that front was presently ruined. I had no idea how to get past this. Could he get past this? I only saw him and Lori in a compromising situation. He had seen me in the process of actually having sex with Dane. I was afraid the damage was far beyond repair all the way around. *How could Dane, Grant, and I ever be close again?* There was too much for all of us to forgive, and nothing would be forgotten. And right now, no one wanted to make any rash decisions. We needed to piece together what the hell had happened and what was still going on.

My head was starting to hurt along with my jaw. I shut my eyes and, same as last night, images of everything flashed again. I didn't want to see anything. I didn't want to feel anything. I just wanted to be numb again, but alone this time. There was so much going on inside my head and it was bringing up some residual shit from my past. I thought I had gotten past it, but there was a reason why I was a workaholic with no time for men. It's not that I wasn't a sexual person. I was. But until Grant, and now Dane, too, there had only ever been one time I went all the way.

I didn't feel like comparing what Tom had done to me to Dane. I was so stupid back then. I let him. Apparently, I hadn't learned my lesson.

"Oh my God," I screeched …

Chapter 11

Well, I Sure Can Shut You Both Up

… to Lori over the phone. "Tom Loft asked me to the prom!" I couldn't believe it. He was one of the hottest guys in school, aside from my boys, but they were like brothers to me.

"You're kidding me!" Lori was a little too surprised for my taste, but there was no way anything could ruin my awesome mood.

"We're going to go out tomorrow night to the movies and dinner. I am so psyched!"

"Well, I'll come over and we can pick out the perfect outfit." Lori knew how to dress for the guys, so I knew she would make it so Tom couldn't resist me.

When Friday afternoon arrived, Lori came over and we picked out a cute little black mini skirt, button down shirt, and boots. She worked on my hair and I did my makeup, and then off she went to flirt with my boys downstairs.

When I came downstairs, Tom was already there and he and Grant were in the corner talking. I wasn't sure, but Grant didn't look too happy. Lori and Dane sat on the couch watching them and intermittently whispering.

"Hey, Tom. Are you ready to head out?"

"Yeah, I think heading out of here would be a great idea." He shot a glance at Grant. Grant came over to me and handed me his cell phone. "Please call me if you need anything." And with that he stormed out of the room. Not sure what crawled up his ass, but whatever.

When Tom and I got into his car, he headed into town and stopped at a strip mall. "Listen, my parents are out of town. Want to get Chinese take out and rent a movie and head back there instead?" All alone with Tom at his house? Hell yeah!

"Sure, that sounds really nice." That sounds really nice? Damn I sucked at this. We went to get the evening's meal and movie. We settled on sharing a few different things for eats and a scary movie that we had both missed in the theater. After we got back to his house and had eaten, it didn't take long for Tom to start making his moves.

"I'm just going to light a few candles and turn the lights off. Better for the movie, you know? Why don't you throw some pillows and blankets on the floor? Make things all cozy."

I made this great little nest ready for a great make out session. I wasn't very experienced with guys, having only gotten to second base before. I wanted to save myself for someone special, for a special night, like Tom and prom night.

When the movie started, so did we. We were hot and heavy, and soon we were down to our underwear. I was so nervous and I hoped I was doing everything right.

"So, you want to do it?" he said smoothly, like he had said it to me a hundred times before.

"I don't know, I don't think this is the right time." But he kept pawing at me and I let him. I was afraid to stop him. He could have any girl he wanted and I wanted him to want me.

When he started to pull at my panties, I did stop him.

"Tom, I'm not ready. I've never … you know." I was seriously blushing at this point. It was pretty hard to resist him. I was fired up, yet scared out of my mind. My hormones were in control now. And this little bit of information seemed to fuel his advances.

"Oh yeah? Well, I can take care of that. I promise to be really gentle." But he wasn't. Next thing I knew, his underwear was gone and he was pushing my face so I was eye to eye with his dick.

"Tom, I'm not feeling comfortable with this."

"Come on, Lanie, all the girls do this. You wouldn't want anyone to think you're a prude, would you?" No. I didn't want that, but this wasn't how I'd pictured this happening. Now he was holding my head and shoving himself into my mouth. I had no idea what I was doing. So I let him. I gagged a lot.

Before he could come, he pulled out, was rolling on a condom and then pushed me on my back. He was on top of me and pulling my panties to the side. He pulled my knees apart and started to push in.

"Tom, stop, I don't want to do this. I'm not ready."

"You feel ready and it's too late. We're already doing it." And with that he pushed into me hard. I could feel myself rip. The pain was insane. It didn't take him long, and for that I was grateful.

When he was done, he rolled off me, put his clothes back on, and said, "Hey, listen, it's getting late. I'm going to take you home."

I should have been upset. I didn't know if this was how your first time was supposed to be. Was he my boyfriend now? Were we still going to the prom? Would he ever call me again?

We drove home in silence. When we got to my house, he stopped the car, gave me a peck on the cheek and didn't even walk me to the door. That was my first time having sex.

And that would have been my first and only time until Grant, and now Dane. *Oh great. Not only am I now a slut, but also a cheater to boot. I think.* I realized it was probably best to not be thinking anymore. I headed down to Samantha. When I got there, Chelsie was back. They were sipping tea at my computer.

"Chels, how's Grant?" I had to know. I really wanted to see him. I really didn't want to see him. It was a bizarre ying-yang thing I had going on for sure.

"He is pretty broken up about what happened last night, too. He gets all testosterony and he goes 'I'm going to kill him!' and then he's all down because he thinks about you. Was that too in-your-face? I really do try not to sound so bitchy all the time. I can't help it." Chelsie smiled and started to play with her nails. Samantha and I just stared at her with our chins on the ground.

"Well, I sure can shut you both up. Listen, Honey, he said nothing happened with Lori. I believe him. But you have to be the one who does, not me."

"Yes. But I don't know what to say to him."

"Then don't talk, just listen," Samantha chimed in. She didn't need to convince me.

"But I need to look more presentable. Want to help?"

Samantha clapped and pulled me back upstairs. She was so easy to make happy. Apparently, she was also a genius with covering things up. I'm sure it was the years of hickies. You couldn't even see the bruise on my jaw. I threw on jeans, a t-shirt, and sneakers. When we got back downstairs, Chelsie was just hanging up the phone.

"I told him to come here. Figured you'd feel more comfortable on your own turf."

"Thanks."

Suddenly there was a loud series of bangs then soft knocks on the door.

"That man is fast."

I looked back and forth between Samantha and Chelsie. We took turns nodding at each other, trying to figure out who should answer the door. Finally, Chelsie had enough and stormed off to let Grant in. When she opened the door, I was shocked to see how terrible Grant looked. *Don't get me wrong; even looking terrible, Grant was a hot piece of ass.* He looked worn, tired, and sad.

He walked right to me, staying about a foot or so away. I felt like I was gravitating toward him but I stayed put.

"Hi."

"Hi."

"Well, love to stay around for the stimulating conversation, but Sam and I have to go. I'm sure we'll hear from you both later." Chelsie kissed us both on our cheeks and walked right out the door. Samantha looked surprised. She made a 'call me' sign with her hand and then waved. Suddenly we were alone.

He wouldn't look me in the eyes. I doubt he would ever look me there again. So we stood in front of each other, staring at our feet. This was getting us nowhere.

"Tea?" I meekly said.

"That would be nice. Have you eaten anything?"

"Toast."

"Sam?"

"Yes."

"Did she offer you chocolate, too? She only pulls out the chocolate covered stuff when it's bad. It can't get worse than this."

I smiled despite myself. Just being in the room with Grant made my heart flutter even under these circumstances. *Hell, it could be the end of the world and he would make my heart feel like pudding.* I wanted him to hold me. I wanted to have some part of me touching some part of him. I wanted to know what the hell Lori was doing at his house dressed in nothing but a towel.

"Lanie, I don't really know how to start."

"Us talking. Right. Yeah, me neither."

"I have an idea. One-for-one?"

"Perfect."

We got our tea and sat down on the couch, on opposite ends, facing each other. I had my knees pulled up to my chest and he just fidgeted. And at the same time, we both said, "You go first." And then we both giggled. Then we did it again.

"You go first, Grant."

"Ladies first."

"Fine. Why the hell was Lori in your room wearing only a towel?" *Guess I was playing hardball.* He asked for it. Although I felt bad, I wanted to know.

"I don't know."

"Tell me that is seriously not your answer."

"Lanie, it's my only answer. I have no clue. I came out of the shower and she was there, like that, until she opened the towel. And then you were there."

"So why did you call her and ask her to come over?"

"I didn't. I told you, she was there when I got out of the shower. I never called her."

"Did you like what you saw?"

"What?"

"Under the towel, Lori in all her naked glory with perfect boobs."

He chuckled. I was not laughing at all. There was nothing funny about any of this. "Lanie, there is no one more beautiful in my eyes than you. You are the only one I want to be towel peeping. Do you understand me? Not Lori, not anyone; only you and your breasts. They're exactly what I like. Beautiful. Every part of you."

I was blushing. I knew it, feeling warm all over. I was suddenly very aware of my cleavage, as was Grant, who was staring at my girls with a crooked smile. "That's a good enough answer for me right now. Your turn."

"I need to know about the, well, you were with Da—I have no idea how to ask you this." He looked down at his feet. He looked like a ball of messed-up hotness.

"I got it." *How the hell was I going to explain this so I didn't mess the hotness up any more?* "Here goes. I thought he was you."

"Tell me that is seriously not your answer."

"Only one I got."

And I braced for something. Not sure what, but I would take it. I would take anything he had to give me. I wish he were giving me some of his hotness right here on the couch. *What was wrong with me? Why was I thinking about sex with him? Damn.* He wouldn't even look at me.

"You thought he was me. So you had sex with him."

"Grant. No, it wasn't like that. I was out of it. I honestly didn't realize."

"So, it was like it is with me?

"No. Don't do that." How could he possibly think that? He looked so hurt. I moved closer to him on the couch and put my hand on his knee. He looked up at me for just a second.

"Look at me."

"Lanie, I can't get it out my head. Seeing him make love to you. If you can call it that." He still wouldn't look at me.

"Grant, please. How can I bleach that from your brain? Tell me how."

"I can't stand the thought of another man even looking at you in the wrong way. Let alone …" I moved closer.

"I felt the same way when I saw you with Lori. Even during dinner the other night. Sweet breast meat my ass!" Now he looked at me and he moved closer. And the discussion got heated.

"You can't possibly compare the two." I moved closer still. We were practically shouting over each other.

"How can you say that?" He moved closer.

"You had sex with him!" Closer, complete frustration on both sides.

"But I thought it was you. I wanted to be making love to you. I still do. Right now."

"So do I!"

Suddenly he reached out and pulled my face to his and his lips were on mine, furious and desperate and oh so good. I feverishly kissed him back and couldn't get enough of the taste of him. His hands slid down my neck to my shoulders and he pulled me tight against him so we were on our knees facing each other. I moaned a bit too loudly. His tongue shot into my mouth, so I shot him back. I curled my hands into his hair and held his face to mine while he ground us together. *God, I wanted him so badly it was like a sea between my legs.* We were panting, staring into each other's eyes, almost daring the other one to start. And then suddenly clothes were flying everywhere. I saw Woof run for cover from the garment storm.

His hands were all over me and I wanted them to be. I grabbed him and began stroking him in my wettest direction.

He groaned and then sucked and bit my neck hungrily, which drove me insane, so I stroked him faster, pulling him closer.

"Fuck, Lanie. I want you now."

Steadying myself against his shoulders, I threw a leg over the couch, giving him full access. He plunged inside me; my entire body flushed with heat and desire as he drove into me. He held me so close.

"Lanie, I want to be the only man you're ever with again. I want to be the last man who's touched you in any way."

I stopped him but didn't want to lose the feel of him connected to me in this intimate way as it made everything feel honest and real. There were no doubts about how we felt about each other at this moment. I held him to me; held him inside me. It must have been torture for both of us to remain still.

"Grant. I only want you, not anyone else. I have only ever wanted you." I poured my soul into his eyes and then released him. He didn't move at first, and then one hand went around my waist and the other around my neck.

Pulling me into a deep kiss, he began slowly moving inside me, making love to me with so much emotion I felt my heart burning in my chest.

He lowered us down so I was on my back and I wrapped my legs around his amazing body. I wasn't ever letting him go and never going to let this moment end. I didn't want to ever be without him.

"Grant. I love you."

This statement alone made him groan deeply. Pinning me beneath him, he made love to me, letting me feel every ounce of emotion he had for me down to my very core. Every cell of my body was on fire for him. There could be nothing deeper. We were one and I finally felt whole.

Time stood still as I felt myself getting lost in him and my body did, too. When my orgasm hit me, it completely washed over my entire body. *I think my brain actually came, too.*

"Grant." His name was all I could say. His body tensed with mine and he came with me, his body shuddering with each thrust deep inside me.

"Lanie, I love you. I love you," he whispered over and over.

"Forgive me. Please just tell me you forgive me." I couldn't stand the thought of him picturing me with Dane. It made me feel like I had betrayed him. He leaned up onto his elbows and looked down at me, pushing a stray strand of hair behind my ear, finishing with a caress down my cheek. His beautiful eyes bore down on me; his face was so perfect. We stayed like that for a long time, holding each other and not letting go.

I felt a flutter in my stomach.

"I can't …

Chapter 12

Slow Down There, Ricochet Rabbit

"… be without you. The thought of it alone kills me. I die a little bit inside every time you leave the room."

"Oh Grant. I have no words. You just made me so happy. Not the part about you dying a little or anything; it just makes me feel so loved."

He laughed his wonderful soft laugh and kissed me. We lay naked together, wrapped up in a cozy blanket on my couch. We stared at each other, holding on and not letting go, until the phone rang.

"Let it ring."

"I'd love to."

"Answer it."

"I'd love to." I grabbed the phone and looked at the caller ID. It was Jack. I hadn't spoken to him since I had returned from traveling.

"Hey, Dad."

"Hi ya, Lanie. Nice to call your old dad once in a while." Grant was close enough to hear.

"I figured you were out fishing or something."

"Yeah, well. I'm not catching anything down here, so I was thinking."

"I love when you think. What were you thinking?"

"I was thinking of doing some cliff fishing. You up for a visit? Maybe have a house guest for a bit?"

"Really? When would you come?" I covered the phone and mouthed, "My dad is coming to stay with me".

"Exceptional. You'll stay with me at my place then," Grant mouthed back and started nuzzling my breasts. This conversation just got more fun.

"I was thinking of coming in a few days." Grant started to move down my body. I immediately spread my legs for him. I could feel him smile against my skin, his breath alone driving me insane.

"Coming in a few days? Not coming sooner?" Now I felt him growl into me as he began making slow lazy circles over my sex with his tongue.

"Oh, you want me to come sooner?"

"The s-s-s-sooner the b-b-better." My stutter made Grant pick up the pace. My girl parts were throbbing in the most wonderful of ways.

"Are you all right, Lanie?"

"Oh yeah, um, Dad. I'm just phenomenal." Grant dipped his tongue between my lips and I arched my back to give him better access. Plus, I couldn't help myself. I was seriously enjoying this phone call. He licked and ran his tongue up and down and in and out.

A quiet moan escaped me and Grant growled again and sucked my lips into his mouth. I didn't know if I could speak.

"Lanie?"

"Dad."

"Lanie, are you listening to me? You sound preoccupied."

"Nope. I'm listening. I just got lost in the view from my living room," I said, watching Grant's mouth on me. He looked up; his eyes dark and lust-filled. He gave a sexy smirk and then dove back in. I melted at both ends.

"So, I won't be coming alone." I rocked my hips and Grant grabbed my ass, holding me to his face, fucking me with his mouth. I was inching towards coming and fast.

"Not *coming* alone," I said breathily into the phone.

"Umm. No."

"Oh!" I was inching closer and closer and Grant was working harder and harder. Speaking of hard, I could see he was enjoying this phone call, too.

"Don't you want to know who's coming with me?"

"Oh God, yes. Yes. Yes. Who else is coming?" I'm sure that answer was probably a bit overboard for the conversation on the phone, but not the one between my thighs.

"Ooookaaay. I'm bringing the Bennetts and the Voights with me."

And that was it. I came hard and my entire body shook. Grant wouldn't release me and he pressed his lips harder to my sex and drove his tongue in and out in time with the waves of my O. I stifled a scream.

"Oh. That's so good. Yeah. Mmm."

"Well I'm glad to hear it's exciting you so much." And a second wave hit me. A multi O. Yes!

As I started to come down, I realized what he had said.

"Wait, what?" I panted. "What did you say? All the parents are coming?" Grant's tongue stopped cold and he cocked an eyebrow my way.

"Yep. We figured we'd stay at our old houses with our kids so we can annoy you, and have some fun. It's been too long."

"Wow. Dad. That's great. And you'll be here this week?"

"We'll all be there Wednesday." *Holy shit.* That gave me only two more days to have Grant in every single room in both our houses, multiple times. There was complete silence on my end, as I was too busy trying to figure out how to sneak out and to make love to Grant every night. It was like I was in high school, except I didn't do that in high school.

"Yeah, we thought it would be great to have the family all together for your birthday. You know, have dinner every night at one of our houses, card games, everything. Let's have some good quality time. And we all want to see how the business is going, too."

Crap. It was the only thing running through my head, and crap, my birthday too. I felt one of my breasts being nibbled on.

"How long are you coming for?" I said while Grant continued to suckle me.

"We figured about a week, maybe two."

"Wow. I have a lot to take care of then. Better let me go."

"Lanie, it's only Sunday. You have a few days."

"But I have to shop and clean and do a few other things."

"Well, don't go all overboard now. That's still like being home for all of us. Can you pass the word on to the boys?"

"Sure, Dad, I'll tell Grant and Dane."

"Hi, Jack," Grant called from my breast.

"Oh, is Grant there? He was so quiet I didn't know."

"He was a bit distracted, Dad, working on something for me." I bit my bottom lip and gave him my best 'I want more sex' eyes.

"Well, you tell him the good news and I'll see you in a few days. Pierre already has our flight info, so no worry about picking us up. Sound good?"

"Sure, Dad."

"Well, um, love you, Lanie."

"Love you too, Dad. See you Wednesday." As I hung up, Grant dove on me. He began showering my body with kisses.

"Babe. We need to talk. I can't talk like this."

"Yes. You seemed a little tongue tied a few times there."

"Every phone call should be like that. I should hire you to sit under my desk all day."

"Gladly." He licked my stomach like a lollipop. It tickled in all the right ways so I grabbed the hair on the top of his head, debating whether to pull him or push him down to dine some more. I pulled him up.

"Ouch."

"Oh, sorry. Let me give you some pleasure with that pain." I kissed him and ran my hands down to his boys, fondling them for a bit until they tightened against his body.

"Please, feel free to pull my hair any time you like, then." He smiled.

"Seriously though, our parents are coming; all of them. How the hell are we going to explain what's going on here? We haven't even spoken to Dane yet."

"Speaking to Dane wasn't what I had in mind," Grant growled, as I was still playing with him below.

"Grant."

"Fine. But not right now. I'm liking the conversations here much better." He drooled the sentence out.

"Do we tell them about us? Or do we wait? What do we tell them about us?" I had no idea where things actually stood. I wanted to know what it meant to him.

"Lanie, we tell them we're in love. That we're together."

"It's not that simple. Wait, we're together? Exactly how would you categorize us?"

Grant smiled and rolled his eyes. "We're going steady. Exclusive. You and me. *Toi et nul autre*. Man and woman as one," he said and then kissed my nose and giggled. "I can dig out my high school ring and you can wear it around your neck if you'd like." A ring from Grant. I got all giddy inside. *It could be a gumball machine ring and I would be in heaven as long as it came from Grant.*

“That’s not really necessary.” I laughed with him, but I still wanted it. “But can we just ease them into it? I’m really not sure how Jack will react. And then there’s Dane to deal with.”

“Slow down there, ricochet rabbit. You’re all over the place. We’ll handle it however you want. But we will tell them. We have to eventually.” Now my mind was really racing. *Why did we have to tell them eventually? Was he in this forever? I sure was.*

“First things first. I think I need to call someone now.” And he gave me a double eyebrow salute.

“Oh, you want to play it that way, huh? Then call your mom.” I smiled evilly and handed him the phone.

“You’re on!” he dared.

He hadn’t even begun dialing and my lips were already wrapped around his length and moving very slowly to drive him insane.

“Holy crap. You don’t play fair.” He began shakily dialing his parents.

“Hello?” I could hear Jennifer’s sweet voice.

“Mmmmom, I didn’t think you’d pick up so fast.” *That’s right.* I was going to make this very difficult for him.

“Grant. Did you hear the good news? We’re coming to visit.”

“Yesssss. I heard. I can’t wait for the coming.” His play on words made me give him a throaty laugh and the vibration made him exhale loudly, so I picked up my pace.

“We can’t wait to see you all. It’s been too long. I’m so happy we could all schedule the same time,” she rambled at him. *That’s not fair.* He needed to speak back, so I bit him gently.

“Mom. Slow down. You’re going to fast for me,” he eyed me and winked. So I slowed my pace again.

"Sorry, Honey. We have so much to catch up on. Oh, remember that nice girl Angela, the one you met when you were down here? I heard she was moving close to you. I was thinking about getting her number for you."

I heard that too and started to suck him harder and faster. He cleared his throat to dislodge the words caught there.

"No, Mom. That's really sweet, but not necessary. I'm—" and I sucked one of his boys into my mouth, "—involved. I'm involved with someone. It's pretty serious."

I heard her squeal over the phone. I gave him a special intense bit of sucking for his comment.

"Who is it? Tell me all about her. Where did you meet? Do we know her?" Jennifer was precious, everything about her screamed awesome mom.

"If I tell you everything on the phone, we'll have nothing to talk about when you get here." He was good at this. I was completely speechless when I was getting my phone call.

"Will we get to meet her?"

"Oh, I'm sure she'll be around a lot."

I needed to do something drastic. I wanted a reaction out of him so I ran to the kitchen. He looked surprised when I jumped up and his eyes followed me. I grabbed a jar of chocolate hazelnut spread and a spoon, and ran back. I straddled him while slathering the chocolatey goodness all over his crème-filled bar. His eyes were wide as I ran my lips over his cocoa-coated shaft, leaning up so he could taste himself.

"Yum," he said out loud, obviously forgetting he was still speaking to his mom.

"Did you just say yum?"

"Oh. Yes, I'm actually at Lanie's. We're having a bit of a tea party, you could say." This made me giggle again and I continued to suck and lick him until he was completely clean.

"Send Lanie my best, Honey."

"Oh, I'll be sure to give it to her," he said in his silkiest voice.

"I have to start packing. It makes your father crazy because I've been packing since last week. We wanted to wait until Lanie was back so we could be there for her birthday."

"Yes, Lanie's birthday is coming up. I'll be sure to pick up cake makings and lots and lots of chocolate icing." Again with the crooked smile and lust-filled eyes. I couldn't take it, so I pounced myself on top of his candy bar and began to bring it on home. This candy bar was definitely satisfying.

"I better go to the store now so I don't forget."

"Don't be silly, Grant. I'm sure Dane's mom will handle baking the cake."

"No one but me is icing your cake," he mouthed to me with one hysterical look on his face. "Of course she will, Mom."

The whole moment had me close to the edge. "I'm coming, Grant," I whispered. And I came hard on top of him. I could feel my walls tighten around him.

"Mom, Lanie just came in the room."

"Ha ha," came out of my mouth, but it sounded more like I had just had great sex than a laugh.

"Well, Honey, I don't want to hold you up. I'm sure you're both very busy."

"Yes. We're very busy at the moment." Man, he sure was a laugh riot today.

"Love you, Grant."

"And I love you." But his eyes were staring into mine when he said it. He clicked off the phone, tossed it on the floor and then tossed me onto all fours sliding inside of me from behind while softly spanking me with each push.

"You were a very bad girl while I was on the phone."

"Oh, God," was all I could get out.

"Oh, God," was all he could get out.

"Let's go shower," I said and I raced up the stairs. I didn't look back but . . .

Chapter 13

I Just Cleaned Those

… I could hear him right behind me. And we did it on the stairs.

When we finally got to the shower, we were spent and tired. The night before, the day's emotions and then awesome sex, had us both ready for some time to relax. I turned the shower on super hot. The bathroom immediately filled up with steam. We stepped in and Grant grabbed the sponge and some soap. He pushed me back against the tile and began gently washing me, taking his time so not an inch of skin was missed. I moaned softly and let him bathe me. When he got to my breasts, he threw the sponge and used his hands, kneading and fondling them for a long time. I now had the shiniest, cleanest breasts in all the land.

When my front was sparkling, he kissed me and spun me around and my back got the same treatment. I returned the favor eagerly, sponging him down until I got to his manliness.

"I think this needs a spit shine." So I did. When he came, I aimed him at my breasts.

"Wow, Lanie. I just cleaned those. Now you've gotten them all dirty again."

"Look at that, I did. You'll have to redo all your hard work." I stood up and washed them off and he quickly pulled me to him and spit shined them again.

"Are you hungry?"

"Why yes, could you tell? You had that chocolate snack, but I'm famished," he winked at me. We played for a while longer and then took turns toweling each other off.

"So, should we just get in bed then?" He smiled a silly smile and I couldn't help but push him onto the bed. "Is that all it takes?"

"With you it is." And we held each other for a while longer, kissing passionately and forgetting about food.

"So, I think it's my turn at one-for-one," I said coyly.

"Of course, anything you want to know?"

"Well, a little birdie, *Chelsie*, mentioned there was more than one pact made. Would you care to elaborate?"

"Lanie, I can't and won't hide anything from you. There was another pact. Dane and I made one."

"And?"

"We agreed that neither of us would ever pursue you. I believe we have both loved you for a very long time, but we didn't want it to become a competition. We agreed to never let it come to that."

"Until now?"

"Lanie, I had no idea Dane still had feelings for you. We haven't talked about it for years. He's been with Lori for months now, and I thought he was serious about her. It didn't even cross my mind to think he did, until now. A couple things tipped me off."

"Like the stables."

"Yes. That was odd."

"You think he and Lori planned this whole thing? Me catching you with her?"

"Yes. That thought crossed my mind."

"We're going to have to sort this all out before our parents get here. They'll know something's up."

"Lanie? He was saying some things while you were making love to him." His face twisted when he said it, like it pained him greatly to pull the words from his throat.

"Don't call it that! It wasn't that at all! I didn't make love to him. I mean, something happened, but I refuse to call it *that.* I told you, I thought it was you." I suddenly felt heated. Now he was heated, too.

"Lanie, then how did it happen exactly?" His eyes pierced into me and I could see all the anger he had pent up inside. I had known this might be coming; it had all gone too smoothly. I just stood there and stared. I didn't know what to say. "Lanie, please, explain it to me. You owe me that. You both owe me that. Because I want to understand what would make you run to another man so quickly without even giving me a chance." He looked more defeated then anything.

"Grant, it was nothing like that. Please, don't think that," I interrupted.

"But then to tell me you thought he was me, and that you were out of it, really makes me think Dane slipped you something." His eyes softened when he spoke to me. They looked empty and he searched my face for the answers he so desperately needed to hear.

"No, Dane wouldn't do that. We were drowning our sorrows together and I just had too many, too fast, I guess." I knew this wasn't what he needed to hear and that it would hurt him because it would mean that I had chosen to be with Dane.

"How many is too many? I've seen you drink Steve under the table. Something sounds off. Do you understand what I'm saying?"

"Yes, I do. I mean, Dane was there after I fell asleep. But I was thinking or dreaming about you. I pulled him to me. I let him. I'm so sorry. I barely even opened my eyes. Oh God. I didn't see at first, and when I did, it was fuzzy, but it was you. I didn't realize it wasn't until I heard you from across the room, and then I saw you. I tried to push him off me. I scratched his face."

"And then he hit you." This time he interrupted me. Grant's entire body tensed. He looked away from me.

"Please don't hate me." My voice sounded like a little girl's, high-pitched and pleading. My eyes stung and my heart dropped.

Suddenly, Grant slumped, staying perfectly still, like a beautiful stone statue immortalized for eternity. I stood just as still, frozen and waiting for his next words. I couldn't breathe and could only hear Grant's slow and deep breaths. He must have noticed I wasn't breathing so turned and looked at me. I must have been turning hues of red, because his expression took on a panicked tone and he said, "Breathe, Lanie!"

I gasped a huge breath in, and then began hysterically sobbing and hyperventilating. *Now I was a little girl who was blubbering like a baby.* He grabbed my shoulders and pulled me tightly to him. I couldn't stop my sobbing and drenched him.

"Lanie, stop. Calm down. Please, love. I don't hate you. I could never hate you." But I couldn't stop. I was devastated by what I had done to him; done to both of them. I had destroyed everything. I tried to speak, but all that came out was hiccupped partial words and cries. Grant took my face in his hands and held it so our eyes met. His grip was strong, yet gentle, and his beautiful eyes pleaded for me to understand him.

"Lanie, I love you. That will never change. Do you hear me?"

"But Grant, I hurt you. How can you ever look at me the same? You'll never trust me!"

He smiled and shook his head. His eyes were closed, and when he opened them to look back at me, they were filled with emotion.

"Lanie, I trust you implicitly and love you completely. This whole thing last night was a nightmare. I wish I could forget it ever happened. I'm really going to try."

"But every time you see me, every time we make love, you'll see me with him!"

"My love, right now all I see is you with a spoonful of chocolate hazelnut spread and a smile." And then he licked his lips.

I couldn't help but smile back. My breathing was ragged and my face was tear-stained. I crushed myself to his lips. I covered them in kisses and said I'm-so-sorries and please-forgive-mes in every breath in between.

He let me throw myself at him and then began to kiss me back. Our kisses became urgent and soon we were locked together, our tongues swirling and my tears running down both our faces. When we finally released each other, we lay down on the bed and just stared at each other. No words were said, we just lay there together drinking each other's souls in with our eyes. Time passed and the light in my room began to dim. We had spent our entire day wrapped in a bundle of intense emotions. This man in front of me had become my entire world in a day's time and my feelings for him deepened to a level I had never known could exist. He reached out to me and ran the back of his hand down my check. It came to rest just below my bruised jaw. He ran his thumb softly over the discoloration. I was sure Samantha's great make-up job had been kissed or rubbed away by now.

"Does it hurt?"

"Only when I laugh," I said dryly.

He smiled and cocked an eyebrow at me. "I'll try to keep the jokes to a minimum."

"Grant, do you forgive me?"

"Lanie, there is nothing to forgive you for. I don't blame you for anything. But if you must hear the words, I forgive you."

"Thank you."

"I do not, however, forgive Dane. In fact, I really do need to have a chat with him, and then I'm going to kill him."

"No, you can't do that. It's my fault. It's not his. Grant, you have to promise me."

"That's not fair, Lanie. You're asking me to do something that I'm really not sure I have any control over. I can't promise you I won't beat him senseless."

"Grant, you have to at least try. Please, for me. I don't want anything bad to happen." He half nodded. It was obscure and I had to question whether I actually saw it correctly.

"Are you still hungry?"

"Want to order a pizza?"

"Mozzarella sticks, too?"

"Anything you want."

"I want you. Forever. I mean that," I purred to him and snuggled myself into his chest so I couldn't see his reaction. He didn't say anything …

Chapter 14

Oh Goody, Another Phone Call

… for a few moments and I could hear my heart beat in my head.

"I've waited forever to hear you say those words to me. It has always been only you for me. Always you." And then my heart crashed into my chest. I put my hand over it to make sure it hadn't actually busted through. He quickly covered my hand and pulled it over to him to cover his heart. I felt his racing even faster than mine. Again, we looked into each other's eyes and no words needed to be said. The phone rang.

"Oh goody, another phone call," he said sarcastically, yet he gave me a sexy grin to go with it. I felt my body drawn to his and watched my hands reach out to touch him without my prompting. Winding my fingers through his hair, I pulled his face to mine and sucked his lower lip into my mouth. His lips parted and his tongue darted out and pushed my mouth open so he could taste me. The phone continued to ring.

"I don't want to answer that. I am perfectly content in the conversation I'm having right now," he whispered into my lips.

"I have speaker phone up here. Could add some spice to that phone call." I was totally egging him on. He leapt from the bed and hit the speaker button. My eyes got wide and my mouth dropped open as I suddenly heard Dane.

"Hello? Lanie?"

"Dane." It was all I could think to say as I watched Grant's demeanor change instantly. His brows knit together and his face tensed up. I could see his jaw muscles flexing. I started to crawl across the bed to get closer to him and the phone.

"I need to talk to you. We need to talk." His voice was cold and emotionless, almost business-like. I imagined this is what he sounded like when he was trying to make someone think the deal might not go through. I felt the need to cover myself up. I grabbed the comforter and wrapped it around me.

"I'm not ready to talk yet."

"Why not? I bet you've talked to Grant, though, right?" Now his voice was more accusatory with a tinge of anger. I lunged towards Grant and put my hand to his mouth knowing he was about to lose it. He relaxed only slightly, so I knew he was cooperating for the moment.

"Dane, what I have or have not done with Grant is really none of your business. Do you understand me?" I said with an extremely bitchy tone. Grant fixed his eyes on me. I could only assume it was keeping him from ripping into Dane.

"I see. None of my beeswax, huh? Fine. Well, I don't really give a shit about Grant. I want to talk about what happened between us."

"What don't you get about I'm not ready to talk to you right now?" my bitchy self continued.

"When will you be ready?"

"Don't push me or I won't ever be ready!" Silence. Nothing. "Dane, I'm getting off the phone now. I'll call you when I'm ready. Oh, and our parents are coming on Wednesday." I hung up. Grant let out a huge, frustrated breath.

"I'm sorry."

"No, you were wonderful. If you wanted to talk to him though, you didn't have to do that on my account. You could have talked. I would have left the room."

"I meant what I said. I'm not ready to talk to him. I need to get my head around this whole drugging thing you and Chels think happened. Around the whole night."

"Wait, Chelsie thinks it, too?" Then the phone rang again. I got a nice little ache between my legs and realized I was already a Pavlov's dog. Phone ring equals sex with Grant. However he wasn't thinking the same thing.

I watched in slow motion as he reached for the phone and shouted into it, "She doesn't want to talk to you!" And then, "No, Sam. She's not mad at you. Yes, I'm sure she'll talk to you. Yes, yes, I'm still here. No, I have no plans of leaving, ever. Things are more than fine, but I'll let her give you all the sweet details." The smile returned to his face as he held the phone out for me. I let out a sigh of relief and then gave a little squeal as I grabbed the phone to let my girls know things were going to be more than okay between Grant and I.

"Samantha!"

"Um, so I am going to assume Dane called?"

"Yes. He made his presence known. But that was about it."

"And how did Grant do with that?"

"Yeah, I didn't let it go there."

"That might be best. Where did you let things go?"

"Nowhere with Dane. But anywhere Grant wanted." And the conversation went to a better place. Samantha and I girlie-gabbed for a bit and then Grant's stomached growled loudly, which made me giggle.

"Sam, I haven't fed this guy any actual food, which I need to do before he has no strength left for dessert, if you know what I mean."

"Yes, Lanie, I know what you mean," she giggled. We said our goodbyes and hung up.

Grant and I proceeded to eat and cuddle and make love for the rest of the evening. We finally settled down on the couch in each other's arms and watched a movie. It seemed so natural. It felt so domestic. It felt perfect and right.

* * *

We spent the next few days rushing around, getting things ready for the arrival of our parents. We shopped, cleaned and got things in order for the business. The business ran smoothly, so that was the easiest thing we had done.

Grant and I had basically been playing house back and forth between his place and mine. At the moment, I was running around his place, trying to make sure none of my undergarments were hanging from lamps or stuffed between the couch cushions. Playing house with Grant had been the most alive I had felt in years.

I knew there were a few other things to take care of before they arrived. I had tried my best to keep Grant and Dane from having any contact with each other. Our parents would all be here tomorrow and I had planned on going over to speak with Dane later on today. I would see if that led to the possibility of the two of them speaking but still didn't think Grant could be trusted to just talk. Anytime I mentioned Dane, he would tense up immediately and begin swearing under his breath about what he planned to do to him, and it wasn't talking.

"Are you sure you wouldn't rather just leave things where they are? It might be fun trying to explain why your panties were under my kitchen table."

"Oh, I'm sure my dad would love to hear that one." I winked and threw them in his direction. He caught them in his hand and brought them up to his face, inhaling deeply.

"Please tell me you didn't just smell my panties."

"Sorry, I can't do that. They smell absolutely delicious. Why don't you come over here and let me get a taste of the real thing?" He reached over, pulled me onto his lap and dove his face into mine.

"Grant, don't get me started." I tangled my fingers into his hair and kissed the back of his neck.

"Oh, but it's so easy. And I miss you."

“We’ve been with each other non-stop for the past few days. How could you possibly miss me? I’m right here.”

“Yes, but you’re not right here.” He moved me so I was straddling him.

“This is where I’ve been most of the time.” I smiled and ruffled his hair again while gyrating into him. He groaned softly and pulled me closer, nuzzling his face between my breasts. He grabbed my hips and pushed against me.

“I have to go talk to Dane. I’m going to go over today.” He stopped. I knew he wouldn’t like it, but it was weighing on me.

“I know it’s something you feel you have to do. However, there is no way you’re going to his house alone. I would prefer you meet him here. When I’m around.”

“Oh, Grant, Honey. There’s no way I’m going to be able to do any talking with you two giving each other the evil eye while wishing death on each other. I’m sure it’d be better if we met alone.”

“Lanie.”

“Grant, are you afraid something might happen between us? Because nothing will, I promise,” I said with my right hand raised and a smile.

“I trust you. I do. It’s him I don’t trust. I don’t want him anywhere near you alone, or in public, for that matter.”

“I understand, really, I do. But this needs to be done. You and I both know it. And I’m pretty much out of time, with tomorrow being parental arrival day.”

“I can hide in the closet. He’ll never know I’m here. I’ll feel much better if I’m close by if you need me.”

“That’s very sweet, but I have it covered. I’ll call you if I need help.” He looked away from me and then tried to slowly lift me off his lap. I braced myself so he couldn’t move me and placed my hands on his shoulders and gave him a soft kiss on his lips.

"Nothing is going to happen to make me ruin anything we have here." I gestured. "I would never let anything or anyone come between us. Do you understand me?"

"I know. I just wouldn't forgive myself if he did anything to you and can't stand the thought of him touching you."

"That's not going to happen. It's not."

"Fine. But you have half an hour. Anything more than that and I'm going to assume the worst and come over."

"You're not putting time frames on this. I'll talk to him until things are settled. Got it?"

"Fine. And I suppose you want to do this now?"

"No better time than the present." He grabbed me suddenly, kissed me deeply and held me tightly. He kept me there for a few minutes and I loved every second of it. He ran his tongue up and down my neck and across my jaw. He ran his hands over my breasts and then down into my pleasure center.

"Are you marking me?"

"Yes. You belong to me. Every part of you, and I'm not letting you go until I have kissed and touched every inch of you."

"As wonderful as that sounds, I think you're just keeping me from going."

"Yes."

"Honey, the sooner I leave, the sooner I get back, and the sooner you can do anything you desire to me, wherever you want." I winked and pulled myself away from him.

He looked like a puppy whose owner was leaving, his eyes looking sad and defeated. I needed to reassure him that everything would be fine; that I was coming back to him, to his arms, his kisses, his bed and his future.

"Baby, I love you more than I have ever loved anyone, and more than I ever will. You have nothing to be worried about."

"Lanie, I have your safety to worry about. I don't trust him. I don't even want his eyes on you."

"You're going to have to do this for me, babe. You have to let me go."

"Fine. But I'm not happy about it."

"And you don't have to be. But you do have to eventually have your own talk with him. And you're going to have to do it today."

I grabbed the phone and dialed Dane. It rang a few times, and he sounded winded when he finally answered.

"Lanie."

"Hey, Dane. I think I'm ready to talk now."

"Then come over."

"No, you come here. We can sit on the terrace and talk." I knew that Grant had a perfect view of my terrace from his house and if he really wanted to, he could watch us. I thought maybe if he had that, it might calm any concerns about what was going on and knew he understood because he gave me a smile, mouthed "I love you" and headed for the door.

"I'll be over in a few minutes," Dane said, and he hung up.

I was nervous and had no idea what things would be like with Dane. I missed Grant already and was sorry I didn't let him hide in the closet. About ten minutes later, the doorbell rang. I slowly went to answer, feeling a pit in my stomach develop along with a cold sweat as I opened the door.

"Dane. Hey."

The door wasn't even completely open and Dane was rushing toward me with his arms outstretched. He threw his arms around me and pulled me into a tight embrace. I tried to pull away but he held me there.

"Lanie, I'm …

Chapter 15

Best Fiends Forever?

"… so sorry about everything. I'm so sorry."

"I'm so glad to hear you say that. Um, you can let me go now." Reluctantly, he released me and pushed past me into the house. I could imagine Grant cringing and on his way over, having seen Dane touch me. I looked out the door to make sure he wasn't. Nothing.

"Are you thirsty? Hungry?"

"No, I just want to get everything out into the open. Talk things through."

"Me too," I said as I headed to the terrace. Dane followed. I positioned myself so I faced Grant's. I knew if he actually were watching, he would be relieved to be able to see me. Dane shot a glance towards Grant's house and then sat down to face me. I wondered if he knew why I chose the terrace.

The ocean breeze was calm and it relaxed me as much as it could for this conversation. Dane and I had known each other our whole lives. He had never hurt Grant or I before. There had to be more to this story. I felt badly because I didn't want to hurt Dane, nor did I want to think badly of him. He must have truly believed I was making love to him. I knew he didn't understand. But neither did I. I didn't understand how he could be okay with Lori and why he couldn't believe Grant wanted to be with me. I didn't want to believe he might have drugged me.

"Listen, I want to know what happened the other night, all of it. So let's start from the beginning." I was ready to have an open mind about everything. I wanted things to be better between us all. I wanted to know the truth.

"Fine. Grant called Lori and told her to come over."

"Don't lie to me, Dane. That's not the way to start this conversation. I know Grant didn't call Lori. I know he didn't, because he told me so." I could see the direction this conversation was going to take and was already getting heated.

"He's lying. He called her." I could feel my face flush and really was pissed about him calling Grant a liar. I trusted Grant. He never liked Lori, not even as a friend so there was no way he started things with me only to jump to her the next night.

"You know he called for sure?"

"Yes."

"Because you answered the phone? You heard him ask for Lori?" I needed him to say it out loud so he could clarify it all.

"Well, no. But—"

"But what? Lori is such a reliable source?" I was speaking to him like an enemy. Right now he was. He knew it. He shifted uneasily in his seat.

"I want to know what the hell is going on here, Dane. And don't try to bullshit me," I spat at him.

"Fine. When we all had dinner the other night, Lori and I realized we were more like BFFs." I rolled my eyes. Lori never just decided things. Lori used people and always had a plan. Shame, I actually hoped Lori had changed and that Dane could be happy with her, for Dane's sake. "Well, no. More like beer, food, and fucking buddies. She's always had a thing for Grant and they were getting so cozy on the couch."

"No, they weren't, they were just talking. Seriously? She was with you and then after one night you both decide you're with the wrong person after months of being together? Are you blind?"

"Couldn't you see it? We coupled off the way it should be. Lori with Grant, you and I."

"Dane, what the hell are you talking about? That's ridiculous. We were all just hanging out."

"No, Lanie. It was more than that. You and I, we were so connected the other night, and then you made love to me."

"No! Dane, it wasn't like that." It broke my heart to say it like that because I knew it would hurt him deeply. "You're my friend. You're like a brother to me. We have always been connected that way."

"Yes, it was, Lanie. You pulled me down to you. You let me undress you. You said you missed me. You called me Baby and said you wanted it."

"I'm so sorry about that. I drank too much or something. I thought you were Grant. I didn't intend for that to happen." I felt so badly. He really did believe I wanted him. Waiting for his response, I already knew it would probably be full of hurt or anger.

"No. You were looking right at me. You can't tell me you didn't feel something. You can't tell me that. I know you have feelings for me. You knew exactly what you were doing." That was not the reaction I expected. He was delusional.

He jumped out of his seat and his lips were on my mine. He shoved his tongue inside my mouth while he held my head. I tried to push him off and he continued his assault. I pushed him back again and punched him as hard as I could. He smiled and rubbed his jaw. "I guess you owed me that. I really didn't mean to hit you the other night. It was just a reaction to your scratching me. I'm sorry. But you can't tell me you didn't feel something just now."

My hand was throbbing for the little damage I had done to Dane. I rubbed my fingers and shot him an incredulous look. I needed to take a few karate classes. Apparently my punch was like a feather hitting a brick wall.

"Are you fucking kidding me?"

"Lanie, we were meant to be together. Don't you see it? It's fate."

"Dane, you listen to me and you listen good. I am in love with Grant. I love him. I love you too, but not the same way. You're my brother."

"I don't believe you, Lanie. I know you. You don't just go around having sex with people, even if it's sex to get back at someone else. You made love to me. You love me. You just got jealous of Lori. You came back from traveling and everything had changed. That's why you think you love Grant. It's rebound feelings. You needed to feel like someone loved you. "

"I can't believe you're saying that. Who the hell are you, lately? You're not the guy I grew up with. Are you hearing anything I'm saying?" I was fuming.

"You're just confused. You just feel dirty because you had sex with him. You feel bad. I felt how much you wanted me. I know you love me."

I was exasperated and couldn't believe he couldn't see things for what they were. I couldn't believe he couldn't see that he had done exactly what Tom had done to me. And more than that, I couldn't believe he just insinuated that I felt dirty having sex with Grant. I mean, we got dirty, but not like that.

"Dirty? I felt dirty because I made love to Grant? So I made love to you instead? That doesn't even make sense!"

"It's the truth. And you didn't make love to him. It was just sex."

"I see. So I just suddenly realized you were the man for me, right after finding my boyfriend with your girlfriend naked in his room. Do you honestly think that having sex with you would make everything better? Does that really sound like something I would do? You said so yourself, that's not like me. I don't just go around sleeping with people."

"Because you realized you and I were meant to be together. Because you wanted me and you love me. We made love. You're just having a hard time because you don't want to hurt anyone. But Grant will understand, because it was just sex for him. You saw him with Lori."

"Let me get this straight. You think you and I should be together and that the other night was romantic love making. That Grant was only using me and that he really wanted Lori? That you're fine with Lori and Grant being together? I thought you had feelings for her. Do I have that all correct?" Now I wanted Grant to punch him.

"Yes. We have a chance to be together now. It's perfect. We can be happy. It was so amazing the other night until Grant interrupted us."

"Dane, I'm really concerned about you. I think you've lost your mind. I'm telling you that I thought you were Grant. He and I are together and it's serious. We love each other. And I did make love to him. It wasn't just sex, for either of us. And what happened between you and I was a huge mistake."

"You made love to me. Why would you do that if you really were in love with Grant? You wouldn't."

"That's a good question, Dane. Why would I? Is there something else you're not telling me?"

"I don't know what you're getting at."

"Let me try and make it clearer for you. Why do you think it was that I thought you were Grant?"

"I don't believe you did."

"Dane, I honestly thought I was making love to Grant. I was out of it. I felt dizzy. I couldn't focus my eyes. Something was seriously wrong. Do you want to think about it for a while and then tell me the truth?" He was losing his mind. None of this was making sense to me. I was positive he had drugged me, but he wasn't owning up to it.

"I am telling you the truth."

I was afraid to come right out and ask him if he had slipped me something. I think I was afraid of hearing he could actually do something like that to me. He was completely off the wall with this entire conversation. Suddenly I wished Grant had stayed. Maybe Grant being here would snap Dane back into reality. If nothing else, it would certainly make me feel more comfortable.

"I will always care for you deeply. You, Grant, and I have been together our entire lives. But I am with him now. And I can tell you, I have no plans for that to ever change. You have to accept it."

"I think you're fooling yourself, Lanie. Grant uses women. He always has. When have you ever seen Grant with one girl in a long relationship? Tell me? When?"

"I haven't." And it was true. I hadn't ever seen Grant in a committed relationship. Only weekend flings. But I believed him when he said he loved me. He told me it had always been me, only me. Maybe he just never wanted to be with anyone else. Maybe he thought he and I would never have a shot. Maybe he just never loved anyone else until now.

"I know you'll come around and realize what a mistake it is being with him. You'll figure out that you love me. You already know it. You just can't admit it."

"Dane. It's not going to happen. I'm sorry. I don't want to hurt you, but there's nothing between us and there never will be."

"You keep on telling yourself that, Lanie, and I'll keep loving you. And I'm not giving up on us. When Grant hurts you, and he will, I'll be here to pick up the pieces. I love you that much. So much that I'd stand aside and let you be with him until you realize what a mistake it is."

"We're getting nowhere. In fact, this is getting worse. I think you should go." This conversation was useless. Dane was in denial and nothing I said was going to change his mind. This was the most bizarre conversation I'd ever had with him. I was so mad I couldn't stand the sight of him. He stood up and leaned over like he was going to kiss me again. "Don't."

"You'll come crawling to me, and when you do, I'll be there. Get rid of Grant. He'll never be able to make you happy, not like I can." He ran his fingers through my hair. It made me uncomfortable. I had never felt that way with him before and needed him to leave, and I needed Grant to be here.

"Dane, I wish you weren't doing this. I wish everything could go back the way it was between us."

"I'll never forget the feel of your skin against mine. I'll never forget the way it felt being inside you. The way I felt when we were making love."

"Dane, please stop. I don't want this." I felt my stomach lurch at his words and was disgusted at the things he was saying. I felt angry and hurt that I was losing one of my best friends. I wished I could just erase everything that had happened with him that night.

"Whatever you say, Lanie. But I know you're thinking about when we made love. I know you are. And I know you'll want to again."

He reached for my hand and I pulled away. I stood up and walked past him to usher him to the door. When he followed me inside, he was right on top of me. I stopped short.

"Dane."

He pushed me up against the wall and held me there. I tried to push him off, but he was three times my size. He knew Grant could see him outside. He ambushed me. I panicked.

"Dane, I'll scream. I'm saying no. This is not what you do to someone you say you love. When they say no, you stop."

He pressed his body against mine. I felt even sicker. He ran a hand down my shirt and started to unbutton it. It made me instantly feel dirty. I struggled to get out from underneath him.

"Dane, stop!"

"Shhh …"

Chapter 16

Cheese Does Make Everything Better

"… you know you want this as much as I do." And with that I gave him my best shot to his junk with my knee as hard as I could. He immediately bent in half with a loud whimper and then was rolling on the floor. I thought about kicking him while he was down.

"Get out. I don't want you. Do you hear me? You are my friend only, and right now that's in question. Get out, before I call Grant or the police."

He eased himself up from the ground, still bent and holding his stuff.

"I'm not giving up on you. Someday we'll laugh about all this playing-hard-to-get you're doing."

I opened the door and pointed. "Get out!" He smiled and walked out. I was furious. I honestly believe what he had just done to me out-crapped anything that Lori or Tom had done put together. I wanted to scream. I wanted to hit him with something very large and heavy, like my car or my horse. I waited until he limped home and was inside before I was out my door and running to Grant's. I was running so fast I was tripping over my own feet. He was already at his door. His arms were open and I flung myself into them.

"Oh, Grant." I didn't know where to begin. I could feel the tears welling in my eyes and all I wanted was to be where I was, in Grant's arms.

"Lanie, are you okay? Did he touch you? Did he hurt you?" His body tensed, yet his embrace was still gentle.

"No. He didn't hurt me." I put my head on his shoulder and took in a deep breath of his scent. I wanted his lips to erase Dane's kiss. I kissed him.

I kissed him hard. I kissed him deeply. He kissed me back, but only for a moment and then pulled us apart.

"Do you want to talk about it?" He seemed concerned, angry and something else, but I wasn't quite sure what.

"I wouldn't even know where to begin. He's insane. He honestly thinks—" I immediately regretted starting my last sentence. I knew Grant would be furious. And I knew I was screwed because there was no way the rest wasn't coming out.

"Lanie, please finish that sentence, and no sugar-coating it." His face was blank; beautiful, but blank.

"He thinks you only had sex with me for sex. He said you only use women for sex, and you were using me."

"And?"

"And he doesn't believe me that I thought I was making love to you. He thinks I knew it was him the whole time."

"And?" This was really not giving me any idea of what he was thinking and it was getting annoying

"He said he and I, and you and Lori, should be the couples. He said he's in love with me and he won't ever give up on us, and that when you leave me, he'll be there to pick up the pieces."

"And?"

"Grant, stop it. I want to know what you're thinking." I was angry with Dane, and now I was getting angry at Grant's lack of emotion. Grant smiled and cupped my chin with his hand. "Is there anything else I need to know?"

"He tried to kiss me. Twice. But I punched him the first time, and kicked him where it counts the second." Now he was laughing. I was starting to worry something was wrong with the water around here. First Dane, now Grant. They both were going insane in the membrane. "You find something funny about all of this?"

"Would you like to take the horses down to the beach with me?"

I just looked at him. I think my jaw hit the ground and rolled away. After everything I just told him, he wanted to go riding. "Really? That's what you want to do right now?"

"Yes." He grabbed my hand and pulled me to the stables. I was dumbfounded. I had spent the past hour with a psychotic friend and now my boyfriend had lost it, too. When we got to the stables, Magic and Century, Grant's horse, were already saddled and Century carried a full cantle bag. I gave Grant a sideways glance with a half-smirk.

"I see you've been busy."

"I thought maybe we might be more comfortable talking down by the ocean. It's very calming, don't you think?"

"I want some of what you had before I got here." He smiled and handed me my reins. I mounted Magic, and he Century, and I followed his lead out to the trail. Once we got there, I pulled Magic up beside him.

The ocean air was crisp and clear. I inhaled deeply, tasting the salt. I was suddenly more relaxed, but maybe that had something to do with the gorgeous man beside me. Grant brought Century to a gallop and Magic matched his cadence. Soon I was lost in the ride. Everything was put into the back of my mind and all that mattered was right now, this moment. We rode through the pine forest, which opened up to the cliff. The horses slowed to navigate their way down to the dunes. Once we got past them, we were on open beach. Grant turned Century to the hitching log, dismounted, and tied him. I was so busy looking at the ocean that I didn't realize Grant was suddenly at my side. Like the gentleman he was, he put out his hand to help me dismount. He was right. When I was by the ocean my soul was at peace. Being here with him, my soul was elated. Once I was down, he grabbed Magic and tied him to the log. He began to unpack the bag, first two large soft blankets, and then a pouch, the contents of which I was clueless. He started to comb the beach for driftwood, which he gathered for a small fire. It was beautiful; green and blue colors danced amongst the flames.

"Lanie, I know you want to talk about everything that happened with Dane, and I want to hear it. But I have limited time with you until our parents get here and we go covert, and I'm not wasting one minute of it on Dane."

He gave me his hand and led me to sit on the blanket, which he had spread out on the sand. Then he unpacked the pouch: a bottle of wine, glasses, a plate of cheeses, little breadsticks, and a plate of veggies and meats. He had made me a picnic on the beach. I couldn't think of anything more sweet and romantic.

"This is just an appetizer to hold you over. Tonight, I am taking you on a real date. If we're going to tell our parents we're together, I have to make sure I've done everything right."

"Grant, you amaze me more every second I spend with you. I would be honored to go on a date with you tonight."

"There's this great new Italian restaurant that just opened in town. We have 6:00 reservations and Pierre is picking us up at 5:30."

"Wow, I get picked up in a limo for our date? I feel so special," I teased. He laughed softly and kissed the top of my head.

"Oh, but you are, love. You mean everything to me. And although I wanted to take things slow and that hasn't actually happened, I want your father to know I'm serious and plan to treat you the way he would want you to be treated. Forever." My heart warmed and my head swooned. I had never had someone treat me with such respect and love. This man was more than I ever could have hoped for.

"Also, consider this your birthday dinner from me. I know we'll probably spend the actual day with our families, but I wanted to do something special on my own."

"Well, I plan on doing something special for you tonight, too." I winked and ran my hand across his thigh.

My birthday was on Saturday and I was not looking forward to it. I never did. But maybe now with Grant being a part of my life this way, my feelings about it and a lot of the holidays might change. I had always found the holidays to be lonely, even surrounded by family something was missing. Don't get me wrong; I didn't need a man to complete me. I had lived my entire life not caring about being in a relationship. I guess I never really understood love. It changed everything. Grant changed everything. Funny, he had been in my life this whole time, but one small step towards each other had changed the whole dynamic.

"Of course, you're not getting your present tonight. You'll have to wait till your birthday for that."

"Oh? You got me something special, did you? You didn't have to, you know. Woof was the best gift. And, of course, you loving me."

"Woof was something to make you stay home."

"And it worked. I'm never leaving again, not without you by my side." I caressed his cheek and then fed him a piece of cheese.

"Cheese does make everything better!" he joked.

"If I didn't think it would burn the crap out of you, I'd cover you in melted cheese."

"Yes, I thought about that. So I opted to bring something I know works," he said as he reached into the bag and pulled out a giant jar of chocolate hazelnut spread and a spoon.

"Oh-my-God! Are you kidding me?" I laughed and dove for the jar. He pulled it away holding out of my reach above his head.

"Oh no, this one is all for me," he said with a sexy grin.

"Oh, it'll be all for you all right, if you give me that jar!" I reached for it again but really only wanted to be closer to him.

"Actually, I have something to go with this." He pulled me onto his lap and handed me the chocolaty bliss.

"Yeah!"

"Slow down there. I don't need you on a sugar high."

"I'm already high on you. Kiss me now, please."

"Well, since you said please."

His tongue traced my lips and his hands slid over my breasts. Immediately all I wanted to do was make love to him here on the beach and spend every minute with him right here like this.

"Grant, I'm so sad that we've wasted so much time. We could have been together for all these years. That stupid pact. Those two stupid pacts."

"Lanie, what are you talking about? We have spent our whole lives together. We can tell our kids about all the holidays and birthdays we've spent together, the prom we went to together, all the summers and winters. We've shared it all. The intimate part—now we have that, too."

"You want to have kids with me?" Out of everything he said, that was what I heard. It meant forever, commitment, the whole shebang.

"Lanie, we can't very well get married and not produce grandchildren for our parents. Of course I think about having children with you. I want everything with you. I'm not moving too fast for you, am I?"

"No. I want all that too, with you. I think I always have. I know I always will."

"I know I always have. I've never felt what I do for you with anyone else. It wasn't ever even a possibility."

"But all those women you've been with, all those weekends. The ones Dane mentioned …"

"They never had a chance with me. I have only ever loved you. Lanie, I didn't think you would let this happen between us. I just could never be with anyone else for long. They weren't you." He ran his hands though my hair and lowered me so I was lying on the blanket. He positioned himself over me and then covered us both with the other blanket. I felt him undo the button and zipper on my jeans and I shimmed them off underneath him. He did the same. My body sunk into the sand and Grant sunk into me.

We made love on the beach, the waves crashing almost in time with out love making. My soul was now certainly at peace and at one with Grant's.

When I felt myself on the verge of bliss, I whispered into his ear, "Grant, I love you." Finally saying the words I know he longed to hear.

"Lanie, I love you more than life itself," he responded.

We spent the rest of our time there, cuddled on the blanket, talking, nibbling on our picnic and sipping our wine. The atmosphere of the fire, the ocean, the picnic and being with Grant made it the most romantic moment ever on this beach for me. I would hold this moment in my heart forever.

"We need to start …

Chapter 17

Tappity Tap Tap

"… heading back. I don't want you to feel rushed for our date," he softly spoke into my ear.

"I think we did this date backwards," I said as I kissed his cheek.

"Oh, but I told you, this was just the appetizer," he growled and pulled me close and ran his tongue down my neck.

"I can't wait for the main course," I purred back.

"And dessert." He handed me the long forgotten jar of chocolate hazelnut spread.

"And breakfast. Chocolate hazelnut spread croissants."

"Don't forget the midnight snack!"

"How could I ever forget snacking on you? I mean with you." I giggled and then bit his lower lip. He pulled back and smiled and I proceeded to bite my lower lip flirtatiously.

He helped me up from the blanket and we gathered everything up and repacked the bag. We mounted our horses and began the ride back to the stables. When we reached my house, Grant slowed Century to a halt. Magic played follow-the-leader and stopped, too. Grant dismounted and gave Century a soft smack on his rear. Century took off and headed to the stables. Suddenly Grant was by my side, taking Magic's reins.

"Wow, dropped off at my door?" I said as I dismounted.

"Yes, Ma'am," he said in his finest southern drawl, pretending to tip a non-existent hat. "I'll take care of the horses. I want the rest of this day and night to be perfect for you. No worries."

Immediately, I felt the warmth spread across my chest. *How did I get so lucky to not only find a man this considerate, but who had charm and amazing good looks to go with it?*

"'You make me feel so special … all the time."

"Because you deserve to be treated this way, Lanie. Don't you know that?" He smiled and planted a sweet kiss on my lips, followed by a soft smack on my rear.

"Now off with you. I'll be here at 5:30 to pick you up for our date. I hope you're still hungry."

"Why not stay and help me work up an appetite?" I could spend all night locked in my bedroom with this man.

"I'd love to, but I have a few things I need to go take care of first." The smile on my face dropped. The words he said were almost the exact words from the night of hell. I was almost afraid to let him leave. He noticed my agitation.

"Lanie, everything is going to be fine. I promise you. Nothing is going to ruin this night. I will be there on time. Nothing is going to keep me from you."

"It's just, I'm being silly, I guess."

"No, you have every right to feel the way you do. I don't blame you. But I won't ever let anyone hurt you again. Especially not me."

I put my hand on his cheek and just took in the pure beauty of his face. His eyes showed me nothing but honesty.

"Okay, Baby. I'll be ready and waiting for you." I turned and went inside. I had a while, so I scooped up Woof, grabbed a soda and headed up to the walk.

The view from the walk was extraordinary today. I don't remember it looking so beautiful before. Maybe it was just the day spent on the beach with Grant. Or maybe it was just having Grant this way in my life. I sat down in my papasan chair and placed my soda by two framed pictures. I picked up the first picture. It was of Grant, Dane and I as kids on the beach. We were all smiling. Grant had his arm around me and Dane was buried to his chest in the sand. We had made a mermaid body on him and put seaweed on his head for hair. He also had huge shells for his knockers. Grant had his arm around me. I smiled. *Maybe he had been giving me hints about his feelings for me this whole time.* I wondered if he felt anything for me back then. I was sad, too. Sad that things were so horribly wrong with Dane. I placed the picture back and grabbed the other. It was of my mom and me. I picked it up and looked at her. She was so beautiful. She was always so happy. Even when she knew she was dying, she never let anyone see how hard things were.

I put the picture back on the table and positioned it so it was facing the view of the ocean so she could enjoy it with me. I still missed her terribly. I had so much I wanted to tell her. So many questions I wished she could answer.

"Mom, I'm so happy right now. I wish you were here with me."

I heard a small tap from behind me and turned. Nothing was there. I felt the hair on my arms stand on end and got a quick chill.

"Is that you, Mom? Are you letting me know you're here?" Again another small noise came from behind me, but nothing was there. I looked at Woof, who was sprawled across my lap. His eyes were focused behind and slightly above me. He didn't seem alarmed. So I slowly turned to see what or who was behind me. There on the small table, the picture of my mother and me was now turned towards the one of us as kids. I was a little more than spooked.

"Okay, Mom. Not sure what you're trying to say here but you've got my attention for sure." Maybe if I asked her some questions I might get a response. It was worth giving it a try. "Um, are you concerned about the three of us?" A slight breeze ran across my body. "You want us to work things out?"

Tap tap

Oh boy, I was seriously creeped-out. I knew, well at least thought, it was my mom, and she would never hurt me, but something about paranormal stuff was just spooky.

"But Mom, what Dane did." Then there was a loud thump on the roof. This had to be my imagination. "Yeah, real asshole move. Sorry I cursed. I'll hear him out again," I said, slightly annoyed at my dead mother's ghost. "And Grant and I? Are you okay with him and I being in love? With where things are going between us?"

Tap

"I'll take that as a yes. Any ideas on how I can break this news to Jack?" No little tap this time.

"Yeah, didn't think so. That's going to be a tough one. No one is good enough for his little girl." I smiled inside, truly believing my mom was somehow reaching out to me.

"But it's Grant. This is different. I love him. And Mom, he loves me back."

Tappity tap tap.

"Mom, do we have your blessing?" And then I felt it. Something touched my cheek. It was tingly and warm. Just as I felt it, Woof jumped up from my lap and scampered out of the room.

"Thank you, Mom. I miss you so much. Thank you." I had tears forming in my eyes. She was there with me. I knew it. It was just all too strange to have been only in my mind.

"I have to go now, Mom. I have a date with Grant. I love you." I got up and left the walk to go get ready for my date. I felt serene. Like my mom would help it all work out.

I went straight to my room and started rummaging through my closet for the perfect thing to wear. Soon dresses were scattered all over my bed. *This wasn't working.* I needed help. Samantha. I grabbed the phone and called her.

"Samantha. I need your help."

"What happened? What's wrong?" Her voice was frantic.

"I can't figure out what to wear on my date with Grant tonight."

"Geez, Lanie, don't scare me like that! What's on your bed?" *Damn. The girl was a psychic.*

"Everything in my closet," I said dryly.

"Relax. I know the exact dress. The slinky black one, the one that clings to all the right places without looking slutty. Oh, and your black platform pumps. I love those!"

"Wow. You're good. And how about my hair?"

"Down. Definitely down. We're going for sexy, not too formal."

"Makeup?"

"Smokey eyes, dark but glossy lips."

"Thanks!"

"My pleasure. But you didn't ask me about underneath."

"I think I can figure out my panties."

"No panties."

"I thought you said not slutty."

"No one but you and Grant will know," she said with what I sure was a shit-eating grin.

"Going now."

"Enjoy!"

I began to preen and primp myself until I was all ready. Time to see how I did in the mirror. *No panty-lines.* I smiled Samantha's shit-eating grin. *Wow, I looked hot.* I was going to knock his socks off and hopefully everything else he was wearing. Not only did I look good, I felt sexy. Tonight was going to be epic; I just knew it.

"Well, Woof, do I have your approval on this outfit?" Woof strutted over and rubbed himself on my ankle.

"Oh sure I do, I'm all in black!"

I heard the doorbell ring and grabbed my purse off the bed. I headed downstairs and answered the door. There, standing in front of me, was the most gorgeous sight I had ever seen. Grant was there with a bouquet of salmon-colored roses. He was dressed in a dark gray tailored suit. My knees felt weak. *This guy was hot.* I felt almost star-struck. I could imagine hundreds of screaming women all wanting a piece of this man. But he was mine. And according to him, he only had eyes for me.

"You look amazing. I mean, beautiful, stunning." He was eyeing me up and down with a huge grin on his face.

I smiled and looked up at him from under my eyelashes.

"You look amazing yourself. Hot, might I add. Let me take those from you and put them inside."

"Just one thing first." He grabbed one of the roses from the bouquet and handed it to me. "I want you to be able to enjoy them all night. This one is coming with us." I blushed and took the bouquet and quickly brought it inside. Within seconds I was back at the door. He held his arm out for me. I took it and we walked down the path together. Pierre was just pulling up. He got out of the car and opened the door for us. We smiled and headed for the limo. But when we went to get in …

Chapter 18

Tonight Is Our Night

… the limo was more than crowded. Inside sat Lori and Dane. *You have got to be fucking kidding me.* Grant suddenly tensed, but held my arm tightly. He shot me a look and then his eyes went to Pierre and then back to me. Pierre was picking our parents up. We didn't need to tip them off. We gracefully got in the limo.

"What the hell are you doing here?" Grant spat at Dane.

"We're on a makeup date. I figured if you could work things out, so could we," he said with a smug look on his face.

"How the hell did you manage to muscle in on our limo?" I said aggressively in Lori's direction.

"I had no idea." She feigned stupid.

"I can't believe you did this, Dane. After everything you said this afternoon?"

"Jealous, Lanie?" Again there was that smug look. I could feel my hand clenching into a fist. I wanted to give him a hard punch to the face.

"Lanie, I said tonight was going to be perfect. I'm not letting lousy limo company ruin tonight." Grant's hand was on my arm. He moved it so he was holding my clenched fist. I released it immediately so I could return his sentiment.

"Of course, Love, you're right. It doesn't matter. All that matters tonight is us." I kissed him.

Dane shifted in his seat and Lori got a look on her face. *I wanted to use her face to wipe the smug look off of Dane's.* The rest of the ride was spent in silence.

Grant did his best to whisper sexy things into my ear and we spent most of our time gazing into each other's eyes, ignoring the other two in the car. Pierre pulled up in front of a sushi restaurant first. *Thank God they weren't going to the same place we were.* Dane and Lori got out and then Dane stuck his head back in.

"Have a pleasant evening," he said like nothing was wrong.

"Yes, you too." Grant's politeness surprised me. *Well, maybe not so much.* He was a gentleman down to the bone. Once the door was shut, we both just gave each other a look.

"I hope they both get some bad puffer fish tonight. Can you believe them? I can't even fathom the two of them thinking it was all right to share a limo with us after everything." I was livid.

"And they just acted like everything was fine. Lori didn't even look at me, let alone apologize for setting me up the other night."

"It's a game. The whole thing is a game to them. They're playing us, Grant."

"Yes, it would seem so. But if they think for one second they're getting away with anything, they are both sorely mistaken."

"Agreed. But what can we do?"

"I've let people pull crap before. But hell if I'm going to let Dane and Lori do anything to destroy what we have. We just have to stay connected, a team, you and I. We can't believe anything they say or do."

"How do we stop them?"

"I have an idea. Let me say this. Dane's parents won't like who Dane has become. I have a plan on how we can use that to our advantage. Keep your friends close. Keep your enemies closer."

"I see where you're going with this. The first thing we need to do is get Dane away from Lori. She's the instigator here."

"Agreed. Dane isn't a cruel person. And for him to be doing these things to us, to you especially—"

"I want our Dane back."

"I do, too."

We spent the rest of our time discussing our plan and how to make it all play out to our advantage. It was ingenious. And it was going to be a lot of fun. When we arrived at the restaurant, Grant spent a few minutes talking with Pierre before coming back and offering me his arm.

"What was that about?"

"Let's just say we'll have the limo to ourselves on the way home."

"Peachy. Shall we?"

We entered the restaurant and were greeted by this drop-dead gorgeous redhead. She made me feel like a flat-chested little girl. Immediately she had her eyes on Grant.

"Please, come with me and I'll show you to your table." She was literally angled towards him and purring her words to him. She shot a glance at me. *Well, I should say at my left hand.* Obviously checking to see if there was an engagement ring or wedding band there.

"That would be fine. Thank you," Grant said in his most formal tone.

Once we got to our table, Grant pulled my seat out and focused all his attention solely on me. I liked it. It made me feel like he and I were alone in a crowded place. I felt confident, even more so than I already did, that Grant was mine. *Only mine.* And would always only ever be mine.

"Can I offer you a drink?" she purred, addressing only him.

"Love, what would you like to drink this evening?"

"I'd love a glass of Chardonnay, Honey," I smiled at him.

"Anything your heart desires," he replied and then turned his attention to the redheaded super model.

"Please, make that two glasses of Chardonnay, house best. Might as well bring us a bottle. We're celebrating this evening."

"Of course. May I ask what the celebration is?"

"We're celebrating her birthday and our anniversary." His eyes were fixed on me again.

"Oh, congratulations and happy birthday. I'll be back with your drinks in a moment." She walked off in a huff.

"Our anniversary?" I said quizzically.

"Yes. It's been two days since you told me you loved me."

"A whole two days? I wish it was twenty years."

"And it will be, I promise. Then thirty. And then seventy-five."

My heart burst in my chest again. It was simply amazing how this man could make me weak in the knees with his words.

"If you'll excuse me, I'm going to go to the ladies' room to powder my nose and then jump up and down like a little girl and squeal a lot."

"Oh by all means. I would never stand in the way of a squealing moment." He smiled his handsome smile and I melted again. He stood up and came around to pull my chair out for me.

"I feel like a princess." I was blushing.

"You're my life, Lanie. I will always treat you with respect and honor. Can you be sure to let Jack know?" He winked at me.

"I'll put in a good word for you. Now I really need to go squeal." I winked back and off to the ladies' room I went.

Once I got there, I grabbed my cell phone and called Pierre. I needed a favor as well. I filled him in on my plan and he was more than obliged to help me out. Then I jumped up and down like a little girl and actually did squeal. When I returned to the table, Grant was holding something in his hands. It was a cocktail napkin. When he saw me, he tossed it on the table and pulled my chair out for me again.

"What's that?" I said, pointing to the napkin.

“Apparently some people can’t take a hint.” I felt a pang of jealousy, which quickly subsided. This was Grant I was thinking about.

“I have another plan. Do you have a pen?”

“Yes.” I dug into my purse and pulled a pen out for him. He jotted something down on the back of the napkin and handed it to me for my approval. I smiled and nodded yes. He placed the napkin in his pocket.

“I took the liberty of doing something else while you were gone.”

“Oh? Do tell.”

“I called the sushi restaurant and had a bottle of their finest wine brought to Dane and Lori with our warmest wishes for a happy life together.”

“Oh you’re good. Can’t wait to see how that goes.” And within seconds of my saying those words, our waitress was back with champagne.

“We just received a call from a gentleman. He said you would know from whom. He asked that we bring you our finest champagne with the message, and I quote, because he made me write it down. ‘To my favorite couple, I look forward to many years of friendship and lots of loving. Game on.’”

Grant just shook his head and I suddenly didn’t know whether to be upset or laugh. *What the hell?*

“I see they’re going to make it interesting. Believe me when I tell you, Lanie, I will not let Dane get away unscathed for what he did to you. I am only honoring your feelings and our families by not kicking the living shit out of him.”

“Noted. And appreciated. But they’ve interfered enough with our date. No more talk of Dane or Lori. Tonight is our night.”

“Agreed. With many more to come.”

We dined on the most amazing Italian food I had ever eaten. The chef was straight from Tuscany, and you could tell. Everything was perfectly cooked and served. We shared every bite. If I had been sitting at another table, I would have been either jealous of the loving going on or sick to my stomach at the couple feeding each other and kissing in between bites. We finally were full and enjoying cappuccino.

"So are you excited about your father coming tomorrow?"

"I'm ecstatic that all the parents will be here. I'm a little nervous about how things will go with Dane, and also about telling every one about us."

"Why, Lanie? Don't you think our parents will love our being together?"

"What if Joe and Jennifer wanted more for you? We have the same business, same house, and now you have the same girl who lives next door. What if they think you're settling?"

"Lanie, that's absurd. My parents love you. And I think my mother has always known I've had feelings for you. She'll be setting wedding plans up as soon as she finds out."

"She's going to have to fight Samantha on that one." I couldn't believe I was sitting here talking to Grant about our wedding and who would plan it. I think I needed to run to the ladies' room for another squeal. All this love was going right through me. I broke the squeal seal.

"I'm sure she'll wrestle Samantha to the ground for it. She might actually win."

"Yeah, I don't think so. Samantha is in some damn good shape. She does body origami."

"Body origami?"

"Yes. *Kama Sutra*, and she shared some with me. Can't wait to try it out."

"Me neither! When can we try it all out?"

"Just you wait for the limo ride home." I licked my lips slow and seductively and I could see Grant break out into a slight sweat on his forehead. I felt the table jump and he repositioned himself in his chair.

"Would you like to go now?"

"Yes, please. Let me take care of the check."

Grant paid and I saw him slip the napkin into the billfold. He got up and pulled my chair out for me and we both shot the waitress a wink and a smile before leaving. When she gathered the check she would have a nice fat tip and a note on her napkin:

> *Lisa,*
> *Thank you so much for your phone number. However, I am very much in love with the beautiful woman you saw me with tonight. If you are interested in a threesome, call us.*
> *Love,*
> *Dane and Lori*

And then he had scribbled down Dane's cell number underneath the note.

Mean? Maybe. Payback? Yes. We were sure Lori might not be too happy when Dane got a call from the super model. *Matchmaking? Maybe.* We hoped she would call him. Dane might look quite nice with her on his arm. When we got outside, we were giggling. It was out of character for both of us to do something like that, but it was fun just the same. Pierre was waiting for us. He smiled and opened the door. We got in and cuddled up on the far seat. Pierre got in and proceeded to close the partition and put on some great mood lighting and music. In the back of the limo were chocolate covered strawberries and more champagne.

"What's all this?" Grant said as he cocked an eyebrow at me.

"I figured we deserved another ally. He's in on it. And he promised not to spill the beans tomorrow morning."

"I just told him to send someone else to pick up the jerky twins."

"And I instructed him to just drive until we tell him to stop."

"Aren't you the little seductress? What did you have in mind for our little road trip?" He growled against me.

I could see he was already getting hard. Well-tailored suits just show everything in the best of ways. I kicked off my heels and jumped into his lap. Now I could feel him, too.

"Why don't you grab that champagne and I'll grab the strawberries." And we each did our job. I popped the end of a strawberry into my mouth and offered it to him. He gave it a nibble.

"Mmm, Lanie, you are especially delicious this evening."

"Maybe I should put that berry somewhere else and see how you like the taste of that?"

He calmly sipped his champagne, put his glass to the side and threw me on my back onto the seat. He positioned himself between my legs and slowly ran his hands up my thighs, raising my dress higher and higher.

"Well, what a pleasant surprise! No panties?"

"That's right, Honey, making things easy on you."

"No, Lanie, you are making things extremely hard on me."

"Goody, my plan worked."

He grabbed his glass, put his lips to my sex and did a champagne shot off me. It was cold and the bubbles tingled as they hit, until his hot tongue lapped up all the liquid. The he grabbed a strawberry, which he ran over me.

"Lanie, you're so hot you're melting the chocolate."

"You have that effect on me, no chocolate is safe." He began kissing all the chocolate off, his tongue darting in and out. I groaned softly and then he did, and the vibrations had a quick effect. He handed me the strawberry without moving his hot tongue and mouth from me. I took it and gave it a nibble while arching my hips up from the seat to give him better access.

"That would be better with some of you mixed in." He growled again and I bucked my hips in response. He feverishly began going to town on me, and within seconds I was coming for him.

"Oh, Lanie, I need to feel you."

“That can be easily taken care of.”

I reached for his zipper and began to take the suit off his bottom half. Once he was stripped down, I pushed him back so we were now on the floor of the limo. I rode him hard and fast and didn’t let up my pace until we were both screaming each other’s names. We heard Pierre hit the horn to cover our noise which made us giggle together.

“Guess that partition isn’t completely sound proof.”

“I guess not.”

We got ourselves back in presentable form and I hit the call button.

“Pierre, you can take us to that location I told you about.”

“Yes, Ma’am. Anything you want.”

“That’s what he said.” I giggled and gave Grant a kiss on the top of his nose.

“You be one lucky man, Mr. Grant.” Pierre said over the intercom.

“Indeed.” Grant smiled at me and pulled me onto his lap. “Where are we going?”

“You’ll see,” I said in a teasing tone.

Soon I felt the limo slow down and then stop. I heard a knock on the window.

“You all decent in dere?”

“I don’t know about decent, but we’re dressed, if that’s what you mean.” Pierre opened the door for us.

I had asked Pierre to take us to the beach Grant had brought me the night of my disastrous prom.

“Lanie, why are we here?”

“Because …

Chapter 19

Kiss Me, It's Prom Night Again

"… I should have been your girlfriend the night you first brought me here. We were meant to be together and I was too blind to see it back then. I want to make it right. I want you to tell our children about how we kissed prom night. Kiss me, it's prom night again."

Grant just stared at me. He said nothing, but he had a small smile creeping over his face. He reached out and caressed my cheek and then slipped his hand behind my neck and pulled me into the most beautiful kiss I had ever received from any man.

When his lips finally left mine, he said, "Lanie, that is the most endearing sentiment I have ever been offered by any woman in my entire life. I would be honored to tell our children our love story."

"I would be honored to be the mother of your children."

"How about we head home and practice?"

"I think I'd love that. We have to get up early and make sure we're not caught in bed when the parental units arrive."

"Maybe that would be the perfect way for them to find out."

"You want my dad to find you in bed with me naked and all sex-messy?"

"We should get up early and make sure our parents don't catch us."

"Like I said …" I laughed, grabbed his hand and pulled him for a short walk down to the water before we headed home to practice.

And we practiced all night. A lot.

* * *

It was a beautiful morning on the cliff. The sun was peeking into my bedroom. My alarm cat was slowly crawling up the bed to wake me. I waited until he was leaning right into my face and scooped him into the crook of my neck for an early morning snuggle. I rolled to my side to see my gorgeous man lying next to me, sleeping peacefully. This was the way I wanted to wake up every day for the rest of my life. And that was my plan. Then I noticed the time.

"Oh crap. Grant, get up. The alarm cat didn't go off early enough."

"Huh? What? Oh shit, what time is it? Is your dad here?"

"It's not that bad," I giggled. "But he has been known to carry a gun."

"I have to go." Grant dove under the sheets. He reached for my hips and pulled them to his mouth.

"Grant, we don't have time." I giggled. "I can't believe I just said that," I mumbled.

"There is always time. I promise to be quick."

"Then come up here so we both get some. God knows how long it'll be until we get a chance again."

"I'll make sure it's tonight and every night."

I pulled him up to me and we had a quickie. When we were done, he rolled back over to go back to sleep.

"No, Grant. We have to get out of bed."

"Lanie, they won't be here for an hour."

"No, it's been half an hour now. Our quickie wasn't so quick."

"Crap. I'm out of here." He grabbed his clothes and slid them on quickly. He planted a kiss on my lips and headed out the door.

As he was galloping down the stairs, I heard him say," See you outside in about ten minutes. I love you."

I threw my clothes on and put my hair up in a messy ponytail. I checked my face. *Crap*. I was glowing. *Shit, shit, shit.* I knew Jennifer would see it on my face in a second. I hoped Grant wasn't glowing, too. *Well, not entirely true.* I hoped he was glowing.

I made my bed, and ran down the stairs. I grabbed two cups of coffee; so glad I put the coffee on the timer last night, and headed out to the drive to do our big family welcome home. My timing was impeccable. When I got there, Dane and Grant were nose to nose, having words with fists armed.

"What the hell is going on? This is neither the place nor the time to be doing this. You want our parents to drive up to you guys fighting?"

They both backed away from each other and stood facing me like two little boys who had just gotten in trouble.

"Not that I don't think you deserve another shot to your junk, Dane. But while our parents are here, you will both play nice! Do you understand me?"

"But ..."

"No, Dane, no buts!"

Grant smiled a smug little smile.

"That means you, too, Mister. No fighting where anyone can catch you. You want to beat the shit out of Dane, fine with me, but you take him for a long ride, far away."

"Yes, Ma'am. Anything you want."

"Good. Dane?"

"But Lanie," he literally whined.

"Not another word. You will act like nothing has happened. And Dane, we're not ready to tell our parents anything yet. If I find out you said anything, I swear to God I'll kick your ass myself. Got it?"

"Yes."

Again, they looked like two little boys who just got grounded for a week. And for all intents and purposes, they did. I handed Grant his coffee.

"How do you want us to handle Lori?" Grant said to Dane. Not that he deserved anything from us, but this wasn't about any of us. This was about our parents.

"I told them I was seeing someone. She'll be around. You can act like it was the night we had dinner together."

"And she will behave herself? Because if she pulls another stunt like the shower, so help me I will rip every hair off her head and then I'll—"

"Lanie, calm down. She'll behave herself."

"I can't believe you're even talking to her, after everything. I can't believe we're even talking to you."

"But I didn't do anything."

"Dane, are you kidding me?" Grant was getting heated again. I thought he was going to take his coffee mug and slam it into the side of Dane's head.

"I didn't."

"You drugged me, Dane."

"I didn't," and he was interrupted by the sound of the limo coming up the drive.

"This isn't finished, Dane. You and I, we will discuss this further." Grant's angry face morphed immediately into a huge grin as Pierre pulled in front of us.

The car wasn't even stopped before the door swung open and Jennifer was jumping out.

"Oh, my babies!" she squealed and grabbed us all into a huge hug. Haley was right behind her and she joined in.

"We've missed you so much. I am so happy to see you all. Oh I'm so happy." Jennifer grabbed us each individually for a private hug and then stopped at Grant and didn't let go.

Haley came over to me and grabbed me into a huge bear hug.

"Lanie, Lanie. You look as beautiful as ever. You're simply glowing."

I shot Grant a glance and blushed.

"Haley, Jennifer, I've missed having some estrogen around here. I am so glad you're home."

"These boys giving you some trouble, Lanie?"

I could feel my dad standing behind me. I spun around and he was there with his arms open. I flung myself into them.

"Dad!"

"Lanie, I missed you." He must have, because he and I weren't usually so touchy-feely. But right now, I couldn't keep my arms from around him.

"Oh Dad. I missed you so much. I'm so glad you're here."

"How about your other dads?" Joe said and he gave me that heartbreaking smile Grant had inherited from him.

Joe and Jeff were now out of the car and we were all together again. The cliff family was whole. I felt my heart grow. I didn't realize how much life they brought when they were here. Everything was going to be better now. I just knew everything was going to work out.

"Why don't we get our bags to the houses and meet for breakfast?" Jeff said. "I'm starving. Plane food just sucks."

"You're telling me," I quickly agreed.

"Lori is at the house getting breakfast ready as we speak," Dane smiled and grabbed Jeff's bags. With his parents here, it was almost like our Dane was here. But I knew deep down that wasn't the case.

"Lori? Your friend from high school?" my father, Jack, directed towards me.

"The one and only. Let's go. I want to get back to everyone," I said.

I almost leaned over to give Grant a kiss but stopped myself and patted his arm instead. Jennifer caught it. She eyed Grant and then me, and then the matching coffee mugs, and a small smile crept over her face. *No. There was no way she was that good.*

I saw her take Grant's arm and start to lead him to his house.

"I guess I'll be taking all these bags …" Joe chuckled.

"Oh, Dad, sorry." Grant ran to grab all the bags.

He looked up at me and smiled a sexy grin. I smiled back and grabbed one of Jack's bags and headed towards my house.

When we got there, Jack walked in and just looked around.

"You've really made this place look amazing, Lanie."

"Thanks, Dad. You want coffee or a snack to hold you over?"

"Just sit with me a while and tell me everything that's been going on around here."

"What? What do you mean everything that's been going on around here?" I said a little too quickly. *Damn, could all the parents be that perceptive?*

"Umm. Yeah. I want to hear what you've been up to."

"Oh. Nothing. Just work."

"Just work. No man in your life? Not dating anyone?"

"Really? You want to talk about men I'm dating?"

"Well, yes and no." He reached into my fridge to get the milk and pulled out something else.

“Lanie, what is this?”

My stomach went into a knot. *Holy crap*. That was not something I wanted Jack to …

Chapter 20

Yes, I Know, Dear

… eat. He was holding my half empty jar of chocolate hazelnut spread. There were nasty-good things put in that jar.

"Oh! That's chocolate spread. But it's really bad for your cholesterol. You shouldn't eat that. Nope. Bad for you."

And I grabbed the jar out of his hands and threw it back into the fridge.

"I'm sure Lori has all sorts of goodies for you. Don't want to ruin your appetite."

"But you just said … forget it. I'll wait. I'm going to go get my things upstairs and then we can head over."

"I didn't change your room. It's still yours. Everything just like it was."

"You didn't have to do that, Lanie. I figured you'd want to move into the bigger bedroom."

"Dad. That was your room with mom. I didn't want to take that away from you. It's exactly like you left it."

He just looked at me. I could tell he didn't have the words. He smiled, turned and headed upstairs.

I was so glad he was here. But in the same moment, I was missing Grant terribly. We had been spoiled, spending every waking moment together. It would be hard not to have him next to me in bed every night; not make love every chance we got. I ran to my room to fix myself up. It looked like I had rolled out of bed this morning. Technically, I had and still had Grant's scent all over me. I planned to keep that for the rest of the day. But there was no way I was going over to Dane's for breakfast looking like a wreck. I was sure Lori would be all spiffed up. I pulled the tie from my hair and let it fall in waves across my shoulders and put some light make-up on and changed into skinny jeans and a royal blue thumbhole shirt. I knew Grant loved me in blue. I stopped to look in my full-length mirror. *Good enough.* I headed downstairs to wait for Jack. He sure was taking a long time. I started to pace. *Damn, I thought it was women who were supposed to take forever getting ready. Come on, Dad. I want to get back to Grant. I don't want him over there with Lori without me there. Come on!*

Finally, I heard Jack making his way down the stairs.

"Dad. What took you so long?"

He didn't answer me. He looked a bit shaken.

"Dad? Is everything all right?"

"Oh don't go worrying about me, Lanie. I guess being home makes me miss your mom a lot more than I thought it would. All her things are still up there."

"Oh, Dad. I'm sorry. I thought keeping everything here would comfort you. Make you feel closer to her. I can move them."

"No need. They do. I guess it just—I don't know. I want you to have what we had. I feel like I left you on this cliff alone. Forced the business on you. Forced the house on you. Now you only have this. That's no life. You should have been able to choose."

"Stop it. I'm so happy here. You gave me everything I needed to have a good life. You provided me with everything. You're the best dad in the world. The best. I love you. I'm so lucky to have you."

"But, Lanie, you're all alone here."

"No I'm not. I have Grant, and Dane."

"That's not what I mean. I mean love. You're alone. You don't have love in your life. No one to share all this with."

Now I was in a shit place. Did I want to tell Jack everything was perfect? That I had more love than he could have ever hoped for? Or did I wait for

Grant and I to tell everyone together? I didn't want Jack to hurt for me. I didn't want him to think he failed me.

"Dad. I … I'm seeing someone." *Crap! How the hell was I going to get around telling him who?*

A huge smile came over his face. "You are? How come you haven't told me about him? Is it serious? Is he coming to meet me while I'm here? He'd better be." *Why couldn't parents just leave things alone without having to know every little detail?*

"Umm, I wanted to wait until it was more secure. You know. It's heading toward serious, yeah, very serious. And I'm sure you'll get a chance to speak with him while you're here."

"Well, tell me all about him. What does he do? What's his name?"

"Dad, we'll have tons of time to talk later. I want to get over to Dane's. I'm famished."

"Yeah, I guess you're right. Let's go get some grub. I'm pretty hungry myself. But I want to hear all about him later. And I want to meet this man."

"Sure, Dad. Come on. Let's get going."

"Oh, one last thing. I noticed this black thing running around. You got yourself a cat?"

"That's Woof. He was a gift."

"Woof? You named your cat Woof?"

Why did everyone have a problem with his name? I loved his name. "Yes. I named him Woof."

"And I supposed he was a gift from whatshisname?"

"Yep. Now let's go."

As we headed over to Dane's, I kept glancing back to see if Grant, Jennifer and Joe were coming. I really didn't want Grant anywhere near Lori. It wasn't him. I just hated her.

"Did you forget something?"

"Oh, no. I just couldn't remember shutting the door is all. Don't want Woof to get out."

"Oh. So when do I get to meet this guy?" He wasn't going to let this rest. I had to figure out how to keep him at bay.

"You'll meet him after I've had plenty of time with just you and me."

We grabbed Dane's mom's knockers, swung them once and then just went in. When we got to the dining room, everyone was already milling around, getting food, and gabbing.

"I thought you two would never get here," Grant said as he came over and handed me a cup of coffee.

I blushed, batted my eyelashes and smiled at him.

"Thanks. That's good service."

"Yes. I'm good for servicing."

Jack cleared this throat and walked over to shake Grant's hand. "Hey, Grant, didn't get a chance to say hello to you when I got here. All these women with their hugging and kissing."

Grant grabbed his hand and then pulled him into a manly back-patting hug. "Nice to see you, Jack. How's the fishing down south?"

"Good, but not like cliff fishing. I hope you'll join us menfolk for a few casts while we're here."

"Of course, wouldn't miss it." I liked watching Jack and Grant. It was altered for me now. They were already bonded, but this was different. Grant was trying to bond with Jack on a completely new level.

I sat down at the table and Jack sat down beside me. I saw Dane on his way over with his plate and suddenly Grant was on the other side of me. I turned and winked at him. Jennifer positioned herself directly across from us. She still had that smile on her face and she was watching us like a hawk. Lori walked over with a plate of bacon.

"Can I offer you something, anything at all?"

"I think I have everything I need right here," Grant raised his eyebrows at her when he said it.

"I see. Fine. How about you, Lanie?" Lori's tone was sweet, but hiding more. That condescending I-am-better-than-you tone.

"No thanks. I'm perfectly satisfied." But my eyes were on Grant when I said it. I heard a little noise from across the table, and when I turned toward it, Jennifer's face was all lit up. *Damn.* She had to know.

I leaned in and whispered into Grant's ear, "Your mom looks like she already knows about her future grandchildren."

He leaned over to whisper back, "Yes, she's annoyingly perceptive. That's why I never got away with anything as a child. I haven't said anything and neither has she, yet." And then his tongue darted out and grazed across my earlobe.

I saw Jennifer nudge Joe with her elbow and then mimic our secret sharing tactics with him. He started to giggle and then looked up at us and immediately whispered something back to her. They both smiled at us and then at each other. *Great. Now they both knew.* Maybe that would be helpful when we needed someplace to make love tonight. My dad was oblivious, which was fine by me. After a while, everyone was just picking and talking and laughing.

"So, how about we order from Hung Lo's tonight and have a huge movie night over at our place?" Joe offered. "A pajama party?"

"Oh that would be great," I heard Jeff say. "I could use some good Chinese food. Lori, breakfast was wonderful. Thanks so much. Will you be joining us for dinner as well?"

"Well, of course I will, Jeff, I wouldn't miss it. Besides, I sort of live here now." She was purring and Jeff was blushing. She had him fooled.

I saw Haley roll her eyes and she looked over to me. I just smiled and shrugged my shoulders.

"Let me help you clean up," I offered and started to grab some of the plates. Grant immediately stood up and started to help me clear the table.

"Wow. Helping with the dishes are we, Grant? This girl you're dating must be an excellent influence on you." And Jennifer smiled at me. I just smiled and shrugged my shoulders again. I turned to Grant so he could see my deer-in-the-headlight-eyes.

"You men go sit down. You always just get in the way, anyway." Jennifer got up and started helping Haley and I gather the dishes.

"We do that on purpose, Haley," Jack said, and quickly retreated to the TV room.

Lori started to grab a few things but Haley quickly stopped her.

"Oh, Honey, you've done enough this morning. We'll take care of the rest. Besides, we want some time alone with our Lanie. She's a daughter to us."

I smiled a nasty ha-ha smile at Lori and she retreated to join the men. I watched her warily, knowing she was making a beeline for Grant. But Jennifer had my back.

"Grant?" she called, "Could you put garbage out for us? I have a feeling it's full of crap and in need of some space." She shot a glance toward Lori's direction and then she winked at me. Haley smiled, too. *Were they all in on it? I loved my moms.* When we got to the kitchen, I was waiting for a ton of questions, but not the kind I got.

"How long has that woman been lurking around my son?" Haley asked, her voice bitter.

"She got here when I was traveling. According to Grant, about four or five months."

"Isn't that the girl who stole your prom date, Lanie? I remember Grant taking the car to go rescue you." Jennifer smiled sweetly at me.

"Yes. Same one. Good thing she did. I was better off without that one. I had a much better night because of it. She did me a favor."

"Yes, I'm sure you did, Dear." Jennifer squeezed my shoulder.

"Well, how do we get her to leave again? I don't like her. I want her hooks out of my Dane." Haley's motherly instincts were sharp. And she had two very strong allies in Grant and I.

"Haley, I'm right there with you. But it's not Dane she's really after. She's after Grant. She's using Dane." I wanted to spill the beans on the whole thing, but I bit my lip instead, literally.

"Don't think we don't see exactly what's going on." Jennifer smiled at me.

"What do you mean?" I stuttered.

"She's bad news, that one. She's a bad influence," Haley added. "And I can already see she's having a bad effect on Dane. He's not himself."

"No, he's not himself. At all."

"Lanie, I need your help."

"Anything you need, Haley. I'd do anything to get her out of here."

"I can see there's a lot of tension between you and Dane. Grant and Dane. And of course lots of tension between you and Grant." Jennifer wasn't coming out and saying anything, but her hint dropping was saying it all.

"Oh? No, Grant and I are fine."

"Yes, I know, dear."

Haley looked up at Jennifer, then over to me, then back to Jennifer. Jennifer gave her a look and Haley grinned and shook her head. Once Grant and I had kids, I was signing up for whatever mom school they went to. I wished Nicole were here to join in on all the looks.

"We'll talk more about all this, but I think we best get back in there, don't you agree?"

"Yeah, sounds good to me." I was desperate to be back in the same room with Grant. I knew garbage detail was more than completed by now, so just knowing he was on the other side of the wall had me heating up and ready to pull him into the bathroom with me for some loving.

We headed back to the men. Dane was sitting on the couch next to his dad, and Grant was sitting with Joe. Lori had positioned herself directly across from Grant and was trying to do her best to get his attention. She made me sick. I wanted to grab her by her hair and toss her out the front door. Instead, lucky for her, Dane's mom's knockers were being fondled, so I went to answer the door.

"Well, hello you guys! So glad you guys came!" I exclaimed as Samantha, Chelsie, Dylan and Steve gave me high fives, kisses, and hugs as they entered the Voight house.

"Where's the little shit and is his bitch still here, too?" Chelsie said under her breath.

"In there. But no one knows. We're all playing nice for the parents. Do you think you could actually try to play along?" I shot Chelsie a please-help-me look.

"Fine. But Steve is ready to …

Chapter 21

This Whole Charade Is Driving Me Insane

"… rip him a new one and I'm going to let him if he does one thing out of line."

"That's right. I'm going to kick his ass. Next to me, he's still a scrawny little fucker." Steve was grinning ear to ear. I guess the thought of Chelsie wanting him to kick the shit out of someone was more like getting the Christmas present he'd begged Santa for.

"Okay, Slugger. He's all yours. But not here and not now."

Apparently this was a huge turn-on for Chelsie, because she was now running her hands all over his huge arms.

"Lanie, you're like a little sister to me. No man is going to hurt you. I can't believe Grant hasn't kicked his ass all the way to Fiji by now."

"Oh he wants to, but she won't let him," Chelsie said, her irritation at the whole thing showing.

"Why the fuck not?" Dylan chimed in as he passed me to enter the house.

"Parents?" I said.

"Well, I'm in. I want a piece of him, too." Dylan gave Steve a low five and they bounded inside to find any leftover scraps from breakfast.

"Samantha, Chelsie, you promised not to tell them. Now you both owe me."

"We couldn't help ourselves. What do you need?" Samantha said.

I pulled Samantha aside and asked her to send Grant to meet me on the side of the house where there were no windows at ground level and to keep everyone occupied.

"Oh, I'm always up for covering for a little nookie break," she giggled and she pranced into the house.

I ran to the side of the house and leaned against the wall and waited for Grant. A short while later I heard running footsteps that slowed as they came around from the back.

"Smooth. Don't ever become a ninja. You're really terrible at it." I smiled at him and as soon as he was close enough, I grabbed him and pulled him into a deep kiss.

His arms wrapped around me and he pressed his body against mine, pinning me to the house. Now this was more like it. I reached down between his legs and gave his junk a little 'hello' greeting. He was hard as a rock and I could feel myself responding immediately.

We were lost in each other. Our hands were touching and rubbing and bringing whatever pleasure they could in the short time we knew we had.

"I barely made it through breakfast without touching you," he said in between kisses.

"I almost kissed you." Then I kissed him again.

"I have to have you. Right now."

"What's stopping you?" I grabbed his hand and started to pull him toward the garage.

"Lanie, where are you taking me?"

"Just come with me and you'll *come* with me."

Now Grant was pulling me. We got to the garage and I grabbed his pants and unzipped them quickly, pushing him up against Dane's car and then getting on my knees to pleasure him.

"Oh God, Lanie," he groaned. "Are you trying to break a time record? Because I think you won." I could feel his whole body shudder with his words. "Holy God. What's this for?"

"To let you know how much I miss you."

"They just got here. Can't wait to see what I get tomorrow."

"I want you, Grant, so badly."

He pulled me back up to eye level and slipped one hand underneath my shirt. He used his other hand to pull the front of my shirt down so he had better access to my girls. He sucked and fondled and kissed them, running his tongue everywhere. He then pushed me against the car, moving his hand between my legs and working me quickly into a frenzy, only to stop short.

"I need more."

"Plenty more where that came from," he said smoothly.

"We have to come up with a plan on when and where to meet so we don't end up in the back of my car."

"We already did it on Dane's car. I can see your ass imprint in the wax. Hot."

"Oh crap." I began to do an unhiney shine. We giggled together and then suddenly he had me pressed back against the car and was desperately kissing me.

"Lanie, I can't be away from you. This whole charade is driving me insane."

"Grant, it's been like three hours. How the hell are you going to make it a whole week?"

"I'm not. Let's go tell them all, now. Please, Lanie; fuck. I can't be without you another minute."

The intensity of his desire to be with me was overwhelming in the most wonderful of ways. But I needed to approach things with Jack slowly. I wanted him to understand that Grant and I being together wasn't out of boredom or being forced or just because. He needed to understand how much I loved this man. How much he loved me back. There was no way I was screwing anything up here.

"Baby, we have time. We have our entire lives together. What are a few more days to tell everyone? Right? We'll do it before they leave. I promise." And I raised my right hand.

"Can I make an ultimatum?

"Of course, Babe."

"You have to tell them on your birthday."

"Really?"

"Yes. Or my gift will be really bizarre."

The little hamsters on the squeaky wheels in my head were going full speed right now. I thought I saw smoke coming out of my ears. *What did he get me that would blow the whole secret? Lingerie? Sex toys? A year's supply of chocolate hazelnut spread, champagne and chocolate covered strawberries? Something more personal? Oh wait, nothing is more personal than sex toys. Gumball machine ring? Hell, it didn't matter.* All I wanted was him. Forever.

"We can tell them on my birthday. Is there a specific time? Or should I just send them a text message first thing in the morning?"

"You'll know when the time comes. I promise." And he raised his right hand.

"One of us has to go back first. You go. I'll go through the back door in a little while."

"You said back door. This is silly."

"Only a few more days, Babe. I promise."

"Fine." He kissed me again deeply and then turned and headed out the door. I sat there for a bit wondering why the hell we didn't just pull our parents aside and tell them now. I was pretty sure Grant's parents already knew. Jennifer did, for sure.

Jack loved Grant, but after his comments this morning, I wanted to make sure that we did it right. I was having a hard time not touching Grant, too. It didn't feel right to sit across from him or not be able to be open with how we felt. We were acting like we were embarrassed, and that was just wrong.

When I felt I was no longer flustered, I headed back inside. Every one was laughing and talking. It was like old times. I even smiled when I saw my dad and Dane talking about the latest draft picks. Jack would put his fist right through Dane's face if he knew what he had done. I shook it off for now. It gave me a knot in my stomach.

I pulled Samantha to the side. "Thanks. I needed that."

"Oh, I understand. You covered for me many times … in high school. Come on, Lanie, what's the big secret for?"

"I don't know, Samantha. My dad, I guess. He seems off. Asking me all these questions about my life and love life. I just want to make sure we do it right. I mean, this is forever, you know?"

And that's when it happened. Samantha did the biggest squeal-scream-jumpy-clappy-noisy-dance thing! Every one stopped talking and stared. Samantha covered her mouth with her hand and just stared at me for help.

"Umm, yep—I got them for half price, and then another 20% off. Can you believe it?"

And that was all it took. Everyone turned and continued on. Samantha was known to go overboard on any shopping deal. I grabbed her and pulled her roughly into the kitchen.

"Are you kidding me?"

"But, Lanie, you just pretty much told me that you and my cousin are forever. I'm assuming marriage? Children? We'll be family for real." And she squealed again.

"Samantha, can you not contain yourself? If you act like this, I will not let you have anything to do with any wedding plans at all."

"Did I hear someone say wedding plans?" My dad was now part of the conversation.

"Oh, Samantha and Dylan's wedding. You know."

"Oh, yeah, right. Let me get out of here, then." He grabbed a beer and literally ran out of the room.

"Wow, Samantha, good thing you're not FBI. You suck at this."

"I get to plan your wedding?"

"He has to actually ask me first."

"Ask who what?" Lori asked as she entered the kitchen.

"Ask the zookeeper what time he's picking you up so all the warthogs are present for zoo day," Chelsie said as she came up behind her.

"Shut the fuck up, Chelsie."

"Shut the fuck up? Are you fucking kidding me? You don't want to mess with me, Lori. I don't play nice like Lanie does. I'll kick your ass."

"Like to see you try."

And with that Chelsie grabbed a container of syrup, knocked it over on the counter, and slammed her fist onto it. The sticky substance exploded all over Lori.

"You bitch!" Lori started to wipe the goop off her face.

"I'm so sorry. I don't know how that happened. Let me help you dry that off." And with that, she grabbed a handful of flour and threw it at her. Now Lori was pretty much tarred and feathered with breakfast makings.

"I'm going to tell everyone you did that!" She lunged at Chelsie. But Chelsie was no pushover, she simply stepped aside and Lori flew past her and landed with loud thump on the floor.

"Really, Lori? Shall we tell them what you've been doing lately? Using Dane, trying to cheat on him with Grant, pretty much throwing yourself at him, setting him up and trying to hurt Lanie? Whose side do you really think they're going to choose?" Chelsie was finally giving Lori a piece of what she deserved!

"What happened?" And now my dad was back in the room.

"We're just having a little fun, aren't we, Lori?"

Lori pulled herself off the floor. Dane was now standing behind Jack, giving her a look.

"Oh that's right, Jack. A fun little food fight. We're just like little kids around each other. I guess I better go shower." Well, she was good at lying; we all knew that.

"You do like your showers. Now you actually need one. I'll just make sure you find your way to the right one this time," Samantha said as she grabbed Lori and pulled her out of the room.

"You kids never grow up, do you? Let me help get this cleaned up." This time Haley was in the doorway.

"Oh no, Haley, this is all my mess. I got it." Chelsie grabbed a sponge and started to clean.

"You did …

Chapter 22

It's Creepy

"… me a favor. I got it." Haley tweaked Chelsie's cheek as she passed her by and then turned and gave Dane the mom-eye. *Oh man, no one wanted to get mom-eye, and Haley had one that grounded you for life.* We did a three-way high five and I left to join the others.

My dad and I were getting ready to head home after a bit so he could unpack and unwind from all his traveling. I wanted some time alone with him. I really wished everything were out in the open so that Grant could spend time with us, too.

"Well, looks like we're heading out. See you for dinner tonight," Jack said, giving a lazy wave as he headed out the door.

"We're heading out, too, let's all walk back together," Grant said, and he grabbed my arm and pulled me out the door with him.

Samantha, Chelsie, Steve, Dylan, Jennifer, and Joe all followed. Mass exodus. Jennifer pulled Chelsie and Samantha back to chat with her. *Damn, those two better keep their mouths shut.* Then Joe caught up with Dylan and Steve. *Crap!* Those two were even worse then their loose-lipped women.

Grant and I shot each other a glance and then smiled. I got up on my tippy toes and whispered in his ear, "The next chance I get, I'm going to make you come so hard you'll forget your own name."

Grant stopped dead in his tracks.

"Grant?" He didn't answer. "See, I didn't even do anything and you already forgot your name." I giggled.

"How about this evening, after dinner?" He gave me that hot smile that made me melt immediately.

"What's this evening after dinner?" Jennifer said as she strolled up next to us and smiled. Her tone was omnipotent-mom.

"Oh, card game. All us kids."

"Oh that sounds like a lot of fun. Can parents join in? Or is this a game of strip poker?" she teased.

"Mom! No." Grant was actually blushing. It was so cute. His mom embarrassed him. *God, I loved him.*

"Well, I guess that all depends on who you're playing with, right, Lanie?"

"Um, no. Yes. I don't know." I shot Grant a look begging for help and he just mouthed 'ha ha' at me. Now I was blushing.

Jennifer just giggled and walked ahead of us.

"It's a pajama party. Will you be wearing something scrumptious?"

"The way you and I go at it, everything I wear lately has been edible."

"Yes, extremely tasty and delectable. Yum yum." He smiled at me and then licked his lips. My girls perked up at just the sight of his tongue and lips. *Damn, the man was hot. Damn, the man made me hot.*

When we reached my house, we all slowed. I took a deep breath in. Life was good. I was happy.

"You guys want to come in for a while?" I said to Chelsie, Samantha and the boys, "Or are you going back to Grant's?"

"We're going to head back home to get PJs for tonight!" Samantha said excitedly.

"I can't believe you're making me wear my night clothes," Chelsie followed. Chelsie never left her house unless she was dressed perfectly, hair and make-up in place.

"Oh don't be such a party pooper. Are you staying over tonight?" Grant gave Chelsie a nuggie when he said it.

"Well, of course. Can't have a card game without shots. And anyway, you need us there tonight. Who's going to make up excuses for why you two are alone in the closet playing seven minutes in heaven?" Chelsie said, annoyed. She swatted Grant's hand.

"Oh are we playing spin the bottle, too?" Samantha giggled.

"No!" Chelsie, Grant, and I all said at the same time. Then we all started laughing.

"Honestly, you guys are adults for goodness sake. Just tell them."

"Chelsie, I will. We will. Saturday. Grant made me promise."

Chelsie shot Grant a knowing glance and they both smiled. Samantha squinted her eyes and looked back and forth between the two of them. She grabbed Chelsie and pulled her toward Grant's house for a secret meeting. Now I knew that Chelsie must be in on Grant's birthday present for me. I did a little hop.

"Guess I'll see you later," I called after them, and then I turned to Grant. He was just staring at me with a silly grin on his face.

"What?"

"What what?" he teased.

"Why are you staring at me?"

"I'm just enjoying the most beautiful view I have ever seen."

"Nope, you can't be. Because that perfect view is right in front of my eyes." I smiled and that's when I almost screwed up. I grabbed his hand and pulled him against me. I could see Jennifer standing behind him, talking to Jack and Joe about some work I had done to the front of the house. She quickly cried out and grabbed her ankle. Both Jack and Joe immediately focused on her.

I smiled to myself and then grabbed Grant into a quick kiss, running my tongue along his bottom lip, then released him and pushed him away. He looked slightly stunned and then gave me a sultry smile.

"Yes, much *much* more of that later. I have plans in place to get alone time with you every night. I promise." He raised his right hand and smiled.

"There's always work. Big presentation we need to focus on. Conference call. Meeting away from here?"

"I love the way your mind works. I love the way your body works even better."

He squeezed my arm and then ran off to play concerned with his mom. I could see him give her a crooked smile when he got there and helped her to her feet. She turned and winked at me.

I started to walk over to play the game.

"Oh my God, Jennifer, are you all right?"

"I think everything is going to be just fine, Lanie. More than perfect."

"I'm so glad to hear you say that." I beamed at her.

"Would you like to have a cup of tea with me later?"

"I think I would love that."

"It's a date then."

I touched her hand and gave her my best thank you smile.

"Come on, Dad, let's go inside and I can show you more of what I've done with the place. And then maybe we can just hang and talk until dinner, okay?"

"Sounds good to me, Lanie."

I waved to Grant. And then when no one was looking, I blew him a kiss, which he dramatically grabbed in his hand and held against his heart. Mine warmed at his gesture. I had never been so connected with anyone in my life.

Jack grabbed a beer from the fridge and went out to the terrace. I made a pot of tea, and when it was done, I headed out to join him.

When I got there, Woof was sitting on his lap and he was affectionately rubbing under his neck. Woof was in heaven and mewing up a storm.

"Friendly little guy, isn't he? You're just the cutest wittle thing. Oh, Jackie woves the wittle Woofy."

"Dad, please stop that. It's creepy."

"Well, then how about you tell me about this guy in your life?" He gave me the dad stare.

Crap. "What do you want to know?" I said nervously.

"Well, what's his name?" He didn't sound anything but curious.

"He has a very prosperous business. Doing very well for himself."

"Uh huh, but what's his …"

"And he is just so handsome and strong and sweet."

"That's all well and good. But what do you …"

"And he treats me like gold. He's romantic and surprises me with things."

"Okay, he's a real giver. But what's his name?"

"Oh, he's a giver, all right; the sex is absolutely amazing!"

"I don't think we need to go there."

"He treats me like a woman, knows every place to kiss and touch …"

"Lanie, you can stop that now. Where's he live?"

"He lives close by, really close by. Close enough to be here every night and every morning."

"So you going to come cliff fishing with us? We're thinking of going out tomorrow morning bright and early."

Yes! I knew if I kept throwing in stuff about sex he'd change the subject.

"What time are you guys heading out?"

"Four o'clock."

"Are you kidding me? The kids are doing shot cards tonight. We'll all be hung over."

"Hair of the dog, Lanie. Just keep drinking."

"Did my dad just tell me to drink all night and into the morning, continue to drink, and then go fishing off the side of a cliff?"

"Yep. Guess I did. So are you coming?"

"Once I wake up I'll be there. I'll bring you guys breakfast."

"You're the best, Lanie. I told Joe and Grant I was going to meet them down at the stables in a bit. Want to come with?"

"I have a date."

"Oh? Is whatshisname coming over?"

"No, Dad. I have a tea date with Jennifer. But I'll walk you down there."

We left the house and headed to the stables in silence. When we got there, all I could think about was the storm and the ride on the beach with Grant. *God it was all so hot, so romantic.* This had to be a dream. It was just all to perfect.

Grant was there; he wasn't wearing a shirt and he was brushing Magic for me. Now my dream just got really smutty.

"Hey."

"Hey"

"Hiya, Grant. Where's Joe?"

"He's still back at the house. Why don't you head on up and get him. Lanie will keep me company."

I gave Grant a secret smile as Jack headed out the door. As soon as he was out the gone, I was on Grant. I threw myself at him so hard we both tumbled back into a huge pile of hay in an empty stall.

"This *has* been mucked right?" I said.

"Mucked but not fucked," his velvety voice beckoned me.

"Not doing all your chores. That's worth a grounding," I mock scolded him.

"Is it worth a grinding?" he growled.

"Indeed. You better get grinding and fu—mucking this stall right away." I giggled and then pulled him on top of me.

"Lanie, I miss your touch. I miss your lips." And then he sucked my bottom lip into his mouth and deeply kissed me.

"Grant, what if they come back?"

"We'll have time. I have a feeling someone will be keeping them busy for a bit." He whispered into my ear and then began to nibble all the way to the back of my neck where he bit into me in the most sensual of ways. My body immediately responded by writhing in pleasure.

"Oh, Baby, yes," I said breathily.

He groaned and began to grind against me.

"Lanie, *yes*." His eye lids were heavy and his gaze beckoned me to make love to him.

"How long do you think we have?"

"Enough time for this."

He began to undress me, pulling my shirt over my head and removing my bra like a pro.

"Hey, you two in here?"

"It's Jack!"

"I got it." He buried us in the hay pile. *Damn, it was really itchy against my bare skin.* "Don't make a sound." He proceeded to fondle me.

"How the hell can you expect me not to make a sound when you're . . ."

"Shhh. Just enjoy." He began to kiss and bite the back of my neck while sliding a hand into my jeans. Now I was ready for more and was also ready to make noise, lots of noise. He was driving me so insane, it was so hard to hold back. I could hear the footsteps coming closer. *Oh shit.* But then they stopped and went away.

Waiting in the hay, Grant continued to pleasure me many ways until we couldn't hear him anymore.

"Let me get dressed!" I whispered. I was now a pro quick-change artist, dressing 0-60 in four seconds.

"That was so worth almost getting caught," he said with a laugh as we snuck out the back way into the paddock.

Jack had just made his way around when we got out there. My heart started racing and I was out of breath. I felt like I was going to get grounded by my dad. *Grounded. Grinded. Grant grinding against me. Oh damn.* Everything I thought became about having sex with Grant.

"Oh, there you are. Joe will be down in a second. Lanie, Jennifer was starting the tea. Better head on up now."

"Yes, sir," I said solemnly.

"Yes, sir?" Jack mused.

"Yes, sir?" Grant laughed out with a half-cocked eyebrow.

"What? I'm a polite daughter." I turned and headed toward Grant's. I passed Joe on my way.

"Hey, Lanie, were you taking a roll in the hay, because …"

Chapter 23

I Have No Idea

"… you have a little something right there," he pointed to my hair.

He reminded me so much of Grant. He smiled that same amazing smile like Grant always did and I melted a little.

"Huh? What do you mean? I mean no. No, I wasn't. Why would you ask that?" He started to come towards me and reached up and pulled three pieces of hay from my hair.

"Oh."

"I guess you just really get into your work."

"Grant and I were just messing around. I mean in the hay. You know, messing around in the hay. I mean we were messing around with the hay." I rolled my eyes at my own stupidity and shook my head.

"I see. Well, I guess as long as you're having fun it really doesn't matter what you do in the hay." He laughed and pulled me into a hug. Then he whispered in my ear.

"Lanie, to me, you're already my daughter. So anything you might be worried about for whatever reason, and I'm not saying you are, well, don't be. Okay?"

His cryptic words hit home. I knew exactly what he meant.

"Thanks, Joe. Noted." I hugged him back and headed for tea with Jennifer. I was nervous. I didn't know why. It was apparent that Jennifer and Joe knew Grant and I had something going on.

When I got to the house, I headed around back knowing Jennifer would be there. Whenever she wanted to have tea, it meant on the veranda in the back of the house. Usually, when she asked for a meeting, it meant she was going to give some sort of speech. I was hoping to get a good talking to.

"Hello, Lanie. I guess some habits never die."

"Hi, Jennifer. No, they don't." I smiled and pulled out the chair and sat down. I started fidgeting with my spoon, my shirt, and the table. I looked at the view of the ocean and suddenly my mind was back on the beach the other day with Grant. *Funny.* Everything led back to Grant. Every memory, Grant was there. Every moment of my life, Grant had been there.

"Are you nervous about something?"

"No. Yes. I have no idea. I—"

"Lanie, you have nothing to be worried about here. Ever. Let's talk. I have some things I thought maybe we should put on the table."

"Okay," I said warily.

"I noticed some interesting things with my son. I don't think I've ever seen him quite … so alive as he seems now. Do you think you might want to clue me in on why? I know he's seeing someone, but he doesn't want to talk about it yet. Maybe you might fill me in. You know, woman to woman."

I wanted to spill everything. Jennifer's tea must have had something in it, truth serum or something. I suddenly felt like hiding things was ridiculous and looked into her beautiful eyes and realized they were the same eyes Grant had. Being so intimate with him made me realize things I had missed that were right in front of me.

"I also heard you're seeing someone, too."

"My dad?"

"Of course. He said you wouldn't tell him anything. He asked me to get the low down."

"I see."

"Now, anything you don't want me to tell him, I promise, stays right here with us. Okay?"

I nodded and waited for the inquisition.

"So. Are you ready to tell me all about you and Grant being together?"

I choked on my tea so badly I couldn't stop coughing. Jennifer jumped up from her seat and began smacking me on the back. When I finally regained my composure, I just stared at her with wide eyes.

"Lanie, it's so obvious."

"It is?"

"Yes. All the stares and secret touches and well, you're not hiding it very well."

"So my career as a secret agent is pretty much out of the question?"

"Pretty much, Dear."

"Jennifer, to be completely honest, I'm in love with your son. I promise you, I'll never hurt him. I want to spend the rest of my life with him. He is just so amazing and perfect and romantic and beautiful inside and out."

She smiled and nodded. She didn't respond for a few moments. I started to regret saying anything. Then, finally, she spoke. "Lanie, Grant has been pining for you since he was three. It's about time he finally did something about it."

"Three?"

"Yes. Even at three he used to refer to you as his wife. He's never stopped, you know. He still calls you that."

"He calls me his wife?" *Oh my God. Grant calls me his wife to his parents!* I felt my heart start to patter at an alarming rate in my chest, so much so, that I could hear it in my head. I wondered if Jennifer could hear it, too.

"Yes, Lanie. Does that surprise you?"

"A little. I just had no idea. All these years."

"Yes, all these years. Nicole and I used to joke around about how we had you both married off as toddlers. We always believed that you two would get married someday."

"Nicole thought that?"

"Nicole *wanted* that. Do you know what her last words to me were?"

"No. Please, tell me."

"She told me to take care of you. She asked me to step in and cover for her when she was gone. I said yes, of course. And then she told me that she knew you and Grant were fated to be together. She wanted so much for you to find love and happiness, and that she knew it was going to be with Grant. She knew it. Even back then."

"So, my mom would be happy that we're together? Do you know how much this means to me?"

"Yes, Dear. Do you know how much this means to me?"

"I don't understand."

"Lanie, all any parent wants for their child is for them to be healthy, happy, and find love. Grant is so different now. He's so alive and happy with you. You do that for him. You are the piece that completes him. The piece that has been missing, despite the fact that it was always there right in front of him, in front of both of you. You are his soul mate. I believe that and always have. I've watched you two for your whole lives. It was so blatant. I can't believe it didn't happen until now."

"So, you're happy?"

"I'm ecstatic! I can't wait for a wedding and grandchildren and to be able to finally call you my daughter, for real." Jennifer's eyes got a bit teary. I could tell everything she was saying was heartfelt and true.

I felt my eyes get moist, too, and got up and threw my arms around her. She laughed and hugged me back.

"Now, can you tell me why you two won't just come out and tell us?"

"It just all happened so fast. It's been so surreal. And I want it to be perfect, and well, there were some other things going on. And it's all tied together and we didn't have time to sort it all out before you got here, and then Dane …"

"Dane? What's wrong with Dane? Isn't he happy for you?"

"Happy. Yeah, not so much."

"But I thought he was with Lori, that slut?" This made me laugh out loud for quite a while. Hearing Jennifer refer to Lori that way was just too perfect. I wish I had been taping this conversation so I could make it my text alert sound on my cell phone.

When I could finally speak, between giggles, I said, "No, she caused a huge problem between Grant and I. I think it was all a plan."

"And Dane?"

Now I got serious.

"Jennifer, he was in on it. And he did something even worse."

"Dane tried to hurt Grant? I don't understand, Lanie; that's not like Dane."

"No, he did something to me."

"He hurt you? What did he do?" I wasn't ready to tell her.

"Jennifer, it's embarrassing. It's terrible."

"Lanie, you do understand you have to tell me everything. Haley won't put up with Dane hurting anyone, especially family. And neither will I. Your father won't be happy about it, either."

"He …" I couldn't get it out. I couldn't say it. I didn't want to believe it had all happened. If I said it aloud, it would be right there in front of me again. I guess I had been trying to block it out. Pretend that Dane hadn't forced himself on me. Kept trying to make it okay, that he didn't deliberately have sex with me knowing I was not in the right frame of mind. He had basically raped me.

I burst into tears. It finally hit home. I had been denying it. He knew exactly what he was doing. And I couldn't say it because I didn't want to believe it was true. I had been protecting who Dane was in my head, not who he had become.

"Lanie? Lanie? Oh my God, what did he do to you?"

I couldn't stop crying. Now I was hyperventilating. I couldn't breath. I was losing it. I saw Jennifer grab her phone and hit some keys. Within seconds, Grant, Jack and Joe were running up the path from the stables.

Grant ran to me and threw his arms around me. As soon as he was by my side, my sobbing slowed. I still couldn't speak.

"Jennifer? What the hell happened?" Jack looked panicked. He sounded panicked. He wasn't very good when I cried. He just stood there with his hands pushed into his pockets. He had shoved them in so hard, it looked like they would come right out the bottoms.

"It's going to be okay. Everything is going to be all right. Shhh, Lane. I'm right here." Grant's voice was soothing. All I could hear were his words. I concentrated on the rise and fall of his chest as he calmly breathed, holding my head against him.

Jennifer pulled Joe to the side and whispered something to him. I couldn't tell what was being said, but shortly, he came over to Grant, and leaned down to share with him.

"No, Dad. I'm not leaving her like this. I can't. It's physically impossible for me to move away from her right now. I can't." He pulled me tighter to him.

Joe put his hand on Grant's shoulder and said, "Son, Jack and I have this covered. Your mother needs to speak with you inside. Now, please."

Grant picked his head up and looked at Jennifer. She nodded.

Grant reluctantly let me go and Joe took his place. I watched as Grant walked away from me. I felt like part of me was being ripped out. I needed this man. I needed him in every way. And I needed him right now.

"Lanie, Honey, can you tell me why you're crying?"

I couldn't. Not with my dad standing right there. I couldn't even tell Jennifer, let alone Joe. I shook my head no.

Seconds later, Grant and Jennifer came out. Grant was back at my side and Joe released me. He put his arms around me again and I leaned into him, my sniffling continued. Jack just stood there, dumbfounded.

"I'm sorry, Jack. This is all my fault. I told Lanie about some things Nicole told me to share with her when she was older. I think it was just too emotional. Heart-wrenching, actually." I gave Jennifer a grateful look and so did Grant.

"Well, I guess that could do it. Look, Lanie, your mom loved you. She'd be pretty upset right now seeing you crying over her." I nodded.

"Why don't we let Grant talk to Lanie right now? Let's give them a minute alone." Jennifer grabbed Joe and Jack by the elbows and pulled them into the house.

As soon as we were alone …

Chapter 24

Are You Willing to Double Down

… Grant pulled my face up to look into his.

"Lanie, tell me."

" Dane, he took, he—It wasn't his to take. He—" I burst into tears again. Grant grabbed my shoulders and pulled me close to him. He dug his face into my shoulder and neck and rocked me. We stayed like that for several minutes before he pulled me back to look at him again.

"Lanie, I've been waiting for this. You were handling it all way too well. What's in the past can't hurt you anymore. It can't—the memories can hurt you, but only if you let them. That's up to you. I won't let anything hurt you now. Not ever again."

I stared into his eyes and swear I could see his soul. They told me to trust in him, that he was explicitly mine for anything I needed. They told me everything was going to be fine from now on.

"But how could he do that to me?"

"In your mind, this whole time, you've thought there was more, yes? That Dane couldn't do that, wouldn't do that. We've known him our whole lives. I am sure there *is* more. I think it's time I had my chat with him, don't you?"

"I'm scared, Grant. I know you want to hurt him. I know it'll end up in a fight."

"Lanie, we can't keep going on pretending things didn't happen. Why are you protecting him?"

"I'm not protecting him. I'm protecting you."

He pondered this for a moment. I could see him weighing his next words quite carefully.

"I'm not going to kill him, you know. I'm going to talk. If it leads to blows, so be it. It's coming. I'm sure of it. But I promise you; I won't be the one to make that first move. Do you understand?"

I nodded. Actually, I wanted him to kick the living shit out of Dane. He deserved it. And Grant deserved to be the one to do it. It was his right. I wouldn't stop him if it were going to happen. I just didn't want it to go so far that one of them ended up seriously hurt or in jail.

"I do, Baby. Just, please wait for the right time. Now is not that time."

"Now pull yourself together for me. We are fine, you and I. And we're getting very close to this facade being put to rest. I can't wait for it, actually."

"Your mom knows."

"I know she does. And she's a very good ally. Not that I think we need one. I think your fears about us are unwarranted. I truly believe everyone, including your dad, will be more than thrilled."

He pulled me to my feet and gave me another hug. I would have been happy just staying like that for the rest of the day. I loved the feel of his body against me. But I opted to head home and have my father give me pitiful looks for the rest of the day.

Speaking of the clueless devil … "Hey, everything okay out here?" he said.

"Yes, Jack, everything is fine now. I think Lanie just needed a moment."

"I guess I just got overwhelmed with everyone being home and Jennifer giving me Mom's message. It was a bit more than I had anticipated."

"Well, okay then. You want to head back home with me?"

"Sure, Dad."

I gave Grant a soft touch on his cheek once Jack had turned to head out.

"I love you, Lanie. Remember that always. I want to be with you forever and nothing is going to stop that from happening. Not anything or anyone," he whispered into my ear.

* * *

I sat on my bed thinking of what to wear for tonight's festivities. I wanted to wear something that would make Grant drool without making everyone else in the room think I was an exhibitionist. I wished I still had Grant's boxers and shirt from our first night together, but we had thoroughly scoured our houses for anything that would be a dead giveaway we were together.

I decided to go cute and threw on a pair of black leggings and a cami with little black hearts all over it. I grabbed my black Uggs and threw them on too. I pulled my hair into a loose bun on the top of my head, letting a few stray tendrils fall. I topped the outfit with some vanilla perfume. I headed downstairs to get Jack and head over to Grant's for Chinese and cards.

"Hey, Lanie, you look cute."

"I do? Thanks, Dad. Um, you too."

He was wearing the matching pajama pants and shirt with bass caught on hooks all over them that I had given him for Christmas five years ago. Guess they never made it into his luggage when he moved. Couldn't blame him. They were hideous. They had actually been meant as a gag gift.

"Thanks, I think. I feel stupid."

"Where's your sense of fun?" I giggled. I grabbed a bottle of tequila and headed for the door.

"Hanging out in my pajamas is not my idea of fun, Lanie."

"But you look so cute, Dad." He just shook his head.

The Voights were walking past and we joined them.

"So, Lanie, I see you brought some libations. I'll go shot for shot with you." Dane was right by my side.

He reached over and put his arm around my shoulder. I pushed him off and he just bumped me playfully like everything was good.

"Really?" I said while shooting him my best bitch-face.

"Hi, Lanie, ready to have some fun tonight?"

I turned toward Lori and almost dropped everything I was carrying. She was wearing a little pink, somewhat sheer on the bottom nightie with her boobs hanging out the top. She had a matching short robe on and feathered high heels as slippers. She wore her blond hair down and it cascaded in curls across her shoulders. I looked like I was doing laundry tonight compared to her. Jack did a shocked double-take and I heard him clear his throat loudly. Jeff just made a whistling noise, not meant as a compliment. He and Jeff shared a look and shook their heads.

"Do you like my pajamas? Dane bought them for me just for tonight."

I shot Dane an evil look and my mouth dropped open. I couldn't think of anything to say. Then he mouthed 'game on' and I could feel my face scrunch up into a tight scowl. I gave him my best bitchface. I bit my lower lip and pushed past him to catch up with Haley.

"Did you get a look at what that girl is wearing? What does she think is actually going to happen tonight?" She was pissed. I was, too.

"How can you not notice it? Everything is right out there on display. Apparently there is no accounting for good taste."

"Were you referring to Lori or Dane?" she said, shaking her head in disgust. "Why would he hook up with that—that whore?"

"I honestly have no idea what he's thinking lately," I said. I shot a glance back at the two of them, laughing together.

I couldn't believe them. This was taking things a bit too far for a family fun night. I couldn't wait to get to Grant's and grab Samantha and Chelsie for some help. I didn't want her dressed like that for Grant to see. I could feel myself heating up the closer we got. I was fuming by the time I got to the door.

We entered the house and I made a beeline for the kitchen and began slamming things around. Grant was immediately by my side.

"What on earth is wrong?"

"Oh you'll see."

"Hi, Grant," Lori purred at him.

He turned toward Lori and I saw his eyes get huge. He looked Lori up and down. I took my finger and closed his mouth with a hard push.

"Like my pajamas?" she cooed.

"I … uh … they're quite nice," he said, and then turned and focused his eyes on me. "Personally though, I prefer something that allows my imagination to work on its own." And he spanked my butt. I quickly smiled at him and leaned my body into his and gave him a little rub with that recently spanked butt. He gave me a double-eyebrow salute and let a little moan escape his lips. I felt his hand brush my sex. I smiled deviously at him. He had shut Lori down with a simple comment, so she turned and focused her attention on Steve, who had just entered the kitchen.

"Hi, Steve."

"Don't even think about it, Bitch." Chelsie stepped in front of Steve, putting herself right between them.

"I was just saying hello, Chelsie. You can't be that insecure."

"Insecure is coming to a family dinner dressed like someone just picked you up on the side of the road for say, a twenty?"

I giggled, turned my attention back to Grant, and we began to rapid fire puns at each other.

"I'm looking forward to *cards* later tonight. You?"

"Yes, I do love a good game of *cards*."

"I'm looking forward to seeing your action."

"Are you willing to double down?"

"I'm not afraid of going down."

"I'm sure we'll both be holding our own."

"I'll do my best to make you raise your anti. The stakes are going to be amazing."

"No limits. I promise my unit will be high."

"Not even a spread limit?"

"Not if I can help it."

"I'm sure you'll enjoy my hand."

"I'm sure I will." He was giving me the sexiest smile and I couldn't help but give it back. I was ready for one hell of a game. *This was the game I was interested in.*

"How long are you two going to do that?" said Dylan. We both turned to look at him.

"Do what?"

"Make sexual blackjack innuendos? I'm ready to surrender now and we haven't even started playing yet."

We smiled sheepishly and returned to setting things up for dinner, all the while, still flirting with each other. I heard a cell phone go off. We all reached for our pockets. It was Dane's.

"Hello? Yes, this is he. I'm sorry, who is this? What? I'm not sure what you're talking about. What note …

Chapter 25

Ouch

"… on a napkin?"

Grant and I immediately looked at each other and began to giggle. I looked at Dane and mouthed 'game on' and gave him my best smug smile.

"Dane, Honey, who is that?" Lori asked as she tried to listen in.

"Shhh," he said, annoyed with her.

"I'm sorry, where did you say we met? No, I haven't been there before, I think someone played a bit of a prank on us both." He shot Grant and I a glance.

"I want to know who that is, right now!" Lori seemed to be getting upset. She actually stamped her foot. I had no idea why since she obviously didn't really care about being with him.

"What did you say your name was again? Lisa? Well, nice to talk to you, too, Lisa. You do sound familiar. Yes, I did send them champagne. Oh, I guess we did speak that night on the phone." He continued talking with the red-headed super model waitress. I had to wonder what she actually called for. I hoped we weren't getting him mixed up with yet another whore. *Who actually calls for a threesome?*

Lori was getting increasingly pissed. She liked to be the center of attention and apparently that included everyone in the room with a dick and a pulse. Dane was her meal ticket and she wasn't going to let him go without a fight unless she had someone else lined up. Her plans of getting her paws on Grant were not panning out.

She tried to grab the phone out of Dane's hand, but he pushed her away. She stormed out of the room.

"Listen, I would enjoy chatting more, but I'm in the middle of a family dinner. Yes, that would be great. So I'll talk with you then." He hung up the phone. He gave us a sideways glance and then proceeded to give Lori chase. Why he did was beyond me.

Within moments they returned to the room with bags of Chinese food. Guess they got as far as the front yard and the deliveryman showed up. *Bet he enjoyed the view.* Still, Lori didn't look happy and Dane didn't acknowledge her at all.

Everyone started to pile their plates with food and grab chopsticks or forks and find a spot on the floor or couch to eat. I planted myself next to Grant and snuggled close. I honestly was growing tired of hiding things and it wasn't unlike he and I to be off in a corner somewhere together. We'd done that since we were kids.

Dane came over and planted himself on the other side of me. I shot him an incredulous look and he just smiled and started shoving food into his face. I looked at Grant and he shook his head. I felt him tense slightly and he wrapped his hand around my waist and pulled me even closer to him.

Then I felt Dane put his arm around my waist and pull me closer to him. Grant turned and glared at him and then grabbed me and pulled me back. Now they were taking turns trying to get closer on either side of me.

"If you two don't cut it out, I am going to throw up. Dane, stop it." He was being pretty brazen. I grabbed my fork and jabbed his hand with it.

"Ouch. Lanie, why did you do that?"

"I'm not on the menu, Dane. Keep your hands to yourself or I'll put it straight through next time."

Grant had won and I was neatly tucked in beside him with a pillow now wedged between Dane and I. Lori had been sitting quietly in the corner, watching us. She was clearly out of her element and we all ignored her. Even Dane.

Around eleven o'clock, the parents all decided it was time to head home or upstairs to get some sleep. The men were going fishing in the morning, so they thought it best to call it an early night.

All of us remaining straightened up and discussed what game would be fun to play.

"Definitely a drinking game; how about quarters?" Samantha chimed.

"Too noisy."

"Blackjack?" Dylan said, smiling at Grant and I.

"I got it!" Steve jumped up and ran to the kitchen to grab some sticky notes and pens.

"We'll play guess who you are." He scribbled something down on one of the notes and plopped it on Chelsie's forehead. It said Betty Boop. We all giggled and started to grab the sticky notes and write names down. I grabbed one, scribbled on it and then slapped it on Dane's forehead. It said Pinocchio. Every one laughed but Lori. Samantha got Cleopatra from Dylan. Grant got James Dean from Samantha. Chelsie wrote one out and placed it on Steve. It said Pee Wee Herman. We all laughed again.

We were all having fun just writing and then finally Lori whined, "Someone do me!"

This made us all laugh even harder. She turned red in the face and then Dane grabbed the pen and scribbled something and placed it on her forehead. We all just stared. You could hear a pin drop.

"Dane, that's kind of mean," Samantha said.

"I think it's quite fitting." Chelsie smiled and pulled Lori to her feet and led her over to a mirror.

We all just watched as Lori looked. I could see her turn bright red now, but not from embarrassment. She was pissed and all hell was going to break loose. On her sticky note Dane had written, Leave!

She turned to look at him. She glared in fact, and then she screamed. "What the fuck is that supposed to mean? Leave? You want me to leave? After everything I helped you do? After everything, that's what I get? Leave? You want me to leave. Fine! I'll leave! But not before I tell Grant and Lanie how the whole shower thing was all your idea! That's right; Dane came up with the whole thing, all to get in your pants, Lanie. Not that I wouldn't have minded a night with Grant, but for some reason everyone wants you, you little flat-chested bitch."

"Get out." I heard from behind me. It was Dane. He was extremely angry and all the veins in his neck were popping out. His fists were clenched and he was getting ready to charge her. Dylan grabbed his arm and Dane pulled away. He started heading towards her and Steve stepped in.

"I don't think so, Dane. She's not a lady, but she's still a female. And I can't let you touch her. Even if she deserves it."

"But I can," I said and I got up and headed toward Lori. I walked up to her and started poking her in the chest so hard she couldn't keep her balance on her heels.

"You came into my world and fucked with my guys and me." *Poke.* "I don't take kindly to that, Lori." *Poke.* "I let you get away with fucking me over in high school, but like hell am I going to let you fuck with me now." *Poke.* "I've let too much happen already." *Poke.* "Do you hear me? You will not ruin what I have." *Poke.* "Get the fuck out of this house." *Poke.* "Get the fuck out of my life and don't let me ever see you near any one of us or this cliff again." And with that, I grabbed her by her hair and swung her toward the door.

Chelsie was kind enough to open it in time before she hit it face first. She fell out of the doorway and landed on her ass in the dirt. She opened her mouth to say something, but Chelsie just slammed the door.

I turned to Dane. "You. You made this mess. You brought that slut back into my life and to this cliff. I gave her a chance for your sake and you used it against me. You used her to hurt me and hurt Grant. You just couldn't be happy for us. Go clean up your mess. Now."

Dane looked at me. He had no expression on his face at all. He looked down and headed out.

I was so angry I was shaking, but damn it felt so good to finally give Lori a piece of my mind. Chelsie and Samantha were on me in a second, giving me hugs and telling me how awesome I was for standing up for myself. I shook my head feeling terrible. It was out of character for me. But I was done. *Done with all that shit.* It felt just as good as it did bad.

I walked back over and sank down next to Grant, who pulled me close to his side and whispered into my ear, "Remind me never to get you mad at me." He gently kissed my cheek. I smiled at him and put my head against his shoulder.

"Shots all around. Lanie, you deserve the first one." Dylan handed me a shot. I downed it quickly and held the shot glass out for another. He filled it again and we all did a shot together for good riddance to Lori.

"How about we get back to the game?" Steve would do anything to get back to a good time.

"Lanie is the only one who doesn't have a sticky on her head yet."

I realized that everything had all gone down and they had all been still wearing them. If anyone had been watching, it would have looked more bizarre than it probably had to begin with.

Grant grabbed a pen and began to scribble. He put it on my forehead and then ran his finger down my cheek. *That's right, there was no one here to hide from.* Everyone in this room knew we were together. I could finally let loose, relax and be with my boyfriend. I curled into him and gave him a deep kiss. I heard Samantha sigh. *So glad my passion for Grant could reach her from across the room.* I giggled to myself and drank another shot.

We got into the game and soon we were laughing and having a great time. It was like old times.

Except something was missing. I ran to the kitchen and grabbed…

Chapter 26

God, I Wish I Was a Sandwich Cookie Right Now

… a package of double-stuffed sandwich cookies.

"You can't have a kid's night without double-stuffed sandwich cookies."

Everyone cheered. *Silly, really, that a bunch of adults were cheering for cookies, but hell, how could you resist sandwich cookies?* Plus, we were all seriously buzzed at this point. We gathered around the coffee table and I started to toss them out to everyone. I grabbed mine and pulled it apart and started to seductively lick it for Grant. As he watched me, I could see the corner of his mouth start to twitch. He licked his lips as I slowly licked the crème filling.

"God, I wish I were a sandwich cookie right now," he moaned softly.

I began to circle my tongue around and around on the cookie, starting slowly and then getting faster and faster. I was completely focused on his reactions. I would lick the crème and then give him a sexy mouth opened 'oh' in between. I was giving him my best sex eyes and totally playing it up. I began to swirl the crème all over my parted lips, moaning and then licking it off again. I sucked my bottom lip in and bit it, closed my eyes and ran my hands down my body.

"Lanie, please," I heard Grant growl, but continued to molest the cookie.

"Maybe we should go …" I heard someone say in the background. I didn't care; I was having fun teasing Grant and not caring who was watching. I grabbed another sandwich cookie and began double dip licking.

Suddenly Grant was on top of me. I looked around the room and it was now completely devoid of anyone but Grant and myself. He grabbed my cami, pulled it up and began mimicking the sandwich cookie taunts on my girls. I squealed quietly and arched my back. Scooping more crème, I rubbed it on myself to offer him a sweet treat. He growled again and began to suck enthusiastically, sucking hard. I moaned and wrapped my legs around his waist and pulled his hips against me.

"We keep having sex with food and I'm going to end up fat."

"No worries, I plan on working all the calories right off you," he whispered into my breast. He licked the rest of the crème off me.

He slid his body down mine and pulled my pants off in one smooth motion. *He was good.* He grabbed the cookie from my hand, licked some crème off and then began to lick me off. I writhed beneath his hot mouth, the feel of his tongue was intense and I wanted nothing more than to feel him inside me. I twirled my fingers into his hair to keep him there and he was totally immersed in what he was doing. He added his hand to the action and he ran his fingers up and down, stroking while he kissed and suckled me. I could barely stand it and wanted to scream out it was so good. He reached with both hands, cupped my ass and pulled me even closer. I was rocking hard against him, barely able to contain myself.

"Oh God, Grant, oh yes, fuck me with your mouth. Oh, feels so good, Baby. Don't stop. Don't you dare stop." I felt so dirty saying it that way but it *was* so good I got carried away.

His hands were now massaging while he penetrated me with his tongue, swirling it over and over again. He slid two fingers inside and began to pump them into me. My entire body exploded with my orgasm and I bit down hard on my lip, holding my breath so I wouldn't scream out. He didn't stop and continued to pump, kiss, suck and lick as my body continued to shudder in pure ecstasy. I couldn't take anymore; it was too much. My legs were shaking uncontrollably.

"Please, Baby, stop. You can stop now. Please, I can't—" and I exploded into another full force O.

"Oh Grant!" I started to scream and he jumped forward to cup his hand over my mouth as body continued to shake with the second O which hadn't stopped yet. He began to grind his hips into me and I couldn't help but grind back against him. I needed him inside me.

"You have to make love to me, right now. I need you inside me. Now!"

He ripped his sweats off and plunged into me thrusting at an extremely fast pace. I grabbed his amazingly muscular ass and pulled him deeper. I bucked my hips into him, our movements completely in sync.

"Oh fuck, Lanie. I'm too worked up. I can't hold back." He came hard, pulsing inside me. We were both completely out of breath, sweating, writhing, and rocking. We groaned softly together, whispering our undying love to each other. Eventually our rocking slowed, until we both lay completely spent in each other's arms.

"Grant, that was amazing. I especially love your O-atmeal cookie recipe."

He laughed softly into my neck and then pulled back to kiss me passionately.

"Remind me to always keep cookies in our pantry."

"You mean in my panty?"

"That too."

We cuddled up together on the couch in our favorite spooning position, talking softy about what happened with Lori and Dane's mysterious phone call. We laughed and kissed until eventually silence and exhaustion overtook us. Grant ran his hands through softly through my hair, lulling me to sleep. We slept so soundly that we never moved up to Grant's room. Sometime early in the morning I was awoken by the sound of talking in the kitchen.

"I'm so glad this isn't our house anymore—look at this mess." It was Jennifer.

"Yeah, me too. Looks like one of their famous high school parties, doesn't it?" Joe said.

"Yes, but we never found that particular couple asleep on the couch together." She giggled.

I rubbed the sleep from my eyes and realized it was still dark out. Joe must have been up getting ready for fishing. It was so sweet of Jennifer to get up with him. I sat up and saw Jennifer coming toward Grant and I with two cups of coffee.

"Good morning, Lanie. I trust you had a good time after we went up last night?" She gave me her warmest smile.

I wanted to snuggle back in next to Grant, but I realized he was supposed to be fishing and that he would have to get up. Then I realized that my dad would be up and notice I hadn't come home. *Why did that make me feel funny, like a teenager who had fallen asleep at her boyfriend's?* I smiled to myself and reached to take my cup from Jennifer.

"Yes, we had a great night. We're one less now." She gave me a quizzical look and I winked at her. "I threw Lori out last night and I think Dane was on board, too."

"Oh, Haley is going to be so happy about that. You'll have to give me all the details. And I want the play by play."

I nodded and then turned my attention to the hot piece of sleepiness curled around me.

"Grant, Honey, you need to get up." I took his mug of coffee and swayed it under his nose. He twitched for a second and then his breathing became deep again.

"Grant, Babe, you have to get up." I ran my fingertips right behind his ear and down his neck.

I heard a low groan, or maybe it was a growl, and he reached his arms around me and pulled me close and started to reach for my gals.

"Whoa there, handsy. We're not alone. Alert, you're mom is watching you try to feel me up."

Grant looked up with one eye, peering back and forth between us.

"Good morning, Mom," he said in a groggy voice.

"I bet it is," Jennifer said with a slight smirk.

Then he reached for me again and pulled me into a deep, passionate kiss.

"Good morning, my love." He was definitely more awake now and I could feel other parts waking up beneath our blanket. I smiled to myself. *Damn morning fishing.*

"Now it's a good morning. I've been waiting to see that happen … for years. And now it's official!" Jennifer giggled and then she ran off to find Joe or to start making wedding plans, whichever came first.

"You need to get up and get ready for fishing."

"I don't want to go to school."

"I didn't say go swim with the fishes." I laughed,

"I see we never made it upstairs."

"I couldn't have even if I wanted to. After what you did to me, I wouldn't have been able to walk up the stairs."

"I would have carried you, you know."

"I didn't care where we were, as long as I was next to you." He pulled me down to him and I snuggled back in. I had to restrain myself from getting all hot and heavy. I was so used to being with him morning, noon, and night. We had been able to not miss a night together last night, but that would not be the case this evening.

"Hey, I'm going to head home. If I stay here much longer, I won't ever leave and you won't be going fishing. Last night was amazing, Love."

"What was amazing was you—the way you stood up to Lori. In fact, yesterday was pretty much epic all around. I am so proud of you, Babe."

"It's you. You give me the strength. You make me who I am, Grant."

"No, Love, you have *always* been a strong, smart, beautiful woman who could stand on her own two feet. Believe it."

"What I believe is that your love has made me whole."

"I feel the same way. I couldn't ever see my life without you in it. It's an impossibility."

"I see the sandwich cookie-whores are up bright and early." Steve was always jokes first and nothing but jokes after.

"Jealous."

"I got mine just fine last night."

"Sure you did, Pee Wee," I teased.

"That's not what she said. She changed my name to Godzilla. Didn't you hear her screaming it out all night?"

"I just heard loud snoring. Wait, that must've been Godzilla roaring," Grant said.

I tousled his hair, leaned down and gave him a soft peck on the lips. "I'll be up to the fishing spot soon with breakfast."

"Will you stay and fish with us?"

"I have to do some work today, go over some ads and trade show stuff. I was going to show Jennifer."

"Bonding with my mother?"

"Well, you'll be bonding with my father."

"Lots of bonding going on around here." Dylan was just making it down the stairs and didn't look like he was awake.

I gave him a high five, which he completely missed, on my way out the door.

"I'll see you guys in a bit. Bringing you all beach sandwiches."

When we were young and hit the beach early, our moms would bring 'beach sandwiches' which were basically a fried egg on a roll and anything else you wanted on it. My favorite was egg, cheese, salt, pepper and ketchup. But everyone had their favorites.

"Cheese, please," Grant called out.

"Not sandwich cookie stuffing?" Steve stuck he finger down his throat and pretended to gag.

"Yuck, that sounds disgusting."

"You seemed to be enjoying it last night."

I closed the door behind me so I could no long hear the banter and headed home to cook. When I got home, I heard Jack milling around in the kitchen, so I headed straight there.

"Still in your PJs, I see."

"Yes, I stayed over last night."

"I figured that out when you never came home."

"Dad, did you stay up to wait for me to get home?"

"Yeah, it's a dad thing."

"You do know I'm in my twenties now, right?"

"Yes, I know, Lanie. It wouldn't matter if you were fifty; you're still my little girl. And I worry and I'm protective. Deal with it."

"Yes, sir." I laughed and he shot me a raised eye-browed glance.

"So are you coming fishing or what?"

"I'm going to stay and make you all beach sandwiches and bring them up later. You want anything special?"

"You know."

"Dad, I don't keep anchovies in the house. And anyway, that's disgusting."

"Bacon, egg, and cheese better?"

"Um, yeah. So I was thinking about tonight." I hadn't really spent any time with my dad alone, and I really wanted to have a heart to heart. It was time to start cluing him in on everything since apparently he was too blind to catch on. Maybe he was just in denial or playing dumb. Maybe he was just waiting for me to come out and tell him. I wanted to wait until Grant spoke to Dane, but I also didn't want to totally blindside him with my relationship.

"What about tonight?"

"I thought maybe we could go out to dinner. Just you and I."

"I heard there's a …

Chapter 27

I Swear to God

"… great new Italian place in town. Want to go try it out?"

"You heard about that?"

"Dane mentioned it last night."

"I see. Well, I ate there the other night and it was amazing. I would love to take you there."

"Oh really? I heard it's pretty fancy. Did you take clients?"

"No, just Grant and I went."

"Oh, I see. Well, if you'd rather go somewhere else …"

"Why would I want to go somewhere else? The food was great. We had a great time. I want to go there with you."

"Then it's a date. Now I have to get up to the cliff before it's biting time."

"Okay, Dad. I'll be up in a little while."

I headed upstairs to get myself ready for the day. Once I was showered and dressed, I headed back downstairs to start cooking. I laid everything out and began my own little assembly line, making various combinations of beach sandwiches. I was also brewing coffee and filling thermoses. I heard my door open, I turned my head to see who it was, and Dane came bouncing into my kitchen.

"Hey, Lanie, where's Jack?"

I shot him my crappy-morning-to-you bitch-face and replied coldly, "He's already at the spot. You should go there, now."

"Good. I was hoping I could get some time alone with him to talk."

"What the hell do you need to talk to my dad about in private?"

"That's between me and your dad, Lanie."

"Dane, I swear to God—"

He interrupted me. "I won't say anything about you and Grant. I'm not an ass, you know," he said defensively, holding his hand over his heart like I had stabbed him there.

"Huh, that's news to me, because you've been a total ass lately." He winced at my words; the truth hurts sometimes.

"Lanie, I backed you up last night. I got rid of Lori for you."

"Dane, you got rid of Lori because she was an unnecessary fixture that was just getting in your way. She wasn't helping you get what you thought you wanted anymore. So don't try and play any kind of games with me. I know exactly what your motive was."

"Lanie, I'm offended. How could you think that about me? I love you. I want to be with you. I'm not out to hurt you." He gave me his best puppy dog eyes, but I wasn't going to let him play me like he had been.

I looked at him in shock. "What the hell kind of crazy pills have you been taking lately, huh? I mean, all of a sudden you're in love with me, out of nowhere. Then you decide you want to be with me, as soon as you found out Grant and I were together. And then you do really dirty things to try separate us. If you really loved me, you'd see I was already in love with someone else and happy, and you would let me be. But no, instead you push and continue to play games."

"Lanie, it's not like that. I've always been in love with you. Always."

"Oh bullshit, Dane. Really? What about Callie? Remember her? You were practically ready to get her an engagement ring for high school graduation. How long did you date? Pretty much from seventh grade all the way through high school and then some?"

"That was different. That was puppy love and then it was just habit."

"Dane, if you hadn't had that stupid, drunken one-night stand at that college party and then got caught, I'm pretty sure you two would be married with at least one kid by now. Instead, she is now soon to be Mrs. Jones. You blew it. And I'm not letting you ruin my chances for a fairytale love story happily ever after. So get it out of your head. It's never going to happen. Even if Grant and I didn't work out for some reason, I just don't feel that way about you."

He looked hurt, but once again, sometimes that's what the truth did. I was really getting tired of all this stupid bullshit. It was starting to get in the way of living my life and being happy. Dane was single-handedly making the beginning of my relationship with Grant, which was supposed to be one of the best times of a relationship, crappy.

"You're wrong, Lanie. You're the one who's in denial. Grant is just sweeping you off your feet because, really, when was the last time you were actually with a man? Tom?"

"I've been on plenty of dates since then."

"If I had been the one to get to you first, you'd be in love with me. Let's face it, Lanie, no one is knocking your door down for romance. You jumped at the first one who did."

"Get out."

"What's the matter, truth hurt?"

"I will not stand here and listen to you tell me the only reason I'm with Grant is because I was hard up. That I would honestly be in love with whoever made the first move. I won't listen anymore. And you know what? I don't have to. This is my house; leave it—now."

"Okay, Lanie, I'll leave, for now. But I told you. I'm the right man for you. I won't give up."

I turned my back and pretended he wasn't there. He got the hint and finally left. I grabbed my phone and text messaged Grant.

L: U have 2 get 2 my dad. D said he needed 2 tlk 2 him alone
G: No worries, babe, Im alrdy w/ ur dad.
L: Asum. I love you.
G: I love you.
L: CU in a bit. <3s

I finished up cooking, packed everything up, and headed to the fishing spot. I actually had butterflies in my stomach waiting to see Grant. I loved that feeling. I felt so alive. When I got there, they were all in a curve along the edge. Some of them were sitting, others were casting, and Dylan looked like he was still sleeping. I kicked him lightly when I passed him by.

"Food. Coffee. You need some." He grumbled something back but it sounded somewhat happy, so I was satisfied with his reply.

I laid a blanket out over a big square-shaped boulder and began taking out breakfast.

"Okay, who wants what?"

"I would love some sandwich cookies, but I'll settle for bacon, egg, and cheese," Grant whispered from right behind me. I got chills down my spine and the most wonderful tickle in my chest. Just him being so close to me made every nerve in my body feel electric. My entire body was humming with a pull toward his.

"You can have anything you want. Everything is on the menu for you," I purred. I reached behind me and pulled him closer until he was right up against me.

"I'll take whatever you've got. At least two of them." Steve was ready to eat and he pulled me out of my Grant-moment for his grub.

I grabbed two sandwiches that had lots of stuff on them and tossed them his way. Joe and Jack were headed over, so I began to pour them both some coffee.

"Thank you, Lanie. I'd like something without all the grease," Joe said. I handed him a plain egg and cheese, and then I immediately grabbed my dad's request from this morning and gave it to him. He gave me a smile and nod. I then brought Dylan something I hoped would help stir him out of his perpetual slumber.

I turned to my attention back to Grant. It was sometimes hard to focus on anything but him. I could always feel his beautiful blue eyes burning into me. They seemed to encase me in all his emotions. *I felt so much love for this man. Why had we waited all these years to give in to these feelings?* I walked over to him and touched his sleeve.

"I'm taking my dad for Italian tonight." I smiled.

"Can I come for the limo ride home?" he teased.

"I think this calls for my car. No limo rides with anyone but you ever again."

"I like the sound of that. How about you meet me at the stables when you get back? Midnight ride?"

"I guess that all depends on who I'm riding," I whispered with a wink.

He reached up and ran his hand down my cheek. He gave a quick look around to see where Jack was and then pressed his lips softly to mine.

"You can ride whomever you choose, but I can guarantee I'm your best choice," he growled at me.

I kissed him softly back.

"Hey, Lanie, what about me?" Dane shouted, hopefully referring to a beach sandwich. I grabbed one, whipped it at him, and beamed him right in the side of his head. Everyone laughed, except I guess I hit him the wrong way, because in a second he was on me and his rage was far more than was called for.

"What the fuck was that for, Lanie? Why would you do that? What the fuck is wrong with you, you bitch?" He was right in my face. I was actually a little scared. His reaction had caught me totally off guard. Jeff and Jack were over in a second trying to back him down, but it was Grant who took over. He grabbed me and pulled me behind him, placing himself in Dane's face.

“Get away from her, Dane; back down now, or so help me …” Grant’s voice was low and threatening; he meant business. I knew he had been waiting to talk to Dane, but now I could see just how volatile he had actually become. I was scared. I tried to get back between them.

“No, Lanie, you need to step back. Please. I don’t want you to get hurt.” He gently pushed me back behind him. My dad grabbed my arm and pulled me to him.

“Listen, boys, I see no need for this over something as silly as a sandwich,” Jack said.

“I agree. Grant, you need to calm down right now.” Joe tried his hardest to reason with him, but Grant put his hand up to his father to let him know this was happening.

Dylan and Steve were behind Grant in a second and Jeff was trying to pull Dane away.

“Dane, your mother and I don’t like who you’ve become. I don’t like this. What’s wrong with you? Why would you lash out at Lanie like this over a sandwich?”

“She’s nothing but a bitch dick-tease lately. Walking around here trying to see who she can get to kiss her ass the fastest!”

Before I knew what was happening, Grant had pushed Dane away from us all and was pummeling him, blow after blow after blow. All Dane could do was hold his arms out to block Grant’s assault. He hit him repeatedly in the face. Dane’s nose was a bloody mess.

My adrenaline was soaring and I stood there, unable to move or speak. I was completely cold and my stomach turned watching them. Everyone else seemed to be having the same reaction: pure shock at what they were seeing unfold in front of them in a matter of seconds. Jeff looked pale, as I’m sure I did, too.

“Don’t you ever touch her again. Don’t you go near her. You’ve hurt her enough, Dane. I’ll kill you before I let you harm her again.”

Grant stopped only long enough to speak, but it was enough time for Dane to get his footing. He went right back at Grant, throwing punches. He caught Grant right above the eyebrow and split it open. Blood started to rain down his face. I reached up to my own face, remembering Dane's shot to my jaw. Grant blocked the next shot and pushed Dane to the ground and gave him a kick to the ribs. But Dane was back on his feet in seconds, lunging at Grant. They were wrestling, punch for punch, grabbing and hitting, growls and curses coming from both of them.

"Steve, do something. Stop them before someone gets hurt. Please!" I begged. I could feel the tears welling in my eyes. I would have tried to break them up myself, but I knew it would only cause Grant to lose focus and open himself up to Dane's blows.

I saw Steve start to react, but as he was heading toward them, their struggle got further away from us, and closer to the cliff's edge.

"Oh my God! Get away from the edge!" I screamed. "Please, Grant, you're too close to the edge!"

Jack, Jeff, and Joe turned to the sound of my voice and then quickly to the edge of the cliff and the scuffle. I saw their eyes get wide and they took off towards them.

"Grant, NO!" I screamed and he turned to look at me. It was a fatal mistake. Dane swung hard and caught Grant right in the jaw and he lost his footing.

Everything else happened in slow motion. I didn't hear anything. There was no sound, only the beating of my heart in my head. It vibrated there, echoing, pulsing.

I watched in horror as the love of my life slipped over the edge …

Chapter 28

Together, Together

… of the cliff. He was grasping furiously at anything he could to save himself. Steve wasn't fast enough. His fingers just slipped right through Grant's as he thrust out to grasp him.

I felt my whole world shift.

"Dane, save him! Please, save him!" I screamed out, begging him with my entire heart, my entire soul.

Dane's arm shot out and he and Grant locked hand to wrist. He held him there. He just stared at him, like he was debating whether to pull him up or not. Grant just stared back, his mouth agape. I saw him mouth the words, 'Dane, what are you doing? For God's sake, pull me up.' His eyes were wide and his face was pale. Dane just knelt in front of him, frozen. I couldn't tell if he didn't have the strength, was in shock, or what was going on. They were eye to eye in some bizarre stare down. I could see their hands starting to strain, the veins in their forearms were popping and their knuckles were white. If he didn't pull him up soon, Grant would fall onto the rocks below.

My heart broke into a million pieces at the thought of losing him like this, at losing him at all. It was a defining moment, which made me realize that, without him, I wouldn't be able to survive. I couldn't, not now that I knew what it was like to have him as mine.

The three fathers had reached them just as Steve scrambled across the dirt to reach for Grant's other arm. Once he had him, he braced himself and began to pull. He couldn't do it. His angle was wrong. He just couldn't get the strength. Jack quickly grabbed Grant's other arm and pushed Dane back so Dylan could grab him for support. Jeff did the same for Steve. They brought Grant back up to the safety of the cliff.

Joe dropped to his knees and grabbed Grant into a close hug. He held him tightly and almost rocked him, his paternal instincts kicking in. I was beside them within seconds. Joe released him and I threw myself into Grant's arms. We sat on the ground, wrapped around each other. I held onto him like it was for dear life; it almost had been. I put my face against his and told him how much I loved him and how I couldn't live without him over and over again. He held me just as tightly, and I could feel our tears mix with one another's. We had almost lost each other.

"Hmm." I heard Jack make the sound. I knew this was too much for him to see and not start asking questions. *Hell, for all I knew, he was aware of everything, just like Jennifer and Joe, and waiting for me to spill it.*

"Baby, are you okay? Are you hurt?" I said as I examined him. I grabbed a napkin out of my jacket, wet it with my tongue, and began to pat at the blood all over his face.

"I'm okay … I'm alive. No thanks to Dane."

And then I could feel the fury building inside of me. I was ready to jump up and rip into Dane, but I didn't have to. Dylan and Steve were on him, and so was Jeff.

"What the fuck, Dane? You could have killed him!" Dylan yelled.

"It was an accident. I didn't realize we were that close to the edge," he said flatly, without one ounce of emotion.

"Why didn't you pull him up? See, that's what I'm seeing as the issue here," Steve questioned.

Dane just stood there, staring at the ground. He didn't speak or move. He didn't even blink. It was like he was in a trance.

"Dane—What were you thinking, son? I don't understand. Grant is practically your brother."

"He's *not* my brother."

"Dane! Grant has been like a brother to you your entire life. This is a family, and you've shamed us all. You've shamed me. I raised you better than what you've become. But to let Grant just—to almost let him die …" Jeff's voice sounded stern and sad at the same time.

"A potential murderer and definitely a rapist. That's what he's become," I heard Dylan spit out.

I felt all the air escape my lungs and my chest began to burn. I looked at Grant and his eyes were already on me. He grabbed me and pulled me closer.

"What do you mean, rapist?" asked Joe. He looked over to Grant and I. I put my head down to avoid eye contact. My eyes would have told him everything he needed to know.

"I didn't rape anyone. And I didn't murder anyone. I wouldn't have let Grant fall. I just … I don't know what happened. I panicked. I just didn't have a good enough grip. If I shifted in any way, I would have dropped him." He looked at Grant and I. His eyes pleaded with Grant for something.

"It's fine, Dane."

"No. No, it's not fine. It's not fine at all!" I was rushing to get to my feet, but Grant held me tight. I shot my gaze to his and he just looked back at me. It was like I could read his thoughts. Now was not the time for me to put everything out in the open. This was a private matter between the three of us.

"But …"

"Lanie—please—for me."

I shut my mouth and looked down. I couldn't even look at Dane. All I wanted to do was get Grant home and hold him and never let him go, ever.

"I think we need to talk. Now. Get your stuff and come home with me," Jeff said to Dane. He was all about the father-tone now.

"Yes, sir." Dane's voice was solemn. He reached down and started to gather his things. He looked up at Grant and I.

"Grant, I'm … I'm sorry." He nodded his head without looking at him.

"How about apologizing to Lanie, Dane? How about her? Or doesn't she deserve an apology for what you did to her?" Steve was always coming to my rescue. Steve had been like a big brother to me since we met freshman year of college.

"I didn't do anything to Lanie that deserves an apology. She knows where things stand between us."

I felt the tears starting again, along with a huge lump in my throat, and I turned my face away from everyone so that only Grant could see. He squeezed my hand and I heard him sigh.

"I think we should all pack it up and head home. Lanie, I think you and I need to have a heart to heart, don't you think?" Jack said.

I gave Grant a panicked look and he mouthed, 'It will be okay,' and then released his hold on me. I stood up slowly, having a hard time moving away from him.

Joe moved toward us. He looked at Grant and then to me. He put his hand on my shoulder and gave me a soft push toward my dad.

"I have him. No worries. You go talk to your father. He needs to know."

I grabbed my breakfast sack and walked over to Jack. I couldn't look him in the eyes. I didn't want to do this. I was afraid to tell him everything. I needed Grant to be there with me. Jack grabbed his fishing stuff and put his arm around my shoulder as we walked back home. I turned and watched Grant as we walked away. He watched me back … until we could no longer see each other.

When we reached the house, Jack opened the door and swung his arm out to show me the way in. *Geez, it was like being a teenager all over again.* Really, it was amazing how parents could make you revert to your childhood no matter what age you were. I looked up at him with watery eyes. I walked in and start to unpack everything.

"Lanie, I'm pretty sure all that can wait. Now come sit down with me on the couch and tell me what the heck is going on around here."

"Dad. I just—it's just—I can't—I don't know how to tell it all without you freaking out."

"Why don't you just try me?"

"I have to go to the bathroom. I'll be right back."

Jack just shook his head, threw his hands up and motioned me to go. I grabbed my cell phone and ran to my bedroom bath. I dialed Chelsie.

"Chelsie."

"Lanie, what the fuck happened out there today?"

"Chelsie, I don't have time to fill you in. I will later, promise. I need help. Jack wants the whole story. I don't want to tell him about Dane yet. And I want Grant to be with me when we tell him about us. Is Grant back yet? Is he okay?"

"He's back. Jennifer is fawning all over him now, looking for broken bones, checking for a concussion, and cleaning up all his wounds. He's shaken up. But all he can think about is you."

"Do you think he'd come over or should I bring Jack there? Is he up for it?"

"Let me ask him. Hold on." She covered the phone and I could hear the muffled conversation. Chelsie, then Grant, then Jennifer and then Grant again.

"Despite Jennifer's wanting him to rest, he's coming to you. Now we need a girl chat later. Samantha and I will swing by. Sound good?"

"Sure. I'll see you then."

I flushed the toilet for believability purposes and then slowly headed back downstairs. But Jack was nowhere to be found. I went back to the kitchen and started to clean up again. I heard the front door open and ran for it.

Once I saw Grant, I couldn't help myself from jumping into his arms and kissing him. I ran my hand over his bruised eye and then focused on his jaw, running my lips softly against it where he took the hit that almost ended everything. My mind wandered back to when he had tended to my bruised jaw. *What the hell had gone wrong with Dane? How could things have gotten so out of hand?*

"So, finally I catch the proverbial cat and mouse with their paws in the cookie jar," I heard Jack say from behind me. Grant and I both jumped and then quickly separated.

"What? Dad, that doesn't even make sense."

"Sandwich cookies," Grant said.

"Shut up!" I said breathily at him, shaking my head. Maybe he *did* hit his head.

We both turned back to Jack. He swung his arm out again, this time ushering us to the couch. We followed and planted ourselves next to each other, facing where he chose to sit.

"So, you two want to tell me something?"

Grant and I looked at each other and then back to Jack. We both went to speak at the same time and nothing came out. Not from either of us.

"Okay. Want to try again? Do I need to ask questions and you two can just nod?"

"No, Dad. It's just, well—"

"We're together. Together, together," Grant managed.

"I see. 'Together, together.'"

"Dad, Grant and I, we're in love. We're in a relationship. We're committed. I mean to each other."

"Jack, I love Lanie. I always …"

"You always have. I know. I'm not blind. Nicole used to tell me this was going to happen. I've just been waiting to see if she was right. I guess she was. How serious is this 'together, together?'"

"Serious. Very serious," I told him and then I grabbed Grant's hand and brought it into my lap. Then I quickly moved it off my lap and just held his hand on the couch and gave a cheesy smile.

"Jack, I want to give Lanie everything you'd want her to have. I promise I won't ever hurt her. I love her. I want to be with her forever."

"I see. Lanie? How do you feel about this?"

"Dad, I'm in love with him. I feel alive, and happy. Everything is just so amazing."

"Right, no need to tell me how great the sex is again, Lanie."

Grant's eyes got wide and he just looked back and forth between Jack and I. I think I heard him choke on his own spit or something.

"I wasn't, but if you'd like to hear about it …"

"No, no. I don't need all the details again, thanks."

Now Grant had a nervous cheesy smile on his face. And that's when it happened. We both got extremely …

Chapter 29

The Your-Dating-My-Little-Girl Speech

… giddy and started giggling uncontrollably. It had to be the relief of not having to hide anymore.

"Would either of you like to tell me what the hell has gotten into Dane? What was that up on the cliff? And why did Dylan call him a rapist?"

And that knocked the giddy right out of our yap. We both went stone cold.

"Jack, I plan to tell you everything, but I need to have a conversation with Dane first. Man to … man. I hope you can respect that and trust Lanie and I on this."

"Well, if you think that's the best way, then I guess that works for me. I trust you both."

"Dad. Are you? Do we? Do we have your blessing? Are you happy we're together?"

"Lanie, I couldn't think of another man that would be a better match for you. I'm very happy. I already consider Grant a son. I think this is great news. Grant, good luck to you there." And he nodded his head toward me.

"Oh my God, I'm so happy to hear you say that!" And I lunged across the couch to hug him. Grant quickly stood up and shook his hand.

"Thank you, Jack. This means so much to me, to us."

"This calls for a celebration. How about Grant and his parents join us for dinner tonight, Lanie? Would that be okay with you? Grant, you feel up to it?"

"I would be honored to have dinner with you both. My mom can keep an eye on me if she comes. I'll call them right now." Grant was all smiles. So was I. Finally, everything was out in the open. Well, almost everything. We still had to deal with the repercussions of what happened on the cliff with Dane, as well as telling my dad what happened between he and I. Grant left the room to call his parents and Jack and I were alone again.

"So, Lanie, this is what you want? This thing with Grant, it makes you happy?"

"Oh, yes. I never realized how perfect we were together. I mean, we've always been so connected, but it's so much more now. I am so happy."

"And you love him? And he loves you?"

"Yes. We're deeply in love. Dad, I mean, this is forever for me."

"Lanie, you guys just started this relationship and things happen, you know. I don't want you to …"

"No. Dad, this is forever. I know that," I interrupted.

"Let's not get all excited about this now. I'm sure you're not jumping into getting married and all."

"Not tomorrow, but not years from now either. If he asked me, I'd say yes. In fact, if he asked me to fly away to an exotic island to get married next week, I'd be packing right now."

"That serious, huh?"

"That serious. Yeah."

Grant came back into the room and Jack and I both clammed up. I knew I was grinning ear to ear. I had a terrible poker face and Grant smiled the second he saw me. He knew I had spoken further with my dad.

"My parents were extremely thrilled that Jack knows about us. In fact, my mom couldn't stop rambling, so I'm sure we'll all be listening to her throughout dinner."

"Oh that's great. Dinner is going to be so much fun."

I heard the front door open and Samantha pranced in with Chelsie right behind her.

"Grant and Lanie kissing in a tree …" Samantha giggled.

"Great. Now we're back in grade school. So, Lanie, can Samantha and I have that girl chat we spoke about earlier?" Chelsie said.

"Sure, let's go out on the terrace."

"Actually, would you mind if I took your dad out there to talk for a while? I'm sure he has some things he'd like to discuss with me, just the two of us," Grant said.

I looked at him nervously and he gave me a reassuring smile. I nodded and grabbed Samantha's hand and started to pull her up to my room. Chelsie followed. We got to my room and we all jumped on the bed.

"What the fuck happened today? Dane almost killed Grant. First he rapes you and then this. We need to get him some serious help and I mean now. And if no one does, I'm calling the police before someone else gets hurt or killed." Chelsie was pissed.

The part of me that remembered the old Dane still tried to find a way to rationalize everything that had happened. But the part of me that almost lost Grant was in total agreement with Chelsie.

"This is terrible. All of it," Samantha said. "Dylan was so angry today. I had to plead with him not to go push Dane off the cliff."

"I wonder what Jeff and Haley had to say to him. Maybe we can have Jennifer call Haley to get the low down?"

"That's a great idea. Samantha, go call her." Samantha made a pouty face and headed into the bathroom so she could hear and Jennifer couldn't hear us.

"He wasn't like this until Lori came along. Dane would never hurt a fly, especially Grant or I. I just don't know what's gotten into him. It's like he's lost all sense of reality."

"Can I talk to him?"

I laughed out loud. "I'll call you in when the cops don't work out. You're my secret weapon."

Chelsie smiled and we both just looked down at the bed, caught in our own thoughts.

"You know. He kind of wasn't the same after Callie left him. I mean, he became obsessed with work and sealing the deal. And he wouldn't even date. He kind of got a bit cocky after that, too," I said.

"True. It did seem to start back then."

"But he really changed after he found out she was engaged."

"That's right. Do you think he's drinking or doing drugs or something?"

"I'd smell the alcohol on him. Not sure about the drugs, but he doesn't ever seem to be strung out."

"Well, we know he has drugs."

"But we don't know if he's doing them."

We stopped and looked at each other. There was too much. There was not enough. We were lost on what the hell was wrong with Dane. We quickly turned our heads when Samantha came back in the room.

"Well?" we said in unison.

"I got nothing. Jennifer had nothing to say. End of subject."

We all just sat there quietly for a long time.

"Grant needs to talk to him," Chelsie said.

"No. You saw what happened last time. Dane could have—he could have killed him. No. We don't know what he's capable of anymore."

"What if it was with all of us? You know, like an intervention?"

"I can't. I'd just be ashamed or something. Everyone would hear. Grant would hear."

"Honey, we all know what happened. And none of us fault you at all," Chelsie said in the sweetest voice. She only used that voice when she really meant what she was saying.

"Yeah, Lanie, you have nothing to be ashamed of. He does." Samantha put her hand on my shoulder. "He won't do anything with all of us there."

"He did this afternoon."

"Lanie, I'm not defending him, but he might not have meant to knock Grant over the edge. That part could have been an accident." Samantha really hated conflict.

"I don't know. Let me talk to Grant about it. Okay?" I said.

"We'll all talk to our significant others. We'll make it a group decision. Everyone in or we don't do it." Chelsie put her hand on mine.

"Agreed." Samantha put hers on top of Chelsie's.

"Okay. But I have a backup plan."

"Spill."

I explained my other plan in a sketchy outline. I knew it was a last resort, but it would be a good one if I could actually pull it off. Samantha actually clapped. Chelsie was less sure, but thought it was worth a shot. I would need some time alone to make some calls.

When we were finished, we all headed back downstairs. The girls headed out and I went to the terrace to find Grant and Jack. They were standing by the far wall. They each had a beer in their hand and my dad was actually doing all the talking. In fact, he was doing a lot of talking. Grant just shook his head and would open his mouth to say something, but Jack would just keep on talking. Grant looked like he should be taking notes. I had to rescue him.

"So Dad, are you trying to talk him out of being with me? You can't tell him awful childhood stories about me. He knows them all already. And he's in all the embarrassing photos, too." I punched my dad in the arm as I said it.

He cleared his throat, said, 'Yep," and just walked away. I looked at Grant and we both broke into laughter.

"What the hell was that all about?"

"The your-dating-my-little-girl speech." He laughed again. He looked at me, smiled, and grabbed a strand of my hair. He twirled it with his fingers.

I was immediately drawn to him and grabbed his shirt and pinned him up against the terrace wall and hungrily kissed his lips until I'd had my fill. We kissed for a long time; a very long time. I only stopped to come up for air.

"Sorry."

And his hands were around my face pulling me into another hungry kiss. He spun me around and pinned me to the wall and kissed until he had his fill. It was so hard to pull away and put an end to this 'conversation' we were having, but we had some things I needed to talk to him about.

I told him all about the intervention and he thought it was a solid plan. I kept my backup plan between the girls and myself. We had all agreed. It was only to be used as a last resort.

"So what's your plan for the rest of the day, Love?"

"Staying with you. What was your plan?"

"I was thinking of heading back home for a while. Maybe rest for a bit. Care to join me?"

"I'd love to." I was tired. Emotionally drained, I guess. I took his hand and we headed over to his place. We stopped to chat with Jennifer, so she could check Grant again for a concussion. Then we headed up to his room.

I sat down on the bed and watched him remove his shoes. Then he began to remove his shirt. *Oh yes. I loved to see that.* Then he began to unbuckle his pants. I felt a ripple go through my body. I watched as he slowly let his pants drop, revealing every single sexy inch of his skin. I bit my lower lip at the sight and held it there while I waited for the briefs to come off. *That's right, Baby, take everything off for me.* I was enjoying my own little strip tease. Everything about his man set me on fire. I was slightly disappointed when my show stopped and he lay down on the bed. I sat there for a minute so I didn't attack him and rip his briefs off and then slowly lay down next to him.

I felt his arms snake around me and pull me close. I reached over to him and put my arms around his neck and pulled his lips to mine. I felt him groan into the kiss and I pushed my entire body against his.

"You're going to nap in all your clothes?"

"Someone was rude and only undressed himself," I purred.

"Please forgive me. It was very unthoughtful of me. Let me make amends."

He proceeded to unbutton my shirt, button by button, taking the time to tease every ounce of new flesh he uncovered. I was already straining not to move things along quicker. He removed my bra and took the time to fondle each breast and give them each a soft kiss. He unbuttoned my pants and slid them down, his tongue trailing just inches behind them. I squirmed under his touch. Every nerve was reacting. He looked up at me when he got to my panties. His eyes were heavy and he gave me the hottest smirk. I was immediately ready for anything he had for me. He pulled my panties off and slid next to me again.

"Nope. You're not done yet."

"I'm not?" He growled into my neck.

I pointed to his briefs. He smiled and promptly removed them. Oh the feel of his skin against mine was pure heaven. I rubbed my body against his so the sensation wouldn't end and then he slowly rolled me onto my back and placed himself gently on top of me. He had an arm on either side of my head and was propped up on his elbows. I let him settle between my legs, and feeing his throbbing hotness pressed against me was torture. I ran my hand long his cheek and shifted my body to bring him closer to entering me.

"I want to watch you."

"What? You want to watch me? Do what, pleasure myself for you?"

"Wow. I didn't even think about that. Raincheck, please."

"Really?" *I mean, seriously? What guy turns that down?* "Raincheck granted."

"I want to watch your face while I make love to you. There is nothing more beautiful in this world to me than seeing you feel pleasure. Because of me." It made my heart melt and other things stir more.

He began to slowly grind against me. I couldn't help but move with him. He held my face firmly in place and just looked over it, from my lips to my eyes to my hair. He was absorbing me into his soul with his eyes.

The friction was driving me insane and I spread my legs to give him access but he stopped at my entrance and just teased for a bit. I was starting to writhe even more beneath him and tried to kiss him, but he shook his head at me and smiled, just wanting to watch my reactions. This whole exercise was hot as hell.

He slid inside of me just a bit and I bucked my hips to try and push him inside all the way. He stayed there, taking his time, enjoying every second of the tease. He might have underestimated his resolve, because after a few moments, I heard him growl and he pushed himself completely and deeply inside me. We moaned together at the feel of it. I wrapped my legs around his waist.

He moved slowly, rolling his hips in a figure eight, hitting all sorts of new and very sensitive places with each roll. I let out a broken breath our eyes never leaving the other's, watching the pleasure on each other. It was intense. I was completely turned on and I understood what he meant. There was nothing more beautiful than his face, at this moment, making love to him.

Our lips were so close I could almost taste him. I parted mine and begged him with my eyes for his mouth to cover mine. He got the message and that hot mouth was on me. He never moved his lips from mine and continued to thrust sweetly into me. I clung to him. My mind was running through thoughts of intense pleasure, pure love for him, and the thought of how close I had been to losing him. I pulled him tighter to me and gave him every bit of my soul.

I could tell he was starting to waiver at his slower pace and he began to move faster. He watched me intently and the thought of what he was doing pushed me over the edge. I let every bit of pleasure show on my face to give him what he desired. I couldn't help but throw my head back against the pillow letting soft sounds escape my lips, and then turned back to him so he could watch pure pleasure washed over me.

It was more than he could take and he exploded inside of me, letting me watch his face in return.

"I love you, Lanie. I can't imagine my life without you."

"You'll never have to. I'm never going anywhere."

He rolled to my side and pulled me close. After a while, sleep took him over. It had been a late 'sandwich cookie-filled' night, an early morning, and an emotional day. All I wanted was to feel his warm body against mine, feeling his heart continue to beat. I drifted off with him.

I'm not sure what woke me, but I rolled over to look at his clock.

"Babe, I'm going to head home and get ready for dinner, okay?"

"Sure. Call me in half an hour to wake me?"

"Okay, Babe."

I got dressed quietly and then I left. The day was starting to fade. I was enjoying the short walk home when I noticed a yellow sports car pull into the gravel drive. As it passed me, I saw …

Chapter 30

Yes, He Is

. . . a redheaded super model driving it. *You've got to be kidding me. What the hell was this going to start now?* I shook my head. I ducked into my doorway and watched her park her car in front of Dane's. She beeped the horn and Dane came running out, hopped in the car, and they took off. I jumped inside and shut the door so they couldn't see me as they passed.

I headed inside to let Jack know I was back and start getting ready for dinner. I was actually relieved to know the redheaded super model wouldn't be working tonight. Game on had turned into this bizarre dynamic, and I was honestly tired of it all. It had almost killed Grant. I was happy we were one step closer to life being good again.

I looked around the house and couldn't find him, so I headed upstairs to my room. I heard something above me, in the walk. I headed up. My father was sitting in my papasan holding the picture of Nicole and me, having a conversation with her. I hadn't seen him up here in so long it made my heart ache a bit. I kept very quiet and watched him.

"Well, Babe, you were right. Lanie and Grant are in love. I guess I should have believed you. I'm sorry I made fun of you. You'd be having a field day with this right now."

Tap tap

I caught my breath. *Oh my God, Nicole was tapping for him.* I saw him look out the window and all around the room, but luckily he didn't catch me spying on him.

"Uh huh. Okay then. So you're going to go ahead and bust on me from up there then. Fine, have at it."

I smiled seeing him talk to her like that. It was unlike him to be emotional. Getting a little glimpse into his relationship with Nicole was sweet.

Tap tap

"Yeah, yeah. I know. But she's so young. I mean, should I have the talk with her?"

Holy crap, no. I was not going to talk about sex with my dad. I mean, I joked about it and used it to keep him from prying when he got here, but no. And what the hell? How old did he think I was? He had to know I had had sex before. Geez.

"I guess not. That'd be real awkward and well, that was your job. I sure do miss you, Nicole. I wish you were here to see all this."

Tappity tap tap

"Well, I guess you already are then, aren't you? So maybe you could just watch out for her when I'm not here. Okay? No need to tap. I know you do."

I felt bad listening now. So I backed down the stairs a bit, waited and then called for him.

"Dad? You up there?" I faked coming up the stairs.

"Yeah, Lanie. I'm here."

"You never come up here. What are you doing here?"

"I think I'm having a conversation with your mother. If you promise not to think I'm crazy …"

"So she answered you too? Tap tap? Nope, you're not crazy. Been there, done that."

"Really? Oh good." He got up, kissed my mom's photo and put it back down on the table.

"Come on. We should go get ready for dinner."

We both headed to our respective rooms and got ready. We met down in the kitchen and headed to the garage to get my SUV to pick up Grant and his parents. Jack actually got out to let Grant sit in front with me. Quite sweet.

We got to the restaurant and were seated by a huge fireplace in the main bar. The place brought back great memories for Grant and I.

"Can we stop and get some champagne and chocolate covered strawberries for later? Or maybe you'd like to try something new. I have a craving for chocolate mousse," he whispered seductively into my ear and then his tongue darted out and gave it a quick brush. It gave me a very sensual shudder.

"You bet," I purred back.

We sat down and enjoyed the most amazing food and conversation. And then everything changed. Out of the corner of my eye I saw a flash of red. Oh please, please don't let it be them. No such luck. In a matter of moments, Dane and Lisa were standing at our table.

"Good evening everyone. I'd like you to meet Lisa. She works here, so we thought we'd come for drinks."

He proceeded to introduce everyone at the table. Jennifer played sweet, but she was shooting daggers at Dane with her eyes and he knew it.

When he got to Grant and I, he said, "I know you've already met Grant and Lanie, but you might know them by some other names." She smiled sweetly and giggled with Dane.

"Would you like to join us?" Joe was being gracious. I knew he was mad at Dane but that's just how Joe was. I actually heard Jennifer kick him under the table. "Or, maybe another time. We don't want to step in on your date; that would be quite rude of us." He sheepishly smiled at Jennifer, who rolled her eyes.

"Oh, no thank you, but maybe Lanie and Grant can join us after for drinks."

"No, I don't think so. We all came together." Grant smiled when he said it. Like father like son, even considering what Dane had done to him just that morning.

"We could drive you home?" Lisa offered.

"Oh, sorry, Grant and I need to stop off on the way home to pick some things up. Maybe another time."

"Yes, you sound like such a fun couple from your note. I thought maybe the four of us could discuss that offer. Make it a foursome."

Jack, Jennifer, and Joe all looked at Grant and I, and then to Lisa and Dane.

"Really, I don't think that's going to be a possibility. Ever." Grant was curt.

"Well, okay, we'll see you later." And they left, giggling again.

Damn it. I knew something was going to rear its ugly head when I saw that sports car. I had hoped it would be different with her. *But alas, another Lori and more games.*

"What was that all about?" Jack asked.

"We'd rather not hang out with Dane right now. I'm sure you can agree with us on that point."

"I don't blame you," Jennifer said angrily. "I'm meeting Haley for breakfast to talk about today's events. She said she and Jeff are very worried about him. Something about him forcing himself on someone, but she didn't know who." Jennifer eyed me. I immediately blushed. Grant squeezed my hand under the table. *Damn Jennifer and her supermom powers of deduction.*

When dinner was done, we headed through town and Grant and I pulled in at a grocery store.

"What are we doing here?"

"Oh we have to run in and get something really quick."

They all smiled. They probably thought we were getting condoms. *Oh geez. If only they knew what the chocolate mousse was for. Cravings … I was craving chocolate Grant. I mean mousse. Grant was hung like a moose. Sometimes I just cracked myself up, even if it was true.*

We only found mousse mix, so there would be some fun in the kitchen when we got home. Jack decided to stop over at Grant's to talk with Joe and Jennifer, so Grant and I ran home to whip up some midnight snacking material. We really did have fun with food. I remembered someone telling me about a spa that had chocolate tubs to soak in. I'd have to do some research and take Grant there for a weekend of chocolove.

"Get the milk, I'll get out the blender," I said. "We don't have much time."

"Oh no, this has to chill for quite a while. I wish you had some nitrous oxide so we could cool it faster."

"Really? Nitrous oxide? I think the freezer will work just fine. No more cooking shows for you."

We mixed it all up and made sure it was nice and thick before we spooned it into a few dessert dishes so it to cool faster. I dipped my finger into the bowl and scooped some out, covering my giving him a little preview of what was coming his way soon. I slowly licked the tip and then continued to swirl my tongue up and down the sides.

"Lanie, you're driving me crazy. You have no idea the effect you have on me," he growled, low and rough.

"Sure I do," I added in some moans and ohs. He started fidgeting. Then we heard the door open.

"Hi, Dad. Did you have a nice time? I'm happy you made your curfew, now off to beddy-bye time."

"Right. What are you two up to?"

"We're going to call it an early night."

"Oh, okay then. Well, bye, Grant, see you tomorrow."

"Dad, Grant is staying over."

"What? No, I don't think so."

Was he kidding me? Grant looked back and forth between Jack and I. "Yes, he is."

"No, he isn't."

"Yes."

Grant would start to move toward the door and then stop, and then start to move and then stop.

"Lanie, Grant has a bed right next door."

"And he has my bed right here. This is my house. And last time I checked, I was pretty sure I was an adult who lived on her own and made her own decisions."

"But, Lanie," he kind of whispered the next part, "You're going to … do things. I don't want to hear."

"Dad!"

"I promise we'll be very quiet." Grant finally spoke up. Great.

"Grant!" He just shrugged.

"Dad, someday, Grant and I will have kids and you'll pretty much figure out we've been having sex. Might as well get over it now."

He cringed and I crossed my arms and bitch-faced him.

"Grant. Lanie. I'll see you both in the morning for breakfast."

"Good night, Jack," Grant offered.

He just shook his head and waved behind him as he headed up the stairs. I waited until I heard his door shut.

"Great. Go grab the mousse."

"Lanie, you heard your dad. He doesn't want to, you know, hear us," he whispered.

Now I bitch-faced Grant.

"How about I grab that mousse and we head on up."

"I'll give you head … on up," I purred and ran up the stairs.

When we got there, he placed the chilled mousse on the nightstand. He turned slowly toward me, smiled and cocked an eyebrow at me.

"Allow me to show you the pleasures of chocolate mousse."

"Oh please."

"Was that considered begging?"

"If you so desire."

"Well then," he said and began to slowly undress me. We fumbled around each other, trying to get the other's clothes off. It was comical and we giggled together, but couldn't get them off fast enough.

When the clothes were on the floor, he lowered me to the bed and grabbed a spoonful of mousse.

"Are you spooning me?"

"Sure am."

I hummed against him as we began to enjoy our dessert and each other.

Luckily, both our mouths were full, so neither of us made much noise at all, as we'd promised Jack.

"I have a raincheck I plan on cashing in tonight," I teased.

"Then you'd better be prepared to …

Chapter 31

Speak of the Devil

"… reciprocate."

"Yes, I believe I can take things into my own hands. I might have to, watching you. It's going to be quite a vision. You're so sexy, Lanie. I get turned on just watching you walk across the room, let alone giving me a raincheck."

"You do? I have that effect on you? I thought it was just me."

"You're seriously kidding me, right? I'm certainly not able to hold anything back when it comes to every part of you. Lanie, I've saved my heart for you; all these years, you've had it. And now I have yours … and your body. I can't get enough of either. I want all of you, all of the time."

My heart began thrumming hard and fast. I moved his hand over it.

"Do you feel that? That's what you do to me. You make my heart race … in every way. You have me. I'm yours, all of me. Forever. Nothing is ever going to change that."

He grabbed me into a deep, passionate kiss and we lay down on the bed together.

"Are you taking a raincheck on the raincheck?" I giggled.

"For now. I may wake up in the middle of the night and ask for it."

"I'll give you whatever you want. Always."

"Then make love to me right now. I want to feel you entirely. Your heart, your soul, your body."

And I gave him what he asked for. We made love. It was slow and passionate and intimate in every way. He told me how much he loved me over and over. I loved this man. Nothing could ever change that.

* * *

We wanted to sleep in, but Woof would have no part of it. He wanted to eat. He started to meow right in Grant's ear.

"Go ask Jack to feed you," he grumbled.

"Oh, my dad—I have to go make him coffee."

He pulled the covers back and exposed his very awake manhood. "You're going to leave this to go make coffee for your dad?"

"Raincheck?"

"Oh yes, please, I'd like that raincheck now. Just let me wake up enough to open my eyes so I can actually watch you." He reached over to grab me, but I was already up and getting dressed.

"I meant I'd take the raincheck this time. Not for nothing, but it's very hard not to enjoy your hard on."

A soft laugh escaped his lips. He got up and pulled on his sweats.

"Oh, Babe, you don't have to get up with me. Stay in bed and sleep longer."

"There is no other place I want to be than by your side, even though it's not here in this nice, warm, comfortable bed." And he fell back onto the bed.

"Well, I'm heading down. So get back up and come with me."

"Get back in bed and come with me."

"Keep it up, Mr. Funnypants."

"I plan on keeping it up for at least an hour if you get back in bed with me."

I knew better than to lean down and kiss him, so I went to the door and gave him my best come hither look.

"Fine. I'm up. I'll be down after I hit the bathroom. I'm sure if Jack doesn't want to hear, he certainly doesn't want to see anything either. And waking up with you makes everything wake up, if you know what I mean."

"Oh, I know what you mean." I left and headed downstairs. My dad was already up and in the kitchen. He had cooked. *Holy crap*. He didn't cook often, but when he did, it was awesome. He had made my favorite: maple syrup French toast. I was in heaven. *Wait*. And bacon, too. *Now* I was in heaven. If only I could bring it back to bed with Grant, then I'd really be in heaven.

"Dad, you cooked."

"What, a man can't cook for his daughter and her, um, boyfriend? Uh, lover? No. How about significant other?"

"Yeah. Dad, you can stop now."

"Speak of the devil. Good morning, Grant. I hope you had a good night's sleep," Jack addressed him.

"Good morning, Jack. Yes, I feel very rested."

"Right. Well, I'm sure you have a huge appetite. Um, 'cause you haven't eaten all night," He threw at him.

"Dad, stop." I could feel my cheeks flush.

"Yes, sir, I'm famished."

"How famished?"

"Dad! Please. Stop." I felt like I was twelve years old and my dad was seriously embarrassing me.

"I could eat this entire platter of French toast," Grant said innocently, having no clue what he was alluding to.

"Grant!"

"What?"

"Why don't we all just sit and eat and say nothing. Okay?" I said, with a bit of an attitude.

"What's wrong with her?" my father asked my lover.

"I have no idea. She should be in an awesome mood," my lover replied.

"How awesome?"

"That's it." I couldn't take it anymore. I took my plate and coffee and went to sit on the couch by myself.

"She didn't used to be this grouchy when she woke up," my dad mused.

"She's usually not," my boyfriend mused along.

"Maybe she woke up on the wrong side of the bed?"

"Nope, she was on her side."

"Ummm, hello? I can hear you over here." They just chuckled, so I took my breakfast and went out onto the terrace. I sat down and looked out over the ocean. I was so lucky. I had everything I could hope for. Everything.

The morning breeze was chilly, but it didn't cool me too much. I shut my eyes so I could feel the sun on my face as I listened to the ocean. I was at peace. Right here, right now. I had no idea what would be coming my way over the next few days, and I didn't care. Right now, I was happy and that was all that mattered. Apparently Grant and Jack didn't quite annoy me enough, because they grabbed their plates and joined me on the terrace.

"So, Lanie, birthday tomorrow. What would you like to do? Go to dinner?"

"Oh, Dad, no. Please don't make a big deal about it. Maybe just a nice family dinner." I forgot when I said it, that family meant everyone.

"Yeah, that won't fly with Samantha. She probably already has decorations and party hats. In fact, I know she does," Grant said as he eyed me for a reaction.

"Well, Haley mentioned she would love to cook something for everyone. I'll give her a call this morning."

"Really? I'd rather we just do something here."

"Sure, sure. It's your day. Whatever you want," Jack said.

"Just something casual, okay? Please don't make a big deal about it."

"*Samantha* … too late," Grant said.

"What do you need? I want to get you something, but I'm not sure what you like these days. I'm thinking dolls are out of the question." Jack usually just sent me money, which I loved.

"Um, Dad, you're joking right?"

"I can help you, Jack. I know a few things she could use."

"I bet you do."

"Are you guys going to start again?"

"I still don't know what she means by that."

Grant just shrugged. I shook my head and proceeded to stuff my face with French toast. *Oh my God, it was so damn good.* I began to actually moan with each bite. Grant shifted uncomfortably in his chair, so I shot him a look and he gave me a sexy smirk. I guess all forms of food brought sex to mind now. I laughed to myself and continued to enjoy my breakfast. My dad took that as his cue to leave.

"Hey, I'm going to go fishing again. Just Joe, Jeff and I. I'll see you two later." He departed and headed inside.

"So, just you and me now. How about that raincheck?" I purred.

"As much as I'd love to, I actually have something I need to take care of this morning," he said cautiously, as if he knew I wasn't going to like his next statement. "I'm going to talk to Dane. Things have gotten out of hand, and with your birthday tomorrow, I feel like now is the time."

"Grant. Don't. Wait for us all to do it together."

"Lanie, I have to do this. You'll understand later. I should have taken care of this the minute I realized what he'd done. I waited only because I didn't want to upset you. But now this is something I have to do. It needs to be done."

"Can you take Steve or Dylan with you? Or both?" I really didn't want him alone with Dane because I had no idea what was wrong with him lately. *Was he out of control?* I couldn't grasp it all.

"Lanie, it'll be fine. I don't think he meant to hurt me yesterday other than a fistfight. I don't believe he would have let me fall. I don't."

"Fine. But at least bring your phone with you. Text me if anything happens. Maybe do it somewhere in public. And no fighting, please."

"Lanie, relax. It's all going to be fine."

He gave me a gentle kiss, grabbed our plates and left me on the terrace. I sat for a while and thought about my secret back-up plan. Now would be a good time to make some calls. I grabbed my cell phone and started to dial. The phone rang and then I heard the other end pick up.

"Hello?"

"Hey, it's Lanie."

"Oh my God, Lanie, how are you?"

"I'm doing great. Well, except for something that isn't so great. It's pretty bad."

"What's the matter?"

"It's Dane. Something's wrong with him. Seriously wrong."

"Lanie, no. Is he sick?"

"I'm not sure. Well, no. I mean, not physically."

"I don't understand."

"I need your help."

"My help?"

"Yes. You're the only one I know who can get through to him."

"I'll do anything I can to help him."

"I knew you would," and I proceeded to tell my *last resort* the whole sordid story. When I was done, we just talked for a long time. And when I hung up, I felt like it could all turn out okay. Like everything would work out. I then proceeded to call Chelsie and fill her in.

* * *

I spent the rest of the morning catching up on work for the business. We had all taken a bit of a vacation since our parents got here and I was behind. I couldn't stop thinking about Grant and Dane. I hadn't heard from either of them. It was hard to concentrate. I grabbed my phone and texted Grant.

L: U OK?
G: It's all good. better thn I exptd
L: Oh thank God
D: Hey B
L: Dane just txtd me
G: I know, he's w/ me
D: ?
L: Hey Dane
G: It's all going 2B OK
D: I'm sorry. 4 everything
L: Ya think?
D: IOU that in person
G: I'll fill you in later
L: I can't do this. I have no idea who I'm txtg
G: Love you
L: Love you
D: Love you

I had to check who I texted my last text to. I was getting confused.

L: What?
D: j/k like sister
L: Really?
D: I understand. IOU Explaining

L: Yeah U DO
G: On my way ovr
L: OK
D: CU L8r

I went back to work and finished everything up and waited for Grant to get home. Grant home. *I loved that.* We were practically living together now anyway. I wondered which house we would end up in. I heard the front door open and I literally sprinted down the stairs.

"Well? What happened?" I think I was yelling.

"Apparently his talk with his parents was quite enlightening. They basically told him they could strip him of everything he has if he didn't straighten himself out."

"Can they do that?"

"They all can. The business is in a contingency contract. They own everything on paper still, legally. Until they sign everything over to us."

"You're kidding me. I had no idea about any of that. I know they still collect money from the company, but I thought they were completely absolved otherwise. My house is in my name, my dad transferred the deed to me."

"My parents transferred the deed to my place, too. I guess Dane wasn't as smart or didn't care."

"So what did he say about yesterday morning?"

"He said he started fighting with me and when he clipped me and I fell, he just froze. He said everything just started coming in flashes. He just couldn't do anything. He just froze up. He said he couldn't get any leverage, that if he moved, his grip would have slipped."

"And you believe him?"

"I want to. But I have mixed feelings about it all."

"And with me? What did he say about that?" I didn't want to bring it up, but I knew I had to. Grant got a pained look on his face. I'm sure the images of me with Dane were going through his mind.

"He admitted to the whole Lori thing. It was a set up. But he still claims that he thought what happened between you and him was real. He thought you wanted to. He denied drugging you. He said Lori was back at the house at some point. He said he thinks it was her."

"It doesn't make sense. But I was so out of it, my entire memory of it could be off."

"He knows we're in love. He's stepping aside. He wants us to be happy."

"And you believe that?"

"I don't know, Lanie. This whole thing with Dane, it's just not right. I'll give him a chance to prove himself because of our history, but one wrong step and I am going to his parents."

"You're going to tattletale on him?" I laughed.

"Yes." But Grant was completely serious. I was having a hard time reading his feelings on this, which was strange, because usually I could read him like an open book. He was hiding something. I just didn't know what. Part of me was glad I had contacted the last resort. I had a feeling we would still need it. This just wasn't sitting well with me.

"Want to go down to the beach?"

"I have to catch up on work." Grant didn't seem himself. I wondered what had really happened. I knew he wouldn't lie to me, so I assumed he really needed to work.

"Want some company?"

"I can't concentrate with you around. I'll just end up taking that raincheck and I'm saving it."

"For a rainy day?"

“No, for tonight,” he growled and then pulled me into his arms. He placed soft kisses up my neck and then along my jaw line. My body responded immediately and I grabbed his face and pulled it to mine. I loved the feel of him against me and started to step things up a notch but he pulled himself away slightly.

“What’s the matter?”

“Nothing, Love. I just have to get to work. You should go into town with Samantha and Chelsie and go shopping. I know Samantha wants you to pick an outfit for your birthday present.”

Grant talked to Dane, and now he was pulling away from me. I started to feel paranoid, but I’m sure it was unwarranted. “Um, okay.” I let my hands drop from his face. He reached up and grabbed mine.

“Lanie, I love you. You look upset. Everything is fine. I just have to take care of some things. You go have fun with the girls. Give them a call. We’ll pick this up later. I promise.” He raised his right hand while placing a kiss on my lips.

I wasn’t happy. But I did as he asked and went to call the girls for a day in town.

When Samantha and Chelsie pulled up, I jumped into the back seat and settled in.

“So, what’s new?”

“Grant and Dane talked.”

“Did he tell you what happened? We spoke to Jennifer, so we already have an idea of what happened with his parents.”

“Do they all know?” I was referring to what happened between Dane and I.

“No. Apparently he wouldn’t say anything about who or what, just that it was a huge misunderstanding and an even bigger mistake on his part,” Samantha said.

"I, for one, am not buying any of this. Not a bit of it. He's an ass in my book and there's nothing more to say on the subject. I'll never be close with him again. Never." Chelsie knew how to hold a grudge. I planned on never crossing her. *Not that I would, but I would never go out of my way to make her mad.*

"So what's the plan?"

"We're taking you shopping for a birthday outfit, one for the day and then something extra special for the night. Meow!" Samantha made kitty claws in the air. She was a pisser.

"Not that it will last very long. The way you two go at it, we should buy you aprons or bibs."

"Ha, ha. Very funny. But totally true."

We shopped at all our favorite stores and they bought me bagfuls of stuff. I kept saying no and Samantha kept saying yes and whipping out the credit cards. We left the lingerie store with three bags full of nighties and honey flavored sparkle dust and well, lots of things. I was actually set for an entire honeymoon. I thought about putting some of the items away for such an occasion. We didn't realize the time and soon it was already six o'clock. We stopped for dinner and drinks. I had one too many and had an awesome buzz for the ride home. They dropped me off at my house; I grabbed my tons of bags and headed inside. It was dark. No one was home.

"Dad? Grant?" I called out. Nothing. "Woof?" And I heard him scamper to me from the other room. I hit the lights and found two notes, one from Jack and one from Grant.

> *Lanie,*
> *The boys and I headed out for dinner and some beers at the bar to catch the game. See you later. I'll make curfew. HA HA*
> *Dad*

Lanie

I had to run out for a bit. Be back later on tonight. Eat something if you haven't already, please. I'll be home for dessert. I love you

Grant

Well, I had the night to myself so I …

Chapter 32

Raincheck?

… headed up to take a much needed bubble bath. My feet were killing me. I started the bath and grabbed a few salts and bubbles to throw in. I waited for the tub to fill up and then undressed and settled in for a long overdue soak.

The water was nice and hot and all my muscles relaxed immediately the second they hit the water. I missed Grant and wished he were here with me. I sighed deeply and closed my eyes.

Suddenly, Grant was standing in front of me, suitcases in hand, saying goodbye. He was leaving. He was leaving me *to be exact.*

"Lanie, I'm sorry, but I have a different life in mind. It's not here on the cliff, and it doesn't include you. "His words stung and I felt my eyes burn.

"I've been here all my life; I don't want to be stuck here. I want more." He turned and walked out of the room.

I could feel my stomach knot at his words and the tears began to flow freely as I jumped out of the tub to beg him to stay with me. "Grant … Grant!" All I could hear was the echo of my own voice. I sunk to my knees and cried.

Then from a distance, I could hear him calling for me. He called repeatedly. I called out to him but he was too far away. I saw a figure down the dark hallway and I jumped to run to him. But when I got there, it wasn't him at all. It was Dane. He put his arms around me and told me this is what he said would happen and that he was here to make things better. That he would love me forever. I clawed at him and tried to get away, but he just laughed and tried to kiss me as his grip tightened around me. He told me he would show me.

He brought me outside into the night over to the cliff's edge on the far side of his house. I could see something below us but it took my eyes a few moments to adjust to the darkness. It was a beautiful house in a small meadow. I was so confused, my head began to reel. There had been trees there for as long as I could remember, not a meadow or house. As we looked down at it, I saw a few children running around in the yard. A beautiful woman came out the front door and called for them. They ran to her. Another figure emerged from the house. It was Grant. He walked towards the woman, put his arms around her and kissed her cheek. The children began to run around them. They both smiled, watching what I can only assume were their children. I felt my body go cold and the knot in my stomach tightened more. I felt like I was going to throw up.

'No, no!' I cried out. This couldn't be happening. Dane just laughed at me. I felt nothing but distain for him. He told me he had been right about Grant. I was only something to pass the time, convenience, not love. He turned me toward him and told me it was him I was meant to be with. I started to run away, my tears blinding me. I could hear myself screaming, crying out for Grant.

I was awakened by someone screaming Grant's name. It was me but I wasn't sure how long I had been asleep. The water was cold and my fingers were pruned. And I was no longer relaxed and felt extremely tired. The dream had been so vivid and real that my heart began to race just remembering it. I let the water drain from the tub and watched until it was completely gone. I reached for my towel, dried off and headed for my room. I had nothing better to do, so I climbed into bed, feeling weepy and lonely. I knew it was only a dream, but it certainly rocked my conscious world. I turned the light to the lowest setting and shut my eyes.

I'm not sure how long I had been there, but I felt movement around me. I was so comfortable and still somewhat asleep. I felt the covers lift and the bed weigh down. I felt arms wrap around me, feeling hot skin against mine. I turned my body around and realized it was Dane in my bed. I began to scream and flail my arms out, pushing him away.

I heard Grant's voice telling me everything was okay. I opened my eyes. He was there with me. I guess my dream affected me more than I thought, and I hadn't been fully awake.

"Babe, are you okay? What's the matter?"

"I thought you were Dane."

"Really, you have to stop getting us confused; we really look nothing alike." I know he was trying to be funny, but it wasn't funny at all. I was actually feeling angry with Grant for finding another love in my dream.

"You—you left me. You left me and you fell in love with someone else. You had children with her. You were happy with her." I smacked at him.

"Lanie, what in God's name are you talking about?"

"I was taking a bath and I fell asleep and I dreamt about you leaving me. You didn't want me and said you didn't want to be stuck here with me. And then Dane was there and he brought me to you to show me how happy you were with someone else. You were there with her and your children. He told me I had to be with him."

Grant started to laugh so I smacked his arm again, then rolling over away from him. He grabbed me and pulled me back.

"Lanie, your dream is only showing you your fears. That's it. Nothing more. There is nothing to them and I'm definitely not leaving you. I'm not stuck here with you. And I choose you. I will marry you and be standing with you and *our* children. Why are you letting a dream bother you so much?"

"I don't know." The tears began to flow. Again Grant laughed.

"Lanie, what's gotten into you? One day away from each other and you suddenly doubt my love for you? It's simply ludicrous. Nothing can change how I feel about you. Nothing and no one."

"Promise me. Please, promise me," I begged him.

"Lanie, you have no idea how deeply committed I am to you and a life with you. Really."

"You didn't promise."

"I promise, Love. I promise I will never leave you and I will always only choose you."

I smiled, rolled onto my stomach, laid my head down on the pillow and snuggled into him. I took a deep breath so I could fill my lungs with his very essence. I felt his hands move up and down my back slowly. His caress was soft and gentle, and it began to lull me back to sleep.

"Oh, Baby, that feels so good. Don't stop."

"I have no intentions of stopping. Not now and not ever. I promised."

I smiled at his efforts to relieve my stress with both his words and his movements.

"Well, you'll have to stop at some point. People might look at us funny if everywhere we go, your hands are all over me."

"If that were the case, I'd never leave the house."

I was getting extremely slick and hot, so I rolled over and smiled at him.

"Raincheck?"

"Another raincheck?"

"No, I was offering to cash in one of yours."

"Hell yes!" he growled.

Finally we fulfilled our rainchecks for each other.

"Oh, Lanie, that was so worth the wait."

"Grant, hold me. I want to feel your body against mine."

He complied quickly and was lying on top of me before I could even blink. He covered my lips and face with soft kisses. I kissed anything my lips could find.

Tomorrow was my birthday. I was excited to see what Grant got me. I closed my eyes and started to think about rainchecks and presents, and sleep soon overtook me.

* * *

I woke up and it was dead quiet in the house. Grant was no longer beside me, and neither was Woof. The light was coming through my window and it looked to be a beautiful day. I rolled over and looked at the clock. *Holy shit, it was nine in the morning. I never slept in.* No wonder Grant wasn't in bed any longer. I was about to get up when I saw a small note and my cell phone on my nightstand.

Good morning, birthday girl!

I love you. Please text me when you are up.

Grant

It's my birthday, damn it! I grabbed my cell and began to text him.

L: I'm up? Where are you?
G: Stay right where you are. Don't move
L: OK
G: I mean it. Unless Bathroom. Then OK.

I jumped up, ran to the bathroom, and once finished, jumped back in bed with a huge smile on my face, waiting for Grant. I heard a soft knock on my door.

"Are you decent, Love?"

"Would you like me not to be?"

"Um, I'm not alone."

Oh crap.

"Then yes, I'm decent."

The door opened, and my dad, Grant and Woof came bounding into the room with balloons and breakfast in bed for me.

"I said not to make a big deal."

"Oh hush up, Lanie, and let your men—dad and boyfriend—guys—whatever, let us spoil you."

"Oh fine, spoil me."

Grant came over and placed a kiss on my forehead as he put a tray of all sorts of breakfast finger foods on my lap. There was a small vase with a single rose.

"Oh, you guys, men, Dad and boyfriend are so cute!" I teased.

"Oh brother," Jack mused.

"You are to sit and enjoy this entire breakfast and relax. I plan on giving you a foot rub while you eat." Grant produced a bottle of massage oil from his back pocket. I clapped.

"And I have your present for you, so you can play, or read, or whatever it is you do with these things."

From behind his back Jack pulled out a white box with a red ribbon. Now, anyone who knows graphics would recognize that box in an instant. Whoot! I grabbed and began to open it. I was so excited. I already knew what it was from the size and shape of the box alone. When I finally got it open, there it was—a brand new tablet.

"Oh my God. Dad! It's perfect. I really, really wanted one!"

Jack shot Grant a grateful look. I smiled, seeing my dad and Grant bonding. This was a great start to the day.

"Well, I'm going to let you enjoy your breakfast and play with your new toy."

"Thank you, Dad. I really love it. It's the best present ever. Even though I wanted a Barbie," I said with a wink.

"I think you got a real life Ken doll. Good luck with that," he said, pointing at Grant as he left.

"Oh, my very own Ken doll. Too bad I only like to undress him."

"There'll be plenty of time for that later. Right now, you get a foot massage and breakfast."

I started to look all over him, in his pockets and around his back.

"What are you doing?"

"Checking to see where your present is." I gave an evil smirk when I said it.

"Oh, you'll get it, when you least expect it." And his grin back at me was just as evil.

"Damn."

"Patience is a virtue, Lanie."

"I lose all my virtue when you're around."

"I know. I love that about you."

I was in complete bliss drinking my coffee and noshing on tidbits of fruit while getting the most amazing foot rub, all the while reading the local news on my newest technology. *Heaven.* If only Grant could rub my feet and other parts all at the same time.

"I'm going to start a nice hot shower for you. Take your time getting ready. Oh, and wear something ridable."

"Something you can ride me in?"

"No. Something you can go riding in. Samantha, Chelsie and I are taking you riding down to the beach."

"Awesome."

I took my time, as requested, not worrying about having to be somewhere or do something. It was actually quite relaxing. I chose a nice tight pair of jeans and a cute t-shirt Samantha had picked up for me yesterday. It said 'Hands off, the hot one is mine!' with an arrow pointing to the right. *I'd have to make sure a certain someone was on my right all day.*

I headed out to the stables. Grant and the girls were there and the horses were all saddled up and ready to go. I mounted Magic and we all set off for a ride down the cliff to the beach.

"Today is going to be epic, Lanie," Samantha sang.

"Samantha!" Chelsie snapped at her.

"What? What am I missing?" I said, looking back and forth between them, and then to Grant, who just had a smooth grin on his face.

"Oh nothing. She's just excited about Lanie-day. Any special occasion is a holiday to her."

"It is not. Well, it is, too," Samantha laughed.

"I love that about you, Sweetie," I said.

"Thank you, Lanie. That's why I don't take Chelsie shopping for *her* birthday."

"No, it's because we have the same damn birthday and you always want all the presents."

As we neared the beach, Grant and Century took off. I looked at Chelsie and Samantha and they both just shrugged. We kept our walking pace, and as we came around the corner, Grant was waiting for us. There was a blanket and champagne with orange juice waiting for us.

"Mimosas?"

"You have to have birthday mimosas on the beach." He cocked an eyebrow at me while giving me a hand dismounting.

"Wow. You went all out."

"I'd do anything for my girl. I love you. You need a great day. There's been so much going on lately."

Samantha and Chelsie each grabbed a glass while handing one to me.

"I'd like to make a toast," Grant said.

We all raised our glasses.

"Lanie, I've known you my whole life. But now, with things the way they are between us, you've given a whole new meaning to what my life is. I love you and there is nothing more I want than—"

Grant was interrupted by the sound of another horse. We all looked up and there was Dane, on his horse, Jane. He rode up to us and hopped off. I heard Chelsie curse under her breath.

"Happy birthday, Lanie. Jack told me you guys were down here. I wanted to come wish you a happy birthday." Grant sort of rolled his eyes and smiled slightly.

"Thanks, Dane. Grant, is there another glass?"

"I think so." He poured another glass.

"A toast, to Lanie on her birthday. May she have a hundred more," Dane said.

"Here, here!" and we all took a sip.

"Grant, did you want to finish what you were saying?" I moved closer to him so he was on my right.

"Oh, Grant, I'm sorry. I didn't mean to hijack your toast."

"No, it's okay, Dane. I can pick this up with Lanie later. Alone."

We hung out on the beach, put our feet in the water and played Frisbee. It was like we were all twelve again. We laughed and joked. It was a good time. We all needed it. Even having Dane here seemed right. He was like his old self again. Dane and Grant even seemed to joke and laugh together, although I think Chelsie enjoyed throwing Dane into the sand to block a catch a bit too much. I think I saw her kick sand in his face when he was down. She smiled. He just got up and brushed it off.

Life was good and I couldn't imagine it getting much better. But it did.

When we decided to head back up, Grant and I lagged behind everyone so we could ride up in semi-privacy.

"Finish what you were saying." I slowed Magic even more to look directly over at him.

"I wasn't saying anything. Do you hear my voice in your head already? I hope it's telling you to bring some chocolate treat to bed with you tonight." He smiled and winked at me. *Yeah, that made me melt a little.*

"Finish your toast. I want to hear what you were going to say."

He fidgeted on Century who gave him a shake. So I gave him a verbal one.

"Well?"

"Just, that …

Chapter 33

Just Romantic Dribble

"… I love you. Just how wonderful my life is with you in it this way. Together."

"But you said there was nothing more you want, and then nothing. Well, then Dane."

"Yes, he has impeccable timing, as usual. It's nothing, Lanie. Just romantic dribble."

"Romantic dribble?"

"Look, I promise you, I will finish that sentence. Just not now."

"Okay." I gave Magic a squeeze and we picked up the pace. I wasn't mad. I just knew if I stayed there, I would have spent the whole time trying to get it out of him. He asked me not to, and I had no willpower when it came to him, so I just had to remove myself. Grant quickly caught up, and soon we could see everyone up ahead.

When we got back to the stables, Steve and Dylan were standing out front, looking like they were hiding something. I turned to look at Samantha; worst poker face in the entire world. She had a huge grin on her face, which she quickly pursed into a bizarre scowl, now trying to not smile.

"Gentlemen, are we all set?"

"Yes, sir!" Dylan saluted Grant, then they both laughed.

"What's going on?"

"Well, let me help you off that horse, Ma'am, and you can see for yourself."

"Oh brother." Chelsie rolled her eyes.

Everyone dismounted and we led the horses into the stables. Steve, Dane, and Dylan took the horses, which was a surprise in itself. Everyone was including Dane like nothing had happened. It was a relief, at least for today, and I wondered if everyone had just called a truce for my birthday. Grant took my hand and led me out the back of the stables and up the path to his backyard. It was a really beautiful walk, as the entire path was lined with trellises and grapevines. He said not a word, but had a smirk on his face the entire time.

When we reached his terrace, the entire place was decorated with tables, umbrellas, flowers and candles. It looked like a restaurant. Every tree was covered in small lights, which were lit, but hard to see in the daylight. I imagined by tonight it would look like hundreds of fireflies dancing in the leaves.

Did I forget to mention there were tons of people there? It was a full-blown party. Pierre smiled, ran up and swept me into his arms for a full on bear hug.

"Happy birthday, my Lanie."

And soon, I was surrounded by friends and family, all hugging me and wishing me well. *So much for not a big deal.* But it was sweet, and Grant just stood there beaming. He looked proud, like he'd been planning this surprise for a long time. I shot him a glance to let him know I was grateful and happy for all his hard work. My dad was finally able to get through the crowd to give me yet another birthday hug.

"I have something for you today from your mom, Lanie. She told me to wait and give it to you when I thought you were ready. You'll get it later on tonight. Okay?"

"Dad, you have something from Mom? How did you keep it all these years? I wouldn't have been able to wait this long."

"Well, she gave it to me knowing I could hold it back. I'm like that."

"Yep. You're a real *enigma,* Dad."

"I guess I am." He placed a small kiss on my forehead.

When everyone had settled into conversations with each other, I took more time to see everything. *Wow, it was truly amazing.* There was a stone fire pit with some sort of meat slow roasting on it. In the corner of the terrace were steps that led down to a grassy area that opened up to overlook the cliff. I looked over and could see Joe and Jennifer placing all sorts of seafood in a big dug out ditch filled with hot coals. It was surf and turf, clambake style. Everyone had gone through so much work and trouble to make this party amazing. It was like a wedding.

"I feel under dressed or something," I said to Grant.

"Don't be ridiculous. You're beautiful. And everyone is casual."

"Grant, this is amazing. How did you do all this without my knowing?"

"I had tons of help."

"He's been working us like slaves." I heard Dylan come up behind me. He was carrying a cooler with Steve, filled with all sorts of bottles of wine, coolers, and beer.

"But today it all pays off, 'cause we get to eat and drink all night long." Steve smiled and grabbed a beer once they put the cooler down.

"You've all been in on this?"

"Hence the trip with the girls yesterday. We spent the entire time stringing lights in trees," Steve said as he rolled his eyes.

"Seriously, Lanie, this man of yours pretty much had the whole town working on this party. He must really love you." Dylan smiled and pulled me into a brotherly hug while giving Grant the double eyebrows.

"Hands off, man. She's mine," Grant growled jokingly. Dylan jumped to my right side.

"Nope, the shirt says she's with me. See the arrow?" He dipped me into a loud, sloppy kiss.

"Eww. You're getting your slobber all over me. Let go!" I giggled.

I spent quite a while making rounds with Grant, saying hello to everyone. We ate amazing food all day. We had amazing music playing. *Did I mention that Grant hired a DJ for this gig?* He thought of everything. When the sun began to set, Grant grabbed my hand and pulled me out onto the path connecting our houses.

"I just want a bit of alone time with you for a minute."

"I like alone time with you."

He led me to my terrace and we stood overlooking the ocean. All the trees were lit up here, too, and it was just beautiful. There were pastel colored lanterns placed all along the terrace wall. He stopped and turned me towards him.

"Lanie, I love you so much, and as you know, I always have. I can't imagine another day in my life if it isn't spent with you as my partner, in every way. So I was thinking that I shouldn't ever be without you. And in order to do that, I—

Suddenly we heard Dane shouting for us. Grant breathed a frustrated sign and turned towards his voice.

"We're over here."

"What the hell does he want? I want to hear what you were saying." I was getting annoyed. That was the second time Dane cut Grant off from telling me something I think I might really want to hear.

"Hey, where have you guys been? Haley told me to find you. They want to do the cake now."

"Cake. Well, I guess cake comes first. Don't want all those candles to start a huge fire." Grant pinched my ass when he said it, which made me squeal like a little girl.

"Grant, maybe we can save some icing for later." He gave me a sultry smile and put his arm around my waist as we headed back for cake.

"Lanie, are you enjoying your birthday?" Dane was like a little kid. He seemed to be his old self. I was completely relieved. But I still felt like we had to work out what happened between us now that things were on the right track. Maybe a new conversation would put this all to rest. At least he was finally stepping down so Grant and I could be together without his getting involved.

When we entered Grant's terrace, everyone was standing around a beautiful cake full of candles. Actually, twice as many candles as my age. Steve was laughing hysterically, so I was pretty sure he was in charge of the candles. They all sang *Happy Birthday* to me. My cheeks flushed a rosy hue. Grant kept his arm around me and I leaned into him, just because I loved him so much, and to hide my embarrassment, of course.

"Go ahead, Lanie, blow them all out! I dare you to do it on one try." Steve was all riled up. He was obviously drunk. I liked him that way. *He was a total riot.*

"Wait, wait. You're so old I might have to get you the fire extinguisher." Chelsie grabbed Steve by the ear and pulled him closer to her. She elbowed him in the ribs, which made him laugh all the more.

Okay, he wanted to play? I could play. I pushed Grant back to give myself room. I took in a huge exaggerated breath and started to blow as hard as I could. I made sure my face got super red and I did my best Dizzy Gillespie cheeks. I hoped I didn't spit all over the cake.

Steve was roaring. He was laughing so hard I thought he might pass out. I blew all the candles out, all fifty of them. Everyone started to cheer. *What? All the candles fucking lit back up again! I just blew them all out.* Now Steve was in tears.

"Oh Grant, I thought you said Lanie could blow really well." This made Chelsie shove Steve, who just fell to the floor, laughing. He was literally rolling. Grant smiled and shook his head. My dad just stood there, looking shell-shocked.

"Sorry, Dad. Steve thinks he's a comedian today."

"Do it again, Lanie, blow them out again. Oh please, one more time," Steve guffawed.

I just stood there, trying to think of a way to put the candles out without passing out. I saw a cup of water and grabbed it. I gave Steve an evil smirk and dipped my finger in and began dousing each of the candles.

"Cheating. That's cheating! Your wish won't come true." Steve laughed out.

"It already did." I looked at Grant when I said it. "There isn't anything more in this world I could ask for. I have the most amazing family and friends, and I found the man of my dreams."

I reached up to Grant's face and pulled him into a deep kiss. All I could hear were claps and ahs coming from everyone. Grant smiled into our kiss.

"I love you, Babe."

"I love you, too."

The cake was absolutely divine. Grant had talked Haley into making a special cake. There were crushed sandwich cookies on the bottom, then vanilla champagne layer cake, then strawberries, then cake, then chocolate hazelnut spread, and another layer of cake all topped with chocolate mousse icing. *It was our sex life in cake form.* I laughed my ass off when he handed me the first piece.

"This is so coming to bed with us tonight."

"There's a smaller version for later. Haley made a special one just for us."

"You're a man after my own heart, stomach and you know …" I gave him double-eyebrows.

"Yes. I plan on making sure it stays that way."

The party started to thin out and soon it was only family and close friends. The music was loud and we were all dancing up a storm. It was one of the best days of my life. Everyone was happy and laughing, including me. My life felt complete. Grant and I danced, drank, ate, and laughed with everyone. It was epic. The entire place was lit up with the small firefly lights. It was like a dream. Grant grabbed my hand and pulled me over to the side.

"Lanie, I really want to steal a few moments with you. Come with me."

"Hell yeah! Where? Stables? My bedroom?"

"I hadn't thought about one of our bedrooms. But not right now. I want to talk to you. Alone. It's important." He was suddenly serious.

"Sure, Babe, anywhere you want. Just take me with you." My dream started to flash through my mind. I knew there was no way he was going to break up with me. Not after planning a whole amazing day like today—but I suddenly got a pit in my stomach. *What did he want to tell me?* He must have noticed my agitation.

"Lanie, you look scared. You better not be worrying. There's nothing bad about what I want to say to you. Nothing. I just want you alone."

I think I must have been holding it, because I let out a huge breath. Grant laughed and pulled me into a hug, and then proceeded to look around like we were going on a covert mission. I looked around with him. Dane was talking to Jeff and Jack; Dylan and Samantha were making out in the corner; Chelsie and Steve were playing a drinking game, and Joe and Jennifer were watching us.

"Your parents are staring at us."

"Smile and wave."

We both waved, gave them a stupid smile and then we took off. We were running and laughing, and I felt like I was going to pee myself I was laughing so hard.

"Where are we going?"

"I have no idea!" And we started laughing even harder.

Finally, Grant seemed to have a direction. He pulled me to the edge of the cliff overlooking the ocean right between my house and Dane's. The trees were all lit up here, too, and I had no idea how in hell they had gotten this all done.

"Grant, this whole night—everything—it's just so beautiful. I mean, you are just so amazing."

"No, Lanie, you are amazing and have been to me since we were kids. I love you. I have always loved you and always will. If you ever decide you don't want this, I will pine for you until my last breath and then some."

"Shut up. Don't say that. I'll always love you. Nothing will ever change *that.* Not ever. Do you hear me?"

He smiled and put his hand on the side of my face, pulling me closer and pressing his lips to mine. *I still got lost in his kisses.* My entire body lit up with excitement and I melted. He pulled back and he looked very nervous.

"What? What's wrong?"

"Nothing, Lanie, everything is perfect. But I want to make it even more perfect."

"Grant, do you want to move in with me?"

"Lanie, I want so much more than that. Believe me, you have no idea."

"No, you're wrong. I do. I can't stand one minute of being away from you. Not one. I want you by my side every second of every day."

"Lanie, do you have any idea how happy it makes me to hear you say that? I feel like my heart is going to explode it's beating so hard for you right now."

"Is there anything else hard for me right now?"

"It's always hard for you. You give me a perpetual hard on."

I licked my lips and tangled my fingers into his hair. Pulling him closer, I reached down between his legs and gave him a soft squeeze. He was right; he did have a perpetual hard on for me. I pushed my body against him and looked at him from under my eyelashes.

"Come to my room with me then." I used my best 'I'll give you anything you want' voice.

"Lanie, I promise to take you up on that very shortly. But first I have something I need to say."

He looked down at me and just had this pure look of total love and adoration on his face. I felt myself blush, my heart began to race and my skin started to get all goose-bumpy.

"Lanie, you have made me so happy. I don't want this feeling to ever end, so—"

And that's when the basketball came and hit Grant right in the side of the head.

"Damn it!"

"Oh my God, Grant, are you all right?" Samantha said as she and Dane came bounding up to us.

Grant had his hand over his face. He let out this grumbling flow of words I couldn't understand. His voice got higher pitched and the words started coming faster.

"Grant? I can't understand you. Are you okay? Talk to me."

At this point, Grant straightened up and uncovered his face. He was laughing so hard nothing was coming out. No sound at all. I started to get scared he wouldn't stop and would pass out. He almost looked like he was about to go all straightjacket on me.

"I'm fine, Lanie. Just peachy."

"Grant, I am so sorry. I really didn't think I was going to even come close to you. You owe me ten bucks," Samantha said as she turned to Dane giggling, and then high-fived.

"You bet Samantha she couldn't hit Grant in the side of the head with a basketball? Really?" *I was in bitch mode.* I wanted to hear what Grant had to say. He'd been trying to say it all day and we kept getting interrupted.

"No. I bet her she couldn't even come close to reaching you guys. She was supposed to roll it. We just wanted to get you guys for some hoops. We're all playing. Even the parents."

"Oh. Well, I guess we'll come play."

I turned and looked at Grant, who was shooting daggers in Samantha's direction. Her smile immediately wiped off her face and she made an O-shape with her mouth. I walked over to Grant's side and reached up to rub his head where the ball hit.

"I feel so bad for you. Can I laugh now?"

"Yes, you can laugh. I did." I giggled simply because the entire day had just been so much fun and I was in the best mood ever.

I didn't want Grant to be in a bad mood now. It seemed he didn't want to either, because the smile stayed on his face and he even giggled a bit more with me.

They were already choosing teams when we got there. Chelsie was one captain and Joe the other. *Chelsie was a total bitch to play against in any game.* She liked to win. I wanted to be on her team.

Chelsie turned to look at me. "I get the birthday girl. Let's go. Play rough."

Joe followed with, "Fine, I get her boyfriend. That way he can distract her. Grant, you're mine. Play dirty!"

I loved when we all played together. It was always hysterical. Chelsie chose me, Dylan, Steve, Jack and Haley. Joe chose Samantha, Dane, Jennifer, Jeff, and Grant. This game was going to be a blast.

We were playing hard. There was shoving and bumping, and even tickling. I went up to take a shot and felt Grant grab my ass and squeeze. I totally missed the basket. I turned and gave him a face, but he was too cute and I couldn't even try to look mad. I saw everyone doing little things to mess each other up. The ball was everywhere and everyone was laughing. Grant went up for a shot and Dane jumped in and poked him right in the stomach. Maybe a little bit too hard, because all his breathe blew out in one huff.

"Damn, Dane, you're killing me today."

"I don't know what you're talking about."

"I go up for a basket; you block me and you're on my team. Every time I try to give Lanie her birthday present, you're there. You just show up like you have us bugged or something."

"I swear, Grant, I have no idea what you're talking about." Their little talk became a bit louder and everyone sort of stopped, backed away and listened.

"Oh please, Dane, at the beach, then on the terrace, and then up on the cliff. Every time."

"Just give her the present. Who cares? I mean what does it matter where or when or who's there? I'm not blocking you."

"Dane, I've been trying to ask Lanie to marry me all day and you are most definitely cock blocking me."

Everyone went completely silent. Grant's eyes got huge. My eyes got huge. Dane's eyes got huge.

"Holy shit," I said in a whisper.

"Holy shit," Samantha followed.

"Holy shit," Grant said in a defeated voice.

"Oh crap," Steve said.

Grant slowly turned around towards me. I just stood there. I couldn't move. He walked over to me, got down on one knee and reached for my hand. I couldn't breathe.

"Lanie, I've been trying to ask you all day. I can't imagine my life without you in it. I never want to again. You *are* my life. You are everything and the only thing I exist for. Would you please do me the honor of spending the rest of our lives together, as my wife?"

I saw Jennifer cover her mouth and Joe pulled her close. In fact, all the couples seemed to gravitate towards each other. Jack was beaming. *Holy shit, my dad was beaming!* Now I understood their talk on the terrace the other day. I felt tears well up in my eyes. I looked down into the most beautiful face I had ever seen in my entire life. His eyes were like a doorway into his soul and all I could see in their depths was pure love, pure love for me. I felt the same. I wanted to be with this man forever.

"Yes, Grant, yes. I want to be your wife. I want nothing more than to spend my life with you. Yes, I'll marry you."

"Is there a minister in the house?" Steve called out and Chelsie just shook her head.

"If there was, I'd marry him right here, right now. Right this second."

Grant reached into his pocket and pulled out a small black box. It looked like onyx with a small gold button at the bottom.

"Press right there," Grant said and he smiled at me. He was still on his knee.

I smiled, and my hand was shaking so badly it took me several attempts to hit the button. Grant grabbed my hand with his to steady me. I gave him a grateful smile. I pushed the button and the top popped open. Nestled inside was the most perfect ring I'd ever seen. A round diamond sat in a high platinum setting. On either side were square-cut, channel-set blue diamonds, which perfectly matched the color of his eyes, Nothing complicated, just simple and perfect, like our love.. He took it out of the box and slipped it onto my finger. I looked from him to the ring to everyone watching us. Grant stood up and pulled me close.

"Lanie. I'm the luckiest man alive. I have you. I love you, Mrs. Bennett-to-be."

"Grant." It was all could get out.

I felt a lump form in my throat and knew if I tried to say anything, I would start sobbing. It was fine, because Samantha was sobbing for me. *She was such a sucker for romance.*

When our lips touched, everyone cheered; even Dane. We stayed for a while longer so everyone could give us hugs and kisses and look at the ring.

"Lanie, we're so happy you're going to be our daughter. Our *real* daughter now." Jennifer pulled me into a tight hug. So tight I couldn't catch my breath.

"Jennifer, I can't breathe."

"Don't kill her, Darling, we actually like her." Joe pulled Jennifer off me and pushed her gently towards Grant. He wrapped his arms around me and whispered into my ear, "Thank you, Lanie, for making Grant so happy. All a parent ever wants is to see their child have everything they want or need. You give him so much happiness and then some. We love you."

I watched my father shake Grant's hand. They shared a knowing smile. Then he turned to me.

"Lanie, Honey, I'm so happy for you two. I can't see you with anyone else. He knows just how to handle you. I feel comfortable with that. Now, I have to give you something from your mom. She told me when this day happened, to let you know she put her wedding dress and stuff away for you. She said you always used to ask for that dress when you were a little girl. She said you don't have to use it, but it's yours if you want it."

"Oh my God. Are you kidding me? I love that dress." It was all too overwhelming. I finally joined Samantha and started to sob, which made her run over and sob with me. Then I-never-cry Chelsie joined in, too. The three of us just held each other and snot-sobbed like a bunch of five-year-olds.

"I love you guys."

"We love you." And we all cried some more. Finally, Grant reached in and pulled me out.

"Love, how about you and I go for that walk? I think I'd like that alone time with you now." I nodded. *It was all I could do.* Haley ran over and handed Grant a container. He smiled and tipped a pretend hat. Every one wished us goodnight and congratulations again; knowing full well we wouldn't be back.

We headed off toward my house. It was like a fairytale. *My fairytale.* We reached my room and I opened the window to let the night air come in while Grant lit candles. He reached into his back pocket and pulled out two forks. We shut out the lights, stripped down to our skivvies and jumped onto the bed with our cake and lots of giggling.

"So, which layer do you want to start with?"

"I think I'd like to start with …

Chapter 34

Why Are You Crying?

"… mousse and work our way backwards." I giggled.

Grant smiled, grabbed me and pulled me over to him.

"Hi, Pretty." He kissed my nose. "Can you believe this is happening? All of this … after knowing each other our whole lives, you're actually going to be my wife. Lanie, I love you so much."

"Grant, I wouldn't want things to be any other way. I'm so happy." And then my eyes filled up with tears and I started to cry again.

"Why are you crying?" he asked, bewildered.

"Because I'm so happy." I sobbed.

"What do you do when you're sad?"

"I cry harder." Which just made me cry harder.

"Are you sad now?" He seemed confused.

"No, I'm still happy."

"I'm confused."

I kept thinking back to my dream about losing him. To lose him now would be impossibly hard. I wouldn't be able to handle it. How could I tell him about my stupid fears when he had just showed me how much I truly meant to him?

"I'm afraid of losing you," I blurted out.

"Lanie." He laughed softly. "That ring on your finger … this man right here in front of you … this all means forever. Do you understand? I'm never going to leave you. I couldn't survive without you. Not now that I've had you this way." He gestured between us.

I felt my heart start to beat a bit faster, and all I wanted to do was make love to him. I needed to make sure this was all really happening, that he was real. I wanted to feel him completely. I wrapped my fingers into his hair and roughly pulled him to me. I ran my tongue slowly over his lips. I tugged on his bottom lip with my teeth. I held his face right next to mine.

"I want you. I need you. All of you."

Grant growled and pushed the container full of our sex life off the bed quickly followed by the two forks.

"I want to fuck you, not fork you." I couldn't help but giggle.

But this was my game, and I wanted to be in control. I grabbed his shoulders and pushed him down onto his back. I crawled over and straddled him.

"Baby, I'm so going to show you how much I love you … and this ring." I held it up so I could admire it again.

Grant put his hands up in surrender. *Sure, what guy wouldn't surrender at this point?* I ran my hands down his chest slowly, using my fingernails to graze his skin. He reached up to touch my breasts and I pushed his hands back down.

"This is all for you." I put my ring on the nightstand and reached in to grab a bottle of baby oil.

"Shouldn't that be olive oil? I mean, given our fascination with food and all," he quipped.

"If you want me to stop and run downstairs to get it, sure." My sarcasm was apparent.

"No, thank you. I've changed my mind," he said with a sultry smile.

"That's what I thought. Now shut it. I'm busy and you're distracting me."

"My apologies. I certainly don't want you to be distracted."

I grabbed the baby oil and just squeezed the bottle so it poured a large puddle over his chest. I smiled evilly. I put both my hands into it and began to spread it out all over. I wanted to touch every single part of his body. Call it marking my territory, but I wanted to be the only one who knew every bit of him.

I let my fingers roam all over him, his pecs, his abs, that awesome part on the side of his hip, the path that led down to my happy place. *Oh yes.* His body was remarkable in every sense of the word. The muscles flexed and relaxed as I ran over his sensitive spots. I leaned my face in so I could watch what I was doing closely and let my breath caress his skin. He shuddered slightly.

I moved up to his neck and his shoulders and then up and down his arms. I rubbed, touched and soaked the feel of him into my hands. If I were blind, I would know it was him no matter where I touched. His breathing became deeper and slower and he closed his eyes and hummed softly for a moment. I reached his fingers and kissed the one that would someday hold his wedding band.

"This is my finger. Don't ever forget that. I might tattoo your wedding ring on it."

"Lanie, they are all your fingers. I've used every one of them on you. Tattoo away." He smiled and kept his eyes closed.

I moved back to his hips and passed over where I knew he wanted my handy work. I heard a frustrated moan, which made me smile all the more. I massaged his extremely muscular legs right down to his cute toes. *Yes, this man even had hot toes. Who would've thought it?* I imagined all the women who would kill to touch this amazing creature this way. *Too bad, he was all mine.*

"Flip over," I commanded.

"Um, you're not done with the front. You missed a part." Again he smiled.

"Oh I can see it. It's standing at attention."

"He wants *your* attention."

"He'll have to wait. I'm saving the best for last. Wait, why are we referring to him as he? Does he have a name?"

"He'll be whoever you want him to be."

"I only want you. But let me think. How about we call him Cannoli?"

"You want to call my manhood Cannoli?"

"Why not, perfect mouth-sized sweet crème-filled treat. And we can call your boys do*nuts*."

"Well, the food names are certainly appropriate." He flipped over for me.

Before I oiled him all up, I brushed my hair softly along his back. Then I had the brilliant idea of rubbing my nipples against his skin, 'cause I was starting to get hot and bothered just touching him. *Any woman would be.* His soft little moans and groans of pleasure were driving me insane. I covered his back in oil and nibbled up and down the side of his neck while letting my girls press and rub against him. I worked my way down and grabbed his fine ass. *Holy God, it was a fine ass.* Then I leaned down and bit it.

"Did you just bite my ass?" He sounded surprised and he clenched his hot little cheeks.

"Yes, and if you don't shut up, I'm going to smack it, too."

"Oh, Lanie, I'm a very bad boy. I deserved to be punished."

I let him have it. I gave him one hard smack. He jumped slightly and then reached back to rub it.

"Remind me never to really get you mad enough to actually spank me if that was only for fun."

"Oh Baby, let me rub it for you." I grabbed the oil and covered his ass with it, smooshed my breasts against it and began to massage with them. He growled and somehow managed to roll over. Now my breasts were smushing into his extremely hard dick.

"You're cheating."

"You said you were going back there, I'm just helping."

I grabbed my breasts, pressed them to either side of him and he began to thrust between them.

"Fuck, Lanie. Every part of you feels so good."

"Ditto."

This was great and all, but the ache between my legs for this man was increasing. I needed some touching. He was irresistible. I'm not sure how to explain it, but when I looked up at him and saw the look on his face, his absolutely drop dead gorgeous face and beautiful eyes, I just melted.

"Hold that thought. I need some loving now."

I turned myself around and now was kneeling over him facing his feet. My very wet sex was now right in his face, just begging to be licked and kissed. I didn't need to say a word before his hot mouth was on me. He just dove right in.

"Yes, Baby, just like that." My voice was breathy and ragged. I was going to go back to what I had been doing, but saw this as the perfect opportunity to dine together. I took him in my mouth and earnestly began to suck. All I could hear was muffled groans, but they felt amazing. I felt myself edging close to an awesome orgasm and he was harder than a rock. I pulled myself away from him. I heard him groan.

"Don't worry. I'm not finished with you yet."

"Oh goody!"

I straddled him and slid him inside me. He felt so good I immediately burst into my orgasm.

"Oh my God. Fuck, Grant."

"Damn, I'm good!" he exclaimed with a huge stupid grin on his face.

"Oh yeah? Feel this!" And I went to town on him. I pounded myself on top of him. Our bodies were slick with oil, and I slid my hips easily up and down him. It only took seconds and he was quivering underneath me.

"Damn, you're good, too!"

I settled myself next to him on the bed and looked him in the eyes. "Grant, I promise to never let that end between us. Every night I'll make sure you're satisfied in every way possible."

"I'm so damn lucky."

"And I'm so damn hungry, so how about some of that sex cake?"

He laughed and reached over the bed to grab our cake and forks, and we spent the next hour forking each other before falling into deep sleep.

* * *

Grant and I spent the next few days with our families in complete and utter bliss. I was on cloud nine pretty much all the time. But today was a little different. Our parents' trip had come to a close. We all gathered as Pierre pulled up to take them back to the airport.

"Lanie, Grant. I'm going to miss you both so much. I can't say this wasn't the most uneventful trip. I'm leaving with a huge smile on my face and Samantha's cell phone number so we can plan the wedding." Jennifer grabbed us into a huge hug.

"Mom, I can't breathe," Grant choked out.

"Neither can I," I gasped with him.

"How can such a tiny woman be so strong?" I heard him croak out.

"I can hear you. You're both talking right into my ears." Jennifer released her death grip on us and showered us with kisses. Joe grabbed me into a hug, shook Grant's hand and then pulled him into yet another group hug. We said our goodbyes to Jeff and Haley, and then I turned to my father.

Grant walked up behind me and put his hand out to him.

"Well, Grant, I guess I finally know what to call you now. You take care of my little girl. You hear me?"

"You know I will, Jack. I promise." He started to raise his right hand and I swatted it back down.

"Dad."

"Lanie, I sure am going to miss you. I guess next time I see you it'll be for the big wedding day. I'm really looking forward to seeing your mom's dress on you."

"Daddy, thank you. That means so much to me. I'm going to miss you, too." I threw my arms around him and felt tears welling up in my eyes.

"Don't you dare cry, Lanie. Grant, you make her stop."

"I don't know where that switch is yet, Jack. But don't worry, I'm working on it."

Jack nodded and got into the limo with all the other parents. The former three musketeers watched as they left. Things were so different now. There were no longer any pacts in place. I turned toward "my guys" and looked at them both. How differently I felt about them now. One I loved deeply. The other I hated. When their car was out of site, Dane turned toward us.

"I know it's a lot to ask of you, seeing as I put you both through hell lately, but I need your help."

"What could you possibly need?" I asked, feeling very skeptical.

"It's the business. I screwed up. Bad."

"What the hell did you do, Dane?" Grant was on the edge of losing whatever patience he had been trying to maintain.

"I lost the SamSyd account."

"What? What the hell are you talking about? That's one of our largest accounts." Grant's patience was gone. *Well, that didn't take long.*

"Dane, why are we just hearing about this now? When did this happen?" I was scared. This was the bread and butter of our company, easy to maintain. I couldn't imagine how he screwed it up.

"I didn't want to say anything with our parents here." Dane looked scared, too. I couldn't help but wonder if this was just another game or if this was for real. I didn't pay much attention to the books, but last I checked, that account was doing just fine.

"That's ridiculous. They secured that account in the first place. Maybe they could've stepped in and made a call on our behalf."

"Dane, you need to tell us what happened. Maybe we can salvage it," I said.

Dane shook his head and looked down at his feet.

"Dane, I'm done playing games with you. You need to tell us right now. This is our business, too. And don't think I'm not aware that our parents still own this company, and that you didn't tell them because you were afraid they'd take you out of the equation." Yes. Grant had had enough. He wasn't going to take any of Dane's crap anymore. It was quite clear he wasn't standing down on this.

"Well, I kind of made a comment to who I thought was a secretary. I called her sweetheart and told her to get someone of consequence on the phone," he began.

"And?"

"Well, seems she was the boss's daughter, and she's taking over the company. She found my remarks rather condescending."

"Dane, you fucking idiot, what the fuck has gotten into you lately? First, you start with dirty tricks and deceit with us, your family. You pretty much raped Lanie. You continually—"

"No. We already talked about this. Why do you keep saying I raped her? You already know it wasn't like that!" Dane and Grant were now yelling at the top of their lungs at each other.

"Seriously? You still think what you did to her was consensual? Really? Because I am seriously starting to doubt it." Grant was laughing, but it was an angry laugh, an incredulous one.

"But it was. I didn't rape her. I told you. I would never do that. Not to anyone, especially not Lanie. It was a misunderstanding. She was drunk. I was drunk. She thought I was you. I thought she wanted me. We were really drunk."

"Dane, you understand I want to kill you right now, right? I've wanted to fucking kill you since the night that happened. But I gave you a chance, I listened to your lies and I believed them because of our past. But this entire time, even now, it still doesn't make sense to me. If it was mutual, why did you hit her?"

"I was drunk, it was a reaction."

"Stop. I want you both to stop. I don't want to hear this. I don't want rehash all this." I felt all the color drain from my face. This conversation was making me sick. I didn't want to go back there. I didn't want Grant to think about Dane and I being intimate. I wanted my life to be happy now, with Grant. I wanted to forget.

"Lanie knows it was all a misunderstanding."

I turned toward Dane, now my face filled with color. I wanted to kill him.

"No, Dane. I don't understand anything. You knew Grant and I were together. You brought that whore into our home and you pitted her against us. That alone should make us hate you. But then you … you drugged me and you raped me. Do you hear me, Dane? You raped me. I didn't want that. I didn't want you to touch me like that. I only ever wanted Grant to touch me like that. You fucked up royally and I'll never forgive you. Never! You took something that wasn't yours to take."

I had admitted to myself that he forced himself on me; but saying it now, out loud to him, made it real. I was finally letting Dane know what I thought about that night. It was finally out there. Now he was forced to come to terms with the truth. He couldn't keep denying it. Grant reached over and pulled me close. His hold was protective and I felt safe. Dane had a stunned look on his face, which then transformed into a look of hurt and pain.

"Lanie, no. I would never force you. Drugs? No! I would never do that. Lanie, Grant, you have to believe me. I wouldn't, not to our Lanie. No!"

He was almost believable, but there was a part of me that just couldn't process his reaction. It would take everything for me to accept this. I couldn't just let him wipe it away with just his words anymore.

"Dane, didn't it occur to you that she didn't want you when she scratched you? When she told you that you were being too rough and struggled, tried to push you off her?"

"Grant, I swear on my mother's life. I never meant for Lanie to think I forced myself on her. Never. I honestly believed she wanted me. I just thought in her drunken state, she didn't care. I didn't realize how serious you two were. You've brought this all up before. I never drugged her. The only thing I can think is it was Lori. This whole thing was her idea. She even had the glasses out. She was at the house. She was hiding in the other room, she was watching. I didn't—"

"You didn't care, Dane. You didn't think, except about yourself. All you cared about was getting what you wanted—Lanie. You're selfish. You took advantage of her and then you continued to fuck with her, with us. Now you have the nerve to come ask us for help when you fuck up again?"

"Wait. What the hell do you mean Lori was watching? That's sick—so sick. How can you say you thought what we were doing was okay when you invited someone to watch? Does that sound normal to you?" I could feel the tears again. Jesus, I was an emotional wreck. Everything made me cry. *What the hell?*

"And now you're making her cry again and that makes me want to kill you even more, Dane. You hurt *my* Lanie. Do you get that? She's *mine*. She will always be mine, and it sickens me to think about how you touched her. I want to retch every time I think about you being intimate with her."

Grant's words stung me. I knew deep down the image of Dane and I together had never left him. I turned my head up to look at him with watery eyes and he immediately saw my pain.

"Lanie, I'm sorry. I don't mean for this to hurt you. I don't want this to ever hurt you again. We have to move past this, and pretending it didn't happen or never discussing it between the three of us isn't helping."

"Grant, how can you be with me? Every time you touch me, you must picture it; think of me with Dane." I had said these words to him before, but I just couldn't shake the feeling he could never forget.

"When I'm with you, it's only about us, no one else. Your touch, your kiss; it erases all the pain I feel about anything, Lanie."

He pulled me tighter and kissed the top of my head gently.

"I'm so sorry. I never meant things to happen like this. I just wanted Lanie. When I realized you were going to break the pact, I wanted her for my own. *You* broke the pact. That meant fair game."

"I'm not a prize, Dane. This isn't a game! This was never a competition. For years, Grant and I kept our feelings locked inside because of that stupid childhood pact. We did it because we didn't want to hurt you! All those years lost. And when we finally take the chance to be together, you try and ruin everything because of what, Dane? Your fucking ego?" I was yelling at him and sobbing in between. It was like the dam had finally burst. "This is supposed to be the happiest time in my life, and you've done nothing but try and fuck it up." I lashed out at him with both my words and my hand, which I slapped across his face as hard as I could leaving a very red mark in its wake.

Dane and Grant both stared at me.

"He deserved it."

"You're right, Lanie, he did. And he deserves much worse from me." Grant's words were extremely threatening. He was staring Dane right in the eyes when he said it.

"I'm sorry. I wish I could take it all back. That night, the morning on the cliff with you, Grant—I don't know what else to say. I'm sorry. I'm so sorry. Lanie, I never meant to force myself on you. It was never that in my head. Never. Grant, you're right. I hurt you both and I deserve whatever you give me."

In a split second, Grant's fist was connecting with Dane's face, and he was flat on his back.

"I know I deserved that, but damn, I think you broke my nose."

"Yes, you fucking did deserve it! And you're lucky I don't finish by breaking every bone in your body. Lanie?"

I looked at my two guys. Dane's nose was bleeding and Grant was waiting for me to make a decision as to how this all played out. I wanted to tell Grant to finish the job and let him push Dane off the cliff, but I couldn't. This needed to be done with, and Dane lived too close and was too involved in our lives to just let him go. Our history was so much deeper than these past few weeks. It encompassed our whole lives; the three of us, intertwined.

"Dane, I can't ever forgive you for what you've done to me."

His eyes were sad and I thought he was going to cry now. I hadn't seen him look that upset since Callie left him, again his own doing. *He was always fucking everything up.*

"But, you've been like my brother for many years. I love you that way, and I can't just pretend you don't exist anymore, so you could say this is your last chance. I need to move on from this. I'm going to marry Grant and we're going raise our children together on this cliff. You are part of this place and despite how absolutely infuriated I am with you, I can't not have you in my life."

"Thank you, Lanie. I'm so sorry, I'm so so sorry. Grant?" Dane looked to Grant for the same. But I could tell by the look in his eyes that Dane wasn't getting it.

“I will always hold you at arm’s length, Dane. I’ll never trust you again. And I’m only doing this for Lanie’s sake, because this is how she wants things. Do you understand me? If you ever, ever hurt her again, I *will* kill you.”

Dane hung his head and nodded.

“Now tell us what the hell happened with the account and how we can make it better,” Grant said with a serious, no bullshit tone.

“The account is not salvageable. There is no way to save it.”

“Oh my God, this is terrible. What the hell are we going to do?” I just couldn’t catch a break. I just couldn’t have my plateful of happiness without a heaping side of shit.

“I have something better. It’s going to double what that account was. There’s only one small glitch.”

“What account is it? And what’s the glitch?” I questioned.

“The client will only work directly with …”

Chapter 35

You'll Skype Me Every Night, Right?

"… Grant."

"Why? Who is this client?" I didn't understand why any Client would only want to meet with Grant. He was a behind-the-scenes guy.

"She's—" Dane began, still rubbing his nose.

"She? The client will only work with Grant and she's a she?" I felt a pit in my stomach. I didn't want Grant traipsing off to meet with some she-client who would only work with him.

"Lanie, there's absolutely no reason to worry. Maybe she just needs someone who's more technical to discuss the business with." Grant's voice was calming.

"Dane, you know the technical side. You can go over everything with her. Who is it, anyway?"

"I don't know enough to answer what she's asking. And it's Tanner Industries. I'm sure you've heard of them. Brianna Stone is the owner. "

"We've been trying to get our foot in the door there for years. How did you finally get in?" I was amazed. This account was untouchable. They'd been avoiding our calls forever.

"I don't really know. Something must have happened, because she called me, out of the blue. I was pretty impressed myself."

"So how did I come into this?" Grant hissed. He hated meeting with clients. Kissing client ass was not his forte.

"She read that exposé they did on us. She said she needed new blood to make her numbers rise. She insisted on meeting with Grant."

"Fine. Whatever I have to do to save our company. Should I call her?"

"She wants an in-person meeting. She wouldn't have it any other way." Dane was looking down when he said it.

"I can see already she's going to be a PITA." Grant rolled his eyes. Not only did he now have to deal with a client directly, but she had to be a needy one, too.

"Fine, when do we all fly out to meet with her?" I was fine leaving again. This time I wouldn't be leaving Grant behind. I'd have to have Chelsie watch Woof.

"No, *we're* not flying out. Only Grant is flying out. She only wants to meet with him. She was quite explicit."

"No. No way. There is no way Grant is going out to meet her alone." I was jealous and there was no hiding it. It was plainly written all over my face.

"Lanie, you have nothing to worry about." He picked up my hand and pointed to my ring.

"Right. There's no engagement ring on *your* finger. How's she supposed to know you're taken? You men planned that!"

"Lanie, you're getting all upset about nothing. That ring is my promise to you. You don't have to worry about her; you just have to trust me. Don't you trust me?"

"Of course I do. I'm just, I don't know. We just got engaged and now you have to leave." I knew he was right. I had nothing to worry about. Grant had proven his love for me. Even if she did try something, he'd never let anything happen. This was all in my head anyway. I was being a jealous child.

"Look, Lanie, you have nothing to be insecure about. This is just business. Brianna Stone is all about the money. And my nose and I can tell you, Grant is all about you."

"I think you need some ice, Dane. Really. Your nose looks bad." I smiled and also winced for him. His nose was blowing up larger and larger the longer we talked.

"Whatever. I'm not a baby. So, the meeting is in two days, so you'll have to fly out to meet with her. I'll set up all the flights and reservations for you with my miles." Maybe he *was* sorry. He was being awfully helpful. But he needed us right now.

"Fine. Lanie, you're coming with me, right? She doesn't have to sit in on the meetings." Grant looked at me and then at Dane.

"I need Lanie here with me to help with a PR campaign to cover for the loss. The news is hitting the industry fast."

"But I want to go with Grant. I can work remotely."

"Lanie, we have a press conference. I need you here. Please. It's all going to be fine now that you guys are helping me." Dane really did seem grateful. He reached his hand out to Grant.

Grant just stood there for a moment, looking at it like it had some kind of radioactive goo all over it. He slowly reached out and grabbed Dane's hand. Dane's face lit up as Grant's face relaxed.

"You'll webcam with me every night, right? How long will he be gone?"

"I guess until she signs the contract. Maybe a week tops."

"A week? Grant," I whined.

"Lanie, this is the last time I will ever leave your side. We'll be together every day for the rest of our lives. It's only a few days, anyway. I promise to leave you with a huge smile on your face. Okay?" He pulled me close and kissed me.

I wanted to run out and get him a puppy and name it Meow or something, so he couldn't leave. I knew I was being ridiculous but this bad feeling just wouldn't quit. I'm not really sure what it was, but I was panicking, and when that happened, it was usually right.

"Can we just spend the next two days in bed? I'm going to make sure you're completely marked before you leave."

"Lanie," Grant laughed, "I had every intention of spending the next week in bed with you. But I'll take what I can get. Two days in bed it is!" He pulled me to him and planted a gentle kiss on my lips. Dane looked away.

"Well, you two look like you have something to get to, so … I'll let you get to it. But I want to say thank you and sorry again. I really am happy for you both. You make a perfect couple and, well, if I can't have Lanie for myself, then I can't think of a better man to be with her to make her happy."

"Um, that's sort of a compliment." I shot Dane with a perplexed look.

"We'll touch base later for the travel plans and our plan of attack. I want to go and just get this over with and get back here to Lanie." Grant grabbed my chin and lifted my face to his when he said it.

There was nothing to be worried about. This man loved me. But the thought of a client only wanting to deal with him and him alone still wasn't sitting well. Just the thought of her thinking about touching him made me mad. I could imagine how Grant felt having seen me with someone else. I would never be able to get over it. I hoped he would.

We headed back to my place and sat down at the kitchen table.

"Lanie, you aren't really worried about my going away for business, are you?"

"Yes. No. Yes."

"Don't you trust me?"

"I trust you, Baby, it's her I don't trust."

"Lanie, you don't even know her."

"Instincts. It's a girl thing. I know we weren't together yet, but didn't you worry when I left for almost six months?"

“Yes. I was afraid you’d meet someone and fall in love before I even got the chance to be with you.”

“Really? You did?”

“I would’ve tried anyway, you know. There was no stopping me. I had to finally let you know how I felt, even if you said no. I had to take the chance.”

“I’m glad you did. I would’ve taken that chance, too. Just so you know.”

He pulled me onto his lap and buried his face into me. “Lanie, I love you so much. I don’t want to leave you.”

“Then let me come with you.”

“You apparently need to be here. Besides, I plan on closing this deal the first day I’m there. I’ll pour on the charm.”

“Don’t pour too much, okay? I just have a really bad feeling. I won’t rest until your plane lands, and you’re back in my arms.” Grant just softly laughed and shook his head. He obviously thought I was being ridiculous too. But something just really felt wrong.

We spent the day looking over the business, trying to figure out when Dane had lost the account and how bad of shape we were in. Grant brushed up on his presentation skills and I put together PPTs and PR statements. Of course we stopped to make love whenever possible.

Around six, the doorbell rang. When Grant opened the door, a young, pimply-faced teenager stood there holding four bags of something that smelled wonderful, whatever it was.

“Delivery for Mr. and Mrs. Bennett?”

“Well, since you’re probably not asking for my parents, and you came here instead of next door, I’ll assume you mean us.”

“What is that?” I asked him.

“Lots and lots of food, Miss. Chinese, Indian, Italian, and Deli.”

“We didn’t order this.”

"I have a note, sir." Grant rolled his eyes when the kid called him sir. I certainly felt like a grown-up with my new ring. He handed Grant the note.

> *Grant and Lanie Bennett*
> *I thought I'd help you 'stay in' before G leaves, since I'm the one who's causing you to be apart. This should be enough to cover you so you can spend more time together. It's all taken care of, even the tip. Again, sorry and thank you.*
> *Dane*

"Hmm," Grant said.

"What? It was thoughtful of him. He certainly went out of his way."

"Right, Lanie, but why is he ass-kissing us? What kind of game is he playing?" Grant spat.

"Because he needs us right now. He stands to lose everything and if you can't land this account, you know his parents will take him out. He needs us so let him ass kiss for a while since lately he's done his best at being a pain in the ass. He *needs* to do this."

"Well, it certainly does help us spend more time alone. No worries about cooking or going out. Fine. I'll take the ass kissing. It's better than what we were getting."

"So, what are you in the mood for?" I grabbed the bags and started looking through them all.

"I don't suppose there's any chocolate hazelnut spread or sandwich cookies in those bags?"

"Alas, no. But they are in my cabinet, so no worries. And we still have sex cake!" I smiled and pointed to the general direction of anything sweet in my kitchen that we could lick and eat off of each other.

"Well then, how about Indian? We can save the deli for lunch tomorrow. And dinner tomorrow is taken care of, too. That leaves one thing for you to have when I leave. So pick which and put it in the freezer."

I grabbed the Italian and tossed it into the freezer. Then I grabbed him and tossed him, so to speak, against the counter.

"You, my love, are not going anywhere. We will be eating and making love all night! In fact, when you pack, I'm going to try and squeeze myself into your luggage."

"You're so petite, I'm sure you'll have no problem at all. And I'd be more than happy to pack you into my luggage. So, about that webcamming you mentioned; there must be a reason to not just email, text and call?"

"Oh, you know why. I plan on making sure you're satisfied even when you're not with me." I ground my body against his. He growled quietly and then picked me up and put me on the counter.

"Baby, I plan on not stopping all night long."

"Oh yeah? Well you might need a short break by the time I'm done with you."

"Oh, you think so? Honey, I'm going to make you come so many times you won't be able to even sit at your computer to webcam me."

"You think so, huh? Well you might want to leave your Cannoli home on ice, because you won't be able to walk when I'm done with it. Oh, and he wants to stay home with me, anyway."

"He told you so?"

"Yes, we talk all the time. He prefers me to you. He's just stuck with you."

"Because he's stuck in you! That's his happy place. And stop calling him Cannoli."

"But I love Cannoli."

"Yes, and he loves you, too. How about we let him tell you all about it? Cannoli proceeded to tell me all about every part of me he loved for the rest of the night.

* * *

I watched Grant go back and forth from his closet to the bedroom with suit after he's-really-going-to-look-hot-in-that suit. I made sure to put out a full set of pajamas for him. No way was he sleeping in the buff without me by his side.

"Lanie, stop unpacking my briefs and putting in boxers. Those things are God awful uncomfortable. And I'm not wearing these pajamas. At least put in sweats." Grant shook his head and went back into the closet.

"Don't forget your phone charger."

"Got it."

"Don't forget your laptop plug."

"Got it."

"Don't forget your passport and your—"

"I've got it. I've got everything, Lanie." Grant was clearly getting frustrated with my constant comments. I did that when I got nervous.

"Don't forget you love me."

"That's something I would never forget. It's a part of me. Trust me, you have nothing to worry about there, ever."

My heart fluttered a bit and all I wanted to do was to go with him. But I had to give him what he needed; and that was my trust. He deserved it. He'd never done anything to make me doubt him.

"I'm not going with you to the airport," I blurted out and then quickly looked at him to gauge his reaction. He slowly turned and gave me a confused look.

"You're not? Why not?" Now he sounded a bit worried. I knelt on his bed and grabbed his face between my hands. Our lips were only centimeters apart.

"Because I can't stand to watch you leave me and then have Pierre sit through the ride home listening to me cry."

"Baby, don't do that. I feel terribly guilty leaving you behind as it is. Especially with you so worried. Please don't make me picture you crying when I leave. It's heartbreaking."

"I don't want to break your heart. I don't. It's just that … I can't be without you."

"Love, we'll be back together before you know it. I promise this will go by fast."

I nodded my head and he slowly leaned in and kissed me.

* * *

I shadowed him the entire morning. I was already feeling empty without him.

I followed him to the car and watched as he and Pierre put his bags in the trunk.

Pierre gave me understanding looks every so often. Finally, Grant turned to me.

"Lanie … I have to go now. I promise you I will webcam every night, and text, and call, too. I promise. I'll be home soon." He raised his right hand.

"I know, Hun. I'm just going to miss you. A lot!"

"Be a good girl while I'm gone. I already had a conversation with Woof, so no parties. Got it? He promised to text me, too."

I smiled and reached out to touch him. He grabbed me and pulled me close.

"I love you."

"I love you."

He kissed me deeply. It was slow but had an edge of urgency to it. He dropped his hands and stepped away from me.

He looked into my eyes. I could see this was as hard for him as it was for me. I gave him my bravest smile and nodded.

He smiled back and got into the car. I watched as they pulled away. I waited until I could no longer see them and felt my heart tighten in my chest. I felt empty and hollow. I felt the tears coming and my face suddenly felt very flushed. I turned and walked towards my house to grab Woof and visit my mom. *Really, what was wrong with me lately?*

I headed straight for the walk. When I entered the room, it was already cold. It was a dreary day outside and the whole room just felt wrong. I sat down in my chair and snuggled Woof close to me.

"Mom? Are you here?"

There was no tapping sound. I waited a moment and repeated myself. Still nothing. *Fine.* If she wasn't going to respond, I'd just talk.

"See my engagement ring? Grant and I are getting married. But I guess you already knew that. Dad gave me your wedding dress. I'm so excited about that—I'm going to wear it. Maybe make an alteration or two. Hope that's okay."

Nothing. No tapping. Even my mom had left me. I crunched myself into a little ball with Woof in the middle and closed my eyes, feeling very alone. Everyone had been here only a few days ago. Now there was no one here with me. I was seriously feeling it, too.

Being alone never bothered me before. Maybe I should just sleep the entire time. I could dream about Grant and I wouldn't know any better. I closed my eyes and drifted off to sleep.

* * *

Tap. Tap Tap.

I was awoken by a series of tapping noises.

"I'm up, I'm up." The walk was still dreary. I felt extremely cold and stiff. Woof was long gone and my stomach began to growl.

"Fine. I'll go eat something. But I really don't feel like it."

I headed downstairs and right to the fridge. I took out the deli meat and a bagel, and slapped piece after piece of assorted meats and cheeses on it. I slathered on mayo and poured myself a glass of soda. I grabbed some chips and headed to the couch to watch whatever channel was there when I turned it on.

I sat on the couch in my sweatpants and ate. I ate like a slob; like a complete and utter pig. There were crumbs on my shirt and mayo on the side of my mouth. I didn't care. I was pretty sure I was experiencing a slight case of depression. I knew after my sandwich was done I'd be eating the chocolate hazelnut spread with a spoon right out of the jar. After a short while, I just stared at my cell phone, waiting for a call or a text from Grant. *What was wrong with me? I really needed to get my shit together.* He'd only just left and I was falling apart. It was so unlike me because I liked to be alone and enjoyed quiet time. But something about this trip was bothering me and I just couldn't shake it.

* * *

I woke up to my cell phone vibrating on my lap. Well, that had to be Grant, who else would vibrate there? Giggling to myself, I grabbed it and checked the number. *Damn.* It wasn't him.

"Hey, Dane." I really didn't feel like talking.

"Were you sleeping?"

"I guess so." I really didn't feel like talking *to Dane.*

"Lanie, we have to start going over all the PR. Have you heard from Grant?"

"No, I guess the plane didn't land yet." I lazily looked at the clock.

"He should've been there by now. How long was his flight?"

"I think it was about 5 hours and 46 minutes and 33 seconds."

"Counting the seconds are we?"

"Yes." Are we done yet?

"Where do you want to work? I can come there or you can come here. Whatever. Just tell me. We have a press conference in two days. I'm hoping we'll have good news from Grant before then."

My phone beeped. I just stared at it. It was Samantha.

"Dane, Samantha is calling. I have to answer," I said very nonchalantly.

"Fine. Hurry back." Now he was getting annoyed with my blasé attitude.

"Hi, Samantha."

"Lanie, turn the news on, now!"

"Why? What the hell could possibly …"

"Turn it on!"

I turned on the news channel to breaking news and almost threw up. Plane crash, and it had departed from our airport, more details to come.

"Samantha! I have to go. I have to go call the airline."

"What flight was he on? They haven't said what airline or flight yet."

"I'll call you back." I switched lines. "Dane, get over here now. There's been a plane crash. I need all of Grant's flight info. Now. Get over here now!"

I was panicking. I couldn't breathe. I knew it. I'd known it all along. It wasn't the client that was bothering me. It was the flight. I never should have let him leave.

"Lanie, Grant left hours ago. I'm sure it's not his plane."

"Dane, get your ass over here with everything you have. Don't question me. Do it." I hung up the phone. I unlocked the front door and headed to my office to check the Internet.

I started my computer and heard Dane come running up the stairs.

"I have everything. Go to Eclipse Airline's website."

I got to the site and immediately saw the alert on their home page. My stomach knotted and I felt the color drain from my face. I started to hyperventilate.

"It's his airline. It's his. Oh my God, Dane. Oh my God."

"Lanie, hold on. They're the major airline out of our airport. There were lots of flights leaving today. I'm going to read you his flight info. Did they post a manifest yet?"

"No, just the flight number."

"He was on flight 3—" *Oh shit! Oh shit!* I was starting to gag. I was holding my breath.

"4—" *No, no, this can't be happening ...*

Chapter 36

Let's Get This Over With

"7—" I just stared at the screen. I thought I had died. My body went cold; I couldn't move. My heart shattered into a thousand pieces. No sounds could escape my lips, because there was no air in my lungs. My eyes started to burn and I couldn't focus on the screen anymore. I felt the room begin to spin. Even the sounds in the room became jumbled and disjointed.

"1." Dane was saying something. My brain had stopped processing everything. *Did he just say one?*

"Lanie, it wasn't his flight." I still couldn't move.

"Lanie? Can you hear me?" Dane shook me when I still didn't respond. "Lanie, it wasn't his flight. His flight was 3471, that one says 347."

One number difference, just one number made my heart whole again. I immediately broke down sobbing. But this sobbing was pure relief. My phone began to vibrate. I didn't remember grabbing it, but it was suddenly in my hands.

"Grant? Grant, please say it's you." I was frantic to hear his voice.

"Yes, it's me, Love. What's wrong?" Grant sounded calm and collected.

"There was a plane crash. Your flight numbers were so close. I didn't hear from you. You should've landed a while ago. Where are you?" I was still frantic. I needed to hear him more to know I wasn't dreaming.

"Slow down, Lanie. Let's see, I can understand why you're freaking out. That's really spooky. I just got to the hotel. Better?" He was still cool as a cucumber.

I took a deep breath in to steady myself. My heart rate slowed.

"You scared the shit out of me. You said you'd call when you got there. I figured I'd get at least a text."

"Sorry, Love. You packed my charger, but I forgot to charge my phone first. Battery died."

"I'm just shaken up, is all. I just had this bad feeling from the start and then the plane crashed."

"It's all okay, Babe. I'm fine. Everything is going to be just fine. On another note, apparently I am meeting Ms. Stone for dinner at the hotel tonight."

"Wow, she doesn't waste any time, does she?"

"Guess not. There was a message waiting for me when I got here. Told me to meet her 'promptly at eight'. And you know how I feel about client interaction. It doesn't matter. Just one step closer to getting home to you."

"Well, we'll webcam when you get back. I miss your face. A lot."

"I miss all of you. A lot."

Dane was sitting on my computer, surfing. He looked toward me when I said something and then pretended not to listen when I turned his way.

"Dane?"

"Sorry, Lanie, I'm just waiting for you. We need to get our PR stuff together. The press conference is tomorrow afternoon."

"We'll be fine. Grant and I worked on it the past two days."

"Is Dane there with you?" Grant asked.

"Yes. He came over with your flight info. We were worried."

"I need to go shower. I hate flying. I'm covered in flight scum."

"Flight scum? Okay. Call me when you get back from dinner. Don't have too much fun."

"I know. I love you."

"I love you too, Babe."

"I love you too, Grant," Dane called out from behind me.

"That's disturbing. Maybe it was *me* he really wanted."

"Eww, Grant, that's a disgusting thought. I have to go bleach that image from my brain right now."

Grant laughed and we said our goodbyes and hung up. I turned toward Dane.

"Well, I have Italian left. Hungry?" I had no idea why I invited him to eat. I could only try to get all the PR stuff out of the way tonight so I didn't have to spend more time with him tomorrow morning.

"Sure. Yeah." He sounded too happy. He had a huge grin on his face.

"We can work while we eat. Let's get this over with." I made sure to dampen his happy demeanor. It worked, too. His grin slowly faded.

I ran down to the kitchen and heated up two plates. I grabbed something to drink and piled it onto a big tray. We ate while we went over the presentation, several times. Maybe he was just trying to make the whole process drag out. We kept going over the same things. He kept nitpicking everything.

"That's it. Make up your fucking mind already. You made me change this three times."

"It has to be perfect, Lanie. This is our company image."

"Oh, go blow, Dane. No one is going to read in between the letters of the words! You're being ridiculous."

"It has to be right. There can be serious repercussions about what they say versus what I say. I don't want some sort of sexual harassment or discrimination lawsuit here. Can you imagine?"

"Well, you should have thought about that before you did something that deserved both! What is wrong with you lately? What time is it?"

"It's eleven."

"Wow. I haven't heard from Grant. Dinner was at eight. He wasn't kidding. He wanted this done fast."

"I'm sure he's doing whatever it takes to close the deal."

"Shut the fuck up, Dane. You're such an asshole."

"What? What the hell did I say?"

"I know what you were getting at. Grant wouldn't cheat on me to close a business deal."

"You're paranoid, Lanie. I didn't mean anything like that at all."

Wow. Was I being paranoid or was it Dane playing games? My inclination was Dane. But maybe I did read into it a little bit. I grabbed my cell phone.

L: Hey, babe. How's dinner going?

I returned to my other conversation. The one I wasn't enjoying.

"Sorry. What's this Brianna person like anyway?"

"Oh, she's a total piece of ass. Wait—she's okay. Ya know, nothing special."

"Dane. I will hurt you if you don't tell me the truth. I have no problem with punching you in your already broken nose."

"Fine. She's hot. And wealthy. And gets everything she wants. She's my dream girl."

"Oh great, the female version of you. You threw Grant to the sharks. Why? Think she'd make a move and he'd leave me?"

"Stop it, Lanie. It had nothing to do with me. She asked for him. I wanted to go. I told you, she's my kind of woman. Ruthless."

"Yeah, you're not helping. Why the hell hasn't Grant texted me back?"

I had checked my phone at least twenty times in the past minute. Maybe he just fell asleep. Grant didn't travel well.

"Look. I'm tired and I'm super-cranky, and I don't really like you right now. So how about we call it a night, huh? I mean, this is perfect. It'll be fine. I can handle it. No one will see your broken nose and everything will be better. This is what I do. Now go home."

"Fine."

He got up and left without saying good night. *Oh, pity.* I didn't give a shit. I wanted to know where the hell Grant was. I went to my room and got ready for bed. I lay down and stared at the phone. I felt it buzz in my hand. I looked at the clock. It was two.

"Grant?"

"Hey Babe. I am so sorry. Ms. Stone doesn't allow media at the table. Unless of course, it's her own."

"Are you kidding me? It's two o'clock in the morning. Dinner was promptly at eight. Where the hell have you been?"

"Lanie, we met at eight and had drinks with her board. I met them all. We then went to dinner, at ten. Very late. We worked through the entire dinner and dessert, and then more drinks."

"Are you drunk? You spent all night with that woman drinking?"

"Lanie, no. I'm not drunk. And yes, we worked the entire time. She's all business. I'm pretty sure she'll sign the contracts tomorrow after the plant tour and lunch."

"Good. Then you can come home."

"After her party."

"Party? What party?"

"She's throwing an industry party. I have to go."

"You have to go. Why is that?"

"Because Bri said she already told everyone that her new 'partner' was coming. And I was pretty sure she meant me. Us. You know what I mean. Lanie, this is all about business."

"Yes, you keep saying that. All business. Bri? You're calling her Bri now?

"Lanie. Look at your left hand and tell me what you see." I looked down at my hand and saw the beautiful ring he had placed here.

"My ring."

"Okay, and what does that mean to you?"

"It means you love me and want to marry me."

"Yes. Now believe it already. I love you. You have nothing to worry about. This isn't like you. What's going on?"

I looked down at the bed, where he'd spent so much time with me. I felt badly for not trusting him. *I was being a total bitch.*

"I keep thinking about how you saw me with Dane. And how that will never leave your mind. And how easy it would be to start from scratch and not have that in your head."

"Seriously?" He sounded completely dumbfounded.

"Yes. Seriously."

"Lanie, that's the most ridiculous thing I have ever heard in my life.

"Stop."

"No, you're being silly. Lanie, I don't picture that at all. I never think about it. Never."

"Really?"

"Really."

"What do you think about?"

"I think about you, only you with me, because that's all I care about. You. I love you."

My heart sank. I was being a royal ass not believing him. I guess I was just so afraid of losing him. I couldn't survive without him. After having this man, no woman could survive without him.

"I'm sorry. I am so sorry. What's wrong with me?" I felt terrible.

"Nothing. I worry constantly. What if you think I'm not enough? What if you feel like you're settling? What if you get into a terrible car accident?"

"Wow. Okay. I don't feel quite as bad now. I just love you so much, Grant. I miss you so much."

"Babe, I miss you, too. I hate being away from you. I hate it."

"Me too. I wish you were here, right now. I'd show you how much I love you."

"Lanie, don't get me all horny. There's nothing compared to you, so I have no release."

"I'm going to get you so hot for me while you're gone you'll run home."

"All I have to do is think of you, your body, what it does to me."

"I love you, babe."

"I love you, too. I'll call you in the morning?"

"The second you wake up."

I fell asleep with the phone clutched to my heart and Woof sleeping on my head. I dreamt Grant was with me all night. His hands were all over me, his lips on mine. Spooning me all night long. When I finally woke up in the morning, I opened my eyes, expecting him to be there next to me. He wasn't and my heart felt heavy. I was still clutching the phone. I looked at the time. Eight thirty. Grant couldn't still be sleeping. I called him. It just rang. I left him a voicemail and decided to text, too.

L: Good morning, babe. Did you sleep well?

I got up and began my morning routine. I headed for the shower, turned it on to warm up and began picking through my suits to find the most appropriate one. Nice gray silk with a knee-length skirt and a white lace cami underneath, gray pumps. *Perfect.* I'd wear my hair up and throw my glasses on for good measure, very business-like.

I made it a quick shower, did my makeup, and hair, and got dressed. I grabbed my phone and headed downstairs to make coffee, noticing there was still no text from Grant. He told me not to worry and I had to trust him. I made coffee and grabbed my tablet to read the news. The crash was all over the headlines, I felt myself shudder, thinking about it, and then realized I had never called Samantha back last night. *Shit.* I dialed her immediately.

"Samantha, I'm so sorry. It wasn't Grant's flight, but I'm sure you figured that much out by now."

"Yeah, thanks a lot, Lanie," Samantha giggled. "It's okay, I spoke with Grant last night around ten."

"You talked to Grant at ten? He told me he wasn't allowed to use his phone."

"Well, I wouldn't stop calling him. That's probably what made the no-phone-rule. I was pretty relentless."

"You? Relentless? Never. I don't believe it." I feigned surprise.

"Ha ha, Lanie. So did you guys webcam last night? I bet it was all hot and chocolaty!"

"Nope. Barely spoke with him. I haven't even heard from him this morning yet."

"Yeah, I heard her in the background. She was purring at him to get off the phone."

"Purring? You heard her purr? How the hell close was she?"

"Well, Lanie, I have no idea. But I could hear her breathing. And she was oh-so drippy sweet."

"Great. This is just great."

"Lanie, what's wrong with you? Grant sounded thoroughly annoyed. He kept shooing her."

"Shooing her? How could you tell?"

"He kept saying 'Bri, please, I'm on the phone and this is very important. Just give me one minute, please.'"

"Well I haven't heard from him, and he only talked to me at two last night."

"Two? Are you kidding me? He was out that late with her?"

"Apparently so. I'm going to go text him right now."

"Don't do that. You'll look needy. You sent him a message; now wait for him to respond, Lanie. That's how you play the game."

"Samantha. This isn't a game. He's my fiancé and I haven't heard from him. I have every right to text and call."

"I'm telling you. Don't call him or text him. Trust me on this. You have nothing to worry about. Grant has been head-over-heels for you since he was a toddler. Why would he ruin that now he finally has you?"

"I don't know. Because you always want what you can't have and now he has me? I'm not a challenge anymore?"

"You're being a jealous bitch, Lanie. Stop. This is Grant we're talking about. Really. Lanie?"

I was quiet for a moment. If anyone else said I was being a bitch, I wouldn't care. But coming from Samantha? *Well.*

"Fine!" I was annoyed because I knew she was right.

"How about I text Grant and I'll let you know if he texts me back? I'll ask him something about the bridal shower. This way I get the whole "getting married" thing in there." *She was good.*

"Perfect. Do it. And then let me know if you hear from him. Hopefully, I'll hear from him before you do."

"Okay. I'll talk to you in a bit. And if I don't hear from him, I'll sick Chelsie on his ass. Bye."

I hung up and checked my phone for a text, nothing yet. He'd better call me soon. I had to get everything ready for the press conference and I wouldn't be able to talk to him then.

* * *

I felt my phone vibrate and grabbed it. It was Samantha.

S: I didn't hear a thing back. He must just be busy.

L: That's bullshit!

S: That's work. Deal with it. He'll call you.

L: Wanna come over tonight? U&Chelsie?

S: OK!

Good. I needed the company. I hated not hearing from Grant and it was apparently making me crazy. I grabbed my phone and called Dane.

"Hey, Lanie!" He answered on the first ring.

"Morning, Dane. I'm going to go over the presentation. Want to come pretend you're the press?"

"Yep. Be right over."

Even hanging out with Dane would make me feel better. The more I was alone, the more I focused on not hearing from Grant. It was one. He was probably at the plant tour all morning, and now lunch. The door opened and Dane came bouncing in like a happy puppy.

"What the hell are you so happy about?"

"You wake up on the wrong side of the bed this morning?"

"No, I woke up alone, which I'm not happy about. I blame you."

"Don't blame me. On another note, I heard from Brianna Stone this morning. She's more than pleased with the progress she and Grant are making. And I quote, 'we're making amazing headway. I'm feeling positive about signing after the party. Grant is quite persuasive.' Seems our boy is taking one for the team."

"You're such an asshole, Dane. He's not taking one for the team."

"What the hell is up your ass today? Didn't you already hear all this from Grant?"

"I haven't heard from Grant since two this morning," I said in the snottiest tone I could muster.

"Well, he was with her when she called me at eight this morning. They'd just finished a work out at the gym and were heading to breakfast and the tour after getting showered."

"He worked out with her? They had breakfast? He's spending all this time with her and has no time to call me?"

"I don't know, Lanie. I have no idea. Why don't you call him?"

"I did. He didn't answer my text or my call." I was starting to feel angry and depressed. I looked away from him and began to play with a tendril of loose hair.

"Lanie, why are you so worried? He's working. There's nothing more to it. You have nothing to worry about. I promise." He sounded sincere, but I just couldn't take comfort in anything that came out of Dane's mouth, and wasn't sure I ever would. We only helped him because it was the business and livelihood. Our parents had worked so hard to build it to the multi-billion dollar company it was today; I intended on keeping it that way.

* * *

By two, I still hadn't heard from Grant. I waited outside for Pierre to pick me up and take me to the conference center. Dane stood beside me even though he wasn't going. I didn't want anyone to see his nose. He was nervous and repeatedly threw reminders at me.

"Lanie, Don't forget to tell them …"

"Dane," I interrupted, "I know very well how to handle the press, so back off. You can watch it on the webcast. Everything will be fine as of tomorrow. I'll take care of your mess and Grant will get the stupid contracts signed and it'll all go back to normal."

"Good luck." He shook his head and walked away.

When I got to the conference center, I was so pissed off it made me all the more ready to knock the bad press right out of the ballpark. Right as I was walking in, my phone vibrated.

G: Hey, babe. I am so sorry.
G: You have every right to be mad at me.
G: This client is relentless and HM.
L: HM?
G: High Maintenance.
L: I see.
G: She requires constant attention.
L: That include working out at the gym?
G: Apparently.
L: So you can't find a second to call me?
G: I'm sorry. She was at my door first thing.
L: Which side?
G: Which side of what?
L: Of your door?
G: The outside!
L: I have to go.
G: Press conference?
L: Yep.
G: We're watching.
L: We?
G: Yes, Lanie. We.
L: I have to go now.
G: Are you mad at me? I love you. I'm sorry.
L: I love you too.

I closed my phone and went to the press conference. They were ruthless, but I was on it having answers for everything. They had nothing, and when I was done, they sat there staring. I think they were scared of me as they well should be. I'd been ready to kick some ass, and I had. I headed out with no final questions, completely comfortable that at least this part of the fiasco was over. Pierre drove me home. He was quiet and only gave me smiles in the mirror. I smiled back and could tell he knew better than to say anything to me. When we pulled up to the house, Samantha and Chelsie were standing outside with Dane. I got out of the car and they all came running.

"Lanie, you were amazing!" Samantha cooed.

"You shut them the hell up! It was fantastic. You should work for the president. I mean you're that good." Dane grabbed me in his arms and swung me around.

"You made me proud, Lanie. I must be rubbing off on you, you were a first class no-bullshit bitch!" Chelsie said in her proudest voice. I *must* have been good for Chelsie to say that.

My phone rang. "Hello?

"Lanie," Grant said, "that was extremely impressive. You were great. And Bri is seriously impressed with you. She said she'd like to meet with you about her company's PR."

"Thanks. Tell her I said thank you. I'll certainly do whatever I have to for the company." I was cold. I should've been happy to hear from him.

"She wants to speak with you now."

"You're still with her?"

"Yes, Lanie, she's right here."

"Fine. Put her on the phone." I saw Dane and Samantha's eyes get wide. I was still in bitch mode.

"Lanie," Samantha said, giving me a warning. I put my hand up and showed her my best 'I'll be very polite' smile.

"Hello?"

"Hi, Lanie, this is Brianna Stone. I knew Grant was perfect for me, but . . .

Chapter 37

It's Not a Date

"… I am now most extremely impressed with you, and your press conference today. It gave me the added confidence that your company is the one I want to sign with."

She didn't sound so bad. Maybe this *was* all in my head. She sounded all business. She did say Grant was *'perfect for me'* and *'the one'*? I guess she just meant work.

"Thank you, Ms. Stone."

"Call me Bri. I think this is going to be a very beneficial partnership for us all. And I really would like to meet with you in person to discuss how you can do some spin doctoring for my company. You were lethal! I loved it."

"Thank you, Brianna … Bri. I would be more than happy to meet. Would you like me to fly out tonight?"

"Now that's even more impressive. Willing to fly out immediately? Amazing. No, I don't think that's necessary. Grant has everything under perfect control here. He has invited me to visit you at your beloved cliff. Apparently there's whale watching there soon. I've always wanted to see them. I think it was so sweet of him to invite me."

"Yes. Very. Well, we'll look forward to seeing you then."

"Oh, you'll see me before that. Didn't Dane tell you? We have a web conference tomorrow at noon."

"No, he hadn't informed me yet." I shot Dane the evil eye.

"Well, Grant and I have to go get his tux fitted, pick up my dress, and then we have to get ready for the ball tonight."

"Oh? Well, let me let you and Grant go to it then."

"Would you like to speak with him again?" she asked with a drippy sweet tone. It made my stomach turn.

"No, thank you. I'm sure I'll be hearing from him later." My voice was cool and business-like.

"Oh, I'll let him know to try and squeeze in a call to you. We'll be very busy for the rest of the night, but I'm sure he can find some time for you." That made my stomach turn even more. *Find time for me?*

"Of course. It was a pleasure, Brianna. I'll see you tomorrow, promptly at ten." I gave her a taste of her own medicine.

"I like that. You're sharp and punctual. You're just what we need. And I thought Grant was all I needed. How wonderful. I'm very excited about this venture." *Who knew she'd like my commands?*

"Yes. So am I. Good bye, and have a great evening."

"Oh, I'm sure we will." I could just picture her staring into Grant's eyes when she said it.

I was fuming. I was also sure Grant was waiting for me to talk with him again. If he wanted, he could call me back but I didn't expect him to. He seemed completely happy without any contact. And if that's how he wanted it, I could play *not available*, too.

"Ladies. We are going to get shit-faced tonight. Let's go raid all the liquor cabinets, shall we? Find our poison?" I blurted out.

"That's my girl! Drink it out." Chelsie put her arm around my shoulder and we headed towards Grant's to raid his liquor. Might as well get tanked on his dime. I'm sure he wouldn't mind.

"Hey, Dane, want to get shit-faced with us tonight?" Chelsie glared at me. Samantha just froze in her spot.

"Umm, sure, if everyone else is cool with it."

Samantha and Chelsie exchanged a glance and then nodded and shrugged.

"You're in charge of dinner. We want something expensive and lavish to celebrate. How about sushi galore?" Samantha clapped her hands and Chelsie just smiled. My girls liked raw fish. So did I.

"Okay, whatever you guys want. I'll get the whole catch of the day!" Dane bounced off.

Chelsie turned and looked at me and threw her hands up.

"What the fuck are you doing, Lanie? Don't you remember what happened last time you got drunk with Dane?" *Ouch. That stung.*

"Yes, Chelsie, I do, painfully. But you'll both be here and everything will be just fine. And anyway, if Grant can go traipsing off with some woman for days and to a ball and not call me …"

"Lanie, you know it's not like that," Samantha said. Her eyes were sincere and I knew she was right, but I was still all feisty from the past few hours.

"I do? No, I don't. All I know is my fiancé flew off to meet some businesswoman and I have not been his on his priority list at all. Two can play that game. I'm sure he won't be pleased Dane is getting drunk with us. That's if he even calls."

"Lanie, watch out. What you're doing … it's dangerous. I'm not sure I like it. It's not you."

"And it's not like Grant not to call me, and be out until two in the morning with some woman he just met."

Chelsie shook her head and walked away. Samantha put her arm around me, and her head on my shoulder. I sighed deeply.

"I know, Honey. It's not like him. But maybe he's just that busy. You don't know, so don't do anything stupid."

"I would never do anything to hurt Grant. I won't do anything stupid. I just want him to feel a little jealous, too."

"And you're going to use Dane for that? Really? Not a good plan." She was right. I suddenly regretted inviting him. Samantha must have felt my anxiety.

"Don't worry, Honey. After we eat all his sushi, we'll get Chelsie to throw him out on his ass. She's been dying to beat the crap out of him." I giggled because I knew it was the truth.

I headed over to Grant's and felt terrible the second I walked through the door. I was so cold to him. I loved him. I didn't want to hurt him. Being in his empty house just made me feel like a complete idiot. But he certainly wasn't making an effort to call me on his own. He apparently needed her permission. Grant was perfect for her. *Fit his tux. Get her dress.* It was like they were going as a couple. Oh and the 'we will' part. Now I was pissed off again. I grabbed Grant's best scotch. I hated scotch, but I was drinking it tonight. And I knew Chelsie and Samantha would like it, too.

"You must really be mad at Grant to be drinking that tonight." Samantha pointed to the bottle.

"I need to." I just bitch-faced her.

"Okay," she whispered.

I got up and headed to the door. I let Samantha pass through so I could slam the door shut. I did, hard. Samantha just eyed me and shook her head.

"Feel better now?"

"Yes. Yes I do." And I did. I felt a lot better.

We got back to my house and Chelsie was getting the dishes ready. I had a full set of sushi ware. *Loved it.*

"Can you guys excuse me? I have to go make a call."

"Yes, you do. Now go do it." Chelsie sounded pissed. I turned and went out on the terrace. I dialed Grant.

Hi, this is Grant Bennett. I'm not available. Leave me a message.

I felt a twinge of anger but it subsided as soon as I could no longer hear his voice.

"Hey, Grant. I thought maybe I'd catch you before you left. Guess not. Well, have fun tonight. Maybe I'll hear from you later. Goodnight. Love you. Bye."

My heart sank. Maybe he was mad at me now. Did I drive him right into another woman's arms? I could feel my eyes starting to well with tears. I didn't want things like this. This was terrible. My phone began to vibrate. My heart started to race to keep up.

"Hello?"

"Fuck, Lanie. I hate the way things are right now." *Damn, we were connected.* "You sounded so down in that message. I was in the shower when you called. I spent the whole day playing drag along. I hate this and want to come home to you. I need you, Love."

Now my heart was really going. I thought it would jump right out of my chest.

"Really? You need me? You want to come home? To me?"

"What? Of course, Lanie—why would you think any differently? Don't you want me to come home?"

"Yes. It's just you've been very preoccupied. You haven't called me. Not anything. Not even a text."

"Love, I haven't had a minute to breathe. This woman is relentless. It's non-stop with her."

"But not even a text?"

"Lanie, please, Love. You have to understand."

"No, you're right. It's just she made comments."

"Everything to her is a possession. You should have seen her eyeing you up during the press conference. Where, might I add, you were fucking sexy as hell!"

"You thought I was sexy?"

"Hell, yes. You were all fired up. You were putting people in their places. It was amazing to watch. You were on fire and it was so hot. God, I want you so badly."

It made my whole body feel better, hearing him talk to me like that.

"So, what time are you leaving tonight?

"The limo is picking us up at seven."

"Picking us up?"

"Yes. Bri is staying at the hotel, too."

"Who else is going with you?"

"Uh, it's just us."

"Just the two of you? Is this a date? Are you her escort?"

"Lanie, I wouldn't say escorting her, and this is by no means a date."

"Does she know that?"

"Lanie, she is quite aware we are engaged. I was literally gushing while you were ripping the media to shreds."

"So, she hasn't hit on you? At all?"

"Lanie, I'll never lie to you. She made plenty of comments about how pretty I was to look at. How easy it was to work with me because I was so easy on the eyes. I understand what a lot of women go through now because I felt like a piece of meat instead of a professional equal."

"She did? I'm going to rip *her* to shreds."

"Lanie, it was harmless. She's simply harmless. She's way too worried I'd turn her down. I brushed off every one of her comments or hints."

"You make sure she knows this isn't a date."

"I promise. Now, what are you doing tonight to celebrate?"

"Chelsie, Samantha, and I are drinking your scotch. And Dane is buying a lot of sushi."

"You're drinking my scotch? You must have been pretty pissed at me for not calling today." *Damn. He knew me too well.*

"Yes. Sorry."

"No, what's mine is yours. Have at it. However, did I hear you say Dane? You're drinking with Dane?" Now Grant sounded insecure.

"Don't worry. Chelsie is all over this. She can't wait to throw him out once we're done eating."

"Lanie, please. I don't trust him."

"It's fine, Grant. I promise. He's just staying for dinner. That's it. And anyway, you'll be off at the ball with your date."

"It's not a date."

"I know. I just wanted you to practice saying it so you had it down to a tee when you have to say it to Bri later."

"I have no intentions of letting her think otherwise. Now you go and have fun. I have to monkey suit up."

"Grant. You're hot as hell in a tux. I had a hard time keeping my hands off you at your prom."

"Shame. I wish you had just reached out and touched. That's the only thing I would have needed to make you mine back then. Just one sign."

"Well, you don't need to look for signs anymore. My love for you is written all over my face."

"I want to kiss that face right now."

"Babe, I miss you so badly. I miss you next to me at night. I dream of you constantly."

"Me too. I miss your skin against mine, Lanie, the feel of you, the warmth of your body. Even the smell of you."

"I smell?"

"You smell like vanilla and I want to eat you constantly." I suddenly got an ache between my legs.

"Maybe that's why we have a food fetish," I giggled.

"Lanie, you drive me insane. I want to reach through the phone right now."

"Grant, you make me so—stop. I don't want you to be all hot when you go on your not-a-date."

"Look, I'll call you as soon as I get home if it's not too late. But I have a feeling you three will be up all night anyway. Please, Lanie, watch Dane. Okay?"

"I promise. And you watch Bri. Okay?"

"Yes, Love. I promise. Talk with you later. I love you."

"I love you, too." I pretty much skipped back into the house.

"Yeah! They're all happy again." Samantha clapped. "Now let's get hammered."

"Let's eat first. I barely touched anything today. I want to enjoy tonight, not puke through it. It's scotch."

"Yes, please, Samantha. I don't feel like watching you drive any porcelain buses tonight."

"Right, Chelsie. Like that would happen. I can hold my liquor," Samantha said defensively.

"Right." Chelsie rolled her eyes.

"No, you can't, Samantha. You can hold beer and vodka. That's about it. I've seen you driving buses lots of times." I loved Samantha, but she wasn't my first choice for doing shots.

"Can you at least call it driving the porcelain Porsche?" Samantha would be mortified to even be seen on a bus. She wouldn't even take the bus to school. Her parents had to drive them in every day.

"Call it what you want, it's still puking in the bowl," Chelsie scoffed.

We all turned as the front door opened. Dane came in with bag after bag of sushi. Dane liked to eat and he had discriminating tastes. He was also a good friend with the sushi chef in town, so we knew what we were going to eat was going to be the very best. We dined on the sushi and sipped on sake, which Dane also thought to bring. Personally, I hated sake, but this was a plum variety, so it went down pretty easy when over ice. Soon we were all watching a scary movie, laughing, and getting drunk. We actually had a good time. Well, everyone else did. My mind kept wandering off to visions of Grant and Bri, arm-in-arm, walking around meeting people. She would introduce him as her date. They would drink. They would smile. They would dance. In my heart, Grant was on a date and it was eating at me. *It was killing me.* My stomach was burning and my heart ached.

"Lanie? Hello? Earth to Lanie?" Chelsie was poking my arm.

"What? I'm here. What?"

"Please, I know where you are. You're wishing you were a fly on the wall at the ball. Let it go. It's a business function. You know those suck. Be happy you're here with us."

"But, I'm sure she thinks it's a date. I'm sure she's hanging all over him. I'm going to text him."

"No, you're not. You're going to have fun and enjoy being with us. I'm sure he's thinking about you being here getting drunk with Dane."

"He knows you're here, too. He has nothing to worry about," I said glumly.

"And neither do you. Now stop it."

"Chelsie, it's time to throw Dane out. I need to just be with you guys. I'm feeling weepy coming on."

Chelsie smiled an evil evil smile.

"Well, Dane, time for the girls to get into t-shirts and panties and have pillow fights and play twister. You need to leave."

Dane's face turned all sorts of colors in a matter of seconds. I could see the hamsters spinning the squeaky wheels in his sorry little head.

"If I promise to be quiet can I watch?"

"Dane, don't make me pick you up and throw you out on your ass. I would love to do that. Can I?"

"Would it add to your fun?" Dane asked. *Where the hell was he going with this?*

"What? Really? You'd let me kick your ass? Would you promise to cry like a baby?" Chelsie was getting excited at the possibilities.

"Lanie, would it make you feel better about tonight if I let you all hit me with pillows and then let Chelsie throw me out?"

Chelsie, Samantha, and I stared at each other. We didn't know whether to grab pillows and start slamming them against his head or do nothing. Suddenly, smiles all around, we each grabbed a pillow and started to wail on Dane.

"Just watch my nose. Please. Grant already broke it. Aim lower." Dane sounded slightly alarmed.

We were relentless. It was a barrage of pillows. Dane just put his hands over his nose. I just kept slamming my pillow into the back of his head over and over again. It was the perfect release. I got out all my frustrations on him and imagined he was Bri and pummeled away. Soon we were all laughing and having a hard time actually making contact. I was laughing so hard I thought I would pee.

"Okay, okay, this is not as much fun as I thought it would be. I've had enough. Uncle. Uncle! Chelsie, please throw me out."

We all stopped dead and just stared at each other again. Chelsie dropped her pillow and grabbed Dane by the ear. She tugged so hard I thought we'd be able to call him Van Gogh soon.

"Ouch, Chelsie. I didn't mean actually hurt me." This made Chelsie smile even more and Dane's eyes got wider.

She grabbed the back of his shirt and ripped him up off the couch. Samantha and I clapped and cat-called. If she was strong enough, I think she would've had him off the ground. She pushed and shoved him ceremoniously to the door and when she got there, she opened it and whispered something in his ear.

"Really? Chelsie, seriously?"

"Yes, please. It would make Lanie very happy to watch." Dane looked at me. I had a huge smile on my face.

"Fine." He bent over with his butt right in Chelsie's direction. If you could wind up a leg, Chelsie did it. She slammed her foot into his ass so hard I heard him whimper and he flew out of my view.

"And stay out, you bitch!" Chelsie slammed the door shut. She looked down at her foot to make sure she hadn't left it wedged in his ass. Samantha and I clapped and cheered.

"Thanks, Chelsie, I needed that."

"Me too!"

"Me three, and now it's time to pull out the scotch."

"What time is it, anyway?" I said, looking for my phone under a pile of pillows.

"It doesn't matter, Lanie. You're having fun here and Grant is having—" Samantha started as she poured us each a glass.

"The worst time in his entire life. He's pining for you and wishing he was here making love to you," Chelsie busted in. And then she downed her first glass.

"I was going to say that." Samantha shot Chelsie a bitch look. And she slammed hers down.

"Holy shit, it's midnight? Where the fuck did the time go? Why didn't Grant call me yet?" I slammed down mine. *Hell, this was scotch, not shots.* We were going to be hurting later. Samantha poured us all another.

"Lanie, it's a ball. He won't be home yet. It's early," Chelsie said matter-of-factly.

"That's not true. They usually have the place until like eleven. It's just like a wedding," Samantha told her.

And that's when Chelsie slammed a pillow into the side of Samantha's face.

"Ouch, you whore. Lanie isn't stupid."

"Yes, I am. I'm completely stupid to think that a man like Grant would ever really want someone like me. Dane was right, it was all convenience. Brianna Stone can give him the world whereas I only can offer him this cliff."

Now Chelsie hit me in the side of the head with the pillow.

"Ouch. You're a whore," I said.

"Lanie, bite your tongue. Grant loves you. You're a hot piece of ass. You already have money. Technically, the same money he has, so no pre-nup needed. You make him happy in every way possible and honestly, the sex part, I know he's totally in heaven. I mean what man wouldn't love food and sex and sex and food? Hell, the way you add chocolate into everything, I want a piece of you, too. Do you go that way? Is it cheating if it's with a girl? Oh my God, would it be incest?"

Chelsie and I just stared at Samantha having no idea what to say. I knew Samantha was a sexual master, but girl on girl? And she was looking at me?

"Wow, Dylan sure is a lucky guy," I said.

"You could get lucky, too." She winked at me. Chelsie was still staring at her with her mouth slightly agape.

"What?" Samantha said, completely oblivious.

"Um, I'm not sure if I tell Grant what you just said if he'd laugh, get jealous, or just stare at you like Chelsie is right now. How much scotch have you had?"

"Not enough to get in that Porsche yet."

"Well, if we keep doing scotch shots, we'll all be fighting for driving rights," I said.

"I want mine to be candy apple red," Samantha chirped.

"Samantha, it's not a real Porsche."

"Look, if I'm going to be driving a Porsche tonight, it can be whatever color I want it to be."

"I'm going to go call Grant. Maybe I can get him to webcam with me tonight." I really missed him. And I just wanted him to be home already. Well, at least back to his hotel room. Alone. And miserable.

As if he was reading my mind, my phone rang.

"Damn, is that Grant? That's spooky if it is," Samantha said.

"It is!" I said. "Hey, Baby. I miss you."

"Hello, Love. I miss you too. What are you ladies doing?"

"We're drinking all your scotch," I giggled, the scotch and my excitement to be talking to Grant all hitting at the same time.

"Is Dane still there?" Grant's concern was apparent in his voice.

"Nope. Chelsie kicked his ass to the curb. Literally. How was your ball?"

"It was boring and exhausting. I'm looking forward to going to sleep and then heading home tomorrow," he said in an exhausted tone.

"Did she sign the contracts?"

"Not yet. Tomorrow during the web conference she said," he said flatly.

"Did you book your flight back yet?"

"Not yet. I'll have Bri's assistant do it for me first thing in the morning."

"Thank God, Grant. I miss you and it's only been two days."

"I know, Love. I miss you terribly, too."

"Want to webcam with me? I promise to so make it worth your while."

"I think I'd like that plenty. Go to your computer; I'll be waiting for you."

"Bye." I hung up. "You girls need to entertain yourselves for a while because I need to go have some fun."

"We're not fun?" Samantha asked.

"Not that kind of fun, Samantha."

"I can be that kind of fun."

"Man, scotch makes you horny, Samantha."

I left them talking and took the stairs three at a time to get to Grant. I opened my laptop and clicked my way to him. Soon his beautiful face was gracing my screen and my heart melted; and so did a few other places. Apparently just the sight of him made me weak in the knees as well as between them.

"Hello, Love. I missed your face so much."

"I missed yours, too. Now take off your clothes and let me show you just how much," I said.

"Computers can do that now?"

"Nope, but I sure can." I slowly started to remove my clothes. Grant licked his lips and began to unbutton his shirt. He couldn't seem to take his eyes off the screen.

"God, you're so beautiful, Lanie. I mean, absolutely breathtaking."

"Wait. I have more." I stripped down to nothing but my panties and sat on the edge of my chair so he had the best view of everything.

“Are you forgetting something?” He pointed at the screen and I could only guess he was trying to point at my panties.

“Oh no. I need to drive you wild before you get the whole shebang.” He smiled and then wiped his brow. He seemed to be slightly intoxicated, but that was okay, so was I. He continued to remove his clothing until he was down to his briefs. I looked over his body, drinking in the sight of him. He was perfect in every way and I thanked God he was mine.

“Tell me what you want me to do. I’ll give you whatever you want.” I gave him a sultry smile and he swallowed, exaggerating for my benefit.

“I’d tell you to touch your breasts, but I don’t want you to cover them up with your hands. Tell me how badly you want me and then show me where.” He grinned.

“Baby, I want you so badly. I need to feel your lips right here …” I pointed to my neck. “And here …” I ran my hand down to my breasts.

He groaned softly and moved closer to the screen.

“More, please, Lanie.”

“But I want you most right here.” I ran my hand down my stomach and playfully pulled my panties to the side to give him the money shot. I heard him growl.

Then I heard something I was not expecting. I shot my eyes back to the screen.

“What the hell are you doing here?” Grant said toward the doorway…

Chapter 38

You're Breaking My Heart

"How the hell did you get into my room?" I grabbed my shirt and covered my breasts, not knowing who he was talking to.

"Grant, who the hell is in your room?"

And then I heard giggling. Female giggling. *Oh no, she was not in his room.* I saw Grant grab his pants and quickly try to put them back on.

"Oh no, don't put them back on; then I'll have to take them back off." It was Brianna Stone. She sounded wasted. *How the fuck did she get into his room? Did she have a key?*

"Is that Brianna? What the fuck is she doing in your room? How the hell did she get in?"

"Just a minute, Lanie. Let me get her out of here," he said quietly toward the screen.

I watched until he was out of camera view and then listened. I couldn't hear, so I turned the volume up as loud as I could. I put my shirt on in the meantime.

"Oh Grant, you're so hot with your shirt off. I just want to touch you."

"Bri, you need to leave. I'm on the phone with my *fiancé*. You have to leave."

"Well, it didn't sound like you wanted me to leave earlier," Bri cooed.

"Excuse me? What the fuck did she just say?" I was starting to get mad now.

"Lanie, please. Just one second."

“Lanie? Oh, is Lanie on the phone?” Her tone was meant to sound innocent but I could hear how fake it was.

“Damn straight I am. You’d better—”

“Lanie, I have this all under control. Bri, you need to go back to your room now. I think you had a bit too much to drink.” Grant was trying to maintain control, but I was about to lose mine.

“Oh Grant, your arms felt so good around me when we were dancing tonight.”

He had his arms around her? They danced? She was in his room earlier? I wanted to throw my computer across the room. I watched Grant and Bri pass in front of the camera. She was wearing a bathrobe and was trying to take it off. Grant was trying to push her back and keep it on her.

“Please, Bri, the bathrobe needs to stay on. You need it to go back to your room.”

“I can put it back on when we’re done.”

“Oh, we’re done. Now please, be a good drunk girl and close up your robe and head on back to your room. Now.” Grant sounded annoyed, yet calm. I was happy to see he wasn’t interested, but I was pissed to all hell she was even there and trying to put the moves on my man. I wanted to say something, but I wasn’t sure what to say.

She crossed in front of the screen and dropped her robe to reveal panties and a bra. I heard Grant gasp; then she took her bra off. *She fucking took off her bra. She was topless in front of my man!*

I saw Grant’s hand reach towards her and she grabbed it and shoved it onto her breast, giggled, and shut the laptop.

What the fuck! I grabbed my phone and headed down the stairs heading straight for the door.

“Lanie, where the hell are you going?” Samantha asked.

"I'm catching the next flight out. That bitch is in Grant's room, and the last I saw, she had nothing on except her panties. She's naked with my fiancé. I have to go … Now!"

"What the hell?" Chelsie shouted. She slammed her glass on the table.

"Lanie, you can't go to the airport like that," Samantha said pointing down at me.

I looked down and realized I hadn't put my pants back on.

"Lanie, what the hell is going on?" Samantha was alarmed and so was I. For all I knew, there was now a naked woman in my future husband's room.

The house phone rang and Chelsie picked it up.

"Hello?" She paused. "Grant, what the fuck is going on over there? What the fuck?" Chelsie was in protect-Lanie-mode. She held the phone out to me so I grabbed it.

"Lanie? Everything is fine. She's gone now."

"Everything is fine? There was a naked woman in your room and you touched her."

"Not by choice, Lanie. She's gone. She had way too much to drink. I'm surprised she didn't puke on the laptop."

"You danced with her?"

"Lanie, she danced with every single guy there."

"Well, last time I checked, you're not exactly single. What the fuck, Grant?"

"Lanie, you listen to me. I have no control over that woman. I told her the deal was off if she was going to continue to act like a slut in my room."

"Why the hell was she in your room? How the hell did she get in? And that deal is off already."

"Apparently she's a very important guest to this hotel. She had them make an extra key to my room. I just called the front desk and told them to reprogram my door. They're coming back with a new key now."

"I'm coming out there, tonight. Chelsie will drive me to the airport."

"Lanie, there's no reason to do that. I mean really, there isn't. By the time you get here, I'll be on my way home to you. Where I want to be."

"You touched her breast. You saw her naked."

"Lanie."

I immediately thought about how he must feel about what he saw me do. I shut my mouth and the tears began to flow freely. I was bawling.

"Lanie, please, don't cry. You're breaking my heart. I would never do anything to hurt you. I'll leave right now and we can forget this whole deal. I don't care. Let the company fold. We have enough to live comfortably for the rest of our lives."

His words bore into me. I knew he loved me. If I said yes, he'd be on the next flight home. I was just about to say yes when my cell phone rang. I grabbed it and looked at the number. I had no idea who it was.

"Grant, don't go anywhere. Talk to Chelsie." I handed Chelsie the phone and she immediately ripped into Grant for not letting me travel with him.

"Hello?" I answered my cellphone.

"Lanie? This is Brianna Stone. I wanted to apologize whole-heartedly for what just happened." Her words were slurred and she was crying.

"You have a lot of fucking nerve calling me, let alone what you did tonight!" I spat at her. "I don't know who the fuck you think you are, but what you did was so out of line. And I couldn't care less if you sign the contracts tomorrow. I don't care about your business that much."

"I completely understand. But I need your business. My company will fall apart if I don't get this contract signed and my father will kill me. I'm so sorry. I didn't realize how in love with you Grant is. All men cheat. Please, is there anything I can do to make this better? I need this partnership. Please, Lanie, you're my last hope."

I thought about what she was saying. I could make this bitch pay by fucking her entire world up right now. I listened to her beg me through her tears.

"I'm an ass for what I did. Please, Lanie, please. I'll double the production; I'll double all the numbers. Anything you want. I need to have this contract go through. Please, my father will kill me. He'll beat me. Do you hear me?"

Now I felt a twinge of sadness for her. I didn't like this woman at all, but I wasn't going to be the reason her father beat her.

"Listen to me, Brianna. I have no intentions of ever liking you, but I refuse to have it on my shoulders that your father hurt you. Why don't you call the police on his ass? I'll do it."

"No. Don't do that. Please. You don't know who you're dealing with. He's a very powerful man."

I had heard about her father. He was a legend in the industry. He was ruthless if you got on his wrong side, but if he cared for you in any way, he would make sure everything you wanted would happen. I didn't want to mess with him. He was a force to be reckoned with. He could tear our company apart piece by piece. I thought about Jack, Jennifer and Joe. What would they do? What would they think?

I took a deep breath in.

"Brianna. I'll allow this deal to move forward. But you will never, and I mean never, work directly with Grant again without me being present. Do you hear me? Never. And we will be doubling all the numbers."

"Deal. Oh, Lanie, thank you. I'm so sorry. I never should have done that. Never. I'm so sorry. Thank you. Thank you!"

"One wrong move, do you hear me? One. Just one and I'll go to your father myself. Do you hear me, Ms. Stone? You're on my shit list. Big time!"

"I know and I deserve it. It was terrible what I did. Grant is just so … hot and perfect. But I understand he's yours. I do. I'll do anything you want. Please don't call my father. Please."

She continued to sob. It was pathetic, really. A rich little brat who was used to getting whatever she wanted. But she was not getting Grant. That bitch would never be able to have him because he loved me. He only wanted me.

"Fine. I'll hold off on calling him. You are to stay in your room for the rest of the night. You are not to contact Grant at all. He'll meet you at the web conference tomorrow. If I see you within three feet of him, I will make that phone call. And believe me, you don't want to fuck with me. I'm sure you've already seen what I'm capable of."

"Yes. Yes, I saw. I promise. And for any future dealings, I'll deal directly with you. Not with Grant, ever again."

"Good night, Ms. Stone."

"Good night, Lanie. I'll see you at the web conference." I hung up and put my hand out for the other phone.

"Grant?"

"Lanie, what happened? Who was that on the other phone?"

"That would have been your attacker."

"Is the entire deal off? Can I come home now?"

"No. The deal is still on. But Dane will need to work overnight with the lawyers to redraw the contracts. Ms. Stone's agreed to double what she was paying us before. The contracts will be signed tomorrow as planned, and you'll be on the first flight home right after."

"I knew I shouldn't have come. Dane should've handled this entire deal."

"No, I should have. Neither of you can apparently work with our female clients. I'll handle them all from now on. Dane's too much of a player and you're way too pretty."

I heard Grant laugh softly.

"Now, I need to see how badly you want only me. So get the fuck back on your laptop and be prepared to make it worth my while." I was totally in work mode. I heard Grant say, 'Fuck, yes.' and he hung up.

I smiled at my girls, and skipped up the stairs, singing something about how I was going to get some.

Grant was already connected to my computer, one of the great things about sharing all our personal pass codes. I couldn't see him.

"Grant? Where are you?"

I saw him come into the camera's view. He had a towel in his hand.

"Did you start without me?"

"No, Love, I had to wash my hand with scalding water since it touched another woman."

My man knew what I liked to hear. He held his hand up and it was bright red. He wasn't kidding; it looked like he'd burned it.

"That hand still going to work? You owe me some hot webcam loving," I purred.

"I owe you anything you want," he growled back.

"Take off all your clothes. Now! Do it. Wait, first go put the chain on your door."

He smiled and got up to bolt the door. Then he reached over, put music on, and lowered the lights.

"What are you doing?"

"Watch."

He began to dance around the room, swaying his hips and trying to look sexy. It almost looked humorous, but damn, even trying to be funny, what he was doing was hot as hell. He began to do his best striptease. I laughed and clapped for him and made sure to make lots of whoot-sounds for him. His face turned slightly red and he threw his briefs towards the laptop, covering the webcam. I booed and hissed. He laughed and fumble with something and then the briefs were gone, restoring my view.

I got an eyeful because his man parts were right in line with the camera. I cheered as he danced away from the camera and gave me the booty shot of all time. I could've slid right off my seat then and there he had me so riled up for him.

"Oh, Baby, if I could I'd give you a dollar right now …"

"Apparently you gave me millions of dollars, since you're a shark when it comes to the media and negotiating our deals."

"Holy shit, Grant. I have to call Dane and tell him about the contracts. They have to work on those tonight."

"Seriously? You'd rather go call Dane than see this?" And he turned so I could see his hot ass again, and he flexed his cheeks extra special for me.

"Mmmm. Well, we've done worse during phone calls, have we not?"

"Why yes, we have."

I grabbed the phone and dialed Dane.

"Hello?"

"Dane, you have to call the lawyers for an emergency meeting. We have to redo the contracts."

"Why? What the fuck happened?"

"Well, I was on the computer with Grant …"

I saw Grant shake his head no.

"Um, and Bri wanted to speak with me."

"Bri? You're calling her Bri now?" *That's right Dane, Brianna Stone was my bitch now. I could call her anything I damn well pleased.*

"Why yes. You don't call her that? Anyway, I basically talked her into doubling the amounts she was going to pay us."

Grant sat down in front of the camera. He smiled quite seductively at me. His eyes were heavy with lust.

"Hold on, Dane."

"What? Not now. I want to hear …" But I didn't hear what he said next. I was taking my top off for Grant, whose smirk got higher on one side of his absolutely hot fucking mouth. I licked my lips and then parted them, moving closer to the screen. He moved slightly back so I could see how happy he already was.

"Sorry. Uh, where was I?" My mind was totally focused on Grant. I looked directly into his eyes; well at least I thought I was.

"You got Bri to agree to double? That part?" Dane sounded like he was ready to screech like a little girl who just got handed a brand new puppy. He loved money.

And I loved Grant. He was all I could think about right now.

"Lanie? Are you going to leave me hanging like this?" Dane was starting to freak a bit. I rather enjoyed it.

I reached in front and unclasped my bra for Grant. He growled softly.

"Yes, I was still on fire from the press conference. I just stuck my chest out and gave it a shot." I heaved my breasts toward the screen. Grant's mouth opened in a huge grin.

"You're being serious?"

"No, I'm fucking around." I grabbed my breasts and gave Grant kissy-lips. He ran his hands through his hair while displaying a very determined look on his face. I smiled devilishly at him.

"Lanie, what are you doing?" Dane said.

I suddenly felt weird that Dane was in the room with us, so to speak. I think Grant did, too. He smiled and shook his head.

"Lanie, go speak with Dane. You can call me back. I'm not going anywhere. And I want your full attention," he said it sexily slow.

"You're on the laptop with Grant right now? No wonder you're not paying attention to me."

Grant waved and turned off the webcam. I let out an annoyed huff and told Dane an abridged version of what we had to do tonight.

"Lanie, you need to be in the meeting."

"No. No, I do not. And I have a phone call I need to finish. I've barely spoken to Grant since he left and I want to do that, not sit in a meeting with a stuffy old law team. That's your gig. You owe me."

"Fine, but at least be on the first ten minutes of the call so we can hear what we need to do. Okay?" I huffed again.

"Give me fifteen minutes. I'll call in to the conference line."

"Ten. Ten minutes."

I called Grant from my cell.

"Grant?"

"Well, this isn't going to be as much fun, unless you plan on talking very dirty to me."

"I'd love to, really, but I need to sit in on the first ten minutes of the lawyer conference call."

"Lanie, please. I'm aching for you right now. It's very hard."

"How hard is it?"

"That's very hard, too. Just thinking of you. Seeing your skin. You have me a mess right now and you can't leave me like this."

No. I didn't want to leave him all hot and bothered, slightly intoxicated with a flasher in the same hotel. Although I didn't think Brianna Stone would be an issue anymore. I turned my computer on and could hear his computer receive the prompt.

I could see his beautiful face on my screen. His eyes seemed to sparkle at me and were full of want and need. I wished I could touch him so I reached out and touched the screen. He smiled at me.

"Lanie, fuck. I need you so badly."

I felt his need. Being away from him made me hurt for him, too. The lawyers could wait.

He was wearing his robe.

"I want to see you, all of you."

He responded easily and opened his robe for me. *Yes. He was so fine.* I eyed every inch of him. His muscular body sent a shiver through me. I removed my shirt yet again, and then everything else for him.

"Lanie, you're so beautiful."

"I want to make love to you so badly," I said softly. "I ache for your touch."

"Touch yourself for me. Please. I can't do it. Close your eyes and pretend it's my hands on you."

I quickly complied wanting to give him anything he requested.

"Lanie, I want more. I want it all."

So I gave him what he asked for. I heard him groan as he watched me pleasure myself for him.

"It's been too long without your touch," I managed to squeak out.

"I want to watch you; hear you, Lanie."

"Oh God, Grant, I wish you were here," I breathily moaned.

"Lanie, so hot, so beautiful. Look at me, Baby."

Our eyes were locked. I'm not sure how long we were like that, but I snapped out of it as soon as my cell began to vibrate.

"We could've used that about three minutes ago," he laughed.

"Funny. You could've just called me over and over again."

"We'll have to remember that for next time."

"No next time. You're never leaving me again and from now on you and I are travel buddies."

"I like that and agree completely. Now you better go take that call; then call me right back."

"Okay, Babe. I love you so much."

"I love you too, Lanie. Don't you ever forget that. No matter what, nothing will ever change that."

I smiled and gave him a wave before closing my screen and dialing in.

* * *

I finished the call an hour later and quickly dialed Grant as soon as I hung up.

Hi, this is Grant Bennett. I'm not available. Leave me a message.

Damn. He must have fallen asleep.

"Hey, babe. You must have been tired. I am, too. But call me if you wake up. Really, don't worry about what time it is cause it's my turn to see more of your sexy self. Okay? I love you. Can't wait till you get home."

I headed off to sleep with Grant replacements: my cell phone and Woof. Sleep would close the gap a little more until Grant and I could be together sooner.

* * *

I literally jumped out of bed at six even thought I'd hoped to sleep until noon so the call would happen and Grant could be on the first flight back. I headed down to make coffee first. It was too early to call Grant, so I figured I'd shower and be ready, wanting look especially hot today to give Brianna Stone an idea of what Grant had waiting at home for him.

The girls were gone, probably sleeping over at Grant's house. Well, I did leave them for websex and lawyers.

I chose a cute little buttercream-colored sheath dress. I'd wear my hair down, with loose curls, and sexy. I chose a cute little pair of matching shoes, not that they could see my feet, but they made me feel sexy as hell. *Hey, I was dressing for Grant, too.* I wanted him to drool over me right in front of her. I jumped in the shower, jumped back out, and got myself all prettied up.

I had no idea what to do with myself. Checking the time I saw it was now seven thirty. *Oh good.* Killed an hour and a half. I ran down to make coffee and called Grant.

The phone rang three times with no answer. I waited for his voicemail to pick up. Then the phone clicked on and then disconnected. *What the hell?*

I dialed again and it went right into voicemail. *Wait. How could that happen?* It was just ringing. Someone picked up and hung up …

Chapter 39

It's Time for the Web Conference

… *Who the hell hung up on me?* I ran upstairs to my computer and tried to get ahold of him there. Nothing. My prompt was never answered. Maybe I just missed him. He couldn't be mad at me. I felt my stomach knot. There was that bad feeling again. I had to get this out of my head. He did nothing wrong. His plane was fine. He thwarted the advances of that bitch, and now another day of not answering me. Maybe they were preparing for the meeting. The lawyers had sent over all the new contracts this morning and I'd emailed him our notes. I'm sure her law team was mulling them over. I called Dane.

"Hey, Lanie. You did some amazing negotiating last night. The lawyers were really impressed with that and the press conference. You're a rock star."

"Yeah, thanks. What time is this webcast?" I asked.

"You *know* it's at ten. You programmed it into your phone. It's in your calendar."

"Right."

"What's wrong with you? What happened last night? Are you going to tell me?" He sounded slightly panicked.

"No, it's not important. Where should we do the call?"

"Your office. You have the biggest screen."

"Fine, get your ass over here then."

"Lanie, it's not for another two hours. You can't reach Grant again, can you?" *Damn. I might be mad at Dane, but he knew me too well.*

"No. I can't." I felt tired. I felt nervous.

"Damn, I can't wait for Grant to get home so you'll be normal again."

"Normal?"

"Well, yeah, Lanie—you've been a wreck since he left."

"I'm sorry. I just want him to come home."

"It's only a few more hours. Want me to check the airlines to see what time his flight is? Will that make you feel better so you can focus on work?"

"Yes, please." I felt weird asking Dane for help, but I'd take whatever I could get.

"Fine. I'll look it all up and then I'll come over. Coffee?"

"Made. Just get over here."

"Okay, Ms. Demanding. Be there in like ten."

I stuck my tongue out at the phone and hung up. Then I called Grant again. It went right to voicemail. *Damn it.* I waited impatiently for Dane. Any distraction would be fantastic.

"Lanie?"

"I'm up in the office. Grab yourself coffee and come on up."

I heard fumbling in the kitchen, more fumbling, and then footsteps coming up the stairs.

"Hey. That was some—"

"I don't care. When is his flight? I want this over already."

"His flight is at six tonight."

"The meeting is at ten. Why isn't his flight until evening? He should leave the meeting and come straight home. It's a long flight."

"Lanie, I didn't make the reservation. He'll be home by midnight or sooner."

"Fine. What time is it now?"

"Jesus, Lanie. I'm not going to sit here and have you ask me the time every two seconds. Here."

He took his watch off and handed it to me. I put it on and stared at it.

"Maybe that wasn't such a good idea, either. Give it back."

"No."

"Give it to me." Dane put his hand out and smiled. Not a happy smile, it was a placating smile.

"Absolutely not. It's mine now. You can buy another one."

"Lanie, you gave me that watch for my 20th birthday."

"I'm a fucking Indian-giver. I want it back. I bought it." I smiled back, shined the watch on my shirt and then admired it.

Dane rolled his eyes and started to set up things on the computer for our webcast.

"I have no idea why you want this set up now. The meetings not for another—"

"I don't want to waste time. This is more efficient. All we'll have to do is sign in."

"You're nuts. You know that? Lately you're nutsssssss." He didn't look at me directly, but his facial expressions at the monitor showed he was kidding, and maybe just a little bit serious. He was right. I was acting certifiable lately. I had no idea why I was being so insecure. I mean really, why would Grant cheat on his brand new fiancé? I was being ridiculous.

"I'm hungry."

"Didn't have enough Crazios this morning?" Dane said, making a circular motion with his finger to the side of his head.

"Shut it, Dane. I need to do something to kill time."

"Basketball?"

"Have you seen what I'm wearing? Does this look like a basketball outfit?" I was being a snotty bitch. Better to get it all out on Dane than to be all twisted inside for the web conference.

I actually couldn't tell whether I had butterflies at seeing Grant or if I felt like ripping into Brianna Stone. I hadn't seen her except for her attempted seduction of my man. However, she was my bitch right now. Maybe I was looking at this all wrong. Maybe it was pure adrenaline that had me so anxious about this webcast. Now she would finally get to see Grant and I interact; that alone could give anyone the perfect impression we were totally connected. Then I could intimidate her. That's right. I'd put her right into her place just like before.

"How about we play war? You won't mess your pretty self up and it'll pass the time."

"You want me to play war with you? Seriously? Yeah. No. Dork."

"Did you just call me a dork? Really? Plainy Lanie?"

"You seriously did not just call me that. Daner the Wolf Trainer."

"Lanie, that's not funny. That was a serious thing. I wasn't faking."

"Right Dane, you saw giant wolves roaming around the woods. Uh huh. Sure you did. You were eight. I still say it was a German shepherd. Or maybe a coyote."

"They were ginormous wolves. I know what I saw." He truly did sound like he believed it. But he'd been telling us about it since we were little. I was sure by now he'd actually convinced himself it happened.

"Right. And it changed your life. I know. I've heard it. Repeatedly." I rolled my eyes and sighed.

"Lanie, those wolves taught me what to be in life."

"Right, cause you're so successful at everything you do." My sarcasm was dripping off the sentence. I rolled my eyes again.

"What's that supposed to mean?"

I shook my head. The list was just way too long to rattle off. There wasn't even enough time before the conference to get half way through it. So I told him so.

"Lanie, that's just wrong. I'm leaving. I'll be back later."

"No. Don't go. I was actually having fun abusing you."

"I'm sorry," he said softly.

"For what? Where did that come from?"

"I'm sorry for what I did to you and Grant. Especially you."

I just stared at him. What was he saying? I didn't know how to respond.

"I would never rape you, Lanie. Never. I'm so sorry you think that. That's almost worse than having done it, because you think I actually could do that to you. To anyone."

"Dane, what did you think?"

"I thought you wanted me. I guess I thought I could be your like, I don't know, rebound guy. Fuck, Lanie. It hurt enough to find out you thought I was Grant. But then to know you both think I raped you? I don't know what to do anymore to make it better. I want to have back what we had before, but you with Grant now. It's where you belong. Together. I know that. In the back of my mind, I always have."

"What do you mean? You always have?"

"I've known he was in love with you since the pact, the second one. That's why I made him make it. I had such a crush on you back then and knew he only ever had eyes for you the entire time. Our whole lives."

"But why? Why wouldn't you tell him it was okay? When you were with Callie; you didn't love me. Why wouldn't you want us to be happy?"

"You were my backup plan." My mouth dropped open and I my eyes widened.

"I was your fucking what? Your fucking backup plan? You thought I'd just be waiting around for you?"

"Look, Lanie, I wanted to apologize, not get you even angrier at me. Please. I just want you to know how sorry I am. I was a complete ass about it. I had myself convinced you were the one."

"Really? And dating Lori was what?"

"A time killer until you got home. But then she wouldn't leave. And she was always eyeing Grant. So we came up with that stupid fucking plan. I'm so sorry. But I never meant for you to think I raped you. Never."

"Dane. I don't really know what to say."

"You don't have to say anything. I know you hate me. You both hate me. Grant will never be the same with me again. I've ruined everything. I've destroyed our family."

And that's what started the longest conversation I'd had with Dane in a very long time. He talked about how bad he felt and I told him how I felt about Grant. Really felt all these years. We talked and time passed and we basically used all the time I was trying to kill before the meeting.

"Lanie."

"Dane, we've talked about so much my head is really spinning. No more."

"Lanie."

"No, Dane. I think we should take a break."

"Lanie, it's time for the web conference."

I looked at Dane's shiny watch on my wrist. *Yep. It was time.*

"Well, sign on already!" I had a huge grin across my face and I was pushing Dane towards the machine.

We sat in front of my computer side by side and started our end. Soon I heard a beep and I knew I'd see Grant's beautiful face in seconds and I'd be aching for him in an instant. Then they were in view, and all I could see was Grant. Smiling at me, that perfect, sultry smile. Oh God. I couldn't wait to kiss that mouth. I needed him.

"Lanie, stop fidgeting," Dane said under his breath. But I wasn't fidgeting. I was sliding on the wet spot that had formed instantaneously between my legs.

"Good morning, Lanie, Dane," Grant said smoothly. I melted. He smiled wider.

"Good morning, Grant. Oh and Brianna. Good morning." I was still having computer eye contact with Grant.

"Good morning, Lanie. Good morning, Dane," Brianna said in the most sickeningly sweet tone. I felt like I'd throw up a little in my mouth.

"Pleasure to meet you face-to-face. Grant." Dane nodded toward Grant, who in turn, nodded back.

We began discussing the details of the contract. My eyes were fixed on Grant. His, in turn, on mine. I could feel the heat between us through the monitor. It was intense.

"I sent you those files last night to your email, Grant. I tried to call you then and this morning, but all I got was voicemail. Why didn't you answer?"

"Honestly, I can't seem to locate my phone," Grant said. He instinctively patted his pockets.

"Oh. I'm so sorry. Grant, I have your phone," Brianna purred.

I immediately felt like my entire body was on fire. I tensed up and Dane turned to look at me. I gave Grant a what-the fuck look.

He looked at me, and then at Brianna, and then back to me.

"You have my phone?"

"You left it in my room last night."

I felt myself breathe in and then hold my breath. My stomach knotted and I looked at Grant. He looked at her strangely. I couldn't exactly get what the look meant. I crossed my arms and pursed my lips. Grant cleared his throat and Dane followed suit.

"Well, let's continue. We don't have all day," Brianna sang.

Dane took control of the meeting and I just stared at Grant. He just stared back, and then at his feet. Brianna and Dane finished, and then it was time for them to sign. I said nothing. Grant hadn't said much, either. Grant and Brianna stood side-by-side. She bumped his shoulder, turned, and giggled at him. Grant smiled and then handed the pen to Brianna. "Ladies first."

She took the pen way too slowly out of his hand, her fingers brushing lightly over his. She kept eye contact with him with a small smirk on her face. I just glared at them. She signed her name, turned toward him and handed the pen back to him. He hesitated. What the hell was that? He took the pen and signed the contract.

"Great. Done deal. We're all finished up here. Now we have a lunch date ..."

"Appointment, a lunch appointment. Not a date," he said, looking at me. I felt the very edges of my lips turn up. In that same instant, it flashed through my mind why he wasn't flying home right after the meeting. He was staying to have lunch with her. That just burned me up.

"Brianna, it was a pleasure working with you and we're extremely pleased to be entering into this venture with your company." Dane was all business. He sensed my agitation and actually put on a very professional cool exterior with Ms. Stone. Was he showing some kind of protectiveness for me?

It didn't matter. She's the one who needed the protection. I was ready to destroy her. Her call was nothing but a lie. She was still making a play for Grant.

"Ms. Stone. Grant, what time can I expect you to be home?" I said in my sweetest voice. Emphasizing the word home.

Grant took a seat on the couch in front of the monitor. He looked at Brianna. "Was your assistant able to move my flight time up?"

"Oh, I'm so sorry. I completely forgot about that. I just had her book lunch." Brianna played stupid.

"Seriously? I was very specific that I wanted to leave right after the meeting." Grant sounded slightly peeved.

"Oh, I'm so sorry, Grant." She reached out and touched my future husband.

"Lanie, I'm sorry. I won't be home until around midnight." Grant looked genuinely disappointed. I knew I was.

"Now don't you worry, Lanie. I'll make sure to put him on a plane home to you once I'm done with him," she said.

"Excuse me?" I was ready to put that bitch back in her place.

"I think we can end this web conference and Lanie and Grant can pick this up privately," Dane interrupted.

"I think that's a great idea. Okay, signing off now. Goodbye." Brianna hit a button, but they were still there.

"Grant?" He didn't seem to hear or see me, but I could see and hear them.

"Brianna, what was that all about?" Grant said. She moved closer to him and around the back. She began to rub his shoulders. He turned to look at her.

"Grant, last night was just so sweet." She cupped his cheek and turned his head toward her and kissed him. Her head was in the way, so I couldn't see what Grant was doing, but he hadn't moved. *Was he kissing her? Was I actually seeing this?* I turned to look at Dane, who was slack-jawed, staring at the screen. I looked back and started to hit buttons, saying "Grant" over and over again. Brianna turned around and touched something on the desk. Suddenly I could see Grant's face turn toward the monitor and pale.

"Lanie," was all he could get out.

"What the hell was that?"

"Lanie, how much did you see?"

"Everything I needed to." I felt the tears begin to well up in my eyes. I was going to start bawling any second. Uncontrollably. I backed out of the room holding my breath, never taking my eyes off Grant.

I ran. I ran out of the house and just kept running until I was looking out over the cliff. My whole world was crashing in. *I was right.* This trip was something bad. After everything Grant and I had gone through in such a short amount of time; it all crashed down in seconds.

I laid down on the edge and just looked at the rocks below, the waves crashing over them. I didn't think. I just looked. I'm not sure how long I was there. I heard Dane walk up at some point, but he didn't stay. He placed my cell phone down beside me and walked quietly away. I didn't touch it. I didn't look at it. I just continued to stare at the angry ocean.

The phone began to vibrate. I didn't move, but glanced to look at it. Dane had conveniently positioned it so I could see it was Grant calling. I turned away. It stopped. Moments later, it vibrated again. I ignored it, knowing if I talked to him now, I would just say something terrible. I didn't know what had happened. It could have been all her. *That bitch. I was so going to fix her wagon. She had it coming.* The phone continued to vibrate on and off. I was finally resolved to answer. I sat up and grabbed the phone. Thirty-three missed calls. *Wow.* I just picked up and said nothing.

"Lanie? Are you there?" Grant sounded frantic. I hesitated.

"Yes." It was all I could muster.

"It's not what you think. I swear. I promise. Lanie, you have to listen."

"I will. But not like this. You need to get your ass home, now."

"I'll be home right after this lunch."

"No, Grant. You'll be home on the next fucking flight. You're not having lunch with that woman. You can call a limo to take you to the airport. Get home."

"I'll leave for the airport right now," he said quietly.

"Fine. Bye."

"Lanie, I love you. Please. Say it." I was quiet. I loved this man, but I couldn't say the words I was so mad at him.

"Lanie, please, Love."

"I love you." I hung up and began to cry. I heard footsteps coming up behind me. It was Chelsie.

"Hey, Babe. Bad day?" She sat beside me so close we were touching.

"Bad couple of days. Can we rewind?" I said through tears.

"Sorry, Hun, can't do that. But this too shall pass. That I can promise you."

"Oh? Really? How's that, Chelsie?" I cried at her.

"Lanie, Grant has spent his entire life only wanting you. Why would he ruin that now you're finally his? I can tell you, that man has never loved anyone but you. Don't you get that?" Chelsie reached out and tilted my head towards hers so she could look me in the eyes. Chelsie was no bullshit. That meant she truly believed it.

"But he kissed her. I didn't see him pull away or push her off. And why was he in her room last night? I know he and I spoke on his cell phone last night and then we were on the webcam. He had to have gone to her room after that."

"Or maybe she was lying." Chelsie spoke of Brianna with complete distain in her voice.

"Why didn't he deny it, then? He just gave her this weird look."

"I'm sure he has an explanation. Looks can be deceiving. You should know that first hand, right?"

Ouch. She did it again. That stung. She was right. But that was before and this was now. In fact, that was also after he was caught with another woman. Now my rational mind thought about how this was probably the same thing. Grant and I had bad luck with this incriminating shit. But then my crazy side thought about how maybe Dane was right. That Grant was a womanizer and our whole relationship had only been about the chase.

Chelsie watched me, and eventually picked up my left hand and stared at my ring. She moved it back and forth in the sun, watching it sparkle. So did I. So sparkly and pretty.

"He's a great guy, Lanie. He wouldn't have put this ring on your finger if he didn't mean it."

"How did you know about all this? Did Grant call you?"

"No. Dane did."

"Dane called you? Why?"

"He said you needed me. He told me what happened. He was actually quite compassionate and concerned—for both of you! He seemed a little disturbed by the whole thing. It took lots of guts for him to call me. What's the turnabout?" Chelsie sounded completely mystified. She didn't sound annoyed and she sounded like she believed him.

"He apologized to me, for everything. We talked for hours this morning about it all. He even told me about all these conversations he and Grant had about me all these years. It was really a very deep and exhausting talk." I truly felt differently about Dane now. He was himself again, the old Dane I loved.

"Well, all I can say is keep him at arm's length and be careful. The way he's been lately, I wouldn't trust him. He has to prove himself again, Hun, but he seems to be on his way."

"Yeah. But nothing is ever perfect for me for long. Just when I thought I could be on my way to happily ever after, this happened." I began to cry again. My heart was breaking.

"Lanie, you're jumping to conclusions. You don't know what happened. Give him a chance to explain everything first. This could all be a waste of both of your hearts feeling a little bit damaged right now. You think he was with another woman and he thinks you don't love him anymore."

"What? I thought you didn't talk to him."

"I didn't. Samantha is on Grant duty. Dane called her, too. I think he called Jennifer as well, in case she needs to fly out here and salvage this."

"What? He called Jennifer? She's probably freaking out. Does my dad know?"

"Oh please, Lanie. Dane showed his girly side, he didn't involve the men-folk." Chelsie rolled her eyes. Now she was talking like Dane was one of the girls. *Great.*

"What time does Grant get home?"

"I don't know. It was supposed to be midnight because he was going to stay to have lunch with her. But then we spoke and I kind of told him to get his ass home now."

"Smart girl. I would have done the same thing. And if you think for one minute if I were in your situation Steve would be innocent before proven guilty, your nuts. His ass would be in so much trouble. You have every right to be feeling the way you are. I'm just saying."

"Can you call Samantha and tell her to find out when he'll be here? I need to clean myself up a bit."

"Oh Honey, of course you do. You need to look like one pissed off hot bitch when he gets here. He needs to grovel at your feet. Kiss your toes even, or maybe a few other places as well. I'd say he should buy you some jewelry, but you just got that rock, so nothing else might be as impressive. Maybe a new car?"

"Chelsie, the only thing I want is for this new nightmare to be false. I've about had it with all this drama. I just want Grant and I to be together and happy, with no one trying to steal one of us away. I mean, really? Have you ever seen as much crap as he and I have gone through?"

"No. But you're both hot pieces of ass, so who could blame anyone for wanting either of you? Hell, Samantha hit on you last night. Geez." Chelsie shook her head and stood up. She held her hand out to me and helped me to my feet. I loved the idea that Chelsie and I would actually be related. It's not like we didn't already feel that way, but it would be all official-like.

As we headed back to my house, I saw Dane waiting outside for us.

"Hi, Chels. Thanks for coming so quickly. Lanie, are you doing any better? Did you get a chance to talk to Grant?" he asked. He really was sounding sincere.

"Yes. Just for a minute. Nothing is better. He's on his way home." It felt weird to be sharing things with Dane. He was on my side now, or so I thought.

"Well, I talked to him. And he is really crushed right now. All he wants is for you to believe in him. Have faith that he wouldn't hurt you." Dane eyed me carefully for my reaction. Chelsie and I just gaped at him.

"Seriously? You're trying to help Grant?" I said. *Well, wasn't this a total change of the tides?*

"Lanie, looks can really be deceiving. I mean, look at what he saw. He saw you and me, well, you know. You just saw them kiss. We were way further than that. And he trusted in you, believed in you. Even though I wasn't a big help … well you know. And you owe him that now. I mean you were harder on him about seeing Lori undressed than he was at you for … well you know."

"Okay, Dane, I know. I get it. Why do all these women just take their clothes off in front of Grant? Who the hell does that? I mean, he is absolutely gorgeous, but that's not the point. He kissed her back."

"Lanie, you don't know that. You have to trust him. Trust is one of the most important things in a relationship. Without trust … there is no relationship. What's the sense of being together then?" Dane put his hand on my shoulder.

"I agree with Dane here. Oh my God, did I just say that?" Chelsie quickly pretended to stick her finger down her throat, and then she smiled and punched Dane in the arm. He smiled back and bumped his shoulder to hers. Well, in the past few hours I'd seen some things I never thought I would. Chelsie and Dane being all sweet to each other, and Grant kissing another woman, and apparently spending time in her room late at night. And that's when I started crying again.

"I'm sorry. Is seeing Dane and I being nice to each other too much for you? It's making me a little sick myself. Quick Dane, do something stupid so I can kick your ass!" Chelsie jumped at Dane and he played scared shitless. Well, maybe not all play. A professional wrestler would be afraid of Chelsie on a bad PMS day.

"How about you guys call Samantha now. Find out when Grant is going to be home."

"Sure thing." Both Chelsie and Dane spoke in unison and both had their phones out.

"You know what, Dane, I like you as one of the girls." She winked at him. Dane actually looked touched.

"Hey Samantha. What's Grant's ETA?" I watched as Chelsie's eyes shifted from me to Dane and then back to me. "I see. I'll tell her. Did he say anything else? Okay. Bye, Sis. Keep me in the know. Better call the boys here. We should all be here tonight."

"Chelsie, what's going on? When will he be home?" I whispered.

"Well, here's the thing about that …

Chapter 40

You Are My Life

"… His ticket was non-refundable. So, he's still on the same flight."

"What? We're made of money. Buy a new fucking ticket. Who gives a shit about losing the money on the first ticket? That's just fucking bullshit."

I was really starting to doubt why the hell Grant was being like this. Not calling. Going to her room at night after the shit she pulled. Not returning my texts. Letting her kiss him. Then not getting his in-so-much-fucking-trouble-sorry-ass on the first flight home.

"I need to go lay down. I have a splitting headache. Will you come stay with me, Chelsie, until I fall asleep?"

"Sure thing, Baby. I'll even rub your neck for you."

"Chelsie, I'll call Samantha and get an ETA on her and the boys. I'm not going to call Jennifer until after Grant gets home, as a last resort, in case it's needed. And I'll order dinner so we can make sure our girl there eats something. Call me if you need anything. Okay?" Dane was still being a good guy. Now this was the Dane I knew and loved.

"Thanks, Dane. I'll call you if anything comes up. Just text me what Samantha says. You can decide on dinner, and thank you." Chelsie reached out and touched Dane's hand when she said it. She smiled warmly at him and then turned, put her arm around me and we headed back to my house. Dane blushed.

"Hey, I'm just going to go up to the walk for a bit. Would you make tea? I feel like a nice cup of Earl Grey." My stomach was in a knot; I was cold and I just wanted something to soothe and warm me up.

"Of course. Anything you need. You want me to kick Grant's ass when he gets home, too?" Chelsie seemed to get excited at the prospect. She really liked kicking ass, I guess. *Poor Steve.*

"Thanks, but no thanks. I can kick his ass just fine all by myself. But you can watch, if you want."

I headed upstairs, changed my clothes and grabbed Woof on the way. I wished I could turn back time to the day I got home from my business trip, so Grant and I could fall in love all over again, and be happy. I certainly would do a few things differently if I had the chance to do it all again. When I got to the walk, I sat in my comfy papasan chair and stared out at the ocean.

"Mom, are you there? Cause I really need you right now."

Tap. Tappity Tap.

"Thanks, Mom. I just needed to know. I'm so upset and confused. I just want to stay here and know you're with me."

Tappy Tap Tap

I felt weak, becoming suddenly exhausted. I closed my eyes and drifted off to the sound of soft tapping. I dreamt.

Grant and I stood on the cliff together. He faced me with his back to the edge.

"Lanie, please, I can't live without you. If you're not in my life, there's no reason to live. I can't be without you. Please."

Grant's words poured out from deep inside his soul; his true feelings plain to see. His eyes showed the great pain he was in. I pulled back even though I wanted to run to him. Anguish twisted his face and I heard a whimper escape his lips.

"No, Grant. You cheated on me. You were with another woman … and we just got engaged. What were you thinking? How could you do that? I could never look at you the same." I was cold and bitter.

"I thought she was you," Grant said blankly.

I just gaped at him. How could he have just said that? My heart twisted in my chest. It felt like he was ripping it out.

"Don't … don't say that," I said under my breath, my words felt like they were choking me.

He smiled at me. It was rather creepy and distorted, and then transformed back to a loving one.

"Lanie, I love you. I would never do that to you."

"But I just heard you. You said you thought she was me." I was seriously confused.

"No I didn't," he said convincingly, like he actually hadn't or had no recollection of saying it.

"But I heard you. You … you just said it," I accused.

"Lanie, you are all I care about. Please, stay with me. Without you, I can't exist."

"I need to think this through."

"If you even question your feelings for me, then there really is nothing to think over. Your decision is made. And I can't be without you. I love you, Lanie."

With that, Grant turned and leapt off the cliff. I screamed, lunged and grabbed for him. But it was no use; he was long gone before I was even close. I threw myself onto the ground and looked over the edge, watching as he fell in slow motion. He watched me the whole time, his arms outstretched as if he was reaching to hold me. He never panicked. He just fell. Right when he was about to hit the rocks, I realized the serious end of it all. Without him, I couldn't survive. There was no turning back. There was no do-over. He was gone.

"Grant, I love you. I'll stay with you," I screamed out to him. I threw myself over the cliff's edge to be with my love forever the only way I could now.

I felt myself falling. The wind blew my hair over my face as I watched the sky above me. It was so beautiful. When I was about to hit the jagged rocks below, I felt my body jump and there was a loud bang on the wall.

"Mom? Grant?" I was in a cold sweat. My body still felt the shock of falling. I kept touching everything to make sure it was real and that falling was the dream. It made me miss Grant even more than I already did. His words echoed in my head in flashes.

I thought she was you. Your decision is made. You are my life. Please. Lanie, I love you.

I could see him falling in my head and it made my stomach turn. I needed to speak with him. I needed to touch him. I needed to feel the warmth of him so that I knew he was okay. I needed to kick his ass for not being home already.

I looked at Dane's watch. I must have been asleep for a while. It was evening. I only had a few more hours until Grant would be with me again. *But would he be with me? Could I be with him?* I was so confused. All I knew was I needed to touch him. The thought of him not being with me, just being out of my reach, was impossible for me. I was resigned to take whatever he had to give me. As long as I could have just a piece of him, my life would be complete. *Fuck that.* I wanted all of him. And I wasn't willing to share, not at all, ever.

I picked Woof up and carried him downstairs with me. Everyone was sitting in the kitchen or the living room, talking, and they all stopped and gave me a sympathetic stare. I lowered my gaze and headed toward Chelsie and my tea, which was probably cold by now.

"Hey, Sweetie, did you get any sleep? Do you feel better? Not sure why I asked you, because I am sure you don't," Chelsie said, handing me my cup.

The tea was still hot. I took a sip and burned my tongue. It actually felt good. Not in an S&M kind of way, it just made me feel awake and out of the dream. I sipped my tea while everyone quietly regarded me.

When I say everyone, I meant it. Steve, Chelsie, Samantha, Dylan, and Dane were all gathered there, watching me. I felt like an idiot, especially with all the perfect couples there. Nothing like what Grant and I had been through lately ever happened to any of them. Everything was always so perfect. The tears began to well and I felt my breath hitch in my throat.

Within seconds, everyone was around me, patting my back or trying to hold a hand. I felt loved. Just not from the person I wanted it from most.

"When, Samantha?" I said glumly.

"I would say in about two hours. His plane is in flight as we speak. He'll be here soon, Lanie, and then we can put all of this behind us. Everything is going to be okay. I promise. Now I'm going to make you some toast with butter." Samantha hugged me and then moved aside for Dylan and Steve, so they could make me laugh.

"You know, Lanie, we could tar and feather him for you," Steve joked.

"More like cover him in chocolate hazelnut spread and then roll him in sandwich cookie crumbs. Hey, that almost sounds good."

I shot Dylan a look and then couldn't help but giggle, but then thought of those two nights and suddenly I was in tears again.

"Oh no, please don't cry. I just hate it when girls cry. That's why Chels gets everything she wants. On with the waterworks and I just can't help but give in." Steve looked concerned.

We all looked at Chelsie.

"You cry? Is that even possible?"

"Steve, shut up. You're going to ruin my bitchy persona." She punched Steve in the arm; he didn't even flinch. That man was a solid wall of muscle. *Muscle.* I thought about Grant's body and how badly I needed to feel it pressed up against mine. I thought about making love to him. I thought about Brianna, topless in front of him, her lips on his. My stomach began to burn and I felt the stress of it all flood over me again.

"Earth to Lanie. Are you there?" Dylan whispered to me. I turned to look at him and the tears started again. *What the hell was with me? I was like a water fountain.*

He put his arms around me and I buried my head into his shoulder. He held me close and tight. I cried hard. Everyone just stood around me, silent, except for Dylan, who continued to hold me while rubbing my back. He whispered how it would all be all right. He stroked my hair. Dylan was a good buddy. I loved him like a brother, and there was something about him that just made everything feel better. He was very calming.

We were all huddled together when I heard the front door. Everyone turned and Grant stood there. He dropped his bags but didn't move. He looked disheveled and tired, and his eyes were red. No one said a word and no one moved.

Tick. Tock. Tick. Tock. Tick. Tock. Tick. Tock.

I could hear Dane's watch like it was on a loud speaker. I couldn't hear my heart beating. It had stopped. I wasn't sure whether it was seeing him in front of me, how drop dead gorgeous he looked even tired, or my fear of what was coming next.

"Welcome home, Grant," Dane said, and he walked over to him and gave him a pat on the back that was more like a push toward me. Grant looked at Dane, his eyes pleading for something to let him know what my demeanor would be. Dane nodded to him.

Grant turned and looked at me. Again with the fucking tears. As soon as Grant saw my eyes tear up he began to move slowly toward me, at first. Then he moved much faster. My perception was so off it looked like he was down a long hallway and would never get to me.

The others all parted like the Red Sea. Dylan and Steve flanked my sides. Grant stopped right in front of me and looked down. He had the same look on his face he did in my dream. He was pained. I felt my lip quiver and I bit it to make it stop. I didn't want him to see me falter. I didn't want him to see me upset. I wanted him to see me angry for what he'd done. But I just didn't have it in me. He knelt down in front of me and reached out for my hands. I pulled them back and refused to look him in the eyes.

"Lanie," his voice was weak and hoarse. I didn't respond. I felt Dylan elbow me in the ribs, so I looked at Grant's knees. "Lanie, Love, please. Look at me. All you have to do is look at me and you'll know," he pleaded. I still couldn't speak. Grant looked to the others for help, but no one had any idea what to do. They looked back and forth at each other and then shrugged their shoulders.

"Please, Baby. I love you, only you. I need you. Please don't turn away from me. Please. All I wanted was to get home to you."

"That's bullshit, Grant! If that were true, you would have called me. You would have kept in contact with me as much as you could. You wouldn't have gone to her room and on a date with her. Danced with her. Kissed her. You would've been here hours ago. But no, you stayed there with that bitch. I don't believe you." My voice was bitter like in the dream, sharp and angsty. I pulled away from him even more. Grant recoiled from my words. He shrunk. I swear to God that if I had a ruler, he'd measure at least a foot shorter. The whole room went quiet.

Tick. Tock. Tick. Tock. The watch again. I took it off and threw it at Dane.

"Hey. That's my good watch. What'd it ever do to you?" Dane grabbed the watch off the floor and put it back on his own wrist.

"Would it be okay if Lanie and I had a moment alone, please?" Grant's voice was soft and smooth, holding no emotion.

Everyone nodded and began to filter out of the room. Grant reached up and tilted my face towards his. As soon as I looked into his eyes, I began to bawl.

"No. Please don't do that. Lanie, please, I can't stand it knowing that I've caused you this pain."

"So it's true? Because you haven't denied any of it. Not one bit. You made your choice when you went to her room and when you kissed her. You didn't choose me. I would always have chosen you. There's nothing more to say here," I muttered under my breath. I reached down and removed my engagement ring from my finger and held it out to him. "This doesn't mean anything to you. I can't wear it anymore. This is a promise, one you obviously really didn't want to make. There's no reason for me to have this." I was staring at the ring when I said it. I felt like it was the end. I was so hurt and angry I wanted to break something.

What I broke was Grant. He collapsed in front of me, throwing himself at my feet and wrapping his arms around my legs. He broke out into loud sobs and spoke in gasps of words. "No. Please, Lanie. No. Don't." No man should ever cry like that. I felt my heart shatter with his. He stood up and pulled me with him. He wrapped his arms around me and cried into my hair. I felt my body lean into his. The desire to kiss him was undeniable. He felt so good. I still loved him and wanted him. It was him who chose another woman. I refused to hold him back. My arms hung limply by my sides and I turned my face away from him. I still held the ring in my hand, but it felt foreign to me. It wanted to be back on my finger.

"Please, Lanie, just hear me out. You have every right to be mad. I … I can't deny anything." He hung his head when he said it. I felt my face flush and my body go ice cold. All this time I thought he would tell me it was nothing. That nothing had happened. I was all ready to feel stupid for even accusing him, for overreacting. But here he stood in front of me, telling me he couldn't deny anything. That meant it was all true.

"So it's true?" And I began to bawl with him. "You cheated on me."

I felt my legs get weak and my head became fuzzy. *Hell, was I going to fucking pass out?* Grant's strong arms wrapped around my waist and held me steady. He pushed his body tight against mine and took a deep breath in.

"I didn't cheat on you. But I can't deny anything else you've said. I …"

"Get out! Get away from me." I pushed at him, but his arms held me in place. "Let go of me. I don't want you to hold me. I don't want you touching me or trying to comfort me."

But I did. He was the only one I wanted comforting me. The only hands I wanted on me. I felt anger, but in the same instant I wanted to feel his mouth on mine. I wanted to grab his hair and pull it hard and kiss him with all the frustration I felt. It needed to be rough and show him how hurt I was. He needed to feel how desperate I was for his love.

"Leave! I can't talk right now; I just can't. Maybe you should go talk to Samantha and Chelsie and see what they think about what you just told me. See their reaction. Just know one thing, you broke my heart, Grant. I'm truly devastated and really have no words. Please go." I turned my head away.

"Lanie, please don't say that. Please don't send me away. I can't live without you. Without you in my life, there's no reason for it." He was crying again.

His words made the blood drain from my face. It was my dream exactly. I was so afraid to let him leave, but I was so hurt. I wanted to hurt him back.

"Will you ever forgive me? Are we over, Lanie?" His eyes pleaded with me.

"I can't keep this." I held the ring out to him again.

"I won't take it back. I will only ever love you. That ring will only ever be on your finger. I won't take it. Please. Don't give it back. Please don't break up with me, Lanie. Don't leave me." He was back at my feet again. His head rested against my stomach and I felt his desperate tears start to soak through my shirt.

"I need you to leave. All I wanted was for you to come home, and now I can't even stand to be near you, knowing what you did."

"Lanie, I don't know what you're thinking. But listen to me. I can explain everything."

"But you can't deny anything. Is that correct?" I interrupted him.

He put his head down and shook it. "No, I can't deny anything you said before. I didn't call you. I didn't text you. I was in her room that night."

"And you let her kiss you. I don't think I even want to know what happened in her room."

Grant stood up to face me. He put his hands on my shoulders and spoke quietly. "I can't deny. I can only explain."

I felt my hand slap him across the face hard enough to make his head turn. His hand went up to where I smacked and he nodded. I felt terrible for striking him. Things would never be repaired now. It was over. I took the ring and placed it on the table, turned and walked out onto the terrace, shutting the door behind me. When I turned back, Grant was gone, the ring still where I had placed it.

I broke into a million pieces. The thought of throwing myself over the cliff's edge was a possibility. I climbed up on the terrace wall and looked over the edge. All I needed was a light breeze. It would be so easy to just lean over too far. I started to lean and I felt a pair of strong hands around my waist.

"What the fuck are you doing, Lanie? Are you crazy? If you slipped, you'd be a dead woman." It was Dane. He pulled me off the wall and back down to the safety of the terrace.

"I can't live without him, Dane. It's over. Without him, I'd have to leave the cliff."

"Lanie, it's not over. Everything will be just fine. Okay? You just need time to cool down and listen to him. You need to hear him out," he said, quite matter-of-factly.

"Oh? On Grant's side, are we?" I spat at him.

"There are no sides. You two are meant to be together. This is just a speed bump, is all. You'll talk tomorrow and everything will be better."

"No, it won't. It won't ever be better. He admitted it. He admitted being in her room that night. He admitted to kissing her back. I hit him." I put my face into my hands and hid from the world.

"Well, you didn't break his nose. He hit me and we're okay."

"It's not the same fucking thing and you know it. Fuck you, Dane!" Venom-filled words spewed from my mouth.

Dane took a step back and looked at me. He put his finger out to point it directly in my face. I wanted to break it.

"That man loves you. He loves you so deeply I don't think there's anyone else in the world with a love that compares or rivals his, except for one; you. Your love for him. When he came back to the house, he was destroyed, Lanie. He was dead inside. Without you … Lanie, he needs you. You need him. You two kids need to work it out." Dane was sincere. I knew after our talk things would be different, but I didn't realize how much. I looked at him with moist eyes. He pulled me into a brotherly hug and told me to suck it up and forgive Grant.

"Damn, Lanie, you even gave me a chance to talk. In fact, you've both given me chance after chance. Doesn't your soul mate deserve the same if not more?"

"I need to be alone."

"Like hell am I leaving after watching you tightrope walk the cliff's edge. No-siree-Lanie. Ain't gonna happen. If it's not me you want here, I'd be more than happy to send one of the other troops over. But you are not to be left alone right now. And neither is Grant. Not in the shape you two are in. Do you think you'd like to talk to him later?"

"No. I don't want to talk to him at all. I gave the ring back."

"Yeah, I know. I saw it on the table. Lanie, please don't let things end with him this way. I've never seen two people so made for each other."

"Then why did he want someone else? And how come you seem fine with the fact he cheated on me? Huh? Did he send you over? Get out of here. Leave!" Dane looked hurt.

"No. He didn't send me. I had to come talk to you. I owe you both. This is me trying to help you. This is me being the way I should have been this entire time. Please let me." Dane grabbed my hand and looked into my eyes. "Lanie, that man loves you. This is Grant we're talking about. You know there's some rational explanation. You just have to know."

"I don't know anything anymore. I just know my life has been hell since I've been with him."

"You don't mean that. You don't."

"I do. I want to be alone right now, Dane. I know you're trying to help, but there isn't anything you can do right now. Not for me and not for him. Nothing. There's nothing that can be done."

"Why don't you eat something? I left a plate on the table. If you want to be alone, take it to your room. But I'm not leaving. I'm making sure you're all right all night."

"Oh I'm sure that'll help things with Grant. Won't it? He was probably getting back at me anyway for what happened between us."

"Lanie, Grant asked me to make sure you were okay. He said, and I quote, 'Dane, go take care of our girl, please.' And then he started slamming shots with Dylan and Steve."

"Oh, I can see how broken up he is. He's over there partying and I'm the fool sitting here broken."

"He's not partying. He's numbing himself. And he's doing it way too fast. He's going to be sick or kill himself at the rate he's going. Steve and Dylan are making sure he does neither."

"I'm going to my room. I'm taking the plate, but I'm not promising to eat. You can stay in Jack's room or have the couch since you won't leave. Thank you, Dane. But nothing is ever going to be the same again."

I went into the house and Dane followed me. He was texting Samantha or Chelsie, I was sure. I grabbed my plate of food, water and a fork and headed upstairs. I put the tray on the bed and changed into a cotton nightgown. I shut my lights off and let the moon light the room. I looked out my window and saw Grant's light was on but knew he wasn't up there. He was downstairs getting trashed, according to Dane.

I sat and daydreamed about the night after we kissed; of all the nights when I was young and hoped he had been watching me in the window. I was lost in the moment, and when I looked back up, Grant's lights were off and he was slumped at the window, watching me. He looked sad. I felt sad.

He ran his fingers through his hair and I wished they were my fingers. The intensity of the draw I felt to him was insane. I stood up and then realized I was giving him a show with what I was wearing, one he didn't deserve. He ran his hand through his hair again and just grasped the top and held it there. I felt like I was teasing him. Maybe I was. Part of me wanted to pull the shades and the other wanted to run to him and make love to him all night.

I turned toward my bedroom, my back to him now. I peered over my shoulder and he was gone so I walked slowly to the nightstand to look at my cell phone. No texts, at least not one from him. Not one from anyone. I waited to see if he was on his way over. Why was I wasting my time? I walked slowly over to …

Chapter 41

Don't Move

… my bed and looked down at it. It looked empty, very empty. I looked back at the window. I looked at my door. I looked back at the bed. *Was I destined to be alone forever?* I would never love anyone enough to replace Grant. I would die a spinster before I would ever engage another man in my life or in my bed.

My heart ached for him, and yet my head cursed him. I turned and walked back to the window. His lights were still off and he hadn't returned to the window. Maybe he was on his way over. Maybe he was feeling as much longing as I was.

I sat down on my bed and waited for him. It would be the right thing for him to do. He should be over here begging for my forgiveness; not giving up. I would forgive him in a heartbeat. I wanted him and didn't want to be without him. I just couldn't talk to him before—I was so shocked and hurt. I know it wasn't fair of me to push him away; he had seen me having sex with Dane. Of course that was so wrong; I didn't mean to. And I didn't know what happened with him and Brianna Stone. Not exactly, but I did know he went to her room and he let her kiss him right in front of me, and he couldn't deny it. But I owed him the chance to explain. I felt terribly guilty for not letting him. Jealousy is a very ugly emotion. It makes you act irrationally.

I was convinced he was on his way to me. I laid myself down on the bed in the sexiest position I could and fixed my hair so it was splayed perfectly around my head. When he got here, I'd make sure I looked so hot and sexy he wouldn't be able to keep his hands off me. I'd show him I was the only woman he wanted. I'd show him what he'd be missing if he didn't fight for me. I'd show him how much I missed him and wanted him, too.

I waited for a while, but he never came. It just showed me how little I truly meant. If he loved me, he would have been over here knocking my door down. But he wasn't. I thought about running over there, but he was the one who needed to run to me. Maybe I had truly hurt him by pushing him away, by taking off my ring.

And that's when it hit me. I was already his for life and there wasn't anything I could do about that. It was just meant to be. So I wasn't going to sit back and let another woman take him. He was mine and I was going to fight for him. If he chose not to be with me, at least I know I did the best I could. I figured I might as well go to sleep. At least I'd be away from this nightmare. But I'd soon learn I wasn't.

I heard a sound beside my bed. When I opened my eyes, Grant was crouched at the foot of my bed watching me. He was dressed in gray suit pants, a button down shirt and a black tie. He looked so handsome. He also looked hungry and desperate. It was the only way I could describe him.

"Grant? What are you doing?" I said groggily.

"Lanie, please let me stay. I just want to be near you," he pled in a whisper.

"I don't want you to leave. I don't ever want you to leave."

A huge grin spread across his face. He started to move and then stopped and looked at me for permission. I felt my heart start to race at the prospect of him touching me and nodded quickly.

He crawled up onto my bed. His eyes pierced through me. He still looked like he wanted to eat me and I felt like prey being approached by a predator. I was unable to move and was mesmerized by his eyes but could feel him before he even touched me.

Soon he was hovering above me. I began to squirm with anticipation. Damn Grant, just touch me already! He leaned over and brought his face close to mine, just inches away. I could feel his warm, sweet breath. The smell of him intoxicated me. At this point, he could have been Casanova, visiting every woman across the land. As long as I had him for this moment, I was okay with that.

"Grant, I …"

"Shhhh." He put his finger up and touched my lips to hush me. I felt a wave of excitement go through my body. I bit my lip in the hopes of being able to taste him. My breath became quicker, deeper as my breasts rose closer to him with each inhale. I wanted to push them against him, throw my entire body against his. Ready for him I squirmed more. He noticed my anticipation and gave a sultry smirk and I melted.

"It's been too long, Lanie. I can't be without you any longer. It's like not having air to breathe. I need to touch you, to have you. Don't move." I nodded my head, wanting him to touch me. I'd do anything he requested right now.

He rested his body beside mine and reached out to touch my hair, pulling a strand of it to his nose and inhaling. His eyes rolled into the back of his head and then closed. I bit my lip, but only to keep myself from pouncing on him.

He removed his tie and ran it over my exposed skin. The tease was intense. I gave his a pleading look with my eyes, begging for his touch. He slowly reached out and touched my face with just one fingertip. He ran it down my cheek. My skin tingled everywhere he touched. I stayed very still, basking in it. His finger traced around my mouth and then my jaw line, down my neck. He ran it across my décolletage and I arched my breasts up towards him.

"No, don't move. Stay very still." My breath hitched in my throat. He traced down to my cleavage, running the tip over every curve. Back and forth he traced, from breast to breast, hovering over my heart each time he passed. I closed my eyes so I could get lost in his light touch.

"Lanie, I'm going to do something now. Please let me."

He reached out and cupped one breast, massaging it and then kissed where my heart laid beating inside my chest. That alone brought me great pleasure. It felt like we were together for the first time again. Each touch, each kiss, shot a jolt of desire through my entire body. He slid his body closer to mine so there was total contact; the heat coming off of him was intense.

"I'm going to remove your clothing now. Please don't stop me." I nodded, and he ran his tongue down my stomach slowly. It was torturous. My sex was throbbing for him. He straightened up, straddled my legs and then began to slowly remove my panties with his teeth. I could feel his breath on me. He was moving so slowly, it was driving me insane.

"Grant, oh, please touch me," I begged him, lifting my hips off the bed.

"Shhhhhh. I will. You'll have to wait," he murmured seductively.

"I've waited too long to feel you again. I can't wait anymore," I whimpered.

"No? You can't wait just a few more moments?" he teased. I shook my head slightly.

He brought his hand between my legs and began to slowly touch. I groaned at the feel of it.

"Oh. Baby, I want to feel your mouth on me."

"Oh and I want to taste you. I'm so hungry for you," he growled. I moaned in response. My man still wanted me. He could have or do anything he wanted.

"Please. Take me. Any way you want. I'll do anything you want." I sighed.

He leaned down and gently kissed my sex, then flicked it with his tongue. My hips bucked gently toward his mouth but he pulled away. I gave him my best pout.

"I want you naked first." He grabbed the front of my nightie and ripped it off of me, the fabric giving way to his strength. His frustration was showing. I began to unbutton his shirt and he stopped me. "No, Lanie. Not yet."

He sat on the edge of the bed and pulled me into his lap so my back was against him. I could feel how hard he was; it pulsed through his pants against my bottom. He took his tie and bound my wrists gently and then slipped them over his head so they were around his neck. It was hot as hell. I was bound to him. It was so loose I could easily escape, but I didn't want to. He wrapped his arms around me and began to run them up and down the front of my body, stopping at various areas to tease and fondle. I leaned my head back against him and closed my eyes and let him have his way. My fingers curled into the hair on the back of his head. He was playing with my breasts and then moved down my body to settle his hands between my legs, where he began to furiously work me. He bit and kissed my neck. Immediately, I was on the verge of an orgasm. My body stiffened against him. I turned my head to kiss him, but he didn't respond in kind. He stopped everything. I suddenly felt very exposed, completely naked while he was fully dressed. But isn't this what I wanted? Him to show me, to come to me?

"Baby, please don't stop."

"But I'm not ready to give you release, Lanie. At least, not like this." After releasing my wrists, he picked me up off his lap, then placed me on my feet, pushing me towards the window. I complied willingly.

When in front of the window, he pushed me down so that I was bent over the sill, my buttocks and sex completely exposed to him. He knelt behind me and took what he wanted. My entire body began to shudder as he dipped his tongue inside me with each pass. I was in heaven, the feeling intense. He smacked my ass and then stood up behind me, holding me in place with one hand while he undid his pants with the other.

Again I tried to turn around to kiss him, but he wouldn't let me.

"Lanie, all those nights in front of the window, watching you, your body, teasing me … this is what I wanted to do to you. For as long as I can remember, I wanted this."

With that he thrust hard inside me. He was moving at an extremely fast pace, being rough, even. I cried out in pain and tried to move, but I was pinned against the sill and he held either side of me to keep me in place. It didn't feel right, it felt degrading and wrong. After a few moments, the pain teetered on the verge of pleasure.

"Oh God, Lanie, so tight." And he continued to drive into me over and over again, until I felt his body tense. He cried out loudly as he came. He turned me around, sat me up on the sill edge and slumped his body into mine, letting the breeze coming off the ocean through the open window cool him off. He kept me pinned against him and the sill.

"Don't worry, Lover, I'm not done with you yet. I have many more things I'm going to do to you, and when I'm done, you'll get yours. Just be a good girl and I'll reward you."

I didn't like where this was going. Grant felt foreign to me. I looked at the large mirror across the room, the image of my love and I wrapped around each other stared back at me. But the image didn't seem tender or loving. I tried to tell myself to wake up, that this must be some terrible dream. I mouthed the words to myself in the mirror. Grant's body moved in front of my view, almost as if he was trying to block my mind. It was a much better sight than the one of my panic. His beautiful strong back and muscular arms around me; but this wasn't the Grant I knew and I saw in the mirror; it was a pseudo Grant.

I tried over and over again to will myself to push him away to leave the room, but Grant would lure me back to him so he could continue to ravage me. It was so easy to stay with Grant no matter how he taunted me.

If he kissed me, I would stay. If he didn't, I would leave.

"Grant, kiss me."

"No, Lanie, I can't kiss you. That would be too intimate. This isn't about love, you know that. We're just about the sex. I only kiss my wife."

"Your wife? What? What the hell are you talking about? You're not married. You're engaged to me."

"Oh, you sweet, demented little minx. You live in a fantasy world when I come to visit, don't you? I can't marry you; you know I'm already married to Brianna. But I could never give up this sex with you. So hot. So good. You have to let this little dream go."

Damn straight I have to let this dream go, because at this point I knew I was trapped inside some sick nightmare.

I willed myself to wake up. In my dream-state, I began to scream. I knew if I could just scream, I'd wake up. I had been here before. Stuck in a night terror, trying desperately to get out. I tried to move, but my arms were pinned to the bed. My body and subconscious were still in the dream, but my conscious mind was awake. I flailed and screamed further in my dream and I could feel my true body just start to respond. I couldn't tell if I were actually moving or screaming for real, until I felt hands on me shaking me awake.

"Lanie? Wake up, Lanie. Wake the hell up. It's just a nightmare."

The hands released me and I heard something click.

"Open your eyes. Open them now. Sit up." Trying to wake from a night terror was really a tough thing. My body wanted to respond, and in the dream, I willed myself to comply. But in the awake world, it wouldn't.

"God damn it, Lanie. Now you're freaking me out. Wake the fuck up."

I felt my body being dragged out of bed and again, violent shaking. Finally, my eyes started to open. My head went back and forth between the dream and consciousness.

"Come on, Lanie, you're almost there."

I felt my eyes flutter open and Dane was hovering above me. The light was blinding. My flailing arms finally listened to my brain and they shot out towards Dane's face. He swatted them away.

"What's ...what's going on?"

"You were screaming. I got here and I couldn't wake you up. Lanie, you need to go talk to Grant now. You two can't be like this anymore. You're over here freaking out in your sleep, and he's over there breaking things and trying to pack and leave forever."

"He's what? He's trying to leave? He wants to leave me again?" I was completely panicking. Partly from the night terror and partly because I believed he was leaving to be with Brianna.

"No, Lanie, he says if you won't be with him, he can't stay on the cliff anymore. He said that would be the worst torture in the world. To know he had you, ruined it, and then to see you every day. He said he couldn't do that for the rest of his life."

"Did he leave? Is he still here?"

"Oh, he's way too wasted to go anywhere. I believe Samantha tossed a sleeping pill in his last drink."

"Is she trying to fucking kill him?"

"He'll survive."

"What time is it?"

"It's 3:33 am."

"I have to go over there. I need to tell him not to leave!" I was frantic.

"That's my girl. Now GO!" Dane handed me my bathrobe when he said it. "Now maybe the rest of us can get some sleep. We've been up all night babysitting the both of you. I had the easier job. You just cried a lot in your sleep and then this night terror. Grant? He needed to be restrained by Steve and Dylan. He's been a wreck."

I didn't have time to listen why. I was already on my way down the stairs and out the front door to Grant's. I busted through the front door, and Samantha, Dylan, Chelsie, and Steve all looked up at me. Chelsie just pointed toward the ceiling. I was gone. I thought I heard Samantha giggle as I took the stairs three at a time, stumbling a few times and giving myself rug burn on one knee. I cursed but kept going.

When I reached Grant's room I was moving so fast I literally fell into it. It was a mess, pillows and books and just stuff thrown about the room. It looked like a bomb went off. Grant was lying on his bed, face down, covered in a sheet. I walked over and sat down next to him.

"Grant?" I whispered softly. I wanted to touch him, but I was afraid he wouldn't know it was me, and from the looks of his room, I didn't want to end up on the floor with the other items. I tried again.

He stirred slightly. And then I heard him whimper my name as if he didn't believe I was here.

"Grant. Turn over and look at me."

"Lanie?" he slurred. "Is that really you or am I dreaming? Oh, sweet sleep, to have you actually here with me." Then another whimper. I was actually amazed he was able to slur so eloquently. And then he passed out.

I sat there and watched him for a while. His sleep was restless and he would murmur my name here and there. I looked around the room. I got up and started to straighten it. I had at it until the room was basically back together.

I turned my attention back to Grant. *He was just so damn beautiful.* I wanted to touch him. I wanted to be against him. I headed towards the bed, climbed in beside him and shimmied my body until I was spooning him. His arm reflectively reached back and wrapped around me. I closed my eyes and rubbed my face gently against his back. I heard a sigh escape him.

“I love you, Grant. I’ll always love you. I just need to understand. And then we’ll figure this out together. I can’t be without you.”

As if I reached somewhere into his mind, he rolled over and took me in his arms. I felt so good there. Safe. Right. Whole. I didn’t want to know what happened anymore. I didn’t care and only wanted him. I felt his lips brush against my cheek and turned my head to let them graze mine where they came to rest. I stayed with him until I heard his deep breaths of slumber. I kissed him softly. It took all my strength not to slide my tongue into his mouth and arouse him in a few ways.

Instead, I let myself drift off into the soundest sleep I’d had since he left. This was my place; by this man’s side. All night long I pushed myself up against him. I was afraid to lose the contact, afraid of waking up and not finding him next to me. When the sun was just starting to light the room, still dim, so early, I felt my hair being moved from in front of my face. I kept still, but my eyes remained closed.

“Lanie, my beautiful Lanie. I would never intentionally betray you,” he whispered, as if he was planting subliminal messages into my sleeping brain.

I began to stir slowly and I heard him take a quick breath in. When I opened my eyes, he was lying next to me, his head propped up on his arm. He just stared at me. His eyes were still full of pain.

“Grant. I’m so sorry. I should’ve listened to you last night … given you a chance to explain. I love you. I trust you. It was so unfair of me to do that to you. I only saw a kiss. After what you saw—”

“No. Don’t you dare do that. Don’t compare the two. They’re nothing alike. You shouldn’t trust me. Don’t ever let a man treat you badly and take it.” His words were sharp and I recoiled from him. I just looked at him with confusion and hurt.

“I’m sorry. I’m to blame for this. This isn’t something you should just accept, Lanie. I want to explain everything and then you can decide. But just don’t forgive me. I deserve your anger.”

“Grant, what did you do?”

"Please. Let me have this moment with you. Just this one last moment like this." His eyes were moist and he looked like someone had just killed his puppy right there in front of him. I couldn't stand to see him like that, but his words were scaring the shit out of me. *Did he sleep with her? If he did, could I forgive him or would I be able to live without him? Did he even still want me?*

"Don't you want to be with me anymore? Don't you want us to be together? What you're saying sounds so final. Grant, you have to tell me what happened."

"Lanie, please," he begged. "We can talk tomorrow, just not now. We need to recover a bit before we go through all this again. The hurt. The tears. Before I break your heart all over again."

I couldn't stand it. He was killing me. But seeing his guilt and hurt, affected me so much more. I needed him.

I grabbed his face and crushed my mouth to his, sliding my tongue over his lips and then thrusting it inside. My need to feel him kiss me back was alarming. I became so desperate I couldn't hold back and was all over him. Throwing myself at him. I needed to feel his desire for me. But more than that, I needed to know it was only me he wanted.

He pushed me back. I was immediately flushed with hurt and embarrassment.

"You don't want me?" I squeaked as the tears began to form in my eyes.

"Oh, Lanie. You have to know I want you. I want to make love to you so badly, so deeply, I'd consume every cell of you down to your soul. I just don't deserve this. I don't deserve you." Again his words tore at me. He was pushing me away. He was making excuses not to touch me back.

"Are you in love with her? Is that why you won't touch me? You don't want me anymore." I blurted my fears right out.

"What? Are you insane, Lanie? How could you think that? What's wrong with you?" He laughed his words out but his entire statement sounded dark.

"Then why? Why won't you make love to me?"

"Lanie, is that what you want? To make love to me and then hear what happened when I was away? Then our lovemaking would be degrading to you. You would regret it instantly. I don't want you to feel that way. I've caused you enough pain." With that, he covered his face and turned away from me.

My heart was racing. I broke out into a cold sweat. What the fuck did he do? Now I was even more in need of his kiss, his touch. I needed to feel him inside me. I would be able to tell everything he was feeling if we were intimate. I pulled my panties off and jumped up on top of him, straddled him and began to remove my nightgown. I literally ripped it over my head. He was wearing only boxers and I could tell my body on top of him was exciting him.

"Lanie, please don't. I can't resist you. You know I can't." He reached out to touch me, but his hands just hovered oddly in front of him. He was holding himself back but I wasn't going to let that happen.

I grabbed his hands and put them on my breasts, forcing him massage them. I ground my hips against him. He would start to respond on his own and then stop. But there was one place he had no control over and I could feel that Cannoli wasn't holding back. I knew I needed to concentrate my efforts on the area beneath me, so I reached down and began to pull his boxers off.

"Lanie. Don't. Please. Oh God, Lanie."

Grant's eyes were pleading, but I wasn't able to process if he wanted me to stop or keep going. I knew what I had to do.

I ran my tongue up his thigh slowly, keeping my eyes on his face.

"Lanie. You know how I feel about that. I want your mouth on me, badly, but I will not let it degrade you."

"Shhh. Don't speak." And now I sounded like he did in my dream. This made me even more desperate. I crawled back on top of him and began to slide myself against him. The heat was so intense. He groaned softly and that's when I knew I had broken his resistance. I leaned over and kissed him, wanting his lips to respond. He didn't move. He lay underneath me like a prisoner being tortured.

"Grant, make love to me right now. And please kiss me back! Show me you still love me."

His eyes widened and his lips parted like I'd said something insulting beyond belief. He grabbed my hips and pushed me down onto him, sliding into me fast and hard. He rolled us over and pulled me so close to him I wasn't sure how we'd be able to move together. I wrapped my legs around him and pulled us closer still. It was like we were trying to pull the other inside.

He covered my face and neck in kisses while he slowly made love to me, pushing deeper inside of me than I thought possible. I felt like he was trying to reach my heart. I pushed back. I wanted it; wanted him to wash any remnants of her off of him with my body. He crashed his mouth over mine and thrust his tongue deep inside. We were totally connected. We had become one. We became feverish; all our emotions poured out into each other. I felt his need and desire for me along with a tear on my face. Now I could feel his love for me, too.

"Babe, what's this all about?" I said when I reached out to wipe another tear away.

"I'm so afraid this is going to be the last time we make love, Lanie. My heart is so full for you and I'm so scared you'll never put that ring back on your finger. I'm sorry I'm being so emotional. I just love you that much. To lose you …would be unbearable." He was tormenting himself, punishing himself for whatever had happened. I began to feel apprehensive about what the truth held and was afraid he had taken things all the way with her.

I wanted to comfort him and for him to know that everything could be worked out, that it would be. I pulled his face to mine, looked him in the eyes and kissed him deeply. We kept the eye contact. I felt him sigh into my mouth and I inhaled his breath deep into my lungs, wanting to breathe him into my soul.

We made love slowly and passionately now. Touching everywhere; not able to get enough of the other.

"Lanie, I don't want this to end. Not ever." Just his statement alone threw me over the edge. We held each other for dear life, not letting go for quite some time.

When the room was completely lit from the sun, I finally loosened my grip on him.

"Grant. I love you more than you'll ever fully comprehend. I need to know what happened now. We need to talk."

His peaceful expression returned to pain and he averted his eyes.

"Let's get dressed and go down to the beach. We can talk there. Is that okay?" He sounded dejected.

"Yeah. It's fine. I need to go back to my place to get dressed. I'll meet you by the path in about fifteen minutes."

He nodded and released me slowly, like he was afraid to let me go. I put my hand on his heart.

"This is mine. It will always be mine. Yes?"

He nodded again. I kissed him and left. I headed right to my room, waving off Dane's questions when I got into the house. I threw on a t-shirt, pair of jeans and my favorite sneakers. I grabbed two travel mugs of coffee and I headed off to meet Grant by the path down to the beach. He was wearing a pair of jeans and a button down casual shirt with a t-shirt underneath. He looked hot and sad at the same time. He looked up at me and gave me a weak smile. I walked up to him, handed him his coffee, grabbed his other hand in mine and pulled him to the path to head down.

We walked in silence. Every time I looked at him he was watching me. About ten minutes later we were on the beach. I sat down in the sand and patted a place next to me. He opted to sit opposite me with his back to the ocean. It reminded me of the first dream in the walk. I was happy we weren't on the edge.

“Lanie, I’m not sure how to start. Please just know that I love you, and will always love you and only you.”

“I know, Babe. I love you too. It’s just … from the way you’ve been acting since you got back … this is going to be bad, isn’t it?”

“Lanie, I’ll understand if you never forgive me. Know I won’t be with another woman again. There is only you for me. It will only ever be you.” What the hell did he mean by ‘I won’t be with another woman again?’

“Grant, you’re scaring me. You sound like you’re saying goodbye. Don’t.”

“You need to hear. You need to know everything before you decide it’s going to be okay.”

My heart felt like it stopped beating and I tried to brace myself for the worst. I nodded for him to begin. I looked down at my ring finger and realized I still hadn’t put my ring back on. Would I after this?

“Lanie, after we got off the phone, Brianna called me. She was hysterically crying and threatening to hurt herself. I couldn’t just turn my back on her. I wouldn’t let anyone stay in that state. So I went to her room to calm her down, to help her. I know you would’ve been upset if I told you, so I just didn’t.”

“I understand. You’re a kind person, Grant. I’m not happy you didn’t tell me, but I get it. And?”

“When I got there, she …”

Chapter 42

I Was Close Enough

"… was very drunk, much more than she was when you saw her on webcam. She was a mess. Freaking out. Something about her father, and you threatening to call him. She kept saying how her life was over and that she should just end it. I couldn't leave any woman like that."

"You're compassionate, Grant. That's not a crime. It was very chivalrous of you to do that." The words that came out of my mouth were true, but deep inside I felt the sharp pang of jealousy that he had gone to comfort another woman. *Was I wrong? Maybe if she hadn't tried to undress for him right in front of me. That woman deserved to be freaking out and crying.* And in the back of my mind, she knew exactly what she was doing. She was a liar and conniver and she had used us both. My anger was totally focused on Brianna right now. I was starting to boil inside.

"Go on." My voice sounded stern. I didn't want it to. I reached out and touched his hand and made an I'm-an-ass-sometimes-and-sorry-face. *Hell, we've all made them.*

"She ended up crying in my arms. And she pleaded with me to stay."

"I see."

"I told her no, Lanie, and she cried even harder. She asked if I would just stay until she fell asleep. So I agreed. I went over to the couch. She went to her bed. I rolled over and put my back to her. I heard rustling and then the lights were out."

"So you slept on the couch in her room? That's what this is all about?" I let out a huff of relief and I could feel a small smile begin to cross my face.

"Lanie."

And all the relief flew out the window hearing him say my name. It wasn't going to be that innocent.

"Okay. Finish." I wouldn't look at him now. I was afraid to. I was afraid for him to see the expression on my face or for me to see the one on his.

"She started crying again. I told her everything would be fine and to go to sleep. She wouldn't stop. She asked me to come over. She said she wanted to feel a human touch. She said she needed to feel warmth from someone, anyone. She went on about her father and how he was going to destroy her once you got done talking to him. I felt badly for her."

My stomach knotted.

"So, I did. I sat down on the edge of the bed. She asked me to hold her. I hesitated. I didn't feel any attraction toward her. She was a mess. I didn't know what harm it would cause."

My head began to throb.

"I laid down next to her and spooned her."

"How close were you spooning her?" It was all I could get out. I was now focused back on Grant.

"I was close enough."

I felt sick to my stomach.

"Why would you even do that? Why? Why would you spoon her?"

"I don't know. I wasn't thinking. I just felt bad. You should have heard her crying. She was lying down and it was awkward to hold her any other way."

"And I guess I'm the bad guy here, right? Making it all okay for you to spoon another woman? Your mean old wife out to hurt her while waiting for you at home?" *Crap. I had referred to myself as his wife.* He shot his gaze to mine.

"No. You were by no means the bad guy. I'm sure you were justified in anything that happened between you two. Well, anyway. I fell asleep, holding her. I was on the outside of the sheet. She was underneath. Sometime in the very early morning, I realized I was under the covers with her. I must have crawled under them in my sleep. We were still spooning. She wasn't dressed."

"You were in bed, pressed up against her, holding her and she was naked." It wasn't a question. I just couldn't fathom what I was hearing come out of his mouth. I thought maybe if it came out of my mouth I would believe it. He lowered his head. I just stared, waiting.

"I became aroused, it happens to guys. I was half asleep, I don't know, Lanie, but the next thing I knew …"

I bit my lip so hard I could taste blood in my mouth. I got up quickly and began to walk away knowing what was coming next. He'd slept with her. He'd cheated on me, so easily. She didn't even have to try. I meant nothing to him if he could do that.

"Lanie, please don't go. Please let me tell you. I have to tell you the truth," he called. I stopped in my tracks. I had to decide if when I heard him say it out loud if I would forgive him and have him in my world, or end it. There was no in between. None. I felt my heart pulling me to Grant. I turned and walked back.

"Please sit back down."

"No. I don't want to sit. Just finish this," I said sharply.

"The next thing I knew she was grinding up against me and for a moment, I responded."

I looked away from him. *Damn, my heart was hurting.* My breath got caught in my throat.

"How much did you respond?"

"I let her. I let her rub against me. And then she started to turn over and I saw her face; it all hit me. I pulled away. It was only seconds, I swear. I jumped out of bed and told her it was a mistake, that I was half asleep. She told me to come back. She told me she wouldn't tell."

I stood there, shocked. Nothing. I was numb. Frozen.

"Lanie, please tell me what you're thinking."

"Did you go back?"

"No! I grabbed my things and I left. I went back to my room and was going to call you. I felt so guilty—I had to hear your voice. But I left my cell phone in her room and there was no way I was going back to get it. Then I couldn't call you. I couldn't. I didn't speak or see her again until that morning at the meeting."

"And the kiss?"

"She came over and kissed me. I didn't kiss her back, didn't respond at all. I thought she would get the idea. Women hate rejection. It was the worst thing I could do."

"You seemed all chummy with her during the meeting."

"Lanie, I was being professional," Grant stated blankly.

"Nothing about what you did was professional." *Now I was pissed.*

"That's all you have to say about all of this? I was unprofessional?" Grant almost sounded disturbingly amused.

"No, that's not all. You were unfaithful, too." I stomped my foot as I threw those words at him. And with that, I stormed away. I began to run.

But I didn't run back to the cliff. I ran the opposite direction, where no one would be able to find me. I didn't want to be found. I just needed to cool down by myself. I had to get my head around what he said. I had a lot of thinking to do.

I walked along a long overgrown path. None of us had used this path since we were young. There were tangled roots beneath my feet, which made me stumble repeatedly because I wasn't thinking about walking right now. I would stumble, curse and then breathe in a bunch of those quick I've-been-crying-and-I-can't-catch-my-breath inhales.

I neared the area of the path that came around the edge of the opposite cliff from ours. I had a perfect view of the ocean and our houses. I was high above the beach and our houses looked smaller from here, like dollhouses. *Well, this place was as good as any.* I sat down on the path with my back against the rock wall. I was glad I brought my denim jacket.

I reached inside the front inside pocket and pulled out my pack of emergency cigarettes. Then I quickly panicked while patting all my other pockets looking for some means to make fire. *Found it, my cobalt blue gem lighter.* It was so gaudy, but I loved it just the same. Grant had given it to me. We had been known to sneak smokes together over the years. My heart wrenched in my chest.

Grant. I lit the cigarette and took a long drag. It made me feel a little lightheaded. It had been a long time since I had one and this pack was probably a little bit stale. I didn't care. I suddenly wished I had a six-pack of beer or something stronger to go with it.

I needed to look at this rationally. But since that wasn't going to happen, I decided to just blurt crap out, out loud. This little exercise began a conversation (well more like an argument) with my head, mouth and heart.

"He didn't sleep with her."

Well, technically he DID sleep with her.

"Fine. He didn't have sex with her. He did sleep next to her."

He slept wrapped around her all night holding her close, spooning even, and she was naked.

Yeah, my head was a bitch.

"Yes. I know. Stop reminding me, because it makes me picture it in my head; her naked against him, rubbing against him. I don't know why he did that. I can't understand why he would not see that as cheating."

Because he's a gentleman and he was coming to the rescue of a maiden in need.

"Make your fucking mind up! Are you on his side or mine?"

Mine of course. I do want to still be with him, don't I?

"Yes. I love him. I don't care. He didn't have sex with her. So he really didn't cheat."

But he showed her an intimate tenderness that is reserved only for you. Isn't that emotional cheating?

"Stop. I can't bear picturing it. I can't do it. He's mine, not hers. She had no right to behave like that with him!"

No reply. I burst into tears. How was I going to get over this? The jealousy in my heart was destroying me. I was broken. But without him I was even worse. How would I ever be able to get past this?

The same way he got past seeing you fucking Dane!

"Shut up! Shut up, shut up, and shut up. Shut the fuck up!" I put my hands over my ears to stop the words. But it didn't do me any good; the words were in my head. Echoing over and over again.

I covered my face with my hands and cried for a very long time. I shut my brain off and let everything pour out. I chain-smoked. I wondered if Grant had done the same thing when he saw me with Dane. I knew it was different. But in matters of the heart, was it really? Was it different in Grant's head? *No.* I'm sure it crushed him. Every time he would make love to me, would he think about Dane being inside me? Would I think about Brianna every time he spooned me?

This led to a whole new line of thinking. *Had it been her that got him hard that morning or was it just a morning thing? Did she feel his arousal and think it was for her? Did he let her rub against him because he was half asleep, and didn't realize it was her and not me? Or did it feel good to have another woman rubbing against his dick and that made him let her continue? Why did he stop her? Did he really stop her? How long is a few seconds? Was he touching her back when she rubbed him?*

I could tell this was going to be a no win situation between me and me. Maybe I did want some help to work through this, but the only person I wanted was Grant. He was the only one who could make this all better. Still wasn't sure he'd be able to. Honestly, it was something I needed to come to terms with on my own. I either had to be without Grant forever, or be able to let go of what had happened. *And if I chose to break things off with Grant, what would become of us? Would we still be close after everything that had transpired between us over the past few months? Would one of us leave the cliff? Would we be able to watch the other fall in love with someone else? Would either of us be able to fall in love with someone else?*

Crap. More questions. I needed answers, not questions. I ripped my cell phone out of my pocket and dialed Grant. I heard him pick up and take a breath in. But before he could speak, I jumped in.

"We're going one for one. But this time, I'm asking all the questions and you just answer. Simple answers. I need answers. Okay?"

I heard nothing for a second on the other end of the phone.

"Grant?"

"Sorry. I just . . . hearing your voice, that you're even just reaching out to me . . . it gives me hope that there's still a chance for us."

I was going for broke here, so I just went for the whole thing.

"Your arousal, was it because it was her or just something different from me? Was it her in particular or would any woman excite you?"

"God no, Lanie. I was half asleep. I was a bit groggy and disoriented. I was dreaming of you." This last part he said under his breath, but I heard it. It was what I needed. But I was sure he didn't want to sound like he was mirroring my 'I thought it was you.'

"So you didn't get hard because she was rubbing against you?"

"I didn't even realize I was until she was rubbing against me."

"And how long did that happen for? How long did you let her?"

"As soon as I realized what was happening, I stopped her. It was for mere seconds only."

"Did you like it?"

"What?"

"Did you like her rubbing against you? It's not that hard a question, Grant!" I was pissed and snapped.

"No! It made me sick to my stomach. When I realized it was her, I wasn't excited anymore. That took even less time." He was aggravated. It almost sounded like he was pissed at me for asking.

"When she did that, were you … touching her? Did you rub back? Squeeze? Kiss?"

"No! Nothing. I didn't do anything."

"You held her all night. Did you think there was something wrong with that? Did you honestly think it was okay to hold another woman like that? Would you like it if I slept in another man's arms? Would you?"

Silence.

"No. I wouldn't like it at all. Not one bit. And yes, I was doubting my decision the whole time. I'm a fool, Lanie. I'm a stupid fucking idiot. I betrayed you." He obviously had remorse over what he had done. He was punishing himself. He must be convinced we were over.

"You did betray me. How can I ever trust you again?"

"I don't know, but you can. The thought of losing you, Lanie, I can't do it. Please. Please don't leave me, Lanie. I'll do anything you want. Anything you need. Please." He was begging now.

"I'm not ready to answer that yet."

Silence.

"Grant?"

"Lanie, please tell me there's a chance for us. I didn't feel anything for her. I was wrong in everything I did. But there is only you for me. The thought of this whole thing sickens me. I know I fucked up; royally fucked up, Lanie. How can I make it better? How can I prove to you how much I love you?"

"I don't know."

"Lanie, I hate to play hard ball, but I'm going to. I have no choice because I have to step up and take any shot I have at this not ending us. I'll do anything not to lose you."

"Be very careful, Grant," I warned.

"Lanie, I believed you when you told me what happened between you and Dane was basically him forcing himself on you, that you thought it was me. I trusted you. I believed it. And believe me, it tore me down to the core to see you making love to another man. Now I understand it's not the same thing here, but in the same respect, I slept next to her, not with her. I did nothing else with her. All you have in your head is an imaginary image, and the feelings of jealousy that I even let it get that far. I, however, will always know you were completely intimate with Dane. That he had you, kissed, touched and fucked you. I have it in my head because I saw it. Now, I don't hold that against you at all. But my head wants to explode every time he's near you. I can feel my blood boil when he even looks at you. And I wonder all the time, did you like it? Do you secretly want him? Do you think about him that way still? When you're making love to me, do you ever think about him? And before you say anything ... Dane has gone out of his way to redeem himself. And I owe him that chance. He's been doing everything he can to help us through this, to help you through this. And yes, I still wonder if it's because he wants you. Now that it's all out in the open, please have at it."

"I ... I don't know what to say." *Fuck.* I didn't. I wanted to rip into him for using that against me. *Who the fuck did he think he was? But hell, he finally told me how it really made him feel.* He was seeing it in his head all the time. *Shit.* How could he still be with me and stand to see Dane and I being friends?

And then I really thought about what he'd said. He was right. This put us on the same playing field. He knew what I was going through. He understood what this did to me. And for the first time, I finally understood what he felt. I finally understood what he'd gone through. Was still going though, apparently. And it sucked. I took a deep breath, stood up and started to head back towards our cliff.

"Okay. You win."

"No, Lanie, I don't want to win. I want everything to be back to the way it was right before I left. I want my fiancé back; want my future wife to love me again. Hell, I want you *to be* my future wife again. I didn't say all of that to make what happened with you and Dane even worse. And I certainly didn't say it to lessen what I did, either. I wanted you to understand that I get it. Does that make sense?"

"Yes. Everything you said made sense," I said as I continued to jog back to the cliff. I was almost there.

"So where does that leave us? I mean, Lanie, do you even still love me?"

"How the hell can you even ask me that? You must really not have any faith in my love for you if you think I could just stop. I mean, mad or not, hurt or not, I never stopped loving you. It just made all the feelings more intense."

Now I was running toward his house.

"Where are you?"

"I'm at my house in the back. Why?"

"I just wanted to know."

"Lanie, where does this leave us?" I was rounding the corner to his back yard.

"It leaves us right here." I was standing in front of him. He looked up at me with the phone still to his ear and slowly lowered it. As soon as he smiled at me, I threw myself into his arms. He immediately responded and covered my face and neck with kisses.

"I love you. I don't want to lose you. I need you. Please don't leave me. Please don't choose another woman over me."

Crap was coming out of my mouth that I didn't even mean to say. I was mad at him. I wanted to yell at him; tell him what a schmuck he was. But I couldn't do it. All the fears came out first. The hurt little girl trying to do what makes everyone else feel better so she doesn't have to deal with a hurtful confrontation.

"Lanie, I love you and never want to lose you, either. And I would never choose another woman over you. Never. Do you hear me? I made an awful mistake. I'll do whatever it takes to make things right."

"No sleeping next to anyone else ever again but me. Never. And you'll never speak to her again. Promise me."

"I'll never speak to her again. I promise you that. I'll never sleep next to anyone but you, and Woof, and our children when they're babies, or afraid of a storm, or having a nightmare. That is, if we're in a place to discuss children."

"Yes. I still want to marry you. Yes, I want to have your babies. But … I think we have a long road of healing ahead of us, both of us."

I was cradled in his lap now. There was no other place I wanted to be in the world. This is where I belonged, with Grant. And I was still pissed to all hell at him for being so stupid and unthinking as to lay with her. Now I was mad again, giving myself whiplash from my massive emotional swings.

"Can we make it through this?" He looked me straight in the eyes when he said it. They were questioning and sincere and it looked like he didn't really know if I was on board or not yet.

"I don't know. But I'm willing to try. I love you that much. But I'm not ready to put my ring back on yet. We have to see if this works first. There's a lot of hurt. I don't know if I can let it go as easily as you did. And speaking of that, you told me you didn't ever think about that night with Dane and I. But then today you threw it in my face."

"Lanie, what was I supposed to do? Tell you how it ripped me to pieces? Tell you when you were at your lowest point? Make you hurt even more? No. I was trying to protect you. I'd rather take all the hurt than have you feel it more because of me."

"But that means you lied to me. Don't you ever lie to me again. If we're going to spend the rest of our lives together then you have to tell me everything you're feeling, whether it hurts me or not. Completely honest and open, all the time. You hear me Bennett? It was never an issue before. Now that we have everything between us, why would you lie about anything? Why start now?"

Grant shook his head.

"Lanie, I just told you why. But you're right, it's another thing I fucked up."

"No. But now you'll know better. Just don't do it again. And thank you for protecting me." I smacked him on the arm but wanted to slap him across the face for sleeping next to that bitch; for letting her get pleasure from him. I wanted to demolish her.

We just stared at each other. And while I looked at him, I plotted on how I was going to take that bitch down. And I was. I was going to make her so sorry she fucked with me. And man, was I motivated. I thought of everything.

I envisioned her coming to visit for whale watching and her just getting a little too close to the edge of the cliff. *Oops. Bye-bye, bitch!* I thought about inviting her to go skydiving with me. *Oh, you go first. Oops, that was my backpack. See you, slut!* I think at one point I must have had an evil smirk on my face and Grant noticed.

"What are you thinking about? You look ... scary," Grant said. His face look worried. A very strange laugh started to come out of my mouth and I stopped myself.

"Nothing. It doesn't even matter. I can't do any of it, anyway," I said, with a twinge of disappointment.

"Do I want to know?"

"No. That would make you an accessory."

He just stared at me. Mouth open, like he was going to say something, but nothing came out. After a few seconds, he started to look like a wax figure. It was creepy.

"No, really. Don't worry about it. I was just kind of zoning out, thinking about something. Don't pay any mind to me."

"Still scary, Lanie. Now, about your ring." He picked up my left hand and thumbed the place where my ring used to be. I thumbed the missing spot all the time. It felt like it was missing. I can't explain it.

"So. How do I go about putting that ring back on here? Where do we go from here, Lanie?" He squeezed my hand and gave me a serious look.

"Well, we're going to have to have some long talks."

"I assumed."

"And no sex. That'll just mask things. Make things feel better. Feel really, really good even. Amazing …"

"You don't sound convinced on that point." He cocked an eyebrow at me and gave me the most adorable smirk.

"Yeah. It's going to be a tough one. But no, you actually have to earn that one back, being like that with me."

"We'll see how you hold up to that one. I do *not* promise not to tempt you. A lot," he said with smooth confidence. He gave me a totally hot smile to go with it. *Crap.* I was already wavering. Mad or not at him, my guy was hot. And keeping my hands off him and not having make-up sex, or even better yet, hot, pissed-off sex, was going to be a challenge. I felt myself start to ache for him. I got up from his lap. He held onto my hand so I wouldn't go far.

"What else, Love. Anything."

"You're going to have to court me. Take me on dates."

"I have no problem with that. When can that start?" His eyes were pleading me to just say *now.* So I did.

"Right now." I looked at him from under my eye lashes." He pulled me closer. Slowly, with each additional inch he pulled me, he'd look for my approval. I let him pull me to him until we were inches apart. My lips were just drawn to his like magnets. But he just kept it slow. I leaned into him; I could feel the heat coming off him.

Our lips touched. It was quick and soft and wonderful. And then I just gave into that part of me, the part that missed him deeply. It needed to have closure, too. He was here with me now, *with me*. And I wanted to feel him. I wanted his kiss.

He crushed his lips to mine and I felt my entire being fall into that kiss. I could feel every cell in his body. It was tender and loving. If it could, my heart would have jumped right the hell out of my chest and into his pocket. *Damn.*

I pulled myself away.

"Remember rule number two. No sex. You keep kissing me like that and—"

"I'll keep that in mind. So, I'd like to invite you to dinner at my house. I'm cooking. Bennett mac and cheese? I think we could both use some comfort food tonight."

"I think I'd like that. I'd like that a lot. But first, there's a small task I have to attend to," I said, as I removed myself from him.

"What are you going to do?" His voice was deep with a slightly humorous, yet accusatory tone.

"I need to …

Chapter 43

Our Little Girl Has a Date

"… take care of something. What time should I be over for dinner?"

"Love, that wouldn't be very gentlemanly of me. I'll come and pick you up at five. Does that work for you? Enough time to do whatever it is I don't want to know what you're doing?"

His eyes were smiling at me and suddenly things felt right again between us. Like they had before he left. I was still fuming, even seriously considering having his wedding band tattooed onto his finger. But no bother, I didn't plan on ever letting him leave without me again, unless it was with Dylan and Steve for a boy's weekend.

"Yes. That should be plenty of time. Plenty." I smiled an evil grin to myself, but apparently it wasn't really to myself, because he noticed again.

"You're looking scary again. Did I mention how grateful I am that you've forgiven me and I'm not on your bad side? 'Cause being on your bad side could be detrimental to a person's well-being."

"Oh, you're on my naughty list, but you can redeem yourself by being extra naughty."

"That made no sense, Lanie. How can I get off your naughty list by being naughty?" I just looked at him until I saw it sink in.

"Oh. Forget it. I'm really slow. But wouldn't that be breaking rule number two?" he teased me.

"I guess you'll have to try and convince me. I don't particularly like rule number two. It's just necessary at the moment. Although I'm thinking that one is going to be hard on both of us."

"Oh it will be. Very hard," he said, with a smile that could melt butter from across the room. "I really do think it's a rule to be broken, mind you. Because it's just inevitably going to have its downfall. Tonight I hope. If not tonight, then … Wait, that reminds me of something I forgot. I'll be right back. I need to give you something. Wait right here. Five minutes tops, I promise." And he raised his right hand.

As soon as he left, I grabbed his cell phone off the table and quickly went through his call list. Yeah, I was being nosey, but I had a right to be. Brianna's number was there. She had called him several times today and I noticed he never answered. They were all missed calls. I'd have to check his voicemails. The first thing I did was block her number from his phone and erase it from everywhere I could find. I switched to his text messages, and with a sigh of relief, noticed they were all from me, Samantha, Chelsie and Dane, and even one from Dylan. That doesn't mean he didn't erase them all, but I knew this was going to be an exercise in trust. I stopped to read through the ones to and from Dane. Everything he said was encouraging Grant to not give up on us. It was all about doing whatever he could to see us through this. This was my Dane. This was the Dane I grew up with. The one who always looked out for me. The one who was Grant's best bro. I had missed him. I wondered if this would change things between them, make them better? I also had to wonder if it was all just another plot. But it didn't feel like it. *I mean, why try to help us get back together just to break us back u*p? That didn't make sense. If Dane wanted me, he had his chance over the past few days. No, I think that glitch in Dane was finally behind us all.

I heard Grant coming back down the hall and I tossed his phone back where I found it. Grant walked in and immediately picked his phone up. *Man, I couldn't hide anything from this guy.* Or he had strategically placed the phone to see if I would touch it and then notice it had been moved? It didn't matter. I got what I wanted. She was deleted.

"Did you get her number off my phone? Block it even? Did you listen to any messages she left? You're perfectly welcome to if it would make you feel better. In fact, I want you to." He held the phone out to me.

"I did everything except check your messages," I confessed, as I looked down at my feet. I felt guilty. He reached out and lifted my head up by my chin.

"I don't blame you. I'd do the same thing if I were in your position. Hell, have at my computer, too. Please, anything you need to make this better. Anything." I smiled at him and he reached out and ran a finger down my cheek.

"So, you have something for me?"

"I have this." He handed me a large manila envelope.

"What is this?"

"It's what I think you and I need. I think we need to get away, alone. Away from everyone and everything. Work on us for a while. If you say no, it's okay. We don't have to go. I can cancel everything."

I opened the envelope and found a brochure to a spa on the beach. But not just any spa, this was a chocolate spa. Chocolate baths and chocolate facials. Chocolate everything. The whole thing was decadent. Two of my favorite things, especially when put together, chocolate and Grant.

"Well, seeing as you and I have such a propensity for adding chocolate into our sex life, I thought you'd get a kick out of this one."

"When are we going? And when did you do this?"

"I actually did it when I was away. I missed you so much and I thought about how wonderful it would be to take a trip with just my fiancé to celebrate our engagement. Of course, since we are no longer engaged, I'd certainly understand if you didn't want to go."

"When do we leave? I mean, when is it planned for?" I asked. I was jumping inside at the prospect of having a completely chocolate-coated Grant. I wondered if they used chocolate hazelnut spread? It didn't matter; I'd bring my own!

"Next weekend." He actually sounded sad. He ran his fingers through his hair, where they remained, and he looked up at me to gauge my reaction.

“So, you don’t think I’ll go away with you because I’m not your fiancé anymore?” I was actually finding this endearing and I felt a little bad. I wanted to be his fiancé, but I also planned on having some fun with making him work for it. That ring was going back on my finger no matter what.

“I don’t expect you to. I would certainly love for you to come with me … in every way.” He cocked an eyebrow and licked his lips quite seductively. I kind of became entranced at the sight of him for a second or two.

“You have one week to convince me. Keep it booked. I’m sure you’ll do your best to win me over.” I smiled, leaned over, and gave him a soft peck on his lips. “I want to go.” And then I whispered, “We’re going!” Grant smiled a huge goofy grin at me. I guess I made him really happy. He did the same thing for me. Now I knew he had been thinking about me while he was away.

“Well, I guess you have something evil to go take care of, so I’ll pick you up tonight. And Lanie?”

I turned back to look at him before heading out the door.

“I love you so much. Thank you.”

“Thank you? For what?”

“For still loving me.”

“I’ll love you forever, Grant. In fact, probably even more than forever, it that’s possible.”

I reached over, leaned down and gave him a kiss on his forehead while running my hand through his hair, then down his cheek. With that, I turned and left. I had to find my bitches, Chelsie and Samantha. I needed their help to take Brianna Stone down. I grabbed my cell phone as I headed out the door, but my girls were hanging by the stables with Dane and their men. They actually looked like they were all having a good time. They were laughing and were in deep conversation. I hated to interrupt; all I wanted was to have fun and for everything to be light. But right now, all I brought was grief with me wherever I went. I didn’t want them to pity me any longer. I was hoping my proposition would bring something fun back to the table.

"Hey," I said as I headed over. They looked up at me, waiting for something. I knew what they wanted to know.

"We're working on everything. Well, I'm making Grant work for it. It's going to be okay. I just know it."

Samantha ran over and hugged me. I hugged her back and she wouldn't let go.

"Hey, Grabby Feely, I can't breathe. Release me, please," I choked out.

"No! I love that you and Grant are still together. Why aren't you wearing your ring?" Leave it to Samantha to notice right away.

"We're not quite there yet."

"Oh poop," she said.

"It'll be there soon. Promise. Now I need you and Chelsie. There's a bitch who needs to go down, and I need *my* bitches to help me plot." I could feel my face scrunch up into a scowl.

"Fuck yeah, now you're talking!" Chelsie was at my side in an instant and I could see the wheels in her head spinning already.

"Hey, I want in," Dylan said. He almost sounded upset that he wasn't included.

"Can you be a total bitch?" I giggled.

"Oh, Dylan's a complete and utter bitch. Sometimes I wonder if he actually has girl parts he PMS's so bad." Samantha kissed Dylan on the cheek and tousled his hair. He just rolled his eyes.

"Yeah, TMI. Okay, you're in. Steve? You want a piece of this shit, too?" I dared him.

He slowly turned and smiled at me. "No, Lanie, I fight for real. Not this girly shit. If you want me to push her down on the ground so you can kick her, just ask. But you guys are on your own. Plot away. Then you can run them by me for another opinion once you think you got it. Why don't you ask Dane? He seems to be pretty good at screwing people over." Steve shot Dane a dirty look. I guess he wasn't over the whole thing yet, but this next thing? This next one shocked my shoes right off my damn feet.

"Steve. That was really mean. Dane, I'm sorry. You've really been trying. Everyone deserves a second chance. It's when they blow it that one last little bitty time that they're done for. I certainly wouldn't want someone to pretend to be doing the right thing and then plotting the whole time. That would be a big issue."

And now Chelsie was back.

"No. It's okay. Steve has a right to feel that way. I was a complete dick. And I got your point, Chelsie. No. I just realized how much I hurt two people I care about. And I didn't like myself very much. And you can believe I'm trying or not, but I'll keep doing it, anyway." Dane gave me his puppy-dog-that-crapped-on-the-floor look.

"Well? You want in, too?" I said directly to Dane.

"Fuck yes! And Steve is right. I can play down right dirty if I want to. And I want to. So let's play." Dane was stoked. He actually looked excited, like it was a game.

"Okay." I said warily. I was actually scared to see how evil Dane functioned. I was kind of hoping he didn't have some kind of multiple personality disorder. *Dane the Bad Ass and Sweet Dane, his fun-loving side-kick.* He shot me a look from under his furrowed brows.

"Don't worry, Lanie. I'm on your side this time. And she made me mad."

I smiled and started walking back towards my house. I stopped and turned back around.

"Well, you coming or not? I only have until four." They all scattered, grabbing their stuff and running behind me. I chuckled to myself. *This was going to be epic!*

When we got to my place I grabbed a bottle of whatever was in my reach and a bunch of shot glasses. We all sat on the floor in my living room and began throwing ideas out and taking shots.

"Well, I'm going to call her father." I took a shot and winced. *What the hell did I grab?* I had to be careful or I'd be wasted for my date with Grant and either puke on him or break rule number two the second I walked through his front door.

"That's your big plan? You're going to tattle on her to her daddy? I'm so glad you asked for our help, Honey," Chelsie said as she rolled her eyes and placatingly patted my hand.

"Lanie, you're too nice. You need to get your revenging-bitch on!" Samantha cooed.

"When you call her dad, you have to make it more than just the jealous fiancé. You have to make some kind of sexual harassment accusation," Chelsie suggested.

"No, that'll piss him off. She has to go for the heart. Cry to him. How the deal was so important and then his daughter made advances at your fiancé. Go for the heart wrenching aspect." Dylan was looking off into a different direction when he said it. Like he was picturing it in his head. I saw the edges of his lips turn slightly up.

"This man is a shark. Really. We don't want him to think he just signed contracts with a weepy chick." Dane had a good point. *How the hell would I approach the subject with this man?* I had no idea what he was actually like.

"Right. Maybe I just play it by ear. Feel him out. Go with the flow. I have all your ideas to use in my head now." It could work. I could play the press, I was sure I could play him.

"But that's just not enough. She has to pay for what she did. We have to make her hurt. Cry, even. I want her to feel ten times worse than she made Lanie feel. I wanna shank her hard!" Samantha really was a bitch when she wanted to be, and an extremely naughty girl, too. I wouldn't want to screw with her. She was a sleeper, all sweet and innocent until you did something to set her in motion. *Dangerous.*

"It's so tough because everything I come up with is totally illegal," Chelsie said out loud. We all just eyed her and slowly moved a little bit away from her.

"What? Like you all weren't thinking along the same lines, right?" She looked at us accusingly. We all mumbled and moved closer. Everyone took a shot.

"What if we dug some dirt up on her? Posted it all over some social media networks?" Samantha suggested.

"Actually, it's traceable," Dylan interjected.

"Fine, Mr. CSI. What isn't traceable?"

"We could send it anonymously to media outlets," Dylan countered.

"Right, but then there'd be bad press for their company, coming right back and hitting us," Dane said. Everyone nodded. We all just sat and thought for a while. Our conversations began to border on murderous ideas with lots of giggles and shots. Finally we got back to business.

"It needs to be personal, really personal. We need to hit home," Chelsie jumped in again and then took another shot.

"Steve, you have anything to add?" I poured him a shot and handed it to him. He poured another shot and handed it to me. We clinked and threw them back.

"Well, since you're asking my opinion, the worst thing you can do to a girl is reject her in public. Make a big scene or something. Or make her think she's a goddess and then never call her again." Steve smiled proudly.

"Really? How do you suggest we do that? Send Grant back out to her?" Samantha chimed in. I made a face and shook my head emphatically no.

"Then we need another guy."

"Who? Who do we know? She only wants Grant." I was starting to feel like I should just give up, call her dad and wimp out on the whole thing. We couldn't find any way to get her back that would work.

"What about me?" Dane offered himself.

"What? Why would you do that?" Dylan asked incredulously.

"She knows who I am. I can contact her and lay on the charm." Dane pulled on a non-existent collar.

"That could work. What say you, Lanie?" Samantha said.

"I don't know. I'm just not feeling it. I just feel like I got screwed and there's no way to get back at her. I want her to feel the hurt I did."

"We could have Dane hook up with her and then we can have him cheat on her so she knows what it feels like. It's perfect." Samantha clapped.

"Really, Lanie, give her a spoonful of her own medicine," Chelsie added.

"I kind of like it," Steve joined in.

"Yeah. It's the only one that's not going to put us all in jail," Dylan chuckled.

"Fine. You guys can all conspire about the logistics. I have to get ready for my date. Grant is picking me up in a little over an hour. And honestly, I need to sober up a bit."

"Lanie, are you going to put your ring back on?"

"Soon, Samantha. I promise." And then a very panicky feeling began to creep over me. I ran to the table. No ring. *Where the hell was my ring?* "Did one of you put my ring someplace safe? It was right here on the end table in the dish from Castelli. Where is it? Holy shit. My ring is gone." My whole body went cold.

"I'm sure it's safe. No worries. We'll look for it while you're in the shower. Okay? It'll turn up. No one but us has been in the house." Dylan assured me.

"Please look everywhere, under the couches and in the cushions. Woof likes shiny things. He might've decided to play with it." I turned to head up the stairs.

"Lanie? What about your phone call?" Chelsie asked, holding out the phone to me.

"Yeah, I have to think about how I'm going to approach that one. Right now, the most important thing to me is getting things back where they belong with Grant. As far as I'm concerned, that woman no longer exists. She's a piece of dust in the wind. I just want my guy back. I want things right again. She can die, for all I care. In fact, I hope she does." I headed back toward the stairs.

Yeah. I had missed Grant. I missed things being okay. I missed not feeling comfortable with touching each other. I missed knowing he'd be sleeping next to me every night. And I missed making love to him, all the time.

I knew tonight was supposed to be a date and nothing was going to happen sexually between us, or at least that was my plan, but it didn't stop me from wanting to tease him just the same. I needed to wear something that looked hot, but casual. Like it wasn't actually my plan to get him all hot and bothered. Now how the hell was I going to accomplish that?

I looked through my closet. Slip dress? It would work, but it was a little too in-your-face. Maybe a pair of cute sweats or yoga pants—great for cuddling and watching a movie, but a little bit too comfortable. I started to look through my tops, hoping something would stand out. And then it hit me.

There in the back was the shirt I would wear for the Women's Heart Disease functions I attended every year to represent our company. It was so cute and would go great with a pair of black skinny jeans. It was a nice deep red, sleeveless, baring my shoulders and my back completely, and secured around my neck with a long sheer tie. It had three long, flowing sheer ruffles across the front, and if I wore it without a bra, it would just give a wonderful hint of what was underneath. *Perfect.* I grabbed my favorite pair of wedgies that looked like sneakers but not as sporty. Actually, I loved them, and whenever I needed to be a little more than casual, I wore these.

I decided tonight to pull out all the stops. I showered and used my vanilla shower gel, shampoo, and conditioner. I never used all three with my vanilla perfume, but tonight, I wanted to smell like waffles or cake. I wanted Grant to drool and try to eat me alive.

When I was all showered, I blew my hair dry and left it in soft waves. I applied smoky eye-makeup to provide extra allure for when I gave him my best sex eyes. I was hoping tonight would go off without a hitch. I put on some toes rings, silver bangle bracelets and a cobalt and silver anklet. I checked myself out in the mirror. I had accomplished my mission. I looked casual but hot, and I was ready to let Grant redeem himself along with making him want me more than he already did. I headed downstairs and my Annihilation Team was still planning and plotting.

"Well? How do I look?"

"You look hot," Dylan said. Samantha nodded her head in agreement. Steve whistled and Chelsie gave me thumbs up. Dane said nothing; I'm sure for fear of everyone thinking the wrong thing.

"Dane?" He just turned and smiled. "Well?"

"I think Grant is a lucky man to have someone who loves him so much and looks hot doing it." Chelsie made a little cute noise.

I still felt like something was missing. I turned and examined myself in the mirror. Then it hit me again. My ring was missing. In fact, it was a blaring reminder that I still didn't know where it was.

"Did … did anyone find my ring? Please say you found it."

"No, Hun. We tore the place apart. Are you sure you didn't put it someplace special? Like a jewelry box upstairs?" Chelsie said, with a lot of compassion.

"No. No! I put it right there. That was a sentimental special safe place. That dish was from when we all went on that school trip with the Italian Club in high school."

"Oh yeah, you and Grant shared a little kiss under the Ponte dei Sospiri in Venice." Dylan chuckled. "I remember, because Grant wouldn't shut the hell up about it for the rest of the trip. He totally believed the legend about kissing your soul mate there."

"And your point is? It worked, didn't it?" I scoffed.

"I stand corrected. But it still doesn't change the fact that we didn't find your ring." Dylan looked sad for me. I felt sad for me. Grant was going to have a cow. He just gave me that ring and it probably cost him a small, no scratch that, large fortune. And it meant everything to him. And it meant everything to me. And here I went and lost it. I could feel the tears welling up and a lump forming in my throat. Samantha jumped up and started to fan my eyes.

"You're going to mess those eyes up. You just tell him nothing. You're not supposed to be wearing it, anyway. Let him sweat it. We'll keep looking. We'll look everywhere." I loved Samantha. Everyone nodded in agreement.

"Lanie, no more tears. We'll find it. We'll look all night." Dane reiterated what everyone else had promised. It didn't matter. Until that ring was back on my finger, I wouldn't care what promises were made. It wasn't good enough. It gave me a bad feeling, like there was some kind of sign being shown to me. *My ring was gone. Did that mean my relationship was, too?* I hated to be superstitious and I knew it was school-girlish for me to even think this way. *Why not just whip out the old Ouija board?* All my answers could be found there. *Ridiculous.* Yet I still tried to remember which closet I had stuffed the board into!

"And we'll interrogate that small black furry thing you gave an identity crisis to by naming him after a canine. I bet he took it and is wearing it on his tail to attract some pussies." Chelsie cracked herself up. We all kind of giggled with her. At ten to five, the doorbell rang.

"Wow, he must really be in trouble if he's ringing the doorbell! We all just get to walk in," Steve said as he got up to answer the door.

"Hey Grant, how's it hanging? Are you here to pick up your date? Now remember, she has a curfew and keep your hands to yourself." Steve was a ball buster.

"Hello to you, too. Is she ready?" Grant entered the house. He looked damn hot in a pair of faded jeans and a tight blue t-shirt that showed every single edge of his outline underneath. His hair was done, but the only way I could describe it was sex hair. It was wild on top of his head and I suddenly wanted to curl my fingers into it and pull him into a deep kiss or whatever else I could pull him into. Namely me. I felt a fire begin below. Tonight was going to be a challenge.

"Oh, she's more than ready for you. I can tell you that. Just look at her!" Steve exclaimed and Chelsie kicked him in the shin.

"Really? Grow up. Our little girl has a date. Now be nice and shut the hell up. Grant, I trust that you'll be a good boy and have our girl home by ten?" Now Chelsie was continuing the faux parental grilling.

"Yes and don't think about trying anything funny, either. Keep your hands to yourself. We'll be watching you." Dylan made the two-finger-eye-to-eye-motion back and forth between himself and Grant.

"Ooh! If I'm watching, put your hands all over her. I want to see everything!" Samantha chimed in.

"You're a real whore, you know that, Samantha?" Chelsie said.

"You know you'd watch them, too. It'd be gorgeous porn. Look at them both!"

Grant made a disturbed face at his cousins and shook his head. I heard a breath come out of his mouth. He looked thoroughly embarrassed. He turned towards me to see my reaction to the peanut gallery. I didn't care. All I could focus on was Grant. I gave him my sweetest smile and felt my entire body heat up.

"Well, they are right. You look absolutely amazing, Lanie."

Grant reached his hand out to mine, and I was about to reach with my left hand when I was suddenly again very aware of the missing ring. So I opted to give him my right hand, which afforded him the opportunity to pull me close to him and give me a sweet kiss on my forehead. I heard them all sigh. *Hell, at this point, I expected them to all whip out their cameras and start taking pictures like it was prom or something.* I pulled Grant toward the door.

"Come on. Let's get out of here. It's getting creepy," I joked.

"I agree. And anyway, I have a wonderful night planned for us, and I'd like to get it started, if that's okay with you. Are you ready, my love?"

"I'm so ready. I'm all yours," I said to him. I turned to my family." I can't promise I'll be back tonight, or how late I'll be if I do. So don't wait up. And thanks for doing that thing for me that you're doing. It means a lot. Thank you for everything. All of you."

Grant shot me a glance and then looked around the room at our family. He gave them a grateful smile and then took my hand and we headed for the door.

When we got outside, Pierre was waiting out front with the limo.

"I thought we were ..." Grant put his finger up to my lips and smiled. He put his hand on the small of my back and guided me toward the limo. I felt an intense heat where he touched me. This was really, really going to be a challenge not ripping every shred of clothing off him tonight.

Pierre bowed and held the door open for me. I turned to look at Grant.

"I love you, Lanie. Please join me for a wonderful night so I can show you how much. It's quite overdue." He motioned toward the door. I turned toward the house and everyone was at the window watching us. It was laughable. We both smiled and I got into the limo.

There waiting for me were ...

Chapter 44

Are You Ready for the Main Course?

… chocolate covered strawberries and an ice-cold bottle of my favorite champagne. I turned and shot Grant a smirk.

"Nice try. It's not going to happen. At least, not tonight."

Grant gave me a sultry smile. "Can't blame a guy for trying, can you? Have you looked in the mirror? You're absolutely stunning. And I did warn you I was going to totally try and seduce you. I plan on standing by that promise."

He shot me an adorable grin and cocked his eyebrows. I melted. This was going to be tough. I was already starting to cave. I stepped into the limo and made myself comfortable. My love got in and slid right up next to me. I was almost right on top of him. He gently pushed me up against the side and put one arm above my head. I was his prisoner and I liked it. He brought his face close to mine. I could feel his breath on my lips. It was so hard not to kiss him—I started to lean in. He brushed his lips softly against mine and then pulled away. I was disappointed to say the least, but I played it off. He produced a strawberry and held it up for me to take a bite. Well, two could play at the seduction game. *Game on!* I looked him in the eyes and licked the strawberry slowly and made a little moaning noise. I put my lips over the tip and mouthed it. I heard a small growl escape him. I smiled and bit the tip off. He chuckled, turned and poured us both a glass of champagne.

"I thought you were making me dinner? Where are we going?" I sipped on the sweet nectar that could be rule number two's demise.

"Just sit back and enjoy the night. It's purely for your pleasure."

“Oh, I’m sure you only had *my* pleasure in mind.” I giggled like a schoolgirl on her first date. Grant turned and knocked on the glass partition. Pierre started the limo and we were off. We fed each other strawberries and sipped our champagne. When the bottle was finished, and my head started to feel giddy, Grant gave the partition another tap. I felt the limo turn and then roll to stop.

“Destination achieved. Madame, may I escort you to dinner?” Grant reached for my hand. I took it and he helped me out of the limo, now parked outside his front door.

“You picked me up in a limo to take me to your house right next door?” I giggled.

“Nothing but the best for my girl. Are you hungry? I’ve been slaving over dinner all day.” He smiled as he opened the front door and ushered me in. The first thing that hit me was the smell of gardenias. Reminded me instantly of Hawaii. Then I could hear soft Hawaiian music playing in the background.

“Are you going for a luau theme?”

“I was going for South Pacific. Tonight we’ll be dining on treats from that locale. I’m sure you’ll enjoy it.” I started to look around the room.

“What’s wrong? What are you looking for?”

“My coconut bra and grass skirt,” I teased. He snapped his fingers like he’d forgotten something.

“That’s okay, Love, I figured we’d go au naturale, like real natives do.”

“Yeah, you’d like that, wouldn’t you? Well, not on a first date!” I giggled some more.

Grant took my hand and led me out to the back, where the terrace was decorated with tiki torches and tons of Hawaiian flowers. There were birds of paradise and hibiscus everywhere.

“How the hell do you do this stuff? You’re like a magician. Where did all these flowers come from? I never saw a florist delivery truck, and you never left the house." I was actually quite amazed how this man managed to get everything done the way he did. He should be a party planner.

"I have my ways. But I can't tell you, or I'd have to molest you."

"Isn't it *kill me*? You'd have to *kill me*, not molest me." I shook my head.

"No, I like you alive, warm and breathing. Molesting is much more appealing." He chuckled. "Now, please have a seat so I can win you back with my amazing culinary skills." He pulled my chair out. I sat down, extremely excited about dinner. This was definitely not going to be Bennett Mac & Cheese.

Grant disappeared and then returned with a tray. I was shocked by all he'd piled on it. He placed it down on a side table and suddenly I was getting lei'd. Well, not the way I was hoping, but fun just the same. He placed a beautiful purple and white orchid lei around my neck. He was wearing a traditional ti leaf maile around his neck. His button down shirt was gone and he was wearing a surf t-shirt. Nice touch. He then placed a ti leaf crown on my head. It was gorgeous. It had small white flowers all woven throughout. I got butterflies in my stomach. My guy had gone all out.

I smiled and said, "Mahalo," and then proceeded to admire my new adornments.

"Madame, for your drink. I wasn't sure what you'd be in the mood for, so I paired a different cocktail for each part of the meal. We're starting off with a delicious Mai Tai." He placed the drink in front of me. This was like being on vacation. I took a sip. *Wow, he made his Mai Tais strong.* He smiled as I shivered from the alcohol. I had a feeling it was all part of some sinister tropical master plan to get me drunk and in bed tonight.

"We'll be starting off with grilled pineapple and coconut shrimp with a sweet and sour dipping sauce." He placed my plate in front of me. It was a nice small portion, which meant he had many more courses planned. There was even an orchid on the plate. *Impressive.* He sat down to join me.

"Grant, this is … amazing. Why did you go through all this trouble? Mac and cheese would have been fine," I said while stuffing pineapple in my mouth. I was starving. I had only had shots all afternoon.

"Lanie, how would making you mac and cheese be trying to win you back?" he mused.

"Have you tasted your mac and cheese? Really? It's fucking awesome!" I was serious.

"Yes, I've had it. And I love it, but I love you more, and you deserved something special. Lanie, I promise to treat you like this forever. Do you understand? I'm never going to stop giving you everything you deserve." He leaned across the table and kissed my forehead.

When we finished our first course, Grant took our plates and disappeared back inside. He obviously knew Mother Nature, because the weather was quite balmy and the soft breeze coming off the ocean seemed to carry the scent of the tropics along with it. I imagined this would be what our honeymoon would be like. When he returned, his tray was filled again. Beautiful presentation, but maybe it was just my own personal hot waiter that made it look so good.

"For our next course, I have a tuna and salmon ceviche paired with fresh guava slices and a balsamic martini. I hope you like it. It was the most difficult part of the meal." I gaped at the plate.

"Grant. This is really amazing. I mean, seriously, four-star restaurant level. You made this for me?"

"Of course. I wouldn't make this for any other woman alive. Not even my mother."

"Better not let Jennifer hear you say that." I giggled.

"You're right, she'd kick my ass, but that's neither here nor there. The point is you're worth it. All of this." I felt special, but I was still angry with him and he needed to work for this. I had to have a backbone and stand up for what was right for me. But the truth was, I was punishing myself keeping him at bay. I wanted to be with him. I needed to be. And it was just as much torture for me to be without him.

I began to eat. "Holy shit, this is so good. You had to have ordered this from somewhere. 'Fess up!" I accused.

"No, Lanie, I did the whole thing right here on my own. I swear to you!" He was actually insulted. It made me giggle even more.

"Fine. I believe you. Chillax. I have to eat this now before I freak out, because it looks so good. Stop talking to me." I laughed and placed a forkful of the tender, perfectly seasoned and marinated ceviche in my mouth. I died, it was so amazing. Grant just watched me, waiting for my reaction.

"Well? How is it?" He was so excited, but I just couldn't rush the exquisite bite in my mouth. I waved him off while I rolled the amazing tastes all over my tongue.

"Stop it, Lanie. You're turning me on," he said, quite seriously.

"No, no. Shh. It's so good. I just want to sit here and enjoy every single morsel."

"You're really making me want to jump you. Stop. Or I will. Now try the martini." He put his elbows on the table and rested his chin in his hands. It was hysterical. He looked like a little boy staring into the window of a toy store. I lifted the glass to my lips. I took a quick whiff. A balsamic vinegar martini didn't really sound great. I looked back at him and placed my lips on the glass and took a tiny baby sip.

"Holy shit!" I screamed.

'What? It's terrible? You hate it?" He was upset now.

"No! It's amazing. And it goes so well with the ceviche. Holy shit. You need to open a restaurant, and I mean like now." A huge goofy grin spread across his face. He was beaming. It was so cute I reached pinched his cheek and then kissed it.

"Kissing the cook? It must be good." He smiled and waved at my food.

“I’d do other things, but you know.” I winked. He frowned. Then we both laughed. I proceeded to spend the next few minutes with the ceviche and my martini; first a bite and then a sip, over and over. I thought I could orgasm it was so good.

After I had a bit of time to recover, Grant reached for my hand and pulled me to my feet. That’s when all those shots and the Mai Tai and the amazing martini hit me. I suddenly realized how buzzed I was. It was a good one, though. I didn’t feel drunk, and I had my wits about me. But I knew at this point I had to slow down. The way I was feeling, I’d be ripping his clothes off or pass out if I took it just one step further.

I smiled at Grant and he pulled me close against him. He felt so good. His body was warm and hard and strong, yet he held me so gently. We began to sway slowly to the Hawaiian music. I began to feel myself push against him. I wanted the contact. I needed to feel him. He responded with a low moan deep in his chest and his arms tightened around me.

We danced for a long time. Actually, I’m not sure if what we were doing was actually dancing. It was more like feeling each other while moving. I felt my hips start to move closer. It was only a matter of seconds before I was grinding against him. I sighed and pushed him back from me. I looked into his beautiful eyes and got lost.

“We have to sit down now. Your seduction attempts are too good.” He smiled and led me back to the table.

“Are you ready for the main course?” The time we had spent dancing had given me enough time to recover from the two courses I had thoroughly decimated. I couldn’t wait to see what he had planned next.

He was gone a lot longer this time. I was starting to think about going in to see where he was when I heard him coming back out. I looked out over the ocean to prolong my excitement. I wanted to see this right up close. I heard Grant clear his throat at my side.

I turned to look up at him but something caught my eye. I shot my eyes back to double check what I’d seen. *Yep. I saw it.* I was staring at his bare calves. He didn't seem to have any pants on. I slowly ran my eyes up his legs and caught site of the apron. I took a quick peek behind him and saw exactly that. His behind and it was hot. I looked at his face and he had a huge grin. Grant was wearing nothing but an apron and his ti leaf maile. However, I will say he was still in theme, as his apron was Hawaiian print. *How the hell did he do all this?*

On this tray were two lobster tails, broiled perfecto perfection, with drawn butter on the side. Next to those was a plate with two raw filet mignons. He placed the lobsters down on the table and turned towards his grill, giving me the best view so far of the night. I suddenly felt flushed. A familiar ache began down below.

"The main course is being served with A Tropical Itch."

"Well, doesn't that sound appetizing," I teased and then took a sip and hummed at how tasty it was. *I was in serious trouble.* This was going to go down way too easy. And he had a whole pitcher of it.

I watched him cook our meal, sipping on my drink, eyeing my lobster, and staring at his backside up and down, wishing he had put the apron on backwards. Life was good. I could barely control myself. He finally turned with our steaks and placed one on each plate. I know I had my best sex eyes going. He was enjoying it, too. He would brush up against my arm while pretending to do something at the table. He finally sat down and began to eat. He was playing me. But two could play at that game.

"I'm going to take a quick run to the bathroom," I said.

"That's cheating, Lanie. You can't take care of things yourself unless I get to watch." He smiled and pulled me over to him and sat me down on his lap. *Man, he was playing dirty.*

"I had no intentions of doing anything of the sort." But I was actually thinking about his lap right now. I could feel him underneath me. I wiggled myself down into him as if I was trying to get comfy, but I heard him sigh and it made me smirk. I got up, making sure to rub myself against him, and headed into the house. I ran to the bathroom, took care of some necessities, and then removed my shirt. The flowers lay perfectly over my breasts. *There.* Two could play at this game. I removed my shoes, too.

When I reached the door, he already had a slack jaw. He was waiting for me. It was endearing. I sat down in front of him and looked up from under my eyelashes and spread a sweet innocent smile over my face.

"You're fighting naked with nakedness? That is so unfair. This is my game and you have to find your own. Wait. I take that back. You didn't take your pants off. Fair is fair." He smiled smugly.

"Fine." I stood up and removed my pants, revealing just a black G-string. I sat back down and smiled smugly back. He swallowed loudly. I was sure it was exaggerated but turned towards my food and began to eat. So did he. He refilled my drink and kept pace with me. We talked about the chocolate spa weekend and all the things we were going to do with chocolate. We talked about places we wanted to travel to, and what would be a great honeymoon spot even though we were presently not engaged. Somewhere in the Fiji Islands in an over-the-water bungalow seemed to be the winner.

When we'd both finished, Grant cleared the dishes and kissed me before heading back inside for dessert. *Follow Grant back inside for some dessert? Oh, I really wanted to, but I made the rules, and dagnabbit, I was going to stick to them.* So I held my ground and sat in his backyard in my panties and lei. *Lovely.* Without him here, it didn't feel as sexy as it did before.

Within moments Grant came back with our last tray and my sexiness. He was now wearing his lei and boxers. He still looked hot as hell. He placed the tray on the side table and I again refrained from looking. He then proceeded to start a fire in his outdoor fireplace.

"Will you please join me by the fire?" I nodded my head quickly, as I was starting to feel a bit chilled. I chose the comfy couch positioned directly in front, and Grant retrieved the tray with our dessert and placed it on the cocktail table in front of me. On the tray were two cups of coffee (the mug rims covered in a dark sugar), a bottle of Bailey's, and the most gorgeous cupcakes. They were piled high with icing and each one was topped with a cherry and an orchid. I couldn't wait to taste one.

"You made me cupcakes? They're so pretty. Now you got these from a bakery, right?" I smiled, knowing he would say they were baked from scratch.

"Oh, no. These are baked from scratch, and they're special ones, too. The base is made with devil's food cake and filled with chocolate hazelnut spread and the icing is double chocolate fudge." He grinned devilishly. I grinned right back at him. Now, not only did I want to eat the cupcake, but also I wanted to rub the icing all over him and lick it off.

He poured Bailey's into my coffee and handed me the cup. I took a deep breath in and exhaled. The aroma was amazing. I grabbed a cupcake and began to slowly lick the icing off like it was spread on Grant. He watched me intently and I noticed the hand holding his coffee was shaking a bit. I made moaning noises and closed my eyes and basically gave him a show of appreciation for his baking skills along with one to turn him on. I could see from his boxers he was enjoying both.

I moved closer to him on the couch.

"These are just … orgasmic."

"I was hoping so."

I offered him a bite and he leaned in, licked off some of the icing, and then took a bite big enough to expose the chocolate hazelnut spread filling. I noticed he had a little bit of icing right on the edge of his mouth. I edged closer and closer. I basically crawled into his lap and straddled him. My panties didn't stand a chance; they were drenched almost immediately. I leaned in and licked the icing slowly from one end of his lips to the other. A soft oh escaped them and he grabbed another cupcake and rubbed the icing all over his mouth. Now a soft oh escaped my lips. I lapped it up and his lips parted for his tongue to dip into my mouth and we began to slowly swirl them together. I moved closer to rub myself against his chest, but he grabbed my arms and pushed me back; so I pouted.

"Lanie, you're entering dangerous territory here. I can't promise you I'll have the restraint you're asking of me if you continue to tempt me the way you are."

"How about we move this party inside?" I beckoned.

"Now you're truly asking for it. I have no resolve when it comes to you and your beautiful body. I'm right on the brink."

I got up and grabbed another cupcake and my coffee and headed inside. I turned and gave him my best come-hither-and-hurry-the-hell-up glance and he grabbed the whole tray and followed quickly behind me.

We settled on his living room couch. He grabbed a cupcake, moved my lei quickly out of the way and smushed the cupcake right onto my breast.

"Oh, no. Look what I've done. I've made a mess. Let me clean that up for you." And he began to suck the icing off me. I arched my back toward him and prayed there were enough cupcakes to cover my entire body and his. God, I loved chocolate hazelnut spread. There had to be some kind of aphrodisiac in it. He grabbed my arms right at my biceps so I was basically pinned to his face as he feasted. I felt my whole body aching for him now.

When every little bit had been cleaned off and I had squeaky-clean breasts, he released me and sat back.

"What? What are you doing?" I said, confused.

"I'm doing the right thing and not letting this progress any further. I will keep rule number two's integrity."

I couldn't believe it. I was letting number two go to pot and he was going to stop it? *Seriously? Isn't this what all the trouble he went to was about?* The whole night, the food, the drinks, the seduction, and now he wasn't going to be a rule-breaker?

"Fine," I said angrily, and tried to pull myself off his lap. Rejection hurt. Was it due to her? That pissed me off even more. Now I could feel a scowl on my face.

"Lanie." He gently placed me all the way back down on his lap. He took my face in his hands and looked me straight in the eye. "I did all this for you. Not just to get you in bed, although I'm not adverse to that at all. But I digress. This whole night was to show you how I would do anything to make you happy. If I just went right in for the kill, what would I be showing you exactly? That you're a great lay? You mean so much more to me than that. I want to follow your rules." He sounded so sincere and I instantly felt like an ass.

"But why all the hot nakedness then?" I really wanted to know.

"Lanie, I didn't say it couldn't be fun. I promised to follow your demands because I thought they were correct. But I can't keep my hands off you. So I have to be a little bad. I hope you don't mind."

"Grant, I love you. Thank you for tonight. For stopping me, I think."

He chuckled and pulled me into a tight hug.

"Lanie, I love you more than you can ever fathom. It's very hard for me to stop. I don't really want to. But I'm doing it for you. How lame does all this sound?"

"It's not lame at all. It's sweet … and thoughtful … and it makes me realize even more how lucky I am to have you." I nestled my face into his neck and immediately started nibbling. He pushed me back.

"What are you doing? I just got us stopped and you're going to get me all started again." He laughed.

"You said we could have fun. Would it be easier to not touch each other?" My voice kind of squeaked at the end. I double eyebrowed Grant. He shot me a hot what-are-you-thinking look. I smiled wide.

"Well, it's touching you that makes it so hard to stop; so what if we just got really close and never touched?" I raised my brows now waiting for his response.

He pushed me off his lap, pulled off his boxers and stood up on his knees, facing me. Then he pointed at me. I won't say with what, but anyone who is intimate with any man knows how they get with their Cannoli whether it's spongy or rock hard. They all have to make it do silly stuff. Like puppet shows, or using it as a stylus for your tablet, and other things it shouldn't be used for. This one was presently a pointer. I had to laugh and if he kept doing things like that, I wouldn't have to worry about how to get myself to stop.

He noticed the look on my face; he blushed and let it drop. "You're turn," he said sheepishly. I shook my head and removed my panties, then knelt the same way in front of him. We moved closer together until we were just an inch or two apart.

He took a deep breath in and then let out a long exhale. His lids became heavy and I could tell mine were, too. We were so quiet, even breathing silently. He leaned his face into mine like he was going to kiss me, but stayed just far enough away to make it torturous. The electricity between us was intense. The pull was so hard to resist. He raised his hands and mock ran them slowly over my body. My skin tingled everywhere he hovered, as if I could feel the energy from his hands caressing me.

I mimicked his movements, but ran my hands over his chest. I moved my parted lips close to it and began to softly breathe across his skin. So hard not to just bite it. I wanted to so badly. I let a small sound escape my throat, which in turn made him groan. We continued to not touch each other until we were both breathing faster and heavier. I looked him in the eye to let him know this was becoming too much for me.

"Lanie, I am so with you on that one. But that should show you I don't even have to touch you to want to make love to you. I'm so worked up I could explode in a second. I need you."

"Grant. Yes. Take me upstairs. Do me on the stairs. Take me right here. But I need you. Now. I need to feel you inside me. I need to be one with you. Please, break rule number two."

He grabbed me and pulled my body against his. The feel of his skin against mine was amazing and I couldn't help but start brushing back and forth against him. I shut my eyes and pushed my hips into him. He stood up, so I opened my eyes to see what he was up to. He reached for my hand and pulled me to my feet.

"Where are we …?" He put his finger over my lips to hush me. He reached down and picked me up and headed towards the stairs. He grazed his nose over my breasts repeatedly as he walked, looking up now and then to make sure we weren't going to crash into a wall. We giggled as he tried to maneuver me. When we reached the stairs, Grant looked up, and then he put me down.

"You're not going to take me to your man-cave?" I giggled.

"Yes, I am, but not holding you like that." He bent over and slung me over his shoulder. I watched in horror as he walked up the stairs; the floor was getting further and further away. Images danced in my head of us losing balance and tumbling backwards. My face, that floor. *No thanks.* I shut my eyes. I knew he was strong enough to carry me. He'd never let anything happen to me, yet the fear existed.

"You can open your eyes now. I know you have them shut, Chicken." He placed me on my feet.

We got into his room, where he quickly offered me the facilities. I took him up on it. I freshened up, and when I got back he had the bed turned down and candles lit everywhere. There was music playing softly in the background. He always had something romantic around the corner waiting for me. I felt loved.

He took a moment as well and I sat down on the bed and waited for him. He came out of the bathroom and was on me before I knew what hit me. His lips crushed to mine and he lowered me to my back. We proceeded to grope and make out until I was grinding against him furiously, anything to get him closer to where I needed him to be. He placed his arm around me and pulled me up to the pillows. I knew I wouldn't be able to hold back. I was ready to make passionate love to him without a second thought about stupid rule number two.

"Lanie, I'm going to …"

Chapter 45

My Feng Shui Is Off

"… explode and we won't have to stop because we're not going to get to that point if we keep going like this."

"Well, I'm not stopping, so screw rule number two. All I care about is being here with you, like this, right now. And possibly all day tomorrow, too." I smiled and pulled him down on top of me. I began to grind into him, my hips feverishly trying to seek out pleasure against his. I was losing control. This whole night just made me realize how much I loved and needed Grant.

"You're too easy, Lanie. I mean … not easy. It's just that you're letting me off the hook too easily. I hurt you. I did something stupid, very stupid. And you're giving in too easy. Not that I mind. The challenge was a lot of fun." He began to slowly roll his hips into mine, parting my legs as he went. I could feel sweet release coming soon.

The room was dark other than the candles and it was extremely hot, or maybe that was just us. I had a thin layer of sweat over my skin, as did Grant, but it just added to the experience.

He slid himself against me while kissing me deeply. I could barely take it anymore. Rule number two was about to meet its demise. And that's when Grant rolled off of me and to my side. He continued to kiss and touch me.

"What are you doing?" I asked, confused and slightly disappointed. I was ready to just jump on top of him and take him.

"Lanie, you have no idea how badly I want to make love to you right now. But the funny thing is … I want this to be right. And although it feels so right, you're still mad at me. And I wouldn't feel so great about it knowing it's the heat of the moment, not your forgiveness that's moving us in this direction. I want you. I do. But I won't make love to you until you've put my ring back on your finger.

Holy crap. The ring! I started to feel panic and a knot in my stomach. *How was I going to tell him I lost the ring?* I sat up rather quickly, pulled my knees to my chest, put my face in my hands and cried.

"What's wrong? Lanie? Please … you're scaring me. Don't you plan on putting the ring back on? Please tell me why you're crying." He pulled my face towards his. He looked distressed and as panicked as I probably did.

"Oh Grant. I don't know where it is. I can't find it! I put it in the dish from Italy, and now it's gone. We all looked for it. No one can find it. I lost it. You hate me now." I proceeded to cry my little eyes out. But Grant laughed. I looked at him like he was insane.

"Why are you laughing? You think this is funny?"

"No. Well, yes. Not that you're crying, but that you think you lost it." He reached into his nightstand and pulled out the original box the ring came in and handed it to me. I opened it and there sat my ring, nice and safe.

"You had it this whole time? Why didn't you tell me? You …you took it back?"

"Yes, Lanie. I took it back. When you're ready, I want to be the one to put it back on your finger. It's just that I want it to be right again. I want you to want it."

"I do."

"Then when you're ready, all you need to do is ask me, and I'll gladly put it back on your finger."

"Grant, I want you to put the ring back on my finger. I want to be with you forever and be your wife."

Grant's eyes lit up and he grabbed me and pulled me close and covered me in kisses. I immediately got worked up again and started to grind. He pushed me back again.

"Lanie, not until that ring is back on your finger. And you're acting like a guy right now. Please, when you're positive you're not mad at me anymore, and mean it, I will give you this ring again. But we need to get through this. I need to know you're past this. I know you love me. But I'm doing this for you, my love."

I wanted the ring back on my finger that instant and I wanted Grant to make love to me. But he was right. I was reacting on the emotions of being with him right now, not on healing the hurt. I needed to do that first. *Screw him for being right. Screw him for what he did or we wouldn't be in this situation. And screw him for being so God damn irresistible that I needed him right here and now.* I groaned and pulled a pillow over my face. Maybe if I didn't look at him this wouldn't be so hard.

I heard him chuckle and he tried to pull the pillow away.

"Lanie, if you think for one second I don't have the biggest case of blue balls in history right now, you're out of your mind. I'm dying over here. They're cobalt blue, they're so blue. And they hurt. Bad."

I thought about rubbing them for him. *Wonder if that would change his mind?* I knew if I just threw myself at him there would be no point of return for him. But again, he was trying to prove to that he loved me and was trying to let me heal. He was already forgiven, but I knew as soon as I made a plan to take that bitch out for what she did, all the feelings would come right back to the surface. It wasn't right for me to make him think everything was okay and then throw it back in his face if I ended up not being okay later. He was right. I needed time.

I rolled over and put my back to Grant and shut my eyes tight, hoping he wouldn't touch me because I wouldn't be able to help myself. Then I hoped he would touch me so I could break this damn rule. I felt him slide up behind me and pull me into him. I sighed and nestled in. I had an ache between my legs that would just not quit, so at the moment sleep was out of the question.

I started to think about the entire night and how wonderful it had been. Everything had felt so right between us. Everything. I thought about how the ring was safe and how badly I wanted it back on my finger. It felt like we were broken up. I didn't like it. And there was a part of me that felt like somehow Brianna had won because I indeed had broken off the engagement. Then my mind just wandered.

Eventually, I fell into a deep sleep shortly after my body cooled down. At first my sleep was restful, but then I guess my mind started to work and I was more aware of everything around me.

Somewhere early in the morning or maybe it was still night, I felt Grant stir behind me. I realized we were still in the same position we'd fallen asleep in and I was a bit sore. I moved a bit and I heard Grant groan. I also felt him get hard against my bottom. I was half asleep, but the feel of him made every nerve in my body come to life. I wiggled my backside against him and he shifted until he was between my legs and he be began to slowly move, cruelly driving me absolutely insane.

I began to move with him and he reached for my girls, gently squeezing them.

"Oh Baby, yes," I purred.

He started to quicken his pace but then my stupid mind decided to associate what was happening here with what had happened between him and Brianna. I could feel my blood pressure start to rise. *Is this what he had done with her?* I was on fire now and I pulled myself away from him and jumped out of bed.

"Lanie, what's wrong?" He seemed shocked.

"I can't do this. I have to go."

"What? What are you talking about? I told you. This isn't going to happen until that ring is on your finger again. We were just playing. Really."

"Oh? Is that what you told Brianna? That you were just playing?" I was pissed. I grabbed his t-shirt and threw it on, suddenly feeling very naked in front of him. I began to pace back and forth across the room.

"What are you talking about?" He stared at me and then I think it hit him as his expression changed drastically. He jumped out of bed and was on me in a second, grabbing me into his arms and pulling me in tight. "I would never do that. No, Lanie, no. It wasn't like that at all. I can of course see how you would think that … the similarities of position, but I was fully dressed and I did not respond like that. This, this was all about you. I'm so sorry. I never … I didn't think."

"You were right. I'm not ready. I thought I was. This whole night just erased everything. The dinner. The romance. The drinks. But I'm still angry and I can't stop picturing it. Just can't get it out of my head. And I can't do this until it's not there anymore." I was in tears now and he held me even tighter.

"Lanie, I love you. There is *no other woman* for me. None. Nothing happened. Not on my end. I'm in love with you. Please. Don't go. I don't want you leaving now anyway. It's the middle of the night." He sounded so disheartened. I was dejected, and I felt myself pulling away.

"Please, Lanie, please. Don't leave." He was despondent now. He gripped me and was not letting go. I started to struggle and he struggled back. He pushed me up against a corner of the room and put an arm up on either side of me so I couldn't leave. He pushed his body against mine so I couldn't move. He began to kiss me desperately, almost forcing them on me. I began to try and push him off me but he wouldn't let up. I would start to kiss him back and then try and turn my head to stop him. I was so confused. I wanted him to stop but I also wanted him, my anger and desire fighting a battle that was never going to be won. He pushed his face into my neck and began to bite and suck.

"Grant. Stop. Get off," I said loudly, but he didn't stop. I started to lose my temper. I just needed to get him to back off a bit so I could think. But he was relentless.

"Get off of me right now. Stop. Don't you know what stop means?" I screamed and then I heard the door open.

"Grant, you need to let Lanie go. I know you're not doing her any harm, but the lady is asking for you to stop. And I really don't want to have to step in." Dylan stood in the doorway, wearing nothing but his boxers. Chelsie stood behind him in a bathrobe. I didn't expect to see Samantha or Steve, as they both slept like the dead.

Grant stepped back and put his arms at his sides. He looked at me apologetically and it was obvious how distraught he was. I'm sure he never meant for things to get to this point. I didn't either, but with Chelsie and Dylan here, the entire dynamic had changed. Grant was a villain. I didn't want him to be. He wasn't. It was just a fight.

"I would never—Dylan, you know I wasn't hurting her. I love her. It wasn't like that." He moved to the side to let me pass. I pulled at his shirt to make sure I was covered. I moved behind Dylan like he was protecting me but I knew Grant was only trying to love me. At this moment he probably felt like complete shit. I felt terrible, but before I could say anything, Dylan pushed me out of the room.

"I'm going to walk Lanie back to her place. Chelsie, this is all you," he said. He gave Grant a small smile to know he wasn't really mad at him. I heard Chelsie's voice as Dylan and I walked down the hall.

"Grant, you really mind-fucked her. Give her time. Don't force it."

"I wasn't. I stopped us so many times tonight, so she'd know I want her to forgive me completely. I guess I really fucked everything up."

I heard his door close. We walked down the stairs and I could feel the tears again. I was really getting tired of crying all the time. Dylan put his arm around my shoulders and walked me home. I left him at the door.

"You going to be okay, Lanie? Do you want me to stay? Maybe have some coffee?" he offered.

"No. I think I want to be alone right now. Thanks, but you didn't have to do that. Grant wasn't hurting me. We were just having a moment," I said.

"I know, Honey. That's why I came. I didn't want things to escalate. You both needed to cool down. Although I do like my angry sex with Samantha."

"Umm, TMI, Dylan. Well I'm going to go in. Neither of us are dressed appropriately for late night gallivanting."

"Actually, we are completely appropriate. Just with the wrong person." He smiled and rubbed the top of my head and waited for me to close the door. I did and started to walk away when I heard a knock. I opened the door and Dylan was still there.

"Did you forget something?" I said.

"Lock the door." He pointed at the locks.

"Why? Who's going to come in? You? Grant? That's silly."

"Please lock the door. And I wanted to say something. Grant fucked up and it'll kill him for the rest of his life even after you forgive him. Lanie, that man only loves you. You have to know that. He can't exist without you." He smiled and waited again for me to shut the door. I nodded my head, shut and locked it. I knew he was right; I just had to get past picturing it in my head. It was ripping my heart out.

The house seemed empty. It was way too quiet. I went looking for Woof.

I found him sleeping by his food bowls. I picked him up and gave him a kiss and brought him upstairs with me. He purred in my arms and I felt comforted. Animals really had something about them; they just knew when you were sad.

When I reached my room, I threw on a pair of panties but kept Grant's t-shirt on. I wanted to feel him close to me and his tee was all I had. I clung to it and Woof as I lay down in bed. I was tired but I didn't think I could fall back to sleep. I wished I were still back at Grant's. I had to get my revenge on Brianna if things were going to change. I needed to hurt her like she hurt me. I just wasn't sure how.

Dane's offer sounded great. But I wanted quick revenge and I was nervous about calling her dad. Who knew if he would rip into me or blow me off? I pondered my choices over and over again and soon sleep took me over.

I dreamt of Grant. I was happy. Everything was perfect. There was no more sadness or anger, just Grant and I and love. I didn't want to wake up. I heard a knocking on my door. I rolled over and pulled the covers over my head.

"Go away." I wanted to go back to my dream. Where everything was perfect with Grant.

The knocking continued. I was getting pissed off. I just wanted to dream.

"I said go away. I'm sleeping. I just want to sleep."

"Lanie?" I heard Samantha's small voice from the other side of the door. "It's one in the afternoon. Are you okay?"

I jumped out of bed. *Holy crap. I'd slept half the day away.* I opened the door and Samantha came in.

"You look like shit."

"You just woke me out of a sound sleep."

"Sleep is a sign of depression. How can I help you, Lanie? I hate things being like this. My feng shui is off."

"Gee, Samantha, I don't want to mess up your fuck shui. I'll run over and kiss Grant's ass now," I said, thoroughly annoyed. Samantha hung her head down and seemed genuinely hurt.

"I'm sorry. I know you're trying to help. I just don't know how to make this all better. I don't know how to get the image out of my head. I can't do it. It's killing me." It really was just the thought of her rubbing against him, like he and I had last night.

"Lanie, it's not about picturing them in your head. Picture you and Grant in your head. You need to let it go. You need to forgive him. How can we make that happen? How can I help?"

"Tell me I'm being stupid. Tell me it shouldn't bother me."

"I can't do that, Lanie. I'd rip the head off anyone who touched Dylan. Oh, I bet that's not helping." *Ripping her head off sounded awesome.*

"I need to bleach my brain. Badly. Can you do that?" I said, really hoping she had a way.

"Vodka is the only bleach I know of," she said with an evil grin.

"Is it too early to start?" I was seriously considering this.

"Lanie, it's the afternoon. We can drink right now." She ran out of the room. I threw on a pair of sweats, knowing today was going to be a lay-around-the-house-drunk-with-Samantha-day. Those were some of my favorite days. I grabbed my phone to text Chelsie to come over, but there were several texts from Grant.

> *G: Lanie? Are you still awake?*
> *G: OK, well I hope you're sleeping. Not not talking to me.*
> *G: I'm so sorry Lanie. Please. Hope I didn't scare you. Never meant to hurt you.*
> *G: I love you.*
> *G: Please text me so I know you're OK.*
> *G: So I know you still love me.*

I felt terrible. I sent him a quick text.

> *L: I love you. I will always love you. We'll figure this out. Drunk girl's day. CYL*

He quickly texted back.

> *G: Watch Samantha. She likes vulnerable girls. :) Thank you. Have fun. Here if you need me.*
> *L: If I do Samantha we'll call it even. OK? j/k <3s*

G: Haha. No. You're mine. And I am yours. Only Yours!
L: I know. I just have to heal. Bear with me.

I texted Chelsie to get her ass over to get drunk with me and in a matter of moments, Chelsie and Samantha were in my room with Vodka, three tall glasses of ice, cranberry juice, and shot glasses. *Oh there was going to be some serious drinking going on.* And it started. We each got a glass with ice and mixed a cranberry and vodka. Samantha even thought of straws. Chelsie lined up the shot glasses and pulled something out of her pocket. There were sweetener packets and lemon juice, just divine: lemon drop shots lo-cal, just perfect. And we slammed the drinks. Shot after shot after shot.

"This one's for Dylan's sexy legs in boxers," I hooted.

"Here, here." Chelsie slammed hers back.

"You should see under the boxers." Samantha slammed hers back. Chelsie and I just made faces.

So the shots were all toasts to someone. Soon I was feeling extremely drunk. I hadn't eaten since last night. But with all the food I'd eaten, I was probably still fine.

"I have to do something," I said.

"Oh goody. Tell us what you have to do!" Samantha laughed out, while mocking me. She gave me a weird, low, guy voice when she repeated me. Samantha could hold her vodka; drink it like water. Still, I could tell she was trashed, too. Chelsie just giggled from the floor. She had been sitting there with all the liquor, playing bartender, but right now she was leaning against the bed.

"I have to kick Brianna Stone's fat ass!" I said. Chelsie giggled some more and held up another shot for me. I grabbed it and downed it. I shivered all over and then grabbed my landline. If I was going to make a call like this, I would have to make sure every word was heard.

"What are you doing, Lanie?" Samantha sounded concerned.

“I have to make a phone call.” I smiled and started to look for the number on my desk.

“Oh, Honey, do you really think it’s a good idea to make that call right now?” Chelsie said from the floor. She was now lying on her back staring at me.

“Yes, because I am backed by vodka. So I have vodka muscles right now. It’s time,” I said without much confidence at all.

“No. It’s perfect. She’s right. She’ll be able to answer on the fly. Lanie’s good like that when she’s drunk and fired up. Go for it, Lanie.” Samantha pointed at the phone. I picked it up and started dialing. I knew I’d be okay because the girls would bail me out if I got stuck. *Maybe I should put it on speakerphone.* I did and it was ringing.

“Mr. Stone’s office. Good afternoon. May I help you?” I heard a very young woman’s voice on the other end of the phone. I was sure she was pretty, too.

“Ms. Lanie Rhodes for Mr. Stone, please.”

“Are you scheduled for a call, Ms. Rhodes?”

“I’m sure if you let Mr. Stone know I’m on the phone, he’ll take the call,” I said with as much attitude as I could. Chelsie gave me a thumbs-up and Samantha did some silent clapping.

“Mr. Stone is quite busy this afternoon. If you’d like to leave a number, I’ll be sure …”

“You will tell Mr. Stone I’m on the phone and you’ll do it now. Do you understand me? Right now.”

“Yes, Ma’am.” Music started to play. The girls waited with me for Mr. Stone to answer.

“Mr. Stone will be with you in just one moment, Ms. Rhodes.” Her snotty little power trip was over. It was butt-kissing time.

“Thank you.” I smiled at my girls.

“Ms. Rhodes. To what do I owe the pleasure?”

“Good afternoon, Mr. Stone. I thought it would be appropriate to call and speak with you directly to tell you how pleased I am with our new partnership,” I said corporately, with just a tinge of sweet.

“Yes, as am I. I was quite impressed with your press conference. You’re a real ball buster, aren’t you?” he mused.

“Yes, I can be,” I said confidently. Score one for vodka.

“So, there really is more to this call than just telling me how pleased you are, I’m sure. I’m just like you. You can’t fool someone on a mission. What’s your mission, Ms. Rhodes?” This guy was sharp. And he was a shark. And I had a feeling this would be a lot easier than I thought.

“Please, call me Lanie.”

“All right. And you can call me Larry.” I took two shots one after the other. I felt sober, but I knew I was far from it.

“So as not to waste your time, I’ll get right to the point. I have a large problem with your daughter, Brianna. I’m sorry if that offends you, but I believe you have the right to know how unprofessional she is.”

“Oh? Enlighten me.” *Oh crap.*

“Well, she made some advances toward one of my partners while the contracts were being negotiated.”

“And that would be with Grant Bennett? Yes?” he said calmly.

“Yes. It would.”

“And if it was so unprofessional, why is Mr. Bennett not making this phone call?”

“Because he’s being a gentleman toward your daughter, although I have no idea why. And I’m sure this news will put our contract on critical status with you. I’m prepared …”

“Ms. Rhodes—Lanie, does Mr. Bennett partner with you in other ways than your company?”

"I can't see how that's any of your business," I said, hoping he would go a different way.

"Really, Lanie, don't try and bullshit a bull-shitter. It doesn't become you. Another try?" Now he was starting to sound like a parent. I looked at my girls nervously.

"Tell him," Samantha mouthed.

"All right, since we're being blunt. Your daughter made advances toward my fiancé and business partner, Grant Bennett. I find it completely unprofessional and honestly it was a shitty thing for her to do. Not only did she show up in his room, undressed, and throw herself at him while I was on webcam with him, but then she pulled another stunt I'm not really willing to discuss. Is this the way you operate your companies, Mr. Stone—Larry?"

There was silence on the other end for a moment. I might have just screwed my company out of a huge contract. The girls and I did a shot. I could feel the alcohol truly setting in.

"Nothing to say, Larry?"

"Lanie, are you claiming sexual harassment here?"

"No, I'm not. But if we're to continue this relationship and make shit loads of money for both our companies, you need to put your daughter on a leash and keep her away from my fiancé. Is that how she closes deals for you? She sleeps with your business partners? Or at least tries to?"

I was actually wondering what the hell kind of vomit was spewing from my mouth. *Oh shit.* I was going to blow this whole thing. Chelsie and Samantha noticed the shift in my demeanor and we all waited for his reply, while holding our breaths.

"Ms. Rhodes, I find your comments to be …" *Oh shit, this was it. I shouldn't have done this.* "… refreshing. Not often does an executive have the balls to call me up and tell me bluntly my daughter is a slut. I like your moxie. This is going to be a fun partnership. I'll put my daughter back in line and make sure your fiancé is well off limits. I'm doing this as a favor to you. I ask in return that, if ever needed, you will handle of my PR *personally*. I think you're a shark in sheep's clothing, Lanie. I like knowing you're an ally. Do we have an agreement?"

Chelsie gave a quick fist pump and Samantha got wide-eyed and then silently screamed. I felt a huge amount of relief and then triumphant. *I won, shit yeah!*

"Yes, sir. I agree to your terms. And your daughter?"

"I'll be switching her to a different company. You'll no longer have to deal with her, effective immediately, and my apologies to you. She's always been a bit of a whore. She takes after her mother. That was a big mistake I'm still paying for. If you have a man who didn't cheat on you with her, I suggest you hold onto him, Ms. Rhodes. Most men crumble at her feet. She's rather relentless. I see she's met her match with you, though."

"Thank you, Larry. I appreciate your tact in dealing with this matter. I look forward to working with you."

"I'm also looking forward to working with you. I have a feeling you're going to be a major asset for this venture. I'm very pleased. Have a nice day, Lanie." He hung up the phone.

As soon as I put the receiver down, my girls and I squealed like little schoolgirls. *Holy crap! I did it. I was totally stoked.*

"Lanie, that was amazing. That man was eating out of your hand and he liked you. He actually called his daughter a whore!" Chelsie said.

"Well she is a whore, a total slut. And now you have exacted your revenge, Lanie. Now can you and Grant go back to being happy?" Samantha pleaded.

"I need to see how this plays out first. But yes, this is a huge step in the right direction."

We all rose yet another glass and did our final shots. The bottle was empty and we were all feeling mighty fine. I felt so much better, but I wouldn't feel my best until I knew Brianna was in hell.

Not two seconds after we put our glasses down, my cell phone rang. I looked at the caller ID.

"Holy shit, it's …

Chapter 46

LIES! LIES! LIES!

"… Brianna!" I said, staring at the phone.

"Well, answer it! This is what you've been waiting for. You wanted to hear her cry and now you get to. Answer before it goes into voice mail," Chelsie urged.

"Lanie Rhodes speaking. Can I help you?" I said in my most corporate tone.

"Don't play all coy, Lanie. You fucking know it's me, you bitch. You called my father!" Brianna spat.

"You've got a lot of nerve pointing fingers. You were supposed to back off from Grant, but you didn't. I told you if you kept pulling your shit I was calling your father. You didn't, so I did," I said calmly.

"You're a total bitch, Lanie. My father removed me from that company and is sending me to one I hate. And I didn't have anything to do with Grant coming to my room. He did that all on his own!"

"I'd rather be a bitch than a whore like you. Quite frankly, I don't believe you. I spoke to Grant about the whole thing and I'm quite aware you called him, crying and begging for him to come talk to you." I kept my cool demeanor. Chelsie was red in the face and kept holding her hand out for the phone. I smiled and shook my head at her. *This call was mine.*

"You're a stupid naïve girl, Lanie. He's lying to you, like all men do. He was at my door on his own. I didn't call him. Why would I? And everything that happened between us, he started. And it was so good," she said, sickeningly sweet. If I had them, my hackles would be up.

"Oh really? Well, maybe the men you frequent are liars and cheats, but not my Grant. And what exactly are you claiming happened, Ms. Stone? I could use the laugh."

"Oh, you want details? He came to my room and told me how sorry he was that he had to pretend to not want me, and how upset I looked. He said he wanted to help me relax. So he started to rub my shoulders, and kept pulling my bathrobe lower so he could touch me more but then he just yanked my bathrobe completely off, fast, and moved right to my tits. He pushed me down on the bed so he could lick and suck on them. It was so fucking good. His hands and mouth are so strong. Then he moved down until he got to my panties and he ripped them off me, with his teeth. He rubbed my ass and then pushed my legs apart and fingered me until I came. I know why you don't want to lose him. He's amazing."

"I don't believe you." I cemented my stand. Of course this whole time I'm picturing everything in my head and the insecure part of me is freaking out. Samantha noticed my face. She put an arm around me and shook her head no.

"Well, it's the truth. He kissed me hard, it was so hot. Then he took his clothes off and got in bed with me. He pushed right up against my back and I felt how hard he was for me all night long."

My blood was boiling. I needed to stay away from Grant for the rest of the day. Not because I believed her, but just hearing her saying the words was enough to rile me up and take it out on him.

"What's the matter, Lanie? Nothing to say? Your man was all over me. He kept telling me how it was the best he ever had. But there was so much more."

"You should write porn. You can make it up so easily. Please, be my guest."

"He held me all night. Every once in a while he'd rub into me or grab my tits or kiss my neck. Then he got worked up and he slid himself between my legs and started to dry hump me. Oh I helped him out too and this time he let me. And when I came again? He held me until I stopped. And then I gave him something. I sucked him so good, he came in seconds, and then I sucked some more. He's a loud one when he comes, isn't he?"

Lies! Lies! Lies! I couldn't stand to listen to her lies anymore. But I had to contain my anger until this call was over. I had to make sure she didn't know she was getting to me.

"Brianna, your father and I have an agreement. You are no longer working with our company and you are no longer to have any contact with Grant. Not that you can, anyway."

"If you think we haven't been in contact since he left, you're out of your mind. I'm very well aware your engagement is off. And I'm not to contact him for business purposes. However, personally, I can do whatever the hell I want. And if you think for one minute I'm giving up on him now that he's free? You're even stupider than I thought."

"Ms. Stone, this conversation is over. Don't call me again. And stay away from Grant. Our engagement is perfectly intact, so, I'm not sure where you're getting your information. Good bye and fuck off." I hung up and threw my phone on the bed.

How the hell did she know Grant and I were not presently engaged? Had she been talking to him? *No. It wasn't possible.* She was just trying to get my goat and she was good at it. I was even madder than before. I wanted to punch her in the face, rip her hair out.

I filled the girls in on every detail of the call. Every single exact word said verbatim with the same tone she used. Samantha looked appalled, which I found amusing for some reason. And Chelsie looked like she was going to kill someone. I swear I saw steam coming out of her ears.

"Are you kidding me? Who the hell does she think she is? I can't believe you stayed so calm through that whole phone call. What the hell, Lanie?" Chelsie shouted.

"I needed her to think she wasn't getting to me. If I let her know anything she said was bothering me, then she won. And that bitch is not winning." I was so fired up. I wanted to go talk to Grant, but I knew I'd only get upset with him because her words hurt me so much. What I should do is go over there and remove rule number two for the whole night. But I needed to cool down first. For one, I was trashed, and I needed to sober up a bit. If I let my emotions run wild, then something was bound to go wrong. I knew myself better than that.

"I need to go take a shower." I got up and started to walk out of the room.

"You're going to go shower? Right now?"

"Yes, maybe a bath. Yeah, I think I'll take a nice, long bath." I heard Chelsie say something about calling Grant. It was fine with me. He'd find out about the call, anyway. I headed right to my room and closed the door. I sat down on the edge of my bed and stared at the picture of Grant and me on my nightstand. *How the hell did this all get so messed up?* Our whole lives we knew each other and nothing like the past few months had ever happened. Were Grant and I cursed? If we were together, would everything always be a struggle?

I sighed deeply and headed for the bathroom, started my water and poured in way too much bath salt and bubble bath. I hoped I'd float away to a happier place. I undressed and stepped in. Immediately, I could feel my muscles begin to relax. I took in a deep breath and tried to let it all go when I exhaled.

It was not going to be that easy. I thought about what she said. Then I thought about why I got so mad last night. *Damn it.* This was just screwing with my head. Last night was nothing like she described. Grant loved me. He wouldn't touch her. *Well, he did touch her, but nothing like she said.* I closed my eyes and tried to clear my mind. I just thought of the color black; emptiness, nothingness.

Soon, I heard a small tapping noise. I dismissed it. My mom would never bother me during a bath. Must be Woof. Then I heard the door open. I kept my eyes closed, waiting for someone to let me know they were there. Nothing. Not even breathing. I opened my eyes and jumped.

Grant knelt beside the tub and his face was only inches from mine. *He scared the shit out of me.*

"Never sneak up on someone like that, especially when they're naked and in the bath. I could have drowned."

"You could have drowned?" He laughed at me.

"Yes. What are you doing here? Not that I'm not happy to see you or anything. I am." I said the last two words softly.

"I hear you've had a busy day. Some good and some not-so-good." He sounded sympathetic.

"Something like that."

"Chelsie told me everything. I'm so sorry, Lanie."

"Why are you sorry? Did you do it? I don't think you did. So don't worry about it," I said flatly. I didn't want to have this conversation in case I lost it on him. It would be so wrong.

"Lanie, if I hadn't done what I did, then none of this would be happening. So yes, I do have something to be sorry for." He pulled back from me. I put my hand over his before he could pull completely away from the tub. He looked at me and repositioned himself so he was sitting next to the tub, holding my hand.

"You look absolutely fabulous. Did I mention that to you?" He smiled his sweet hot smile and I thought about pulling him in here with me, clothes and all.

"So I'm bubbilicious? Is that it?" I smiled and placed my arms on the edge of the tub. Grant immediately started to blow the bubbles off my chest. I covered them back up.

"Hey, what do you think you're doing?" I teased him and sunk myself into the water again.

"I find it very hard to keep my hands off you." He smiled and reached into the tub, feeling for things.

"Looking for the soap or something?" I handed him the soap and my loofah. "Think you could just get my back for me?" Grant growled and grabbed the items from my hand. He furiously soaped up the loofah and turned me so my back was facing him. He began to scrub. I thought about Brianna's words: 'He was rubbing my shoulders and then he just kept getting lower and lower.' Yeah, that killed the mood.

"Grant, Brianna said something on the phone I wanted to ask you about," I said timidly.

"Ask me anything, I have nothing to hide," he said confidently.

"She said you've been in contact since you left. Is it true?" I asked. He stopped scrubbing. *Shit.*

"I promised you I wouldn't lie, and I won't. Yes, she has contacted me."

"But I blocked her number from your phone. I have to remember to block her number from mine, too, apparently."

"Lanie, there's still email. And she tried to webcam me the other day, too," he said, like he was afraid of what my reaction was going to be.

"You've been in contact with her," I said out loud, even thought it was meant for myself.

"I said she tried to contact me. Not that I had responded. I haven't. "

"How many emails?" I said. I don't know what difference it made, but I wanted to know.

"To be honest, I'd have to say at least one or two a day since I've been back. She's really quite persistent. I haven't replied at all. I just delete them." He was looking down at the floor and then quickly looked into my eyes so I could see he was being honest.

"Well, the first thing you need to do is block that email address. And I mean now. Today, as soon as you're back at your computer. Hell, do it from my phone. It's right there on the counter." I pointed.

"Okay." He grabbed my phone.

"Grant. Really. Are you trying to prove something to me?"

"Yes, Love. I'm trying to let you know you have nothing to worry about. I'll do whatever makes you comfortable. If ignoring and erasing her messages isn't enough, I'll do whatever it takes until it is. After speaking with her today, your imagination must be going insane."

"My imagination? Last time I checked, you actually did go to her room and sleep next to her and hold her all night. That's not my imagination." *Yeah, this wasn't going to go well.* I was too mad at Brianna. I wanted him here, but I knew it would be better for him to leave.

"I think you need to go. I want to be alone right now," I said as I pulled the bubbles toward me to cover myself.

"You want me to go? Lanie, please, I don't want to be away from you. Everything was going perfectly last night and then it was all ruined. I thought we were headed in the right direction." He sounded upset and I didn't really blame him.

"No, I don't want you to go. I don't. But I'm angry, and you're the only person here I can take it out on, and I don't want that to happen. So you should go."

I pulled him into a deep kiss, soaking his front. He kissed me back feverishly and then pulled away.

"You know, Lanie, I've been waiting for your forgiveness and I understand why you're upset. I do. And I could understand if I actually cheated on you, which in a way, depending on how you look at it, this could fall under that category. But this *not mad, mad, not mad, mad* is literally making my head spin. Either be mad at me or forgive me. Because honestly, I can't handle the ups and downs of not knowing whether you love me or not, or whether we're together or not. Either put the ring back on your finger, or break things off completely. I love you. I want to marry you. But I can't take this roller coaster anymore, Lanie. I stood by you when it was the other way around." He shook his head, got up and walked out of the room.

My face felt flushed and my heart dropped. I was so confused. I didn't know how to react; I didn't know what to think or say anymore. I didn't want to hurt him. He was right. I had exacted my revenge, but then Brianna's phone call had just made it all crap again. What if there was something more to what she said? I mean, it was so similar to what we'd done last night. And she had been contacting him, every day since he'd left. But worse than anything, he had just walked out on me, upset.

I sank myself under the water and held my breath for as long as I could, hoping it would spark my brain into something—anything—but where it was. Not sure how long I was under the water, but when I surfaced, I expected to find Grant waiting for me. He wasn't, so I was pretty sure he'd meant what he said.

Damn, I hadn't even caused any of this, but suddenly it was all on me. What could I do to make things better? I had to forgive my fiancé. I had to put that ring back on my finger. I needed to make things right.

I got myself out of the tub with every intention of heading over to Grant's to make amends. I started out, but realized I should probably get dressed first, although I was sure he would be pleased if I showed up in my towel. I dried off quickly and threw on a pair of blue sweats and a tight white long-sleeved tee and my favorite blue sneakers. I towel dried my hair and didn't bother with any make-up.

I ran down the stairs and out the door. I had no idea where my drunk girls had gone, but I didn't check the floor when I left, so they might have been passed out there.

I was a girl on a mission and was almost to Grant's when I ran into Dane, heading towards Grant's house, too.

"Hey, where are you off to?" I said as I edged up beside him. "I'm heading over to Grant's. I need to put an end to all this crap between us already. It's stupid. What are you doing?"

"Well, I just got quite the email from Brianna. Something about you calling her dad and her being moved out of the company; and then I got a detailed description of some stuff. I was on my way to Grant to discuss it," he said. I already knew what she told him. I wanted to see how different it was than what she told me.

"Really? Care to elaborate?" I said with a sing-songy tone.

"Umm. Not really. I need to talk with Grant first." *How cute.* He was trying to protect Grant.

"You know, I already spoke with her today. I got quite an earful, as you can imagine."

"Lanie, I don't think you understand."

"I'm pretty sure I know exactly what she told you. I got the same story, details about their supposed night together. I don't believe her. Do you?" I chuckled, thinking he would realize it was such nonsense.

"Lanie, there were some things she said. I need to talk with him. Can you just give me a few moments with him before you do anything?"

I was starting to get worried. What did she tell him? I had to know.

"Hey. I want to know. Can you please tell me?" I stopped and grabbed his arm. He wouldn't look at me.

"Lanie, I want to talk to Grant first. It's not right for me to tell you and put him in a bad place. Those days are over. Grant is like a brother to me and I am trying to act like it for once," he said.

"What am I? Chopped liver?"

"It's the bro code, Lanie. You wouldn't understand. Plus, I owe him. A lot. Now can you please hang back or something?"

"No. I can't. Sorry, it's the girlfriend code. You wouldn't understand," I said as I pushed past him. I started running to Grant's. Dane started to run, too, and he grabbed my arm and pulled me behind him. So I pushed him. So he tripped me. We continued like that for the next ten feet to the door. I grabbed the handle, opened the door, and he knocked me out of his way so that he was now in the doorway. I tried to get in, but he wouldn't let me by.

"Lanie, please. Just wait here and let me talk to him. Please?"

"Fine." I headed toward the kitchen to see if there was any wine. I grabbed two glasses and found a great bottle. I dug through the refrigerator to pick at any leftovers from last night, but at the moment, found my appetite was MIA.

I sat at the table and waited. I heard nothing, so it wasn't a heated conversation. Then I heard Dane come down the stairs.

"I was about to kick Grant's ass, but I think there's something you need to see," Dane said as he motioned me to come with him. I felt a pit in my stomach. I got up slowly.

"Hurry up, Lanie, I need you to come right now." I picked up my pace, but right before I sprinted up the stairs, Dane slowed me and gave the shush finger.

We quietly ascended and headed toward Grant's office. I heard two voices coming from the room, Grant's and a female voice. The pit became a knot, and I felt like I was going to throw up. I knew the voice. It was Brianna.

I started to move quicker and Dane slowed me again. I followed him until we reached the door. Then everything became quite clear. I could see Grant at his computer. He was on his webcam. And on the other end was a scantily clad Brianna. I was fuming. Dane held me back again. I tried to break free, but his grip was freakishly strong.

"Grant, you know we're meant to be together. The way you touched me. The way I felt when we were together. This whole thing is a mess. We have to get this right."

"Brianna, I—"

"I know, Baby. You want to be with me, but we can't until you end things with her. Then you can fly back here and we can be together."

I was just about to break in when I heard Grant break into this bizarre laughter. I turned to leave, but the freak held me in place. He spun me around and shoved me slightly into into the doorway.

"Brianna, what kind of drugs are you on? How many times do I have to tell you? What happened meant nothing. You mean nothing. In fact, nothing actually happened. And nothing ever will. I've known Lanie my whole life; and that's not an exaggeration. And I've loved her the entire time. Finally, she sees me the same way. And there is no one who will ever come between us. It's not possible for me to love another woman. I can't. I feel nothing toward any other women and never have. It's her. She's my soul mate. So stop! Stop trying to ruin what I've tried my whole life to obtain—Lanie's love."

"But she's done with you. It's over, Grant. You cheated on her with me."

"No, Brianna. I didn't. I was there for you because you needed someone. I would do that for anyone, but not at the expense of my relationship with Lanie. Get it through your sick, delusional skull. You mean nothing to me. You never will. If Lanie chooses not to be with me, then I'll spend the rest of my life trying to win her back. She's all that matters."

Dane let go of my arm, which I was sure was bruised by now, and gently pushed me into the room.

"Grant," I said. He turned quickly and stared at me. I ran to him and threw myself into his lap. I twirled my fingers into his hair and we kissed. Everything else in the world stopped. There was only he and I. Wrapped in each other. Although I did hear a disgruntled noise come from the computer. All I wanted to do was feel his lips on mine, swirl my tongue with his. I was ravenous for him. I had to fulfill my desire to feel him, to absorb him. This was my guy. My Grant. And there was nothing that could keep me away from him ever again.

"Lanie," he said as I crushed my mouth against his.

"Shhhhh. Kiss." I shot my tongue into his mouth to silence him. All men should be silenced that way. They actually get it.

But right now, I knew everything he wanted to say to me. No words were needed. I could feel his love in that kiss. He said he had loved me his whole life and always would. And I felt the same. Our kiss became slow and passionate. I was lost in it. Nothing else mattered.

Grant pushed me back. We were both out of breath, and on the edge of jumping back into more loss of oxygen. He had to talk quick or I'd be right back on his sweet lips. The taste of him drove me insane. Everything about him drove me insane. I was his, down to my very core.

He put me on my feet and jumped up beside me. In an instant he was on one knee. He'd already asked me to marry him, but there was something about hearing him say it again that just made every single girly part in me squeal. I felt my face flush.

"Lanie, please. I want and need you to be by my side for the rest of our lives and then some. Please, marry me. I want to have babies with you and grow old together." He stood up quickly and brushed his lips against my ear and growled. Every nerve in my body jumped. He pulled back from me, but the intensity of what was between us ... there were no words to describe it.

"Grant. There's nothing more I want in this life than to be your wife. Yes. I'll marry you. I'd marry you every day for the rest of our lives if you wanted me to. Does that even make sense?" I giggled.

"Yes," he said, his loving stare had me hypnotized. I smiled at him. He grabbed me and pulled our bodies together. We were once again locked in a kiss. I could hear Dane clapping in the background and Brianna huff and curse. It was done. Revenge was never as sweet as this kiss. I heard the computer disconnect. *Okay. It just got sweeter.*

"I love you, Lanie. And no one, not one single woman out there, could ever take your place."

"Dane, you need to leave now. Grant and I have a rule to break," I said, staring into Grant's eyes with my best sexy expression.

"What the hell does that mean?" He was clueless. He backed out of the doorway.

"Dane?" Grant called after him. "Thank you."

"I don't know what you're talking about," Dane lied.

"I have very, very good hearing. And I could see you in my monitor," Grant smiled.

"You're welcome. Now go do whatever. I'm going to spread the good news."

"Dane?" I stopped him again.

"Yeah?"

"Tell Samantha to call Jennifer. This wedding is a lot closer than we think. They have to start planning," I relayed.

Dane was out the door before I knew it; and I was all over Grant. All I wanted to do was make love to him. The heavy atmosphere between us was completely gone. Everything felt right. There was no anger or hurt. I heard my guy tell that whore off loud and clear, and there were no doubts in my mind that everything was going to be all right. Grant was innocent.

I started to remove his clothing, knocking us against a wall because I lost my balance. I was moving too fast. We giggled and each tried to undress the other, becoming entangled in our shirts, with pants stuck on shoes. After a bit of wrangling and wrestling, I gave up and just wrapped my arms around Grant's still struggling body and kissed him. We crashed to the floor.

"Well, at least we're horizontal now. This was all part of my evil plan to destroy rule number two. Oh and just for the record, all the rules are rescinded." I smiled and tried to get my arms out from under him so I could remove his briefs.

"Well, I still would love to continue to woo you. I was kind of enjoying your reaction to my romance."

"I kind of love your romancing. You treat me like a princess. Not sure I deserve it."

"Lanie, you deserve to be treated like a goddess. Any man would be lucky to have you. I just happen to be the luckiest of them all. Do you know how long I've waited for this? Dreamt about this?" He was no longer playing around. But I was having fun and didn't want the mood to shift back again. We'd been too serious of late.

"What? You dreamt about being hogtied by our clothing and basically stuck on the floor? We might need some help getting out of this. I'd say call Samantha, but she's kinky and might like it too much. Steve and Chelsie would just laugh at us. Dylan's our best bet. Can you dial with your nose?" I giggled out.

"So, you want to get married soon?" Grant pulled me even tighter to him.

"Where did that come from? Was I even talking about that? Maybe it's this whole being bound thing."

"Lanie, please. Be serious. When do you want to get married?" He looked me directly in the eyes and I could tell this was one time he didn't want some snarky reply.

"I see no reason to wait. We've known each other our whole lives. Let's just go for it!"

"Then let's set a date." His eyes were sparkling. I wanted to be his wife. I wanted to make babies with him, too, lots of babies, and lots of practice trying. I wanted to grow old with him. I wanted it so badly, all of it.

"How about …

Chapter 47

I Wanted You to be Mine

"... we get married—" My cell phone rang.

Grant and I struggled to get a hand free to answer it. He was able to grab and bring it close enough to my face, but my hands were still wrapped underneath him.

"Shit, can you see who it is?" he asked.

"Well, whoever it is has crappy timing. Maybe we can ask them to come untangle us first," I giggled and looked at the caller ID.

"It's Samantha. Grant, just push it a little farther—I think I can answer with my nose." Grant stretched. I could feel the clothes that bound us get tighter and all I could reach with was my tongue. I turned it on.

"Wow, I am one lucky man. That is one talented tongue!" Grant said in his smooth sultry voice.

"Excuse me? Did Dylan tell you that?" Samantha said loudly over speakerphone. I saw Grant blush and roll his eyes. *So damn sexy.*

"Nothing, Samantha. You just caught us at a bad time. Well, good time for us, bad time to call. What's up?"

Grant's eyebrows shot up, I'm sure because I was actually taking this phone call. I smiled sheepishly and tried to shrug my shoulders.

"I heard we're back on and ready to set a date. Jennifer and I want to know how long we have to plan. I want to start today," she said excitedly.

"You're going to have to. I decided to move things up a bit. Why wait, right?" I stared into Grant's eyes. *Hell, I hadn't even been able to tell him what I was planning, but I knew he'd be fine with anything I chose.*

"Well? I'm waiting," Samantha said impatiently. I could hear her tapping her foot. Not quite sure why she was so excited about planning my wedding when she'd been planning hers for the past two years with two more to go.

"So I was thinking exactly one month from today." I heard a scream come from the other end of the phone and then nothing but babbling. I couldn't tell anything except for the few expletives I could make out. Grant, however, had the most ginormous grin on his face. I couldn't help but smile back and mouth, "Are you cool with that?" He nodded his head with zest.

"Are you fucking kidding me? You're giving us a month to plan a huge wedding? Are you trying to kill me? Jennifer is going to have a cow. What's the rush? You preggers or something?"

"No, Samantha, I am not preggers. I just can't wait for this man to be my husband. Apparently, all the women want him, so I need to tie him down."

"Well, you already seem to have that covered." Grant growled.

"Are you two having sex?" Samantha said bluntly.

"No, at the moment we're on the phone with you instead of breaking all the rules," Grant said, slightly annoyed, but with a tinge of humor.

"I just don't see any reason to wait. I love him; he loves me and I want to start our lives together. You can pull it off, Samantha; I have the utmost faith in you. Now we have to go. We're kind of in the middle of something." Grant chuckled and used my shirt to shift my breasts closer to his mouth and began to use his teeth to gnaw at my bra. It shot an electric wave through my body and I started to groan.

I couldn't wait any longer. Staying away from him had been too hard; keeping my hands off him when we were together had been even harder. *Heck, I almost pulled him into the tub with me earlier. Why the hell hadn't I? Oh yeah, I was being an ass.* Now all I wanted to do was make love to him for the rest of the day through the night.

"Samantha, can we talk later? I have to go, right now," I said simply, not really paying attention to her anymore. At this point I was totally focused on

Grant and how to escape from our current situation and get into a more intimate one.

"Lanie, we need to start pla—" And then she was gone. My nimble tongue had disconnected the call and was now licking Grant's earlobe. His lips were on mine in a matter of seconds.

"Lanie, if we don't figure out how to get out of these clothes, I might not make it. I'm very excited already," he said, grinding his hips into mine. I was right there with him. I felt like a teenager in the back seat of a car.

"Grant, I want you so badly, please get us loose." I began struggling to get myself free. My phone started to ring again. I could hear the riffs of my favorite song playing. We both stopped and stared at it.

"You didn't shut it off? Good thing I like your ringtone."

"My tongue had other ideas and was rushing." I giggled and then began to try and get one shoe off with my foot so I could get out of my sweats. My struggling soon became writhing as Grant used each of my moves as a sexual tease. I was dying. He was so damn hot.

"Lanie, I promise to buy you a new one," he said as he ripped my shirt to free me. My hands flew right into his hair, grasped and pulled his face to mine.

He slid his tongue into my mouth and the taste of him intoxicated me. All the stress being apart brought everything to a higher sensitivity. I was blissful, soon to be in ecstasy.

I took one hand and used it to finally remove my shoes and then shimmied out of my sweats. Grant helped, as he was doing the same with his free hand. His other hand held my head and my mouth to his. He sucked on my tongue and lips, like a man who was lost in a desert and had just found water. He couldn't get enough and neither could I.

Soon we were skin-to-skin and rubbing non-stop against each other, unable to get enough friction. I wanted him inside me, but I was enjoying soaking in every bit of him. I wrapped my legs around his waist and ground into him. He pulled himself up so he was on his knees, held me to him and slowly began to crawl across the room.

He managed to get us over to his reading chair. He plopped us down so his back was against the chair and he was on the bottom. I released my legs from around his waist and straddled him as he bent his knees to support my back. I slid myself up and down over his length as we kissed deeply. He reverently ran his hands over my body, taking his time, watching his fingertips glide across my skin. He brushed my hair gently out of the way and began to softly kiss my neck. I closed my eyes to concentrate on the feel of his touch. He groaned as his hand moved down my neck and hovered over my heart, as though he was counting each beat.

I wanted to show him how badly I wanted and missed him. We had been walking on eggshells lately, and honestly, he must have felt like I didn't love him as much as he loved me. I didn't ever want him to feel that way and wanted him to know the unbreakable bond which existed between us now and forever.

Needing to be physically connected to him, I grabbed his face and kissed him with everything I had. I lifted up so he could guide himself inside of me and he hovered at my entrance as though waiting for my cue. I heard a small sigh of pleasure escape him and it made my body shudder as I pushed myself down on top of him. His response a bit louder this time, telling me how much he loved me. It made me die a little inside it was so damn sexy. That was the end of Rule Number Two.

We tenderly made love for the rest of the day, stopping only for food and other necessary things. When we weren't making love, we were staring into each other's eyes, no words needed. Eventually we snuggled up together in his bed.

"Lanie, we have plans this weekend, remember?" He smiled while we snacked on what we'd raided from his fridge. Presently I was eating multigrain crackers with peanut butter and chocolate hazelnut spread. *Yum!*

"How could I forget? You dipped in chocolate all weekend long. We have to get a few more jars of this to take with us," I said, trying to scrape the last bit out of the bottom of the jar.

"Oh Honey, you have no idea how much dipping is going to be happening this weekend." He sucked his cheeks in a bit and did this really sexy thing with his mouth when he said it. I bit my lip and pushed him back down and started all over again. I thought about what I should pack and then realized not a lot of clothing would be required.

When it had gotten quite late, we decided it was time to head downstairs and grab a real bite to eat. We grabbed a few items and cuddled up on the couch. He flipped through the channels and I spent time looking over all the packages in the chocolate spa brochure.

I was so content and if this was what life would be like every day and night with him, then I was the luckiest woman in the world. There was nothing like having some hot eye candy sitting on the couch next to me. He noticed me staring at him and gave me a side-glance.

"What are you thinking and should I be scared?" He reached out and caressed my cheek. I leaned into his hand and gave it a quick kiss.

"Nothing, babe. I was just thinking how lucky I am. Any woman in the world would kill to have you, or other things, as we already know. But why am I so lucky? What did I ever do to deserve you?" I really wanted to know.

"Lanie, it's not what you did or didn't do. I have just always known it was you. There was never a time I doubted my love for you. I only doubted we would have a chance to actually be together."

"Why would you think that? Oh wait, the pact? Or should I say pacts?" I had actually forgotten about them, since they were pretty much void now.

"Well, those were one reason, but not really. I didn't think I was worthy of your love, Lanie, why would you want me? I was just like a brother to you. I just assumed bigger and better things were waiting for you. Someone out there who could give you things I never could. Do you know what I mean? It's hard to explain." He looked away.

"No, it's not. I could say the same thing. You could have any woman in the world you want. I was convinced some woman would come along who'd take you away from me for good. That you'd realize there was an entire world beyond this cliff."

"Lanie, there is no choice for me. I have always belonged here with you on this cliff. And I always will. In my heart, there's no room for anyone else to exist."

"Grant, you have to have known I've felt the same way for so long. I tried so hard to not love or want you because of that stupid pact. And I thought you liked me, but that things would never happen. Don't you remember that Christmas party we threw? The one where you and Dane made that bet about who could get the most women under the mistletoe? You guys were like kissing bandits. I was so jealous every time you grabbed another girl to kiss."

"And then Dane got you under the mistletoe and my heart broke." Grant smiled at me as he touched his heart. I wanted to hold him I felt so bad.

"But then after everyone left and Dane was so drunk, you were standing under the mistletoe while talking to him. I got you. Remember?" I reminded him.

"How could I ever forget? It was the first time you kissed me."

"You kissed me back for a second. I was hoping you'd grab me and slip me tongue. I wanted it to go somewhere so badly. But you pulled away. Why?" I said almost sadly. I remember the feeling of rejection.

"Lanie, I only pulled away because if I hadn't, I would have never let you go. My entire body was aching to hold you tight against me and show you how I really felt. But I wouldn't have been able to stop myself. I pulled away for you, out of respect."

"I thought you didn't want to kiss me back. I went to bed thinking about you, hurting that you didn't want me. You kissed all those other girls and then when it came to me, a peck. I thought you only looked at me like a sister then."

"My love, if I had known you felt that way, I would've taken you upstairs right then and there. We both would have had a different first that night. But you never have to feel that way again. I promise to always kiss you back. Passionately and very, very deeply," he said as he raised his right hand. I raised mine, too. He leaned over and pulled me closer so I was basically right up against him. Our faces were so close and all I wanted was to feel him kiss me.

"Shut your eyes," he said.

"What? Why?" I asked as I complied.

"Think back to that night. Be there right now. I want you to kiss me. I want to show you how I wanted to kiss you that night. Do it exactly like you did it. Can you do that for me?" he said as his thumb rubbed up and down my cheek. My heart melted a little bit right then and there. I actually felt a small flutter of excitement in my chest. My heart started to beat faster and so did Grant's. I could feel it.

I leaned up and put my lips close to his just as I had so many years ago. Back then I was afraid he'd pull back. He didn't, but he held his kiss at bay. Apparently. I moved so slowly. I could feel his breath on my face. It was ragged. My memories started to flood back. He was breathing just like this that night. He didn't move. He just stood there frozen … waiting. He did the same thing tonight. I moved closer until my lips softly brushed against his. I just kept them there and then slowly pressed harder. His lips felt like heaven.

And I felt like I'd gone back in time.

I could hear a Christmas song playing in the background. The room was decorated floor to ceiling. Haley and Jennifer always went overboard for the annual Cliff Christmas Party. It was a huge event, spanning all three of our houses. Everyone was there. Dane, Grant, and I stuck together like we were glued. It was so late at night, or maybe early in the morning, depending on how you looked at it. We had all been drinking. Dane had grabbed me and done a dramatic dip and kiss, smashing his mouth to mine, but in a mock kiss. Grant had smiled. But now thinking back, it wasn't a happy one.

Dane had continued to drink, toasting all the guests when they left. He was totaled. He fell over the couch, rolled right off and passed out on the floor. It was only Grant and I. We were standing at the back of the couch, giggling at Dane and enjoying the revelry. I looked at Grant and realized he was standing under the mistletoe. I don't know what came over me, but in seconds I was right in front of him, against him. I could feel the heat of his body and I wanted to fling myself at him. But I slowed myself and felt heaven when my lips touched his.

I was suddenly very aware that Grant was holding back his kiss tonight. I started to move back from him and his hand thrust out and entwined into my hair. He grasped the sides of my face and pulled me back to his lips. He crushed his mouth against mine, moving his lips in the most amazing way. I was lost in it.

His hand reached around the back of my head and held me in place as he slid his tongue between my parted lips. A fast tingle ran through my body and I instantly grew warm. I began to kiss him back, desperate for more, but he released me. I was dazed for a moment.

"*That* is how I wanted to kiss you back that night. I wanted nothing more than to show you exactly how your kiss made me feel. But Lanie, how could I?" he whispered sweetly.

"How could you hold back, Grant? If you had kissed me like that back then, we'd have been together all these years. You should have."

"I was scared," he said with a smile.

"You were afraid to kiss me back? Why?" I looked at him incredulously.

"Because it was you and I wanted you to be mine so badly. What if you didn't want it? I was already aching for you in every way possible."

"I would have kissed you back and would have been yours. But I am now and that's all that matters." I touched his heart. "We still have all those memories."

"I have another memory of that night." He leaned his head down and raised an eyebrow at me.

"Oh?" I uttered, knowing fully well what he was referring to. I had given him a little window show that night. I wanted to show him what he was missing, so I had purposely removed my dress in front of it. The lights in my room had been dim, so he got just a hint of my silhouette, but I actually had stripped down completely that night.

"Yes, the view from my room was beautiful. I saw everything," he said provocatively.

"Everything?"

"Yes, Lanie. Your dim lights illuminated you more than you might have thought. You were breathtaking. I spent a few moments that night with that image in my head and other things in my hand. If you know what I mean."

"Raincheck?" I guessed.

"Yes, Sexy Girl, I rainchecked all over myself."

I blushed and had no idea why. Grant and I had done things to each other recently that were just, well, overly intimate. Why I was blushing now after so many years, I had no idea. He had seen everything up close and personal, very up close. The thought of him pleasuring himself to thoughts of me all those years ago made my heart thrum in my chest and other places get all warm and achy.

He smiled at seeing me get flustered.

"You're still stunning."

"Would you like a repeat performance?" I offered.

"Uh, hell yes!" Grant relayed quickly.

I stood up reluctantly, but only because I didn't want to leave his side. But I knew it would only be a second or two before he was pouncing on me. I moved throughout the room, turning lights off, and then closed his terrace door blinds. I decided to make that my stage, so I repositioned one of his floor lamps behind me. He jumped up and turned the stereo on so there was soft music playing in the background.

I faced him and began to slowly remove each piece of my clothing. I actually didn't have much on besides one of his t-shirts and a pair of his boxers so this would be a quick show.

I started with the shirt and teased him by bringing it up to below my breasts a few times. His eyes grew wider each time the shirt got higher. When I finally pulled it over my head, I allowed the shirt to pull my hair back in a sexy display. I heard a little gasp when he saw my breasts. I smiled because he had seen this so many times, but for some reason, he was feeling reminiscent like I was. We were back in time on Christmas night.

I twirled slowly for him so he could get an eyeful before I removed his skivvies from my bottom half. He sat mesmerized; almost as though he had never seen me like that. When I was sure he was starting to fidget enough, I turned my back to him and glanced at him over my shoulder. He took a deep breath in and gave me a libidinous stare. I knew I had to make this part seductive as hell. I wanted to please him.

"You're going to hide those luscious breasts from me?" He sounded slightly disappointed. *Men and boobs, what can you say?*

"It's more risqué this way. Don't you think? I'm trying to spice it up for you. You just sit back and enjoy." I shook my little ass for him and I heard him moan. I began rolling my hips as I held the briefs, which basically helped me shimmy out of them quite quickly. I let them drop to my ankles and I nimbly stepped out of them. Again I heard a small gasp from across the room.

Grant and I were teenagers again. Is this what it would have been like that night had he kissed me back? *I don't think so.* We probably would have been much tamer.

I had planned on turning around and giving him the full Monty, but I felt his arms slip around me. He pressed his body into my back and we began to sway to the music as his hands roamed all over me. I turned my head to the side to plant a kiss on him and his lips were there to meet mine. He pulled me tighter and he drove his tongue deep into my mouth. He moved us backwards until we reached the couch and laid us down so I was still on top of him. He proceeded to kiss my neck while his hands lingered playfully.

"I love you, Lanie." He sounded like he was telling me for the first time.

"Oh, Grant. I love you, too." I felt like it was the first time. I wished we could go back in time and redo all those years just like this. But since that wasn't a possibility, I was more than happy to begin the rest of our lives together as soon as we could.

And that would be a month from today, a fall wedding. The leaves on the trees would be reaching their peak when we said I do. Everything was right in my world.

* * *

"Have everything you need?" Grant called from downstairs.

"Yes, I have everything," I called back.

"Are you sure? Pierre will be here in about half an hour and I want to be ready to go. I don't want to waste one minute of our confectionery weekend," he called back up, already acting like my husband. We had been going back and forth between our two houses. We really had to make a decision as to whose house we were eventually going to settle in.

"No worries. I won't let you miss a thing. Can we stop off for coffee when we head out of town? I don't want to have to make a whole pot," I told him.

"For you, anything, my love. I'll even make it a mocha java to get you all psyched on the way up."

"Honey, I'm already stoked to spend this weekend with you. We have so much to talk about on the trip, too. Like, where do you want to go on our honeymoon? Hawaii? Tahiti? Fiji? Australia?"

"I thought we already decided on Fiji? We can get one of those over-the-water bungalows. It'll be paradise there with you. I'm sure we can find something very private. I wish we had our own island so I could make love to my wife whenever and wherever I wanted to."

"I don't see that being an issue. We can stay in our bungalow and never leave for all I care. As long as I'm with you, that's all that matters. Can you grab those travel and bridal magazines that Samantha dropped off his morning? They're on the coffee table. I swear if she doesn't get off my back about picking out a wedding gown, I'm going to smack her." I hauled my over-packed bags down the stairs. I knew I wouldn't need half of what I brought, but I was a woman, and if I was going to wear anything at all this weekend, I wanted choices.

"Can I help you pick out the wedding gown?" he suggested.

"I thought you weren't supposed to see the wedding gown?"

"I'm not supposed to see you in the wedding gown before the wedding. But that's all a superstition. You and I, we're not going to let some silly wives' tale get in our way, are we?"

Hell, if he wanted to look at bridal mags with me on the trip up, more power to him.

"Sure, Babe. I'd love that." I wasn't lying. I was more than happy to let him help me. I was wearing the gown for him, anyway. And he knew what I looked good in. "Do you want to pick out my wedding night lingerie, too?"

"No, let Samantha pick that out. I want to be more than surprised when it comes to that." He growled and pulled the bags from my hand, dropped them to the floor and pulled me closer to place a sweet kiss on my lips.

"Dane is taking care of Woof while we're gone, right?"

“Lanie, cats are pretty much independent, and really we’ll only be gone for a few days. Is this going to be what you’re like every time we leave our children?”

“Woof is my child. Well, a furry child. I’d shove him in my bag if I could.”

“Dane has everything under control. He can handle it.”

“It’s nice to hear you and Dane getting along again. It’s nice to be back to the way we used to be. I still can’t believe all that happened,” I declared.

“I don’t want to remember any of the bad things that happened. As far as I’m concerned, it was a small blip on the radar. We can leave it at that. Deal?” Grant held his hand out to shake on it. But I had other ideas. I grabbed his hand and pulled him to me.

“Deal.” I kissed him deeply and then heard the knock on my door. “Pierre is here. Let’s go get covered in chocolate and make love all weekend.”

“I like the sound of that, my bon bon.” Grant grabbed our bags and we headed out the door. He placed everything in the trunk and we got into the limo, where champagne and chocolate covered strawberries awaited us.

“Is this going to be our limo meal from now on?” I asked, grabbing two glasses.

“I had nothing to do with this one,” Grant responded. There was a small note next to the strawberries. Grant picked it up to read it.

To the happy couple,

Enjoy your weekend! We’re all so happy you’re back together.
Now pick out a wedding dress already.

Love,

Samantha, Chelsie, Steve, Dylan, and Dane

“Oh my God! That was so nice of them. How did they know about our limo meal? Oh wait, I told the girls all about it.”

“You limo-dined and told?” Grant accused.

“Some things are just too damn hot to keep to myself.”

He poured our champagne and we settled back in for our long drive. Soon I was sitting in his lap feeding him strawberries and thumbing through bride’s magazines. He pointed to a gown he thought would look hot on me, and I pointed to ones that would be too hard for him to take off me that night.

We giggled a lot and everything was perfect again.

“Hey, speaking of our wedding … did you decide who your best man is going to be? Dylan? Steve?”

“Neither. I’m going to ask Dane.” I was shocked.

“Are you serious?”

“Lanie, so much has changed. He’s who he used to be, and that’s my brother. He’s always been my brother. And everyone deserves a second chance, right? We’ve both had our issues and forgiven each other. I feel like I can trust him again. Don’t you?”

“I do. I really do. In fact, I think he’s grown up a lot lately. He’s different. He’s not as self-centered anymore. Which gets me thinking about something I need to do,” I stated.

“Oh no. Lanie, you have that look on your face that scares me. What are you planning?”

“When all that stuff that shall remain a blip was happening, I made a phone call as a last resort. I think it’s time to call that last resort back, but for a different purpose.”

“Who’s the last resort? And why?”

“It’s …

Chapter 48

I Think There's Chocolate in my Hoohoo

"… his future wife. Or at least she was supposed to be. I think I can make it happen."

"Callie. He was happiest when they were together. Isn't she engaged to someone else now?"

"She was. But when I spoke to her last they weren't heading in the same direction. He was focused only on his career and she felt she was taking a back seat. She was more than interested to help me out with Dane. I hope I didn't scare her. She knows everything."

"Even about … that night?" Grant said with a look of concern. "That would blow everything for a second chance for them."

"It could, but I don't think so. She was so worried about him; she was ready to drive out right then and there. Is it okay if I—?" I held my cell phone up.

"Absolutely. Make the call. I have things to keep me occupied," he said as he started to unzip my pants. This should be a fun call. I found Callie in my contacts and hit send. Ring ring.

"Lanie, I was wondering when I was going to hear back from you. How is Dane?" Callie sounded very worried, so I wanted to put her mind at ease immediately.

"He's great, Callie. Everything is so much better. *He* is so much better," I assured her.

"Oh, I'm so glad. Was he sick? Was it just something wrong in his head or was it physical?"

"Not sure. I personally think he was hanging on to being young while everyone else was growing up. I just think he was confused. But now …"

"What? What now?" Callie was interested. I could tell she still had feelings for him.

"How are things going with you and Heath?" I asked, ignoring her question.

"Over. All he cared about was working. He never had time for me anymore. He was traveling all the time and even when he was home with me, he wasn't with me. It's better this way. I'm not sure I really loved him."

"But you were sure that you loved Dane when you were with him?" I asked.

"Where are you going with this, Lanie?"

At this point, Grant was doing a great job of trying to distract me from my phone call. His lips were delicately kissing above the band of my thong. My eyes rolled back slightly in my head and I almost forgot to answer Callie's questions.

"Lanie, are you still there?"

"Oh sorry, yeah. Dane has really grown up in the past few months. I think he's ready to make things right all around. Would you be willing to go see him? Maybe? I know he needs a date for my wedding next month, and you're already getting invited." I left the last sentence more like an open ended-question.

"You're getting married? You and Grant are finally getting married? Hell, I knew it when we were kids. You guys were always sharing hot glances at each other. I never understood why you never dated."

"We did? We were? Well, you were right, and yes, we're tying the knot next month." This made Grant pull my thong down more and begin to lick his way lower. I tried to push him back, but I really didn't want to. He giggled into my panties.

"I'd love to be there. And I'd love to see Dane. But how do I approach him?"

"I have an idea if you're willing?"

"Anything. I've never really gotten over him. He was the only true love of my life. I think I was just settling for Heath. What did you have in mind?"

I began to tell her about how Grant was going to ask Dane to be the best man. I thought it would be pretty cool to have Callie deliver the request this evening at his front door. She got giddy on the phone and we even planned her outfit and what she would say. She promised to give me a call tomorrow morning to let me know how things went. When we got off the phone, I called Dane.

"Lanie? What's wrong? Why are you calling me?" Dane said as soon as he picked up.

"Nothing. I just wanted to let you know that I have an important wedding item getting delivered tonight. I have to make sure it gets there. So I told them to bring it to your house and that you have to sign for it. Is that okay? You didn't have plans tonight, did you?"

"Um, no. Nothing. I was going to grab Woof and hang out all night and watch movies. He seems to be the only company I have lately when you and Grant aren't here." He sounded sad. Which made me seriously happy.

"Well, Woof is great company, although he tends to talk too much, so don't let him monopolize the conversation. He also likes to wake you up at the break of dawn, so you might want to take him home before you go up to bed. Okay?"

"Okay, sounds good. Now go get all chocolaty with your future husband. No reason to be wasting one second on the phone with me. I'll take good care of your package and Woof."

"Okay, talk to you later. Bye." I hung up the phone and did a little happy dance, and then sunk into my seat so Grant could make the ride way more enjoyable. We'd be at the spa soon.

After much playful teasing on our ride, we finally reached our destination. Chocolate spa loving was awaiting us right on the other side of the limo door. I couldn't wait! Three things I loved most in this world coming together for a full blown weekend of bliss: Grant, chocolate, and sex with Grant and chocolate. *Could life get any better?*

Once Grant and I had retrieved our bags and checked in, we headed to our room. It was the most amazing hotel room I had ever seen. We had four rooms to ourselves, including a living room with an eat in kitchen, a huge bedroom with master bath, a Jacuzzi room and a treatment room with two massage tables side by side. We literally never had to leave.

"So when do we start? I want to spend every second of this trip eating you or chocolate," I said excitedly, stuffing one of the many chocolate items placed around the room into my mouth. Everywhere you looked there was a candy dish filled with a different type of chocolate, caramel or truffle. I was in complete heaven and would need at least a week to work this all off so I could fit into my wedding gown. Well, maybe not; Grant and I would have plenty of working-it-off time this weekend, too.

"Our first appointment? And what is it?" I already had a sugar high and was raring to go.

"Relax, hyper. We have our first treatment in about twenty minutes, just enough time for me to take your clothes off with my teeth. We both need to be naked for most of everything we're having done."

"I want to know. Ple-e-ease?" I dragged out the word for a very long time until I ran out of breath. Grant rolled his eyes.

"You don't want to leave anything for a surprise do you? We start today off with lunch in our room. I've already ordered that, so you'll have to wait and taste. Then we have our first appointment for a chocolate facial and massage, followed by a hot fudge bath in our Jacuzzi, and then lots of sex. And then we have time to hit the gym or the pool before dinner. We're having dinner someplace I know you're going to love. Then I thought you might like to take a walk through the gardens. There's a ton of waterfalls and koi, and we can round the night off there with chocolate martinis. How does that sound?"

"Lots of sex sounds amazing. Everything else sounds fantastic, too. What about tomorrow?"

"Okay, tomorrow we're both getting the couples chocolate fondue wrap, followed by the whipped cocoa shower and a sugar scrub massage and lots more sex. Oh, and breakfast and dinner in bed. We're also going to the amusement park tomorrow. I thought it'd be fun. Our fondue isn't until five. And then more sex, breakfast in bed and back home to find your wedding gown and book our honeymoon. And then the bridal shower and bachelor party, and most importantly, our wedding," he said in one breath and at super hyper speed.

"Okay, I think you have forever all planned out. I love it. I'm so excited. Let's start getting ready. I want to be in that big comfy robe in the closet when lunch gets here. You, too. Something about you being naked underneath during lunch is totally turning me on."

He smiled at me and pulled me down onto the bed with him. He hovered over me and removed every stitch of my clothing with his teeth. It was really quite impressive. He would grace each area he uncovered with a kiss. When I was completely undressed, he removed his clothing, grabbed our robes and returned to lay on the bed with me. The feel of his skin against mine made the fire between my legs start to roar. Just as I leg-hitched him, there was a knock at the door.

"Food is here. Quick, put on your robe." He donned his and went to answer.

Lunch was served at a small table on our balcony overlooking the gardens. We shared an appetizer of crab and baby shrimp spring rolls, followed by a large metal pot containing paella. We dined to soft spa music while sipping on a honey amber wine. *I was in heaven.* For dessert we had individual chocolate soufflés filled with molten chocolate. It took everything I had not to start smearing the chocolate all over Grant. But I knew we had our first treatment shortly and I wanted to make love to him slowly, not in a rush.

After our tray had been removed, our masseurs came to start our first treatment. They dimmed the lights, prepared our tables and lit many chocolate scented candles around the room. It was scrumptious. We started with our chocolate facial, which was like having chocolate hazelnut spread put all over our faces. I looked over at Grant and giggled. He looked back and gave me a crooked smirk.

"Something funny, Lanie? You know I've seen you look like that before, but it was a lot more fun getting you that way." We both giggled and then were lightly reprimanded by the technician about letting the chocolate mask cure. Soon I knew what a chocolate covered strawberry probably felt like and I wanted to be eaten by Grant just like they were. *Lucky strawberries.*

I felt my face start to freeze up and I tried to smile at Grant to no avail. He did the same. Soon our technicians were using a scrub to release the mask and we were on to our massage.

I lay face down on the table with nothing but my towel. Grant was the same. Lucky for me, but not for him, we had been sent two very hot masseurs to give us our chocolate massage. Grant and I reached between the two tables and held hands and turned our heads towards each other so we could have eye contact. I noticed Grant trying to look back every few minutes to make sure Rowan, my masseuse, was being completely professional. I had to giggle.

The massage was pure pleasure, with oils scented with cocoa, caramel, sugar, and layer upon layer of yummy smelling creams. Once we were done, we headed to our Jacuzzi for our hot fudge bath. It smelled and looked like a huge cup of hot cocoa with frothy cream on the top, good enough to drink. I looked to Grant to make the first move. He smiled, removed his robe and got in slowly. I spent my time waiting, staring at his ass.

"Are you looking at my ass?" He chuckled.

"Hell yes, of course I am. Any woman would be." I dropped my robe and entered the giant cup of cocoa. It felt smooth against my skin, and my already relaxed muscles went completely limp. Grant reached for our chocolate cake shooters, which were sitting on the side table. The hot tub had bowls of chocolate-dipped fruit sitting in ice baths all around. I reached in, grabbed some pineapple and settled in. Grant took a sip of his drink.

"Holy shit, this tastes just like chocolate cake. I want to order these for later so I can pour it over you and lick it off."

"Feel free to lick anything you want off me," I purred.

"Your breasts look like marshmallows floating in hot chocolate," he growled.

"Thanks for reminding me I need a tan." I giggled.

"You're beautiful any way you are. But right now, Lanie, I can barely stand not touching you."

"Then why are you sitting all the way over there? Get your marshmallow-nibbling butt over here."

Grant moved closer and his lips were immediately on mine. I moved my hands under the chocolaty mixture and began fondling him playfully."

"Fuck, Lanie," he groaned and leaned back to give me better access.

"That's the plan, for you to fuck Lanie." I couldn't take my eyes off his face. The pure beauty of seeing him in ecstasy was mesmerizing. He was so handsome, even more so when he was being pleasured.

"Lanie, if you keep doing that, this hot cocoa bath is going to have marshmallow fluff all over the place."

"Yum." Was all I could get out amid the hysterical laughing. I couldn't hold in.

"What's so funny? Forget it. Please continue pulling the taffy." I just continued to laugh.

"And don't forget my malted milk balls, they get upset when you ignore them," he said casually, like it was every day conversation. I was dying, but I still couldn't keep my hands off him.

"You're like a granola bar, filling and satisfying."

"I'd rather be more like a jawbreakers at the moment," he said as he side-eyed me. I giggled and pulled myself on top of him so I was sitting in his lap with my back to his front. I could feel his Twizzler becoming more like rock candy. I smiled to myself, leaned back and just enjoyed the moment with him. There was nothing better than this. We drank our drinks and nibbled on candy and each other. Soon I started to feel a bit lightheaded from the heat of the hot cocoa we were floating in.

"How about we get cleaned up and head out for that walk in the garden you promised me? I also want to check in with Dane and find out if our package arrived."

"You really want Dane and Callie back together, don't you? I know they were really happy together for so long. It'd be nice to see Dane settle down like us, maybe get married." That's when it all hit me. I was getting married in less than a month, to Grant. I was the luckiest woman in all the chocolate-loving land.

We hit the shower and began to get dressed. I decided on a cute cotton sundress and Grant threw on a pair of board shorts and a t-shirt. We were off to the garden for a walk, then dinner and then chocolate martinis. I giggled. Probably the sugar high I was on. I grabbed my cell phone and called Dane on the way down.

"Hello?"

"Hey Dane. Just calling to check in on Woof. How is he?" I said, sounding totally like I was not calling about Woof.

"Woof? He has a new friend. Won't leave her alone. Your package came, by the way." Dane just played along.

"Oh? Did you open it?"

"Yes, I made sure it was intact as soon as it arrived. Okay, enough of this. Thank you. Thank you for calling Callie. We've been talking all day and hopefully all night. She's staying for dinner. I'm cooking," he said excitedly.

"No. Do not cook for her. You want her to stay around, don't you?" Dane was great at ordering dinner, but cooking was not his forte."

"No worries. Callie is cooking with me. We want to give it another go, Lanie. She's not with Heath anymore. We have a chance together and I'm not letting her get away again. We have some things to work out, but I think we're going to be okay. I really do. We still love each other deep down. I want to tell you that I know I didn't deserve this, from either of you. But I'm pretty stoked that I have people who love me so much that they can let me fuck up and then forgive me." He was heartfelt. And it made me warm and fuzzy all over. I gave Grant the thumbs up and did a little jumpy dance in the elevator.

"Well, Grant is holding his hand out for the phone so I'm going to let you guys talk. Bye Dane. And you're very welcome." I handed the phone to Grant.

"Hey, Dane, all going well there?" Grant had a sweet smile on his face like he was genuinely interested in things going well for Dane. "There was something I wanted to ask you, a favor, so to speak. I wanted to know if you would stand beside me when I marry Lanie. You know, be my best man." Grant held the phone to his ear and nodded his head to no one who could see it other than myself. "No, Dane. Really. You're my brother. I don't want to think about any of that anymore. Don't do that. I just know it wouldn't be right to have anyone up there but you. We're the three musketeers, ya know?" Then there was more shaking and nodding and smiles. "I think a new pact would be perfect. When we get back, we'll all have dinner and make it official. I think Lanie would love that. Have a good night with Callie and I hope it turns into a good weekend. Bye."

"So? What did he say?"

"He got choked up. Said he didn't deserve to stand up there with me and it sounded like he was crying."

"Are you kidding me? He cried? What a wimp!" I laughed and then hugged Grant. Everything was right. Everything was perfect. I felt the tears well up in my own eyes and just knew everything was how it was meant to be.

"So do you want to hear about the new pact?" Grant said into the top of my head right before planting a kiss there.

"I think I already know what it is, but you can fill me in over dinner."

We dined at a restaurant that sat in the center of a large pond with koi fish everywhere you looked. We walked the gardens with our chocolate martinis and enjoyed all the beautiful views. But the only thing I could think of was getting Grant back to our room and making love to him the entire rest of the night.

"Babe? Would you mind if we went back to the room? I just need you, all of you. It's been too long," I said as I pushed him up against a tree and playfully groped him.

"Lanie, this isn't Hedonism. If you keep that up, I'm going to take you right here and now." He turned his back to me and it looked like he was texting something into his phone and then spun back in my direction.

"Well, it's pretty isolated. I mean, what's stopping you?" I teased.

"Nothing," he said, with his signature sultry smile. He grabbed my hand and pulled me to the side of a gorgeous waterfall where we would be shielded from anyone on the path. Not that anyone would be out this late. He lay me down in the grass.

"Grant, what are you doing? What if someone walks by?" He didn't answer with more than a growl. I looked at the stars above our heads as he kissed and bit my neck. It was beautiful and surreal.

"Holy shit, someone's coming," I whispered and tried to push him off of me before we were caught making out like two teenagers.

He giggled, but didn't stop his relentless kissing. He seemed not to care if anyone caught us. In moments I heard the footsteps stop right on the other side of the fall. I froze, but Grant just kept kissing. I heard a clanking and then the footsteps faded away.

"That was so close. They had to known we were here." Grant just smiled, got up, and disappeared around the side of the waterfall. When he returned, he had a blanket, a bottle of champagne and two glasses.

"Where the hell did that come from?" I figured out who he had been texting.

"I have my ways. It's so beautiful here, and since it seems we have the place to ourselves, I thought it might be nice to stay for a bit longer."

Was this guy for real? What guy was that romantic?

I spread out the blanket while he poured and then handed me a glass of champagne. He cuddled up with me on the blanket and we spent the next hour or so talking about our wedding and what we would name our kids.

Eventually, we headed to our room to finish the rest of our night making love in bed, and on the floor, and in the Jacuzzi and on the massage table. Sleep came deeply for both of us.

We got up early and spent the day at the amusement park and it reminded me of all the times we had gone when we were kids. We rode the roller coasters the most because we were both huge buffs. But there wasn't a ride we didn't hit, or a game we didn't play. We took silly pictures and ate a lot of cotton candy. This was almost as much fun as spending time with him in the sheets.

Soon we headed back to our room for our chocolate fondue wrap. We undressed, and our technicians, the same from yesterday to Grant's chagrin, began their magic. First we got a sugar scrub to detoxify and after a quick rinse, we were ready to become dessert. We were covered from the neck down in a thick, chocolate paste. It was probably just like a mud mask, but all I could smell was the sweetness of cocoa, like I was being iced.

"I think there's chocolate in my hoohoo," I said as I was being wrapped in some kind of foil.

Grant glared at my technician who seemed a bit nervous after that, because his wrapping was much quicker. Soon we looked like some kind of space-aged food wrapped in tin foil. I began to feel the wrap heat up and closed my eyes to wait for the treatment to take full effect while Grant whispered dirty things from his table to me. I giggled back, and I would've jumped him, but I couldn't move. After our treatment, we had a shower and spent the rest of our weekend in our robes, making love before, during, and after dinner. But soon our weekend of chocolaty bliss was over and we needed to head back.

"So, did you enjoy having me as dessert all weekend?" I questioned as Pierre loaded our luggage into the limo.

"Babe, I'd love you covered in tar."

"And feathers?"

"Of course, can't forget the feathers. Lanie, I can't wait to spend the rest of my life with you in every way possible. And when we get back, you won't have much time before that happens. You'll be Lanie Bennett soon." He kissed me and helped me into the limo. About half an hour into the ride, Samantha and Jennifer started to text me. Yep, this would be my life for the next three weeks. But I didn't care. All that mattered was marrying my love, my Grant.

* * *

I opened my eyes and the sun was just coming up. It was my wedding day. I jumped out of bed to find …

Chapter 49

You May Kiss Your Bride

… dozens of salmon colored roses all over my room. Next to my bed was an envelope. I grabbed it and looked at the handwriting on the front.

To My Future Wife

Grant's handwriting. *How the hell did he get all these roses in here without waking me up?* I looked around the room. They were everywhere. I know brides are supposed to be nervous on their wedding day, but I wasn't at all. All I wanted to do was be with my guy for the rest of my days, and maybe then some. I slept like a log last night. I ripped open the envelope.

Lanie, my love,
I have waited, literally, my whole life for you. In a few hours I will finally have everything I have ever wanted in this entire world. You. I love you. I cannot wait to be your husband and call you my wife.
Grant

My heart burst out of my chest and I could feel everything wonderful most people take for granted. Hope and love. There was nothing more I could want in life, except a child or two with Grant. I was happy, truly happy. I ran down the stairs, looking at the clock, and seeing it was only a bit past six in the morning. No one else was up. Well, that wouldn't do at all.

"Dad? Are you up? Get the hell up; your daughter's getting married today! Samantha? I cannot believe you're not up already. Get your asses out of bed!"

I headed for the kitchen and found yet another note.

Please open me

It was Grant's handwriting again. I smiled and ripped it open.

To whoever gets this note first,
I can't have my bride sleepy or hungry at the altar. You'll find breakfast in the fridge and fresh Kona coffee brewing (I set the timer). Please make sure you tell her I can't wait to see her today and I love her. I'll be waiting for her, the handsome one in the tux.
The Not-So-Nervous Groom

I felt tingles run through my body and I grabbed a mug and poured three cups, light and sweet for Samantha and I, black for my dad. I ran to the fridge and pulled out breakfast; bagels, lox and all sorts of cool toppings. On the table, which was set for four, sat a jar of chocolate hazelnut spread with yet another note.

This is for my wife. No one else touches it!
Lanie,
Bring whatever's left for our wedding night. Wink wink. I love you.
Your Husband

I popped my bagel in the toaster oven and picked out strawberries to put on top of my chocolate hazelnut glazed bagel. *Yum.* I sat down and sipped on coffee calmly while waiting for everyone to get downstairs. Samantha was the first to arrive.

"Here comes one of your Maids of Honor! Where's our bride?" she chimed.

"Over here stuffing my face!" I mumbled with a full mouth of chocolaty goodness.

"Well, are you ready to be my official cousin? Are you nervous, excited, cold feet, ready to run off and elope?"

"Uh, no, yes, no, no. I think I covered it all. What's first on our agenda? Whatever you say goes. I'm all ready."

"Wow, you're going to make this easy, aren't you? Okay, well, make-up and hair. Then get dressed and the photographer will be over to do the before pictures with us. Then it's time to get married and party the night away. Then you and Grant need to consummate …"

"Yes. I know. No worries there. We'll have no problem consummating anything. I'm looking forward to it. We plan to consummate all over the place. And then tomorrow it's off to Fiji."

"Is your luggage all packed?"

"Hell yes. I've been packed for a week. I even got a second set of make-up so I don't have to worry about last minute anything. I am all ready."

"I can't believe you and Grant are going to be gone for a whole month! You're a lucky bitch," Samantha said with love.

"You can visit the last week," I teased. "Why don't you and Dylan go there on your honeymoon?"

"We're touring Europe. Paris, Italy, England, Spain. It's going to be amazing." Samantha looked off as if she was dreaming about it all.

"Now if you'd just set the date …"

"Shut up. I know the date. I just haven't told anyone yet."

I heard someone coming down the stairs slowly and grabbed Jack's cup and held it out behind me. I felt him take it and he joined Samantha and I at the table.

"So, Lanie, this is the big day. You and Grant, finally, after all this time. Your mom would be so happy today."

"Dad, she is. She is happy. And so are you, right?"

"Of course. Grant's already like a son to me. This just makes the holidays easier. No worrying about in-laws I hate. I like your in-laws a lot already. Hell, I have since grade school."

"Well, that's good. Eat something. The cocktail hour isn't for hours. I've heard your stomach growl. It's loud. I don't want it to ruin the wedding," Samantha said as she shoved the plate of bagels towards him.

I giggled. Of course, this morning I was giggling at everything. I was on a giddy-high. Well, more like a Grant-high. I sat and thought about everything we'd been through together, from our childhood to recently. There was so much it was overwhelming, and suddenly there were tears in my eyes.

"What's wrong?" Jack said nervously.

"There's nothing wrong. She's just full of emotions today, happiness and excitement. It's a lot. Right, Lanie? Nothing's wrong, right?"

"No, nothing's wrong. I just have so much history with Grant. And today, I'm marrying him. It's just … I have no words."

"You're where you're meant to be. You and Grant, you were fated to be together. Written in the stars," Jack said as he slurped his coffee. I just looked at him, poetic, aside of the slurp. It touched my heart to hear my father say it.

We heard grumbling and all turned toward the noise. Chelsie. She looked like she'd been side-swiped by a truck. Her eyes were half-closed and her make-up from the night before was smeared across her face. Her hair was all over the place. Apparently she and Steve had seen some action after the rehearsal dinner last night. They were both toasted. Samantha had insisted on not drinking a lot so everyone would look great for pictures, but I think Chelsie and Steve had actually gotten sentimental and spent most of the night reminiscing about their own wedding, which was only two years prior.

"I need coffee and a shower. Now," she mumbled as she slumped herself into a chair.

"You're looking lovely as ever this morning, Chelsie," Jack said as he handed her an extra large mug of coffee. Samantha and I giggled as Chelsie flipped him off and took her cup.

"Nice, Chelsie, after I give you coffee and a compliment." Jack kept at her. She side-eyed him and took a long gulp of the dark, hot brew.

"Come on Chels, give us a big smile for the bride," Jack continued. Despite her obvious morning grumpiness, Chelsie cracked a smile on one side of her scowl.

"Aw, thanks for the huge effort there, Chels," I joined my dad. She flipped me off, too.

"Now, now, Chels, that's not the way to treat the bride on her big day." Samantha couldn't help herself.

"Fine. I'll be all cheery if you stop talking to me. Okay?" Chelsie was starting to perk up and I'd have my second Maid of Honor in a few moments.

After a nice breakfast, we all headed up to start getting ready. Samantha spent an hour twisting and braiding my hair and adding small stephanotis to it to prepare it for my veil. Chelsie was in charge of make-up and she gave me dramatic smoky eyes and my lips were a deep java color. I looked hot so far and didn't even have my gown on. My dad was getting nervous and started to run in and out of the room making time announcements and letting us know when the flowers, caterer and photographer had arrived. I could only imagine what he'd been like the day I'd been born.

"Gown time. Where is it?" Samantha said nervously.

"It's up in the walk. I wanted to get my mom's vibe all over it before I put it on."

"Okay, I'll send Jack to get it."

"No, I'll get it. My mom should see me on my wedding day and I want to thank her for the dress. I know you think it's weird but … it's something I have to do." I smiled and headed up to the walk in my bathrobe and wedding undergarments.

"Mom? I just want to let you know it's time to put your gown on. I tried not to change it too much. I hope you like it."

Tap Tap Tappity Tap Tap

I reached for the gown and felt a hand on mine. I pulled it back instinctively and then moved it back to the dress. I smiled because I could feel my mom all around me, like she was holding me. I put my arms over my chest as if to hold her back. Everything felt warm and tingly.

"You'll watch the wedding, right? It's a perfect view from up here, right there on the edge of the cliff.

Tap Tap Tap

"Okay, Mom. Well, I have to get ready to marry Grant. I love you. I wish you were here."

Tap Tap

I smiled because I knew she was. I headed downstairs and Samantha helped me get into my gown. It was an off-the-shoulder with a plunging back gown that was fitted in the waist and opened back into a full-skirted bottom, not poofy, with a semi-long train. There wasn't a lot of decoration all over, just a single line of rhinestones along the neckline and the hem. I looked at myself in the mirror and felt my eyes tear up.

"No. What are you doing? There's no crying. You'll mess up that amazing job I did on your eyes!" Chelsie freaked. She was immediately at my side with hairspray and fanning hands. She fanned at my eyes and then hair sprayed my face.

"There, that should keep everything in place."

"Including my eyes glued shut."

I heard her giggle and then I turned back to the mirror as Samantha placed my waist-long veil in my hair. She was suddenly under my skirt sliding up the borrowed garter and taping six pence into my shoe.

"While you're down there …"

"You'll have to wait for your husband for that," she mused as she put a final stitch into my gown.

"Think you have all the superstitions covered?" I said with raised eyebrows.

"I just want all the bases covered. I even put the Irish travel coin in your luggage. We're still missing one thing though, something blue."

"Oh, wait, I have that. Lanie, Grant told me to give this to you once you had the dress on," Chelsie said as she handed me a blue velvet box. I opened it up to find a beautiful platinum chain with a Tanzanite heart dangling from it.

"It's beautiful." I took it out of the box and held it out for Chelsie to put around my neck. It was perfect. "Why did he do this?"

"He said it's your wedding present. It reminds him of the color of the ocean he's stared at with you almost every day of your lives together. He wanted to capture that ocean and give it to you. He said you'd understand."

I did. When we were young, I would tell Grant how I would gather all the stars and give them to him in a jar like fireflies. One star for every wonderful thing he did for me. I told him it would be the entire sky because he was always so good to me. He told me he would collect every drop in the ocean to give back for every time I made him smile. I laughed when I thought about the cuff links Dylan was giving him today. They were diamond encrusted with a note to Grant about the stars. I felt the tears start and then realized Chelsie had clogged my tear ducts with hair spray.

Chelsie and Samantha looked gorgeous in their cobalt blue gowns. They were pretty basic, but elegant and classy just the same. Strapless fitted gowns with a sweetheart neckline and a dramatic slit up the front. They each wore their hair up with Blue False Gilia throughout their hair. I heard Jack clear his throat.

"Come on in, Dad."

"Lanie, the photographer is—" And he stopped dead. He just stared at me.

"What? What's wrong? Is my epidermis showing?" I giggled. He didn't answer but I watched as his eyes filled with tears. He smiled and nodded his head. He thought I looked beautiful.

"Okay, when you can speak again, you can send him up."

* * *

When the photographer had left to set up for the ceremony, I waited anxiously to go down to the cliff to marry my love.

"You have to pee?"

"Are you thirsty?"

"Are you ready?"

"Nervous?"

The questions were coming from everyone and incessantly. I just smiled, shot a glance at the clock and knew it was time to head out.

"I hear the string quartet. I think it's time."

I peeked out the door to see the entire grounds decorated in white, blue and salmon flowers. There were tables with white linens, crystal, and china all over them, and in the center was an arrangement of flowers in a large conch shell surrounded by other shells. All the trees were once again lit with miniature white lights. It was a fairytale view; something every bride would want for her wedding day. The band was setting up and I could see the wait staff doing last minute touch-ups. I couldn't see the actual area where the ceremony would take place from my vantage point, but I knew it was beautiful. I could hear the string quartet and could see some of the guests heading over. My heart was racing. I was ready to just run out and marry Grant. It was all that mattered and I was becoming increasingly impatient.

"It's time," Samantha said excitedly. I could hear the string quartet begin to play the wedding march in the distance. I watched as Chelsie and Samantha joined Dylan and Steve and began to walk towards the ceremony area.

"Are you ready, Lanie? I'm not going to ask if you're sure you want to do this and help you sneak out the front door or anything. I know you want this. I know you want him." Jack smiled and held out his arm. I grabbed hold and clutched my bouquet in the other. Okay, so maybe the bride-nervousness was there just a little. But I had not one doubt in my mind. Jack and I set off and step-by-step we got closer. I tried to get a quick glimpse of Grant before everyone stood up and blocked my view before we rounded the corner.

And then—I saw him. He was a vision of complete perfection and happiness. The grin alone on his face was priceless; he was beaming. He looked extremely hot in his black tux. I couldn't take my eyes off his. Suddenly there was no one else there, just Grant and me. I couldn't hear the music anymore. We got closer and closer and soon I felt my dad release me, saw him shake Grant's hand and then take mine to put in his. I felt him place a soft kiss on my cheek and tell me he loved me.

I could feel the energy between us where our hands were touching. His eyes were glistening and sparkling; so I can only imagine the emotions were building up for both of us. I smiled and he told me he loved me with no words. The priest did his whole we-are-gathered-together speech and I could only focus on Grant, the man who would be my husband any second now.

"I understand the couple have prepared their own vows. The rings, please." Samantha and Dane pulled the rings out and each handed us one. Grant and I had promised to keep the vows real, from us, and from the heart.

I turned to Grant and placed the ring on his finger.

"Grant, my love, you have been by my side since the day I was born. You have been one of my best friends and a part of my family for as long as I can remember. Today you'll become a part of my family forever. You bring the best out of me every day. You pull me up when I'm down. You make me laugh when I'm crying and you make a damn great bowl of chicken soup when I'm sick. I couldn't imagine another person in this entire world I would want by my side for the rest of my life. I know you'll make the best father ever and I can't wait for the day I see you hold our child in your arms. I want to be that old couple everyone sees walking hand in hand down the beach, still in love. Thank you, Grant, for choosing to love me. Thank you for wanting to be my husband. I am the luckiest girl in the world and you make me so happy, in every way. I promise to never stop giving back. I will never give up on us and I'll live every day like it's our wedding day and honeymoon." I winked. "I love you."

Grant wiped a tear from his eye and had a cute smirk on his face. He took my ring and placed it on my finger.

"Lanie, there is no other woman on this earth for me. There never has been and there never will be. I have saved my heart and soul for you and I am so damn happy to be giving it to you right now. It's yours, it always has been. You give me everything any man could ever want in life. Not the material things; the things that everybody wishes they could have and spend their whole lives searching for. Unconditional love. I know I have that with you. I promise to be everything you could ever possibly want from a husband. You make me feel alive and you complete me. I will never let you fall. I will always be by your side. Yes, we'll be that old couple walking down the beach. I love you so much, Lanie. You are my life. I love you." He leaned down and kissed my hand. I felt my cheeks blush and I could hear the ahs from the guests.

"By the power vested in me and in the eyes of God, your family and friends, I now pronounce you husband and wife. You may kiss your bride."

Grant smiled and I did a little jumpy dance. He grabbed me and crushed his lips to mine as he spun me around to a full-blown dip. I could hear everyone cheering in the background and our kiss went on forever. When Grant finally pulled back he whispered in my ear, "Wait till we make love tonight. That was nothing. Unless of course you'd like to run off and consummate right now?" He kissed my neck and pulled me up so I was standing beside him.

"Ladies and Gentlemen, I give you Mr. and Mrs. Grant Bennett …

Epilogue

I Will Be With You Forever

I sat on the terrace watching my nine-month-old daughter struggle in her Uncle Dane's arms. Grant and I just smiled and took the moment to sit back and eat something without a squirming baby in our arms. Uninterrupted bliss.

"Oh, give her to me. You love Aunt Callie, don't you? Yes, you do." Callie took Randi from Dane and immediately the tears stopped. Callie was six months pregnant with their second child. Samantha was three months pregnant, too. Samantha and Dylan had finally married a year after Grant and I had moved into my house. I just couldn't imagine not having access to the widow's walk and Nicole whenever I wanted. I knew she would want to hear the patter of her grandchildren throughout the house, so we had chosen to live there.

Callie and Dane had married about a year after them. They lived in Dane's house. Chelsie and Steve were in the process of building a fourth house on the cliff. The plan was to be moving in within the year. They needed a larger place now that they were working on adding to our cliff brood.

"Can you see the other two?" Grant asked.

"I can see them. They're sitting on the beach. They're just hanging out and talking. Wait, one of them just got up. Looks like they're heading back this way."

I saw my son, Chris, get up and take Dane's daughter, Emily's, hand. They were always together and I believed they always would be. They were inseparable. I turned and smiled at Grant and he gave me a half smirk back, because he knew what I was thinking and I knew he agreed. Even Callie was on board. *Dane?* Well, Dane had become the overprotective father. He said he knew what guys could be like first hand. *You think?* He didn't want to think of his daughter having any kind of feelings for a boy. Any boy. But he always followed up with, if he could choose any boy, it would be Chris. *Oh, how times had changed.*

A few moments passed and soon Randi was reaching for me. I shot Grant a glance and smiled. He tried to take her, but like her daddy, she only wanted me. I liked it that way. She curled into my arms and began to twirl a stand of my hair against her cheek until she was blissfully asleep.

"Hey buddy, where's Emily?" Grant quizzed Chris when he walked onto the terrace. Chris had all the charm and amazing looks of his father. His copper hair was stylishly messy and his eyes always sparkled. He was a very good-looking boy and he reminded me of Grant when we were younger.

"I don't want to talk about it, okay?" Chris snapped.

"Well, you know that's not going to fly," I snarked.

"She went home to get ready for her date." We could all hear the anger in his voice, but we kept silent. We just stared at him. I watched Dane shift uneasily in his chair and clench his jaw.

"She's going to the movies with some guy from school who's been after her since the beginning of the school year. I don't like him. He's two-faced and a user. I told her not to go and we got in a fight and now she's not speaking to me."

"Oh, Baby, I'm sorry. Why don't you tell her how you feel about her?" Callie said.

"I don't know what you're talking about. We're like brother and sister. Nothing's ever going to happen between us. We agreed on it," Chris said.

Dane, Grant, and I all giggled and shared a knowing look. Chris just looked at us, shook his head, and stomped off to his room. I thought about heading after him but Grant took the lead and headed into the house first.

"Who the hell does she have a date with, Callie? Did you tell her she could go?" Dane was starting to fume.

"It's just the movies. Relax. I don't see the harm in it. Lighten up, Dane. You and I both know she's not our little baby anymore."

"I don't want her going out with some guy I don't know. Guys are all scum," Dane ranted.

This made Callie and I bust out laughing. I put my hand on Dane's arm and smiled at him. "Seriously? All guys are scum? What about my son? He's not scum."

"I have no problem with Emily being with Chris. He's respectful. He loves her."

And there it was. Dane knew Chris loved his daughter and apparently he was on board with them being together, too. Now my mind was racing. *What could we do to help make this happen?* I didn't want to see Emily and Chris waste all their time like Grant and I had. *Don't get me wrong; I wouldn't change anything for the world.* But I wish we had all those times when we were younger, the first kiss, going through all the bases together and of course, the first time making love. I wanted them to have it all together. They had plenty of time for all of that, but I still wanted them to have what Grant and I didn't. I put my plan into motion with Callie and Dane. Now all I had to do was get Grant in on it so I headed inside to find him.

"Absolutely not, Lanie. We're not going to do it. I'm not doing it," Grant said, semi-joking, but mostly not.

"I could convince you, you know. I have my ways." I fluttered my eyelashes at him and then pushed my body against his.

"Stop. You know I can't resist you. Don't do this right now. How long will Randi be sleeping?" Grant caved.

I slowly pushed him out of Randi's room and backed him down the hall to our room. He mocked holding back, but his movements were surefooted. He liked where we were going.

"How do you intend to convince me, Love?" he smoothly said with a smirk.

"With every inch of my skin. Do you think that will work?" I feigned stupidity.

"I most certainly do not," Grant quipped.

"Oh? Is that a dare?" I purred.

"That is most definitely a triple dog dare," he said, his eyes burning into mine. It didn't matter how much time passed, Grant would always have the same effect on me. I wanted to throw myself on top of him right there in the hallway. I was positive we would be the friskiest old people anyone ever met.

I began to pull my shirt over my head and heard a soft ah escape his lips, yet he still pretended to be fighting me off. I must be very strong, because I had no problem pushing him into our room. I smiled and began to shimmy out of my jeans; this time a low growl rumbled in his throat. He reached for me and I pulled myself away from him, only to receive a pout in return.

"No Sweetheart, you're supposed to be resisting, remember? This is why we don't ever have kinky role-playing sex," I mused.

"No, we don't do that because I only want to be kinky with you even when you're not being you. Plus, I want you to only think of me." Grant chuckled. I smiled and swiftly shoved him onto the bed and straddled him.

"Oh. No. You pinned me to the bed with your hot fucking body. No. Please no. Let me up," he said flatly with no emotion at all, while barely moving his arms to try to escape.

"You could at least give me a bit of a challenge, Grant. You're making this no fun. Well, it's fun. Making love to you is always fun, but I do like the challenge of trying to convince you." He quickly grabbed my wrists and soon I was in his place on the bed and he was straddling me.

"Lanie, why do you bother? You know I can't resist you at all and you know I'll do whatever you ask. I have never said no to you in any way at all. Now these must go." He grabbed my panties and ripped them off of me. He was a bit gentler with my bra. I reached for his pants and unbuttoned them. *Stupid button-fly jeans, such a pain in the ass, but damn did they look good on him.* I thought they'd look better on the floor right now. He was a gentleman and assisted me in undressing him and soon we were skin to skin on the bed. He was too willing of a captive, but it didn't matter. The whole point of this exercise was moot anyway. This was now about making love. He brushed his lips across my collarbone and worked his way up to my ear.

"Lanie, this moment could happen a hundred times over and my desire for you would never lessen. I'll do whatever you want as long as you'll always be here by my side."

"You know I'll never leave you. I'll always be right here beside you." And it was true. Grant and I were never apart again after the Brianna incident. We never traveled separately and never left the other for any extended period of time. I had not spent one night without Grant beside me in bed. We were truly connected in every way. I wasn't even sure if I could breathe on my own without him anymore. I know my heart beat for him. We were one.

He kissed my lips gently and I felt the urge to have all of him, so my game ended and soon my tongue was deep between his lips, hungrily feeding on him. I could feel him smile and he slid his hand into my hair and pulled my face even closer to his so we were locked in our kiss.

My body couldn't hold back. I wrapped my legs around his waist and began to grind my hips against him. I dragged my fingernails down his back to his buttocks and squeezed. The feel of him against me drove me wild.

"Are you trying to communicate something you want me to do, Lanie?" he said breathily into my ear.

"Go fuck yourself! Well actually, do me instead. I need you, Grant. Make love to me right now," I begged with a giggle. He was immediately sliding inside me; our bodies reconnected, our souls one. The feel of him was as intense as the first time I ever made love to him. I could never get enough of this man and wished we could stay here alone together all day.

"I love you, Lanie. I will always love you."

"And I'll always love you, Grant."

* * *

"Anything yet? Has Chris called?" Grant said, pacing. "No, Emily is still in labor. Callie was in with her when he called. She said it looked to be a long night. Relax. This is our third grandchild. Why so anxious? Shannon is on her way, and it's only a matter of time before you get to hold her in your arms."

"Is Randi coming home this weekend?" Grant sounded distracted.

"Hun, she'll be here. She and Joe are coming to look at how the house is coming. Didn't you speak to her this morning? Look, how about we head up to bed? It's been a long evening and I know I'm tired. You have to be exhausted. You didn't sleep at all last night." I grabbed Grant's hand in mine and pulled him towards the stairs. "Callie will call us if anything happens. Let's grab the chocolate hazelnut spread on the way up." I winked at him. All the wrinkles on his face seemed to lessen and he smiled and pulled me to him. We were well beyond our youth, but he was still so handsome.

Sometime during the night, I felt Grant's lips softly kiss me, and then his side of the bed lift. I rubbed my eyes and opened them only to see him at the window looking out over the cliff.

"What are you doing up, Babe? Come back to bed. It's cold and lonely without you."

"Lanie, I'm always with you. I'll always be with you forever. You know that, right?" he whispered softly without turning to look at me.

"Grant, you're making me nervous. Is something wrong? Do you feel okay?" I was scared. I couldn't live without this man, and we were old now. It was only a matter of time before our health began to fail. He slowly turned towards me and smiled; his eyes sparkled in the dark. I saw him young again in that instant, and my heart began to race at the sight.

"Lanie, are you all right? You look a bit pale," he said as he slid back beside me into bed. He curled his body around mine to spoon me, wrapped his arms around me and pulled me as close to him as he could.

"I'm fine as long as you're right here next to me." I closed my eyes and soon sleep fell upon me.

I dreamt that night, of being young again, with Grant and Dane on the cliff. We were running along the shoreline, laughing together, not even teenagers yet. Grant and I held hands and Dane ran behind us. He lagged back to throw stones in the ocean.

"Grant? I'll love you for eternity. There will never be a love like you and I have. If anything ever happens to the other, let's make a pact that we'll wait to be together again," I said.

"I'll wait forever for you. I promise," Grant said as he raised his right hand and smiled. I did the same. "Nothing can ever keep us apart, Lanie. Not time or space or even death. We'll always be together. Forever." I felt his lips on mine. I felt them. And it woke me out of my sleep.

"Grant? Are you awake? I swear I just felt you kiss me. Grant?" But I already knew. His absence was so apparent. I rolled over and he looked like he was only sleeping. I knew he had gone. My love was no longer with me in this world. I felt my eyes well with tears, my cheeks burning, my heart already aching for him. There was only half of me left in the room.

I heard the phone ring and knew it must be Callie with news on Shannon's birth. I answered, tears of joy and tears of complete devastation pouring out of me. How could I ever survive without my love? When the call ended with Callie, I dialed Chelsie.

"Lanie? Did the baby come?" Chelsie said groggily.

"Chelsie." It was all I could get out.

"Lanie, what's wrong?" Now I could tell she was wide-awake and panicking.

"Grant. He's … he's gone." And that's when it hit me. I broke down and threw myself onto his body.

"No, Grant, no. You promised. Please don't leave me. Please, Grant. I can't do this without you." I don't know how long I begged him to come back, but soon I felt hands on me, pulling me into a big bear hug. It was Steve.

* * *

"Grandma, are you sleeping?" Shannon whispered in my ear as she crawled into bed beside me.

"No, my love, I'm resting my eyes. I'm just very tired today. Come snuggle with me."

Shannon was my girl. She was six years old now. How time had flown since Grant had left me. I had always felt a part of Grant's soul in her. Like somehow it had jumped from him to her the moment he passed and she was born. She and I were inseparable.

"Grandma, you can sleep. I'll be here right beside you. I'm not going anywhere," she said with a smile. She had her grandfather's eyes and smile. I drifted off, seeing him through her, and before long I was asleep.

I felt his lips on mine. I felt them. And it woke me out of my sleep. I opened my eyes and knew I must be dreaming, because Grant was standing over me, smiling. He was young and so beautiful to see. It reminded me of the day of the nor'easter at the stables. My heart began to race in my chest.

"Hello, my love. Are you ready?" he said smoothly. "You're so beautiful, Love."

"I'm sure I'm not." But the voice I heard was mine from many years ago. Grant held his hand out to me, and when I reached to touch him, to see if he was real, my hand was young, too. I had no idea what was happening, but I knew I needed to be in his arms again. It had been too long since I had felt him and I knew I would feel him now. I jumped out of bed, something I had not been able to do for a long time.

He laughed and threw his arms around me and pulled me close. I took a deep breath just to inhale his scent. His lips were on mine in an instant. I felt his love flood over me and everything was right again. I was whole again.

"I promised you I'd wait, and I did. Now there is no end, because we can be together forever, my love. I love you, Lanie. I've been here beside you every day. Every night. I have never left you. Did you feel me?"

"Yes. Every time Shannon touched me. Every smile from her. Every laugh. Grant, I love you so much. I've missed you so much." I wanted to cry, but there was nothing but happiness inside of me.

"It's time to go, Baby. We have a lot of catching up to do." His eyes. They were burning into mine again like he had never been gone. It was just like so many years ago, even before our children and grandchildren existed.

"Do they let you catch up in heaven?" I giggled and winked. He gave me a double eyebrow raise and smiled his sultry smile.

"You bet they do."

He slipped his arm around me and we walked out to the cliff's edge, to be with each other forever.

About the Author

Christie A.C. Gucker lives in NJ with her husband, two daughters and a menagerie of pets. Being a mother is one of the greatest joys of her life. She has worked in the advertising industry for over 20 years as a degreed artist, but also works in the fine arts, especially sculpting out of stone or snapping photographs. Christie is also a singer and musician, and can be found singing on a few CDs.

After the death of her father, Christie searched for something to fill her desire to make a mark in this world. Her love of the arts and creativity allowed her to search for a new medium, which she found with a pen instead of a brush. Being an avid reader her whole life, and with her family cheering her on, she decided to take her shot, and began writing.

Fascinated by the supernatural and sharks, Christie studies both avidly. You'll be sure to find something spooky lurking somewhere in her stories. Her greatest joy is sitting on a beach with her family while surf fishing, flying kites or building sandcastles with her girls.

CPSIA information can be obtained at www.ICGtesting.com
Printed in the USA
LVOW041926111012

302502LV00003B/31/P

9 781938 397318